MORTAL SIN

Also by Paul Levine

False Dawn
Night Vision
To Speak for the Dead

MORTAL SIN

Paul Levine

William Morrow and Company, Inc.
New York

It is the policy of William Morrow and Company, Inc., and its imprints and affiliates, recognizing the importance of preserving what has been written, to print the books we publish on acid-free paper, and we exert our best efforts to that end.

Library of Congress Cataloging-in-Publication Data

Levine, Paul (Paul J.)
  Mortal sin / Paul Levine. — 1st ed.
    p.   cm.
  ISBN 0-688-12717-7
  1. Lassiter, Jake (Fictitious character)—Fiction.   2. Lawyers—
Florida—Miami—Fiction.   3. Miami (Fla.)—Fiction.   I. Title.
PS3562.E8995M6   1994
813'.54—dc20   93-30662
                                                     CIP

Fic.

Printed in the United States of America

First Edition

1   2   3   4   5   6   7   8   9   10

BOOK DESIGN BY LISA STOKES

To the memory of John D. MacDonald,
whose tough love for an embattled Florida inspires us still

Acknowledgments

I gratefully acknowledge the assistance of attorneys Roy E. Black, Terrence Schwartz, and Edward Shohat, oenophiles Michael Goldberg and Gene Rivers, medical examiner Dr. Joseph Davis and deputy medical examiner Dr. Emma O. Lew, computer wizard Lourdes Perez, and expert in multitudinous matters Luisa Vázquez-Mora.

Special thanks to my agent, Kris Dahl, and my editors, Paul Bresnick and Lisa Wager.

The most bitter remorse is for the sins we did not commit.
—Mexican proverb

I long ago come to the conclusion that all life is six-to-five against.
—DAMON RUNYON, "A Nice Price"

Chapter 1

Thy Client's Wife

On a stifling august day of becalmed wind and sweltering humidity, the Coast Guard plucked seven Haitians from a sinking raft in the Gulf Stream, the grand jury indicted three judges for extorting kickbacks from court-appointed lawyers, and the Miami City Commission renamed Twenty-second Avenue General Máximo Gómez Boulevard.

And Peter Tupton froze to death.

Tupton was wearing a European-style bikini swimsuit and a terry cloth beach jacket. Two empty bottles of Roederer Cristal champagne 1982 lay at his feet. His very blue feet. Two thousand six hundred forty-four other bottles—reds and whites, ports and sauternes, champagnes and Chardonnays, Cabernets and cordials—were stacked neatly in their little wooden bins.

A high-tech air-conditioning system kept the wine cellar at an even 56 degrees and 70 percent humidity. Hardly life-threatening, unless you wandered in from the pool deck sopping wet, guzzled two liters of bubbly, and passed out.

Cause of death: exposure due to hypothermia. Which didn't keep the *Miami Journal* from seizing on a sexier headline:

ON YEAR'S HOTTEST DAY,
ENVIRONMENTAL ACTIVIST
FREEZES TO DEATH

The medical examiner reported that Tupton's blood contained 0.32 percent alcohol. If he'd been driving, he could have been arrested three times. But he'd been swimming, then sipping mimosas on the pool deck. When he stumbled into the wine cellar, he must have kept drinking, this time leaving out the orange juice.

Cheers.

"He was a most disagreeable man," Gina Florio said, dismissing the notion of the late Peter Tupton with a wave of the hand. It was a practiced gesture, a movement so slight as to suggest the insignificance of the subject. When the hand returned, it settled on my bare chest. I lay on my back in a bed that had a bullet hole in the headboard. The bed had been Exhibit A in a case involving a jealous husband and a .357 Magnum, and I picked it up cheap at a police auction of old evidence.

I stared at the ceiling fan, listening to its *whompety-whomp* while Gina traced figure eights with a blood-red fingernail across my pectorals. A crumpled bed sheet covered me from the waist down. Her clothing was simpler; there wasn't any. She reclined on her side, propped on an elbow, the smooth slope of a bare hip distracting me from the hypnotizing effect of the fan. Outside the jalousie windows, the wind was picking up, the palm fronds swatting the sides of my coral-rock house.

A most disagreeable man. In earlier times, she would have called him a dickbrain.

Or if there were clergy on the premises, simply a birdturd.

But Gina was a sponge that absorbed the particulars of her surroundings, the good, the bad, and the pretentious. Lately, she'd been hanging out with the matrons of the Coral Gables Women's Club. Finger sandwiches at the Biltmore, charity balls at the Fontainbleau, tennis at the club. Discussions of many disagreeable men. Mostly husbands, I'd bet.

"A swine, really," Gina said. "A short, bald, lumpy swine who mashed out his cigarettes in my long-stemmed Iittala glasses."

"Iittala, is it?"

"Don't mock me, Jake. Finnish, top of the line. Nicky likes the best of everything."

"That's why he married you," I said, without a trace of sarcasm.

"You're still mocking me, you prick."

Prick. Now, that was better. You can take the girl out of the chorus line, but . . .

"Not at all, Gina. You're a name brand. Just like Nicky's Rolex, his Bentley, and . . . his Iittala."

"What's wrong with my name, anyway?"

Defensive now. She could play society wife with the white-shoe crowd at Riviera Country Club, but I'd known her too long.

"Nothing," I said. "I've liked all your names. Each suited the occasion."

"Even Maureen? Rhymes with latrine."

"I didn't know you then. You were Star when I met you."

She made the little hand-wave again, and her butterscotched hair spilled across my chest, tickling me. Her movements hadn't always been so subtle. When her name was Star Hampton, she jumped and squealed with the rest of the Dolphin Dolls at the Orange Bowl. She had long legs and a wide smile, but so did the others. What distinguished her was a quick mind and overriding ambition. Which hardly explained why she chose me—a second-string line-backer with a bum knee and slow feet—over a host of suitors that included two first-round draft choices with no-cut contracts and a sports agent who flew his own Lear. Then again, maybe it explained why she *left* me.

We were together two years, or about half my less-than-illustrious football career, and then she drifted away, leaving her name—and me—behind. When the gods finally determined that my absence from the Dolphins' roster would affect neither season ticket sales nor the trade deficit with Japan, I enrolled in night law school. By then, Star had sailed to Grand Cayman with a gold-bullion sales-man, the first of three or four husbands, depending if you counted a marriage performed by a ship's captain on the high seas.

I hadn't heard from her for a few years when she called my secretary, asking to set up an appointment with Mr. Jacob Lassiter, Esq. She wanted her latest marriage annulled after discovering the groom wasn't an Arab sheikh, just a glib commodities broker from Libya who needed a green card. We became reacquainted, and Gina—though that wasn't her name yet—kept drifting in and out of my life with the tide.

Sometimes, it was platonic. She'd complain about one man or

another. The doctor was selfish; the bodybuilder dull; the TV newsman uncommunicative. I'd listen and give advice. Yeah, me, a guy without a wife, a live-in lover, or a parakeet.

Sometimes, it was romantic. In between her multiple marriages and my semirelationships, there would be long walks on the beach and warm nights under the paddle fan. One Sunday morning, I was making omelets—onions, capers, and cheese—when she came up behind me and gave me a dandy hug. "If I didn't like you so much, Jake," she whispered, "I'd marry you."

And sometimes, it was business. There were small-claims suits over a botched modeling portfolio, an apartment with a leaking roof, and a dispute with a roommate over who was the recipient of a diamond necklace bequeathed by a grateful thief who had enjoyed their joint company during a rainy Labor Day weekend. And, of course, the name changes. She had been born Maureen Corcoran on a farm somewhere in the Midwest. A mutt name and a mutt place, she said long ago. So she changed her name and place whenever she deemed either unsuitable. She called herself Holly Holiday during one Christmas season, Tanya Galaxy when she became infatuated with an astronaut at Cape Canaveral, and Star Hampton when she dreamed of a Hollywood career.

Finally, she asked me to make it official: Maureen would become Gina.

"It goes well with Florio, don't you think?" she had asked. "And Nicky likes it."

Nicky.

What was he doing today? Making money, I supposed. Wondering whether he was going to get sued by the estate of one Peter Tupton. Maybe worrying about his wife, too. Had Gina said she was going to see her lawyer?

Their lawyer, now. I could see Gina cocking her head, asking Nicky if it wouldn't be sweet to hire Jake Lassiter. *You remember Jake, don't you, darling?*

Sure, he remembered.

Before he was filthy rich, Nicky Florio used to hang around the practice field. He was hawking someone else's condos then, and he'd deliver an autographed football at each closing. If he couldn't get Griese, Csonka, Kiick, Warfield, or Buoniconti, I'd sign my name. And theirs.

Nicky was a great salesman. He pretended to love football, always looking for the inside dope on the team. Injuries, mostly. How had practice gone? What was Shula's mood? I'd give him a tip now and then, knowing what he was up to, but I never bet on games. Well, seldom. And I never bet against us.

Nicky probably balked when she mentioned me. *I need another lawyer like I need another asshole. Besides, your old boyfriend's just an ex-jock with a briefcase.*

He was right. I don't look like a lawyer, and I don't act like a lawyer. I have a bent nose, and I tip the scales at a solid 223. My hair is too long and my tie either too wide or too narrow, too loud or too plain, depending on the fashion of the times. I've hit more blocking sleds than law books, and I live by my own rules, which is why I'll never be president of the Bar Association or Rotary's Man of the Year. I eat lunch in shirtsleeves at a fish joint on the Miami River, not in a tony club in a skyscraper. I laugh at feeble lawyer jokes:

How can you tell if a lawyer is lying?
His lips are moving.

And I do the best I can to inflict the least harm as I bob and weave through life. Which made me wonder just what the hell I was doing with Gina yet again.

If Nicky had said no, Gina would have waited, then tried again. When the neighbor sued over the property line, *Give Jake a chance.* I picture Nicky Florio running a hand through his black hair, slicked straight back with polisher. He'd squint, as if in deep thought, his dark eyes hooded. He'd shrug his thick shoulders: *Sure, why not, he can't screw it up too bad.* Putting me down, building himself up. Hire the wife's old boyfriend, something to gloat about at the club, tell the boys how he tacks a bonus onto the bill, like tossing crumbs to a pigeon. To Nicky, I was a worker bee he could lease by the hour. He could buy anything, he was telling me, including Gina.

Well, who's got her today, Nicky?

Was that it, I wondered, my infantile way of striking back? Hey, Lassiter, old buddy, what *are* you doing in bed with Maureen, Holly, Star, Gina? Don't you have enough problems, what with the Florida Bar on your back? What would the ethics committee say about bedding down a client's wife?

With all the single women available, what are you doing with a married one? South Beach is chock-full of unattached women, leggy models from New York, Paris, and Rome. Downtown is wall-to-wall professionals in their business-lady pumps, charcoal suits, and silk blouses. The gym has an aerobics instructor plus a divorcée or two who brighten up when you do your curls. So what's with this destructive, nowhere relationship mired in the past?

"Jake, what are you thinking about?" Gina asked.

"Star Hampton," I answered, truthfully. I rearranged myself on the bed to look straight into her eyes. "Do you remember the time you hit me?"

"Was it only once?"

"Yeah. You were leaving me for some cowboy. A rodeo star named Tex or Slim."

"It was Jim. Just Jim."

"No, Jim was the Indy driver."

"That was James," she corrected me. "Or was he the tennis pro?"

"You hit me because I didn't beg you to stay."

"I don't remember," she said.

But I did.

We'd been living together in my apartment on Miami Beach. She stepped out of the shower, her hair smelling like a freshly mowed field. She kissed me, soft and slow, then said she was leaving. I told her I'd miss the wet towels balled up on the bathroom floor. She let fly a roundhouse right, bouncing it off my forehead, cursing as she broke a lacquered nail.

Good kiss, no hit.

She dressed quickly and tossed her belongings into a couple of gym bags. Then she said it to me, a parting line I was to hear time and again. "Maybe I'll see you later," she said, heading out the door. "And maybe I won't."

*   *   *

"Slugged anybody lately?" I asked.

She laughed. It was the old laugh. Hearty instead of refined. "Gawd, I was so young then. Did you know I turned thirty last April? You think I need a boob job? Am I starting to sag?"

She sat up, stretched her long legs across the bed, and hefted her bare breasts, one at a time, her chin pressed into her chest. The streaked blond hair hung straight over her eyes. Outside, the wind was crackling the palm fronds. Only three o'clock, but it had gotten dark inside the bedroom. I peered out the porthole-sized window. Gray clouds obscured the sun as a summer squall approached from the west.

"Jake! You're ignoring me."

So was Nicky, I thought. Maybe that was why she was here. Or was it just for old times' sake?

"Can we be friends again?" she had asked when she showed up at my office for a lunch appointment.

"Friends?"

"Friends who screw," she explained.

Which, come to think of it, is what we had been from the beginning. After all these years, I was still dazzled by her beauty, the granite cheekbones, the wide-set deep blue eyes rimmed with black, the body sculpted by daily workouts with a personal trainer. Attention must be paid to such a woman, I thought.

She dropped her breasts, which, as she well knew, sagged not a whit. "Jake?"

"Tell me more about Tupton," I said.

"Ugh! No more talk about business."

"I thought that's what this was about."

"Come on, Jake. That was an excuse. I missed you."

She rolled on top of me and grabbed a handful of my sunbleached hair. "You get better-looking every year. I don't know why I talked Nicky into hiring you. You're too tall and too tanned and too damn sexy."

"That's why you talked him into hiring me. And here I was hoping it was for my legal acumen."

"It's for your amorous acumen." She let go of my hair and began nuzzling my neck.

"Look, Gina, you're just bored. It's an occupational hazard of the *haut monde* wife."

Her teeth were leaving little marks on my earlobes. She whispered in my ear. "If you think I don't know what that means, you're *très trompé*. My second husband took me to Paris. Or was it my third?"

"C'mon, let's do some work—unless you want me to charge you two hundred fifty dollars an hour for—"

"A bargain at twice the price."

"Gina. I'm serious."

"I know you are. You're suffering from postcoital guilt."

"Really?"

"I've had therapy," she said proudly. "My next-to-last ex-husband was a big believer in self-growth."

"C'mon now, tell me more about Tupton."

She sighed and rolled off me, her hair trailing across my chest. Her back toward me, I admired the twin dimples at the base of her spine. Then she turned to face me, her full lips pouting. "We invited him to the pool party to soften him up. Nicky's bright idea. Why fight the guy, waste thousands on legal fees—"

"What better use for your money?"

". . . when maybe we could reason with him, show him the good life, serve him some grilled pompano—"

"And chilled champagne."

"Jake, stop it! If you don't want to fool around anymore, treat me like a client."

"You want me to pad the bill?"

"No, I want you to screw me."

"Gina!"

"Okay, okay. Fire away."

"So you invited Tupton to a pool party."

"Along with a bunch of stuffed shirts, Friends of the Philharmonic, the opera and ballet groups. I haven't seen so many bobbed noses and tummy tucks since the Mount Sinai Founders Ball."

"A society crowd."

"Business, too. With Nicky, a party can't just be a party. We had some of the big growers plus a Micanopy chief or two. Nicky always says if you want to do business in the Everglades, you've got to make friends with the Indians and the sugar barons. And, of course, we invited Tupton, the turd."

Dropping all Gables Estates pretenses now. More like Star Hampton, who once shared a two-bedroom Miami Springs apartment with five stewardesses, none of whom could scrub a pot.

"I've seen his name in the paper," I said. "What did they call him, an 'environmental activist'?"

"A turd!"

"The *Journal* said he was executive director of the Everglades Society. A pretty nice obituary."

"A shithead."

"I assume he wasn't fond of real estate developers the likes of Nicholas Florio," I said.

She placed a hand on my stomach. "All Nicky did was send some surveyors onto the Micanopy Reservation. He's been doing business with the Indians for years."

"The reservation's in the Big Cypress Swamp, so Tupton was probably concerned that—"

"Who cares! I mean, the Indians have something like seventy thousand acres out there. It's all mucky. Yuk! Who would want it?"

"Nicky, I guess. He's probably going to improve the environment by draining the groundwater, chasing out the birds and alligators, and building ticky-tacky condos on rotten pilings."

"Jake, that's not fair. He's got a planned community on the drawing board. Something that would enhance the environment. That's what the brochures say."

"Maybe the buildings would even last until the first hurricane."

"Don't let your feelings about Nicky interfere with your good judgment, Jake." She let her fingers do the walking, or maybe it was a slow dance under the sheet, a soft stroking of me farther south. "Anyway, Tupton files a suit against Nicky's company for not having all the right permits. But Nicky wasn't dredging or anything, just surveying, for crying out loud! I gotta tell you, Jake, these bird-watchers and gator-loving econuts are real wackos. They've protested against the oil companies for making seismic tests and the airboat tours for disturbing the tadpoles. And Tupton, talk about holier than thou, he comes to our house wearing jeans and a chambray shirt with the sleeves rolled up, like some urban fucking cowboy. I'll bet the dipshit makes thirty-five K a year, tops."

"*Made*," I said. "He's not cashing any more checks. And I remember when you shook your booty for fifteen bucks a game at the Orange Bowl."

She withdrew her hand and studied me. "You disapprove of me, don't you, Jake? You never say it, but I disappoint you."

I listened to fat raindrops plopping against the window. The wind whistled through gaps in the barrel-tile roof. "Nothing and nobody ever turns out the way you think."

She turned away from me, either to express her displeasure or to show off her profile. "And what did you think, Jake, that I'd be doing brain surgery now? I just count my blessings that I'm not dancing tabletops in one of those dives near the airport."

In the distance, a police siren sang against the wind. "Maybe I'm just jealous that you're with Nicky, and this is the way I show it."

"You? Jealous?" She laughed a throaty laugh, her breasts bouncing. "Since when? You never cared. You never once said you loved me, not even when it was just the two of us. We were close, Jake, or don't you remember?"

"I remember everything," I said. "The Germans wore gray. You wore blue, and I missed the boat."

"The boat?"

"The one to Grand Cayman—others too, I imagine. I never could keep up with you."

She turned back to me and brought an elbow down into my stomach. Not hard, but not soft either. I let out a *whoosh*. "Jeez, what's that for?"

"You jerk! You big, dumb jock jerk! You never asked me to stay. You think I wouldn't have stayed? You never cared!"

"Who says I didn't care?"

"Me! I say it. You didn't care."

"I cared," I said softly.

"Then you're a double dumb jerk for never saying so."

Gina sat on the edge of the bed, craning her long neck and blowing cigarette smoke into the air. She'd been quitting smoking ever since we met, probably longer. Self-discipline was not her strong suit. It took her another half hour to tell me the rest of the story.

She had put on what she called her sweet face and served Peter

Tupton a pitcher of mimosas to loosen him up. Nicky lent him a swimsuit, and before you knew it, there he was frolicking in the pool with a couple of Junior Leaguers from Old Cutler Road.

"Is there a Mrs. Tupton?" I asked. Without a wife and kids, the value of the wrongful-death case would plummet.

"There is, but he didn't bring her," Gina told me.

"Why not? Were they separated?" An impending marital split could limit the damages, too.

"Tupton said something about Sunday being her day to spend at Mercy hospital. She's a volunteer with child cancer patients."

Oh shit. When the surviving spouse is an angel, tack another digit onto the verdict form.

"Any little Tuptettes?"

"No. They'd been married a couple of years. No kids yet."

Be thankful for small blessings.

"How'd he get into the wine cellar?"

She exhaled a puff into the draft of the ceiling fan. "Beats me. When he first arrived, Nicky gave him a tour of the house, including the cellar, which isn't a cellar at all or it'd be under five feet of water. It's a custom-built room off the kitchen. Lots of insulation, custom wood shelving, a couple thousand bottles. He must have come back into the house from the pool. Maybe the jerkoff wanted to steal a Château Pétrus 1961. Or maybe he was looking for a place to pee."

I was trying to figure it out, but it made no sense. There was plenty to drink outside, where it was also warm, and tummy-tucked women in bikinis lounged poolside. "Why would he wander into a freezing room soaking wet, settle down, and drink two bottles of champagne? Did he lock himself in?"

"Impossible," she answered, tossing me the hand again. "The bolt slides open from the inside. Apparently, he didn't want to leave."

Or *couldn't*, I thought.

The rain had stopped, and the wind had died. Outside the window, the late-afternoon sun peeked from behind the clouds, slanting shadows of a palm frond across the room. In the chinaberry tree, a mockingbird with white wing patches was yawking and cackling. *Mimus polyglottos*, Doc Charlie Riggs called him, using the bird's

Latin name. Mimic of many tongues. My mocker is a bachelor. They're the ones who sing the songs. Maybe that's what I was doing, too.

"Who was the last person to see Tupton alive?" I asked.

Gina looked around my bedroom for an ashtray. She seemed to consider the question before answering. "Nicky, I think." She appeared lost in thought. There being neither an ashtray nor Iittala glassware on the premises, Gina dropped the cigarette butt into the mouth of an empty beer bottle. Her eyes brightened. "Sure, they were both sitting in the kiddie pool drinking the mimosas, Nicky trying to charm him. I remember thinking that Nicky must be making progress, maybe getting through to him. Then they walked toward the house together, going into the kitchen. That's the last I saw him. You'll have to ask Nicky what happened next."

I intended to do just that. As Nicky's lawyer, I had to be ready for anything. I had to "zealously" defend my client. It's in the *Canons of Ethics*, you can look it up. Just now, the lawyer inside me—the guy who sees evil and deception, artifice and mendacity—had a lot of questions to ask. And so would the state attorney, I was willing to bet.

The death of Peter Tupton was just a bit too bizarre. Words like "inquest" and "autopsy" and "grand jury" were popping into my head. And motive, too. What was it Doc Riggs always said? *When there's no explanation for the death, always ask,* cui bono, *who stands to gain.*

Hey, Nicky Florio, this may be more trouble for you than just a wrongful-death suit that's probably insurance-covered anyway. You could be up to your ass in alligators.

Gina was up and getting dressed. She wriggled into her ultratight jeans and shot me a look. "Jake, why are you smiling?"

"Didn't know I was."

"You were. Your blue eyes were crinkling at the corners, and you had that crooked grin you used to sweep me off my feet."

"So that's what did it. I thought it was my witty repartee aided by ample quantities of Jack Daniel's."

She was looking around the room for her bra. "No. It was your smile. That and shoulders I could lean on."

"Since then, one's been separated, the other dislocated, and I've torn a rotator cuff."

She found the bra, red and frilly, in a tangle of bed sheets. "Just now, you were almost laughing. What were you thinking about?"

"The *Canons of Ethics*."

She gave me a shove. "No, really."

"Okay, then. The Ten Commandments, or at least one of them."

"Which one?"

"Something about thy client's wife," I said.

Chapter 2

Self-Inflicted Pain

"How long have you known mr. lassiter?" asked wilbert Faircloth.

"Since he was a pup," Doc Charlie Riggs answered.

"May we assume that constitutes many years?"

"We may," Charlie said, wiping his eyeglasses on his khaki shirt. His old brown eyes twinkled at me. "When I was chief M.E., Jake was a young assistant public defender. Well, not as young as the others, since he'd spent a few years playing ball, though heaven knows why. He wasn't very good, and he blew out his anterior cruciate ligaments." Charlie scratched his beard and shot me a sidelong glance. "Anyway, when he began practicing—law, not football—we were on opposite sides of the fence. I'd testify for the state as to cause of death, the matching of bullets to weapons, that sort of thing, and Jake would cross-examine on behalf of his destitute and very guilty clients. He always did so vigorously, if I may say so."

"No one is questioning Mr. Lassiter's competence," Faircloth said.

Good. Not that it was always that way. New clients, particularly, are suspicious. They want to see your merit badges—diplomas from prestigious universities, photos with important judges, newspaper clippings laminated onto walnut plaques. I don't have any. No letters from the Kiwanis praising my good works. I don't have a family, so no pictures of the kiddies clutter my desk. If anyone wants to examine my diploma from night law school, they can visit my house between Poinciana and Kumquat in Coconut Grove. The sheepskin isn't framed, so the edges are yellowed and torn, but it serves a purpose, covering a crack in the bathroom wall just above the commode. I like it there, a symbolic reminder of the glory of higher education, first thing every morning.

I don't give clients a curriculum vitae or a slick brochure extolling my virtues. I just tell them I've never been disbarred, committed, or convicted of moral turpitude, and the only time I was arrested, it was a case of mistaken identity—I didn't know the guy I hit was a cop.

I keep my office walls bare except for a couple of team pictures and a black-and-white AP wirephoto from some forgotten game. The sideline photographer caught me moving laterally, trying to keep up with the tight end going across the middle. The shutter must have clicked a split second after my cleats stuck in the turf. My right leg was bent at the knee in a direction God never intended. Nobody had hit me. It's one of those rare football photos where the lighting is perfect and you can see right through the face mask.

My eyes are wide, mouth open.

Startled. No pain yet, just complete astonishment.

The agony came later. It always does.

What had been perfectly fine ligaments were shredded into strands of spaghetti. Doc Riggs gave me the photo on the day I retired, which is a polite way of saying I was placed on waivers and twenty-seven other teams somehow failed to notice. Because he always has a reason for everything, I asked Charlie why he went to the trouble of having the photo blown up and framed.

"Why do you think?" he asked right back. Sometimes, his Socratic approach can be downright irritating.

"You want me to remember the pain so I don't miss the game so much."

"No, you'll do that without any prompting. As Cicero said, *Cui placet obliviscitur, cui olet meminit.* We forget our pleasures, we remember our sufferings."

"Okay, so why—"

"Most of the pain we suffer we inflict on ourselves," he said.

I still didn't understand. "You want me to be cautious? Doesn't sound like you, Charlie."

"I want you to examine the consequences of your actions before you act. *Respice finem*. You have a tendency to . . ."

"Break the china."

"Precisely. And usually your own."

I knew I'd never be a great lawyer. I lost most of my cases as a public defender. The clients—I didn't start calling them "customers" until they could pay—either pleaded guilty, or a jury did it for them. Occasionally, the state would violate the speedy-trial rule, or witnesses wouldn't show, or the evidence would get lost, and someone would walk free, at least for a while.

I can still remember my first jury trial. *State of Florida* v. *Monroe Shackleford, Jr.* Armed robbery of a liquor store. Abe Socolow was the prosecutor. More hair then, but same old Abe. Dour face, sour disposition. Lean, mean Abe in his black suit and silver handcuffs tie. "Can you identify the man with the gun?" he asked.

"He's sitting right over there," the store clerk answered, pointing directly at Shackleford.

Outraged, my saintly client leaped to his feet and shouted, "You motherfucker, I should have blown your head off!"

I grabbed Shackleford by an elbow and yanked him into his chair. Sheepishly, he looked toward the jury and said, "I mean, if I'd been the one you seen."

Wilbert Faircloth appeared to be studying his notes. "Dr. Riggs, did there come a time when you and Mr. Lassiter became friends?"

Charlie fidgeted in the witness chair. He'd been in enough courtrooms to know that Faircloth was attempting to discredit Charlie's favorable testimony by showing bias. It's the oldest trick in the cross-examination book.

"I took the lad under my wing, showed him around the morgue," Charlie admitted. "He watched me perform a number of autopsies, didn't toss his lunch even once. It took a while, but Jake learned the basics of serology, toxicology, and forensic medicine."

"The question, Dr. Riggs, was whether the two of you became friends."

Charlie turned his bowling-ball body toward me. He had a mess of unkempt graying hair, a bushy brown beard streaked with gray, and eyeglasses mended with a fishhook where they had tossed a screw. He wore brown ankle-high walking boots, faded chinos, a string tie, and a sport coat with suede elbow patches. He gave the appearance of a bearded sixty-five-year-old cherub. Charlie never lied under oath or anywhere else, and he wasn't going to start now. "Yes, I'm proud to be his friend, and as far as I know, Jake's never done anything unethical."

"Ah so," Faircloth said, mostly to himself, smiling a barracuda's smile. Wilbert Faircloth was in his mid-forties and razor thin, even in a suit with padded shoulders. He had a narrow black mustache that belonged in Ronald Colman movies and an unctuous manner of referring to the judge as "this learned Court." After a mediocre career defending fender benders for a now-bankrupt insurance company, he became staff counsel of the state bar.

Now Faircloth was making a show of thumbing through his yellow legal pad. He rested the pad on the railing of the witness stand and fiddled at his mustache with the eraser of his pencil. "Would grave robbery be ethical to you, Dr. Riggs?"

"Objection!" I was on my feet. "Your Honor, that's beyond the scope of the bar complaint. It's ancient history, and no charges were ever filed."

Faircloth looked pleased as he approached the bench, cutting off my view of the judge. "The witness opened the door, and as this learned Court knows, I may walk through it if I please. In addition, I will demonstrate a pattern of misconduct."

Judge Herman Gold peered into the courtroom, empty now except for my old buddy Charlie, the slippery Wilbert Faircloth, and little old grave-robber me. Judge Gold had retired years ago, but you couldn't keep him off the bench. He accepted appointments to hear disciplinary cases against wayward lawyers, bringing as much of the law as he could remember to the deserted courthouse after hours. It was past 9:00 P.M. now, the grimy windows dark, and little traffic sloshed through the rain below us on Flagler Street. With its ceiling of ribbed beams and portraits of judges long since deceased, the huge courtroom was cold and barren as the old air-conditioning wheezed and cranked out dehumidified air.

"Overruled," Judge Gold pronounced, squinting toward the clock on the rear wall. He had missed the opening of jai alai at the fronton on Thirty-sixth Street and was not in a pleasant mood. "Past actions are relevant in aggravation or mitigation of the present transgression."

"Alleged transgression," I piped up.

Judge Gold ignored me and gestured toward Charlie Riggs to answer the question. I sank into my chair, armed with the knowledge that I had a fool for a client.

"What was the question?" Charlie asked.

"I'll happily rephrase," Faircloth offered. "To your knowledge, did Mr. Lassiter ever commit the crimes of trespassing, grave robbery, and malicious destruction of property?"

"It wasn't malicious," Charlie answered, somewhat defensively. "And it was my idea. I was his partner in crime. . . ."

Great, Charlie, but they can't disbar *you*.

"And besides, it was for a good cause," Charlie Riggs continued. "By exhuming Philip Corrigan's body, we were able to ascertain the identity of his killer."

"But Mr. Lassiter didn't obtain court permission for this so-called exhumation, correct?"

"Correct."

"Just as he didn't obtain court permission for the blatantly illegal surreptitious tape recording in this case, correct?"

"I'm not familiar with this case, Counselor."

"Ah so," Faircloth said, as if he had elicited a devastating admission.

On his way out of the courtroom, Charlie patted me on the shoulder and whispered, "*Vincit veritas*. Truth wins out."

Damn, I thought. Truth was, I committed a crime.

We took a brief recess so the judge could call his bookie. When we resumed, my backside hadn't even warmed up the witness chair when Wilbert Faircloth announced, "Mr. Lassiter, you have the right to counsel at this hearing. So that the record is clear, do you waive that right?"

"Yes."

"Do you do so freely, knowingly, and voluntarily?" Faircloth asked in the typical lawyer's fashion of using three words when one will suffice.

"Affirmative, yessir, and friggin' A," I answered. One of these days my sarcasm was going to get me in trouble. Maybe this was the day.

Faircloth seemed to puff out his bony chest. "The hour is growing late, so I suggest we cut to the chase without further ado."

"I'm all for skipping the ado," I agreed. Judge Gold gave me a pained look, or maybe he just had stomach gas.

"Now, sir," Faircloth continued, "did you or did you not surreptitiously tape-record your own client, one Guillermo Diaz, on or about February 12, 1993?"

I remembered the day. It was cool and breezy. I should have gone windsurfing. The black vultures soared effortlessly around the windows of my bayfront office, lazing in the updrafts. Thirty-two stories below, the predators in double-breasted suits were toting their briefcases to the courthouse. Birds of a feather.

Guillermo Diaz was chunky and round-faced with a nose somebody hadn't liked. He wore loafers with elevator heels, a short-sleeve knit shirt that was stretched taut against his belly. He had soft white hands and hard black eyes. He was harmless-looking, which made him better at his job. His job was killing people.

Diaz worked with a brute named Rafael Ramos who was twice as big but only half as tough. Together they were hired to shake down a horse trainer in Ocala who borrowed sixty thousand dollars from their boss at 5 percent interest. A week.

The trainer figured he'd pay it back quickly out of winnings, but his nags had an annoying habit of either finishing fourth, tossing their riders, or suffering heart attacks in the backstretch. With interest accumulating at three thousand a week, before compounding, the debt soon reached a hundred grand. When the trainer couldn't pay, Diaz and Ramos headed north on the Turnpike in a blue-black Lincoln Town Car.

Diaz joked that they should lop off the head of Ernie's Folly, a three-year-old filly, and leave it in the trainer's bed. "Just like in the movie."

Ramos was puzzled. "What movie?"

"Jesus, with Pacino and Brando. 'I'm gonna make him an offer he can't refuse.' "

Ramos stared blankly at him.

"You know, you gotta get out more," Diaz said.

Guillermo Diaz hated working with someone so stupid. He had to do all the thinking himself. What can you talk about with someone like Rafael Ramos, who sits there cleaning his fingernails with an eight-inch shiv? Playing Julio Iglesias tapes all the way up the turnpike. *Jesús Cristo!* Julio Iglesias.

Make him an offer he can't refuse. Though it started as a joke, riding through dreary central Florida past the orange groves and into the scrubby pine country, the idea sounded better all the time. Outside of Okahumpka, Diaz aimed the Lincoln toward the exit ramp. Ramos didn't even notice. He was humming along to "*Abrázame.*" Diaz found a hardware store in a strip shopping center and bought a chain saw from a pimply clerk who tried to sell him tree fertilizer plus fifty pounds of mulch on sale.

Back in the car, Ramos asked, "Fuck we need a chain saw for?"

"The horse."

"What horse?"

Diaz explained again, and Ramos started whining about his new white linen *guayabera*, and what a mess it would be. Diaz was so tired of the bellyaching, he agreed to forget about the horse—they'd just use the saw to scare the guy. The noise alone would make him shit his pants.

"No need to chop him into pieces," Diaz said. "Not like in that movie with Pacino and the guy in the shower."

"The movie with the horse?"

"No, different movie. Pacino's a *Marielito* in this one. More Cuban than you. Smarter, too."

They stopped at a service station, and Diaz filled the small tank on the chain saw, dribbling gasoline onto his patent-leather loafers. At the horse farm, they found the trainer in a barn made of telephone poles set in concrete. A light rain was falling, pinging off the barn's tin roof.

The trainer was a gray-haired man in his fifties, lean and wiry, with the blue-veined nose of the drinker. They backed him into a corner, where he stumbled over a pile of Seminole feed bags and nearly impaled himself on a pitchfork. The two enforcers felt out of place here, nearly intoxicated from the ripe, earthy smells of the barn, the distinctive tang of horse sweat, the sweetness of molasses from the feed mixing with the aroma of manure and urine, sawdust and creosote.

It took Diaz half a dozen pulls to get the new, warranty-covered Black & Decker chugging. He threatened to cut off the man's head if he didn't pay up. Diaz yelled this, because sure enough, the little machine made a hell of a racket. The trainer was crying, begging for more time to pay. All the while, two golden palominos and a paint were kicking and snorting in their stalls. Ramos cursed and lifted his left foot, a moist glob of excrement sticking to his tasseled loafer. Flies buzzed around Diaz's ears. Not little houseflies. Big, blue-winged monsters that looked like they could suck blood. By the quart.

Diaz felt ill. He would rather be in Miami, banging a guy's head against the asphalt in a back alley. He lived in a two-story stucco apartment building just off José Martí Avenue in Little Havana. The smells there were of cooking pork and steaming espresso. There were no horses with ugly square teeth and jackhammer hooves pounding the sideboards. He wanted to do the job and get the hell out of there.

While the trainer was pleading for another twenty-four hours, Diaz decided to send him a message. Take a little chunk out of the man's shoulder, just as a warning. Maybe get the guy to find a safe with some cash in it underneath the manure piles. In a movie, he saw the bad guys chop off someone's little finger. He couldn't remember if it made the man talk.

Diaz lifted the chain saw with both hands. "No!" the trainer shrieked, his eyes filling with tears.

"Ay, be thankful it's not your *pinga*," Diaz yelled over the roar.

The saw was bucking, and the man was screaming, and the horses were kicking the place down, and Ramos was saying something he couldn't hear. Diaz tried to gently tap the wailing machine against the trainer's shoulder, but he missed. The churning blade came to rest against the man's neck, where it bit through his carotid artery, splattering Ramos's white linen *guayabera* a rich scarlet and spraying the two palominos, turning them into pintos.

A week later, on that cool and breezy day, Guillermo Diaz sat in my office. "Grand jury meets this afternoon," I told him.

"Big fucking deal. They got no witnesses."

"Ramos turned state's evidence, testified yesterday. You're going to be indicted for Murder One."

"That's bullshit. Where is the chickenshit *cobarde*? Where's he now?"

"In protective custody.

"*¿Dónde?*"

"How should I know? And what difference does it make? You think you can get him to change his mind?"

"No, I think I can kill him."

Outside the windows, a buzzard landed on the ledge, spreading its six-foot wings, then folding them in that familiar hunched-shoulder look. The ugly birds fly south each winter and perch outside the windows of high-rise lawyers, reminding us of our ethical standards.

"You're not kidding, are you Guillermo?"

"You get to take his statement, *¿verdad?*"

"Right, a pre-trial deposition."

"You tell me when and where, it's over real quick."

He stood up and paced to the window. Spooked, the buzzard spread its wings and soared away. I leaned back in my chair, put my feet up on the credenza, and flicked the button on the Dicta-phone. A little red light blinked on. "Let me get this straight, Guillermo. You're asking me to set up Rafael Ramos, so you can kill him."

"Ay, Counselor, I do it with or without your help. What other choice I got?"

"Yes," I told Wilbert Faircloth. "I recorded my conversation with Mr. Diaz."

Faircloth let his voice pick up some volume. "And did you have a court order permitting you to conduct this recording?"

"I did not."

"Was the recording made in the course and scope of a bona fide law-enforcement investigation?"

"No, I did it on my own."

"And, as a lawyer, you are familiar with Chapter 934 of the Florida Statutes, are you not?"

"I know the gist of it."

"The *gist* of it," Faircloth repeated with some distaste. He paused, apparently considering whether to press me on the particulars of the law. "Do you know, sir, that the statute forbids tape recording a conversation unless all parties to that conversation have consented?"

"Yes."

"Did you know that on February twelfth, 1993?"

What would be better, I wondered, denying knowledge of the statute and therefore admitting incompetence, or conceding I knew my conduct was felonious? Probably the former, but damn, it would be a lie. They couldn't prove it, of course. No perjury charge. Still, one of Lassiter's Rules is not to lie to the court.

"Yes, I knew the law at the time."

"May we assume you obtained your client's permission?"

"You may assume it, but it wouldn't be true."

"So then, you did not have Mr. Diaz's consent to tape-record his conversation?"

I can't stand it when lawyers posture. "You expect me to ask permission to record his threats to kill a witness?"

"No, Mr. Lassiter. I expect you to follow the law."

Touché.

"Look, my plan was to record Diaz, withdraw from his case, and warn him that the tape would be turned over to the state attorney if anything happened to Rafael Ramos. The idea was to force him not to kill a man."

"But you were his *attorney*, Mr. Lassiter. You owed Mr. Diaz the duty of unyielding loyalty. The conversation was privileged. What gave you the right to act as his conscience?"

"*My* conscience," I answered. "Besides, once he disclosed the plan to commit a crime in the future, I believed the privilege was lost."

"Did you seek an advisory opinion from the bar to confirm your so-called belief?"

"No. There wasn't time."

"So you proceeded to knowingly violate Chapter 934 and to also breach the privilege by contacting the state attorney?"

"Yes. Diaz fired me when I wouldn't agree to set up a murder. I contacted Abe Socolow after Ramos was found with three bullets in his skull."

"Do you have any regrets about your conduct?"

"Yeah. I regret not calling Abe before Diaz killed Ramos."

"Now, isn't it true that Mr. Diaz was never convicted of that crime?"

"Right. There was a profound lack of witnesses."

"And you have no proof that Mr. Diaz committed this crime, do you, Mr. Lassiter?"

"No. I mean, yes, I have no proof." I hate questions phrased in the negative.

"And do you have an explanation for your behavior?"

"It seemed the right thing to do at the time," I said.

Faircloth couldn't suppress a snicker. "It *seemed* the right thing to do." He shot a look at the judge, trying to figure if he was scoring points. When he turned back to me, his smirk announced he was three touchdowns up with a minute to play. "Is that how you live your life, Mr. Lassiter, doing what *seems* right at the time?"

I didn't have to think about the answer. It was just there, the simple, stark truth. "As a matter of fact, that's exactly what I do."

Chapter 3

Goblins in the Night

CHARLIE RIGGS WAS WATCHING A LITHE YOUNG WOMAN IN BLACK Lycra shorts and a bikini top whirl through a pirouette on her Rollerblades, smack in the middle of Ocean Drive. No drivers yelled. No horns honked. A white stretch limo politely pulled around her. Four bearded guys gunned their black Harleys in an admiring salute as they gave her room. Two Miami Beach cops in khaki shorts weaved in and out of traffic on their bicycles, looking tanned, fit, and friendly, despite the Sig-Sauer nine-millimeters on their hips.

"Fascinating," Charlie said, as the young woman sped down the center line.

"Her abdominals, or the aerodynamics of the sport?" I asked.

"Dying of hypothermia in Miami in August," he answered, dipping a piece of pita bread into a bowl of pureed eggplant with garlic. We were sitting at a sidewalk table of the News Cafe, gathering spot for artists, actors, models, and assorted junior-varsity wannabes. A light breeze from the ocean, a few hundred yards to the east, cut the midday heat to manageable levels. To the west, storm clouds gathered over the Everglades. In the summer, lunch is followed by midafternoon thunderstorms nine days out of ten. I was wearing jeans, running shoes, dark glasses, and a Hawaiian shirt festooned with orchids. Charlie had on baggy pants that he must have worn while painting his house, a green surgical smock, and a fisherman's vest with various hooks and flies attached. He wore a shapeless canvas hat to keep the sun out of his eyes. To the casual observer, he was either the hippest guy on trendy South Beach or a demented professor.

Charlie took a sip of his lemonade and said, "A few years ago, a body turned up in Bayfront Park. It was July. A lad in his late teens, frozen stiff as a board and banged up a bit. Nobody could figure out what the deuce had happened. We checked the local meat lockers, ice plants, that sort of thing. I did the autopsy. Cause of death was asphyxia. Checked the inventory of his pockets. No wallet, no ID, no nothing except an Eastern Air Lines schedule and a hundred colóns in Costa Rican currency. Of course, that solved the mystery."

"It did?"

"The poor wretch had no visa and no money for a ticket, so he crawled into the wheel well of a jet at the airport in San Jose. There's space up there that a man—well, not someone your size, but this fellow—could fit into. The wheel well isn't pressurized, and if the lack of oxygen hadn't killed him, the temperature would have."

"The fall probably didn't do him any good, either," I speculated.

A group of Hare Krishnas chanted and bangled their way along the sidewalk, sweat glistening on their shaved heads. I took a bite of my cheeseburger. South Beach overflows with chichi cafés where the pasta is al dente and the tuna rare, but I'm still a burger-and-brew guy. I'm as health-conscious as the next guy, as long as the next guy is sitting on a barstool, but there are limits. It doesn't bother me if someone waxes poetic about the joys of bean sprouts. If a scrawny woman feasts on grapefruit and lettuce, fine. If a guy is a vegetarian jogger, that's great, too, though most look as if they couldn't buck a force-three wind. I don't tell other people how to live, and I appreciate reciprocity.

Once when I was chomping a cheeseburger with a side of fries at an outdoor café in Coconut Grove, a fragile-looking guy in a gold velour warmup suit and white bicycling helmet stopped short at my table. "I'd hate to see the inside of your arteries," he said somberly.

"Fine," I responded, taking a long swallow of my chocolate shake. "I'll tear your heart out, and we'll look at yours."

He blinked and took a step backward. "Eat yourself to death, if you want. All that animal fat leads to cardiac arrest, and the excess protein causes kidney failure."

"So does a good left hook," I advised him.

I don't believe in being judgmental. You eat your tofu, I'll eat my T-bone. Today, though, it was a rare burger with purple onions, ripe tomato slices, and tangy mustard on a fresh-baked roll. A nice slab of melted Jarlsberg cheese to keep the juices in the meat. With all the pasta and sushi places, it isn't easy to find a good burger any more, so it's a real quiniela if the same place also serves Grolsch, the Dutch beer.

"You say Mr. Tupton had been drinking?" Charlie asked.

"Heavily."

"And the room temperature was in the fifties?"

"Fifty-six, right on the button, and Tupton was soaking wet."

In the street, several young men carried a banner protesting discrimination against AIDS victims. The Miami Beach bicycle cops patiently directed traffic around the demonstrators. Charlie smoothed his beard with the back of his hand. "That could do it. Once in a while, in the winter down here, with the ambient temperature in the fifties, we'll see a homeless person die of hypothermia. If there's been excessive alcohol intake, vasodilation is the killer. The blood vessels dilate, body temperature plummets. All kinds of complications can result, metabolic acidosis, elevations in serum amylase, and pancreatitis." A shirtless man walked by, a bright green mynah perched on his shoulder. Hardly anyone turned to stare. "How long was Tupton in there?"

"Twelve, fourteen hours. The maid discovered him in the morning. When the paramedics arrived, his body temperature was seventy-seven degrees. No respiration, no heartbeat."

"Ventricular fibrillation was the likely terminal event. Seems like he died of natural causes, so what's the problem, Jake?"

I shrugged. I didn't know. It was just this vague uneasiness. I took a bite of the burger and drained the beer.

"Any surprises in the autopsy?" asked the man who had performed twenty thousand before retiring to a life of fishing and reading medical texts in their original Latin.

"M.E. says no. Nothing unusual in the system other than the elevated blood alcohol. No signs of a struggle, no toxins, no puncture wounds . . ."

That made us both pause. I can't read minds, but Charlie Riggs had to be thinking about a twenty-gauge hypodermic track in the buttocks of rich old Philip Corrigan. Dead old Philip Corrigan, but that's another story.

"The report confirms what you said, Charlie. Ventricular fibrillation caused by hypothermia."

"So all you're dealing with is a wrongful-death suit. Just another dispute about money."

"Right. Social-host liability."

Charlie seemed to be studying the man-made sand dunes on the beach across Ocean Drive. "Who's the plaintiff's lawyer?"

"Henry Thackery Patterson."

"H.T.'s good, though a trifle flamboyant for my tastes," Charlie observed.

"He's already filed a boilerplate complaint. Simple negligence for serving alcohol to an intoxicated guest. I'll file an answer with the usual affirmative defenses, comparative negligence and assumption of the risk."

"Blame it on the victim, eh?"

"Sure. The old defense gambit. The plaintiff caused his own harm, so don't point the finger at the party hosts who had to keep the hors d'oevres moving."

Charlie shook his head. "Whatever happened to the concept '*de mortuis nihil nisi bonum*'?"

"Damned if I know."

"Speak kindly of the dead," Charlie translated.

"Why? They're the only ones who can't sue for slander."

Charlie tut-tut-tutted and finished cleaning his plate of the eggplant goo with a swipe of his pita. "I still don't know what's troubling you. Talk to me, Jake."

"Too many questions don't have answers. Didn't they miss Tupton at the party? Didn't anybody see him go in there or see his car parked all night in the street in front of the house? How about his clothes, still hanging in a closet in a guest room?"

Charlie wrinkled his forehead. "You're talking like a prosecutor now. You've been retained to defend a simple civil suit. Just do your job."

Charlie was right. I should file my pleadings, take my depos, make my motions, and eventually settle the case before trial. The usual old soft-shoe. I was trying to treat this like any other case. I really was. But my mind was buzzing with other thoughts. Gina. Nicky. Tupton.

"Is there coverage?" Charlie asked.

"A million in homeowner's, another five-million umbrella policy."

"So, you have no downside. Win, you're a hero. Lose, the insurance company pays. Why go looking for goblins in the night?"

"Hey, you're the guy who taught me not to accept things at face value. 'Things are seldom what they seem, skim milk masquerades as cream.' That was you talking, Charlie. And how about this little ditty, 'Seek the truth,' or however the hell you say it."

"*Quaere verum*," he instructed me. "And you're the lad who told me that isn't the lawyer's job."

"It isn't," I said. "My job's to take the facts handed to me and present the best case I can. I'm not supposed to dig for stuff that'll hurt my client."

"Like in Philip Corrigan's grave."

"Thanks for reminding me. Can you believe that's coming back to haunt me now?" I mimicked Wilbert Faircloth's weasel voice: " 'Would grave robbery be ethical to you, Dr. Riggs?' Jeez, Charlie, I'm in for a public reprimand, maybe even a six-month suspension."

"Precisely my point. Why go looking for trouble now?"

"Why should *now* be different? Look, Charlie, I never liked Nicky Florio, and I never trusted him."

Charlie Riggs harrumphed and rearranged his bulky body in his chair. "You never liked him because he married Star Hampton." He paused, and a light flickered in his deep brown eyes. "Jake, you're not seeing her again, are you?"

"Her name's Gina now."

"Your answer was not responsive, Counselor. Haven't you got enough trouble with the Bar as it is? Talk about conflicts of interest." Charlie stared toward the ocean, screwing his face into thought. The clouds from the west were nearly overhead now, and the temperature was beginning to drop. Intermittent gusts tugged at the café's umbrellas. "I never thought that girl was for you. She combines dependency on a man with an ability to manipulate him. She's a user, Jake. I know the effect she had on you, and I only hope it's over. You've got this flaw, you know. . . ."

"Only one?"

"Where women are concerned, you're attracted to the birds with the broken wings. You want to mend them, make them whole. But Star, or Gina, or whoever, is a predator, a hawk, not a hummingbird. Let the Nicky Florios of the world deal with her kind."

I always listen to Charlie, but sometimes I don't follow his advice. This time, I kept quiet.

Charlie leaned back in his chair and eyeballed me from under his canvas hat. "You can't represent Nicky if you're seeing his wife. You understand that, don't you?"

I stayed buttoned up. The Fifth Amendment was always dear to me.

"Are you listening, Jake? A meretricious relationship affects your judgment. You should be planning Nicky's defenses, and instead you sit here implying that maybe this accident was really . . ."

"Say it, Charlie. That Peter Tupton was aced, offed, zapped, rubbed out."

I had raised my voice without knowing it, and Charlie's bushy eyebrows were arched as he appraised me. "You've been under a lot of stress, Jake. Maybe you should let one of your partners handle the suit, take some time off. From what you tell me, there's no indication of a homicide."

I signaled the waiter for another beer. "Motive, Charlie. It's what you taught me to focus on. Tupton could cause Nicky a lot of trouble, cost him a lot of money and time fighting lawsuits instead of building his plug-ugly condos. Nicky invites the guy to a party, tries to soften him up, but it doesn't work. . . ."

Charlie scowled and harrumphed in disbelief. "So he gets Tupton drunk and drops him in a chilly room. Really, Jake, if you're going to the trouble to kill someone, you'd use a method that'd be sure to be lethal, and you probably wouldn't do it in your home."

Just then, Charlie's beeper went off. He extracted it from his belt and squinted at the digital readout. "State attorney's number." Charlie balled up his napkin, stood, and headed inside the restaurant, looking for a pay phone.

While I waited, I mulled it over. The old sawbones was right. If Nicky wanted to kill Tupton, he wouldn't do it himself, and he wouldn't use a method that might just give the guy a cold. In this town, there are semipros who'll ace somebody for a new outboard motor or a three-day pass to Disney World. And Florio could afford the best. But then, if everyone who committed a crime was so smart, nobody would ever be caught.

I was still thinking about it when Charlie toddled back to the table, his brow furrowed, one hand absentmindedly stroking a cork attached to his fishing vest by a 3/0 hook. "Abe Socolow," he announced, gravely, "asked if I'd take an appointment to assist the M.E. in a suspected homicide."

"So?"

"I told him I have a potential conflict of interest."

Charlie hadn't told me, but I knew. The state attorney was looking into the death of one Peter Tupton, a guy who didn't fall out of a wheel well of a jet but still froze to death in Miami.

"Where's your conflict?" I asked. "I haven't retained you as an expert."

"The conflict is that I'm your friend, but if you don't have a problem with it, neither does Abe."

"Why does he want you?"

"Metro Crime Scene tried to lift prints off the corpse with the plate-glass method. See if somebody carried Tupton into the wine cellar. They came up with something on the wrists, but they're not good enough to match up, though they seem to exclude the paramedics. Socolow wants me to oversee a methyl-methacrylate test."

Charlie was too modest to say it, but he's the old coot who invented it. Getting latent prints from the body of a corpse was tricky stuff. Moisture, the breakdown of tissues, and the surface of the skin itself were major problems. Sometimes, prints would show up by rolling a piece of glass across the body, but usually it didn't work. Charlie came up with the Super Glue method. Convert the glue into fumes and tent the body. The sticky stuff settles on the skin, and *voilà!*, if someone manhandled the body, prints appear in the glue as the fumes condense on the skin.

"I don't mind, Charlie. Take the job."

"I don't need the money," he said.

"C'mon, take it. I'd rather have you on the other side than some yahoo who doesn't know what he's doing. Remember, I'm supposed to be seeking the truth."

"No, you're not, Jake. You're supposed to be representing Nicky Florio."

Chapter 4

Playing Footsie

"JUST WHAT IS YOUR NET WORTH, MR. FLORIO?" H. T. PATTERSON asked.

"Objection," I called out, slapping the table with a palm. "The defendant's financial resources are irrelevant."

"Irrelevant!" Patterson boomed, as if there were a judge and jury to appreciate his righteous indignation. "Dare you say irrelevant?"

"I dare. And while I'm at it, I dare say immaterial, inadmissible, and just plain none of your business."

Patterson feigned outrage and turned to the court reporter. "Has the stenographer recorded every word of this obloquial colloquy? When we bring this before the Court, I shall seek sanctions."

The reporter, a heavyset young woman, nodded silently. Patterson was decked out in a white linen three-piece suit, which was set off nicely by his cocoa-colored skin. He was short and trim, a native of the Bahamas and a former fundamentalist preacher at the Liberty City Baptist Church. After law school, he continued his Holy Rolling, only in the courtroom.

Five of us sat around the conference table in Patterson's law office—Nicky and Gina Florio, the court reporter, Patterson, and a big lug who used to wear number 58 in the aqua and orange and was now squeezed into an off-the-rack, 46-long seersucker suit.

* * *

Before we started the deposition, I sat in H. T. Patterson's office as he slid a videotape into a VCR. The television screen flickered to life, a helicopter shot of the Miami skyline. Then the music came up, a strident beat stolen from *Miami Vice*. Finally, two men appeared on the screen, a beaming interviewer and a super-serious Peter Tupton. They sat in straight-backed chairs on a carpeted riser. Between them was a coffee table on which sat an artificial rhododendron, and behind them a logo, ¿QUÉ pasa, MIAMI? One of those Sunday morning public-affairs shows you watch when the hangover is so bad you can't bend over to pick up the remote control.

The tape was marked Plaintiff's Exhibit Seven, and Patterson intended to introduce it at the trial. Under the rules of discovery, I could see it first.

"What's the relevance of this?" I asked, as the interviewer was telling us Tupton's background.

"Two weeks before his tragic death, Peter Tupton gave this interview. Thanks to the wonders of modern technology, we can show the jury that this was a *man*. Yea, more than a man, a towering figure of vision, courage, and honor."

"I'd like to listen to your client before you canonize him," I said.

I watched for a few minutes. The towering figure appeared to be a short, overweight man in his late thirties with receding pale hair, horn-rimmed glasses, and thin, grim lips. He wore a safari jacket over a blue chambray shirt. The pants were khaki, and when he crossed his legs, I could see one hiking boot stained with mud. I quickly learned that Tupton had studied petroleum engineering at a university out West, that his first job had been with an oil company, and after an explosion and fire on an offshore rig, he had been so shocked by the ecological destruction that he had quit. Tupton didn't say anything about the men who had been killed, but the loss of fish and birds really seemed to frost his buns. He went back to school, picked up a master's degree, and became involved in environmental protection, first with the government, later with the Everglades Society.

The interviewer asked about the history of the Everglades, and Tupton used its Indian name, *Pa-hay-okee*, grassy water, a reference to the tooth-edged saw grass in the shallow, vast stream. He talked about the diversity of the Glades, the shallow sloughs and gator holes, shell-filled beaches and tangled mangroves. He decried development, claiming it had caused the drought, turning parts of the Glades into a prairie. He talked about the ecosystems, pine rocklands, mangrove swamps, hardwood hammocks, bayheads, and cypress heads. He bemoaned the sugarcane fields, sucking up nutrients from the saw-grass peat that accumulated over thousands of years. He criticized the man-made irrigation channels that artificially restrict the natural cycle of dry winters and flooded summers.

On the screen, a file videotape showed a variety of animals in their natural habitat, and Tupton gave a voice-over narration in a calm, measured voice. He described the endangered species in the Glades, and we looked at crocodiles and turtles, manatees and panthers, a bald eagle, a wood stork, a pair of snail kites, and a peregrine falcon.

"We must keep ever vigilant," Peter Tupton said. He radiated sincerity, seriousness of purpose. "When there are threats to the environment, we must respond with protests, lawsuits, political pressure, every tool at our disposal."

The interviewer asked, "Aren't people much more aware of the environment these days?"

Tupton nodded. "Twenty-five years ago, some so-called regional planners proposed building a huge jetport in the Big Cypress Swamp smack in the Glades. They publicly announced that entire cities would be built around the jetport, as if that was something to be proud of. Before anyone knew what was going on, they dredged and even built a trial runway. That's how close it came before the public rose up and shut it all down. Now there's a local developer who wants to build a town out there."

Next to me H. T. Patterson chuckled. I listened some more.

In the space of thirty minutes, interspersed with public-service spots and commercials for every Jim Nabors record ever made, Tupton told everything I wanted to know about the Everglades, and then some. I concluded that the judge would allow the tape into evidence and that the jury would like Peter Tupton.

Maybe not *like* so much as respect. Patterson knew what he was doing. Wrongful-death cases with a surviving widow involve two kinds of plaintiffs. The regular guy—*No, ladies and gentlemen of the jury, this was not a special man. This was not an extraordinary man. This man was not an Eagle Scout or a high public official. He packed bags at the Piggly Wiggly, but he was someone special to his wife, because this was the one man in the world who had fallen in love with her, who had spent his life with her, who had shared her joys and her sorrows all these many years. . . .*

That kind of case was tough enough to defend, but Patterson was going after something else. The special person—*Yes, ladies and gentlemen, this was a special man, a man who made a difference in our lives. While we went about our daily chores, oblivious to our surroundings, he was there fighting the good fight to assure we have water to drink, to bathe our children, to wash our cars. He fought to make sure our grandchildren can enjoy the majesty of the southern bald eagle. This was a man who was our keeper of the lighthouse. He kept a watch out for us all. He was a special man. . . .*

Oh, my, how H. T. Patterson could play this one.

Now, barely ten minutes into the deposition, we were hung up on the issue of the plaintiff's right to details of the defendant's financial condition. "If you persist in your mulish intractability," Patterson announced, "we shall forthwith and with due dispatch move to amend the complaint and add a claim for punitive damages. Thereupon, the issue of the defendant's net worth is relevant, admissible, and if I may say so, quite instructive to the jury in assessing damages."

He was doing his best to intimidate Nicky, trying to convince him that the discovery process would be so burdensome and invasive of his privacy that he should settle the case. Trouble was, Nicky Florio didn't intimidate easily.

I was about to make my objection when Florio spoke up: "You guys can keep on yapping and running up the bills, if you want. I don't give a shit. I'm not gonna answer questions about my finances to you, the judge, or even my beautiful wife."

Across the conference table, Gina giggled.

I put my hand on Florio's arm to hush him up. Refusing to answer questions sometimes backfires. Once, in a divorce case, I asked a flagrantly unfaithful wife if she had stayed with a particular gentleman at a hotel in New York.

"I refuse to answer that question," she reponded.

"Did you stay with the man in Los Angeles?"

"I refuse to answer that question."

"Did you stay with the man in Miami?"

"No," she answered proudly.

Florio quieted down, and I turned my attention to Patterson. "This isn't a case for punies, and you know it, H.T., so until I see your motion, and until the judge grants it—which should be the same time Tampa Bay wins the Super Bowl—you can forget about prying into financial resources."

Patterson kept blathering as if he hadn't heard me. "Your client is guilty of gross and glaring negligence, willful and wanton misconduct, egregious and intentional deviation from the standard of care imposed on social hosts. Thus, we are entitled to what is euphemistially called smart money in an amount sufficient to make the defendant smart, i.e., feel pain. Hence, your objection is obdurate and obstinate, ornery and obstreperous. Your conduct is predictably perverse and consistently contumacious. You . . ."

When H.T. lapses into his seductive singsong, even I stop and listen, usually tapping my toe on the floor, keeping time with the rhythm until he runs out of steam.

". . . thwart justice by defending actions that are depraved and degenerate. If you continue this iniquitous and unscrupulous stonewalling, we shall have no recourse but to take this matter before the judge and apply for sanctions."

"H.T., chill out."

His eyes lit up. "That's just what your client's tortious misconduct caused to occur. The terminal chilling-out of a dedicated citizen, a man who put civic duty above financial reward, a man who spent his all-too-brief life fighting the robber barons and the well-connected. A man who walked through the valley of greed and gluttony, cupidity and corruption, and sought the straight-and-narrow path.

"Save it for the jury, H.T."

"A man cannot indiscriminately let flow a river of demon rum to his guest," H.T. continued, impervious, "then abdicate his responsibility. No, he must be made to pay, and pay till it hurts."

Nicky Florio's olive complexion was beginning to color. He drummed his well-manicured nails on the tabletop. His black hair was slicked straight back, his dark eyes blazing at H. T. Patterson. Florio wore a jet-black suit, a white-on-white shirt, and one of those expensive Italian silk ties that looks like a bouquet of flowers and costs more than most small appliances. He leaned toward me and whispered, "Do I have to listen to this shit? Jesus, let's get it over with. I got a business to run."

I calmed him with a hand on his shoulder and turned to my opponent. "H.T., you're wasting a lot of valuable time and paper. I'd swear you were getting paid by the word instead of your usual forty percent."

"Blasphemer! I have promised a percentage of my fee to the Everglades Society, so that Mr. Tupton's grand works can continue after his untimely passing."

"How thoughtful. I don't suppose the group is returning the favor by helping you with the lawsuit, is it? And what percentage are you contributing, Henry Thackery? A tiny morsel, a single digit, no doubt? It'll be good for a tax deduction and a mention of your generosity in the newspapers, probably at the time we're picking a jury."

"Counselor, you vex me."

"Good. We're even."

I yawned and decided to keep quiet. Maybe if I ignored Patterson's diversions, he'd get back on track. I stretched my legs, locked my hands behind my neck, and cracked my knuckles.

Something touched my left leg.

At first I thought that Nicky, seated to my left, had bumped into me under the table. He hadn't. I glanced at Gina, sitting directly across from me. She wore a sleeveless red leather minidress. Too hot for Miami in the summer, but it covered so little, maybe it didn't matter. A gold zipper ran diagonally from the hem to the neck. It was unzipped to the middle of her breasts.

Something touched my leg again and moved upward.

Gina's foot.

Unless you were watching, you wouldn't notice her slipping slightly lower into her chair as her foot inched upward along my leg. A small smile played at her lips.

Risk.

Danger.

Fun.

They were all the same to her. Sex was enhanced if she was bouncing on the deck of a pitching boat during a gale. Preferably with a man who was not her spouse. She drove too fast, drank too much, partied too long. She liked men who risked their bodies and their bankrolls. She skied on slopes too steep and dived in waters too deep. She jumped off bridges attached to a bungee cord and told me it was her second-favorite sport. And now, with her husband two feet away, her toes crept toward my crotch.

"Just how much did you serve Mr. Tupton to drink?" Patterson asked.

"I didn't serve him anything," Nicky replied. "We have servants for that."

"Servants!" Patterson sang out. "As it is written in Matthew, 'The dogs eat of the crumbs which fall from their masters' table.' "

I knew where he was going. This wasn't a lawsuit but a class war.

"How convenient you have servants," Patterson continued sarcastically. "Pity they're not slaves."

"Objection!" I yelled. "Move to stri-eeek!"

The ball of Gina's foot had found a part of me that was totally unconcerned with the rules of evidence. Patterson was looking at me, puzzled for once.

"That is, move to stroke, ah-chem, *strike* the provocative and inflamed, I mean . . . inflammatory comment of counsel."

I felt my face redden. Nicky Florio shot me a sideways look that seemed to ask whether I was competent. At the moment, I was not.

"You intended to get Mr. Tupton intoxicated, did you not?" Patterson asked.

"No," Florio answered flatly.

"Did you ask him to come to the party without his wife?"

"No, that was his choice."

"Isn't it true you provided him with female companionship?"

"There were single women at the party, if that's what you mean."

Patterson thumbed through his notes. "Do you know a Ms. Amber Lane and a Ms. Marcia Middleton?"

Gina's foot had miraculously withdrawn from my crotch.

"The ladies work for me. They take reservation deposits on new condos at Rolling Hills Estates."

I knew the place. Located on a former marsh about six feet above sea level, the only hills were made of swampy landfill, and the estates were town houses crammed sixteen to the acre.

"Were the *ladies* wearing those very skimpy bikinis," Patterson asked with obvious distaste, "the ones designed by Satan himself, the ones called—"

"Tongas," Gina piped up, with a lascivious grin.

"Hush!" I told her.

From across the table, Gina winked at me.

"It was a pool party," Nicky Florio said. "All the women were in appropriate attire. As I recall, a few were sunbathing topless near the seawall."

"No!" thundered Patterson. "You violated Coral Gables ordinances, to say nothing of the law of the Lord. As Peter observed, 'Thou shalt abstain from fleshly lusts—' "

"C'mon, H.T.," I implored. "Keep to the point."

"And was it the job of Ms. Lane and Ms. Middleton to spend the day entertaining Mr. Tupton?"

"All the employees are encouraged to socialize," Florio said.

"Socialize," Patterson repeated, as if the word turned his stomach. "Did that include playing"—again he consulted his notes—"pool tag? Where the person who's 'it' must tag the next person, regardless of sex, exactly where he or she has been tagged."

"There were games going on in the pool," Florio said. "Nobody seemed to be complaining, and I didn't keep track of what everyone was doing."

"Just as you didn't keep track of how much Mr. Tupton drank."

"Look, fellow. There were a hundred people at my house. I'm not a nursemaid. I'm a businessman. These were all consenting adults, if you know what I mean. If somebody slips into the cabana with someone not his wife, it's no business of mine. If a guy chooses to get sloshed, that's his prerogative. During a party, I'm working. I've got to entertain county commissioners, tribal leaders, sugar growers, zoning lawyers, subcontractors, plus the usual Ocean Club crowd. I'm sorry about Peter Tupton. I really am. But he drank himself into a stupor and wandered into the wine cellar. It's his own damn fault, and that's all there is to it."

Not a bad speech. We could clean it up a little, make it seem not so harsh, a little more sympathetic to the deceased, then use it at trial. With enough rehearsal, it would seem appropriately spontaneous.

Patterson pretended not to have heard a word. He had taken mental notes, I knew, sizing up the opposition, figuring just what kind of witness he had to deal with, and then he went back to work. "Now concerning your business, you lease several thousand acres in the Everglades from the Micanopy tribe, do you not?"

"Yeah, it's a matter of public record."

"And you run the Micanopy bingo games, correct?"

"Right. My associate handles that."

"Your associate being Rick Gondolier?"

"That's right."

I had seen Gondolier's picture in the newspaper lots of times. Handsome, mid-thirties, he was usually wearing a tux, his arm around a woman in an evening gown at one of Miami's endless social events. Gondolier came from Las Vegas, where he had managed a couple of hotel casinos. There'd been a scandal, skimming cash, bribing local officials. Some indictments, an immunized witness who disappeared, no convictions. Gondolier made a splash when he bought into Nicky Florio's businesses. A few major charitable contributions and membership in the right clubs brought contacts and society-page publicity. In Miami, a shady past doesn't hamper careers. Hereabouts, the only sin is being poor.

"And what are your business relationships with Mr. Gondolier?" Patterson asked.

"Objection to the form the question," I said. "Vague, overbroad."

The court reporter noted my objection, and Patterson thought about it. "I'll rephrase. Are the two of you partners?"

"Objection, irrelevant."

Patterson gave me his patronizing look. "If they're partners and this pool party was a business event," he lectured, "then Mr. Gondolier is equally liable for the negligence of Mr. Florio. Jake, didn't you did take Business Organizations in law school?"

"Twice," I told him. I turned to Florio. "Go ahead and answer."

"We're not partners. All the relationships are corporate. We each own fifty percent of the stock in Micanopy Management Company. That's the subsidiary that runs the bingo business. Gondolier's got a minority position in the parent company, Florio Enterprises, which develops our real estate interests. He's got an option to purchase up to half the stock. I'm the president and CEO of each company. He's the chief operating officer of the bingo business. Anything else you want to know?"

"Was Gondolier at the party?"

"Yeah, and so was the archbishop. Want to sue him, too?"

Patterson ignored the crack. He was good at it. "Now, concerning the several thousand acres you lease from the Micanopy tribe, you and Mr. Gondolier plan to build apartments and town houses on the environmentally sensitive land, do you not?"

"So what? It's perfectly legal. I've been this route before. I've got the best lawyers, the best consultants, the best lobbyists."

I remembered what Gina said about her husband. *Nicky likes the best of everything.*

Patterson leaned over the table, closer to Nicky Florio. "You knew that Mr. Tupton's group opposed your plans?"

"Sure, he told us. A hundred times. He told the newspapers. He wrote letters to the governor and the cabinet. His fax machine must have blown a gasket over this thing. Gondolier and I talked about it. We were searching for areas of common ground with Tupton."

"Such as a bribe?"

Oh shit. What was this all about?

"Objection!" I sang out. "Argumentative and irrelevant." Buying time now.

"Jake, Jake, Jake." Patterson's tone was condescending. "You know that objection is preserved for trial. As for the present, there's a question pending." Patterson turned back to Nicky. "Now, Mr. Florio, did you offer Peter Tupton a bribe to drop his opposition to your plans?"

"Don't answer," I instructed my client. "Time-out, H.T. I need to confer with my client."

"Confer or coach, Jake?" Patterson stood up, smiling.

He left the room, bouncing on his toes, a satisfied look on his face. The court reporter stood, opened her purse, grabbed a pack of cigarettes, and went into the hallway. I was left with Nicky and Gina.

"What's going on?" I asked.

"Tupton must have told his wife," Nicky said.

"Told her what?"

"But there's nothing in writing."

"Told her what?" I repeated.

"I could say *he* solicited a bribe, and I turned him down. Who would know?"

"I would," I said.

His look was razor-sharp. "Don't start playing Boy Scout with me over a harmless little talk I had with that self-important sack of shit. I know about you. I know all about you."

Gina cleared her throat. "If you boys are going to play, I think I'll go take a pee. Excuse me . . . powder my nose." She wriggled back into her shoes—one or two wriggles more than seemed necessary—stood up, and left the conference room.

Nicky Florio and I just sat there staring at each other. What had he meant? *All* about me. Professional, personal, or both? The grievance proceeding, or Gina, or a guy I once decked in a bar? I didn't know. All right, so maybe I'm the bull in the china shop when it comes to tact and subtlety, but basically, I like to think I'm considered almost respectable by my peers. Unfortunately, there are no sophisticated electronic devices to measure character, and all of us see ourselves differently than those around us. Our reputation is created out of earshot.

I try to go through each day wreaking as little havoc as possible. I am unfailingly polite to bone-weary waitresses who deliver my potatoes fried instead of mashed. I never park in the handicapped space or toss gum wrappers on the sidewalk. I don't shoot little furry animals or curse at telephone solicitors. I help old ladies across the street, feed stray cats, and recycle beer bottles. For the past several years, I worked the cafeteria line at a homeless shelter on Thanksgiving, scooping out the gravy to haggard men and women, thanking the powers of the universe for the cosmic luck that gave me a sound body and semisound mind.

In the practice of law, a sea inhabited by sharks and other carnivores, my ethics are simple. I won't lie to a judge, steal from a client, or bribe a cop. Until recently, I wouldn't sleep with a client's wife, but since I knew Gina before she married Nicky, I figured I was grandfathered in, if I figured anything at all.

Other than that, I believe in drawing blood from the opposition, but not by going for the knees. Hit 'em straight on, jawbone-to-jawbone. Which is why I didn't like the slippery scruples of Nicky Florio, who sat there glaring at me with his dark, piercing eyes.

"Okay," I said. "Forget about my principles. I sometimes do. Think about this. Maybe Tupton was wired when you talked."

"That'd be illegal, wouldn't it?"

Now it was getting too close to home. "Not if it was part of a law-enforcement investigation. Or maybe he did an affidavit after the conversation or told it to the newspapers. Maybe the grand jury is looking into it."

"Abe Socolow runs the grand jury, doesn't he?"

"Yeah, he's the prosecutor in charge of corruption probes."

"He was at the party. He's all right."

"He's better than all right. Abe's tough and honest, and he could eat your canapés all night and subpoena you the next morning."

Florio smiled. "Don't worry. He's on our team."

"What does that mean?"

"He's running for state attorney, right? I'm helping him out with his finances."

"Look, Nicky, I've known Abe since he was prosecuting DUIs and I was defending shoplifters. You can't buy him. Now, what the hell was going on between you and Tupton?"

If Nicky had to think about the answer, he was a quick study. "It was no big deal. I offered him stock in Micanopy Management Company at a special rate, that's all."

"A special rate?"

"Yeah, like for free."

"You didn't!"

"The company's a gold mine. We've got the management contract for the Micanopy bingo hall. You ever see the place?"

I shook my head.

"Out on the fringe of the Glades. You could play the Super Bowl in there, and it's a real cash machine. Gondolier does a great job. We bring in the retirees by the busload from all over. St. Pete, Naples, Lehigh Acres, Cape Coral, Sunrise Lakes, Bonita Springs. Jeez, we gotta have a cardiologist on the premises, we get a couple tickers stopping during the hundred-grand game on Saturday nights. Now we've got the video pull-tab games, French bingo, do-it-yourself bingo."

"What's it got to do with Tupton?"

"Nothing, until, as a friendly gesture, I offered him the stock, that's all. Plus a seat on the board. He could pick up some spare change in director's fees."

"This is bullshit, and you know it. You were trying to bribe him."

"Hold on, Jake. He wasn't a public official. There was nothing illegal about it. Okay, so I wanted some cooperation. But I never said he had to do anything for me in return. That's not a bribe, right?"

"Right, there's no bribe unless there's a quid pro quo." I haven't hung around Doc Riggs all these years without learning something.

Florio smiled, thinking about it. I wouldn't want him smiling at me like that. " 'Course, if he took the quid and didn't give me the quo, I'd have killed the son of a bitch."

"But Tupton didn't take it, did he?"

"No, he refused."

"So how come the son of a bitch is dead?" I asked.

Chapter 5

The Fox and the Henhouse

I AIMED THE OLD CONVERTIBLE WEST ON TAMIAMI TRAIL BUT NEVER got out of third gear. From Brickell Avenue westward, the Trail cuts a straight, if congested, path through Little Havana. Once out of the city, the road splits the Everglades heading straight toward Naples on the west coast. Eventually, it bends to the north and hits Tampa.

Tamiami, Tampa to Miami, get it?

My old beauty, a canary-yellow 1968 Olds 442, growled and groaned, anxious for wide-open spaces. But now, as the afternoon sun glared down, Charlie Riggs and I were stuck somewhere between Thirteenth and Twenty-second avenues. At least that's what they used to be called. Thirteenth is now Luis Medina Muñoz Marin Avenue, and Twenty-second is General Máximo Gómez Boulevard. If that's not confusing enough, Tamiami Trail is better known as Calle Ocho, since it is really Eighth Street, in case you're counting.

Salsa music poured from open storefronts, the neighborhood a potpourri of cultural confusion. The sign above a medical clinic: VENAS VARICOSAS. A furniture store: GARANTIZAMOS LOS PRECIOS MÁS BAJOS. A nightclub: EXÓTICO, ARDIENTE, ESPECTACULAR. Delivery vans blocked the right-hand lane. Shoppers and tourists and kids in souped-up Chevies crept along, engines heating up, radiators threatening to blow. Yesterday, on the TV news, one of the weather guys with the pasted-on smile tried to fry an egg on the sidewalk. He got some sizzle, but the yolk was still runny.

In front of us, a Metro bus downshifted and braked, belching black smoke. "Damn, Charlie, is it getting hotter every summer or is it just me?"

"The greenhouse effect's a fact, my boy, and it feeds on itself. As the atmospheric temperature rises, more carbon dioxide is released from the forests and grasslands. So, global warming stimulates more global warming."

"Then we're cooking ourselves to death," I said, inhaling a dose of bus exhaust. On the back of the bus, a billboard extolled the virtues of Rolling Hills Estates, a Florio Enterprises community. Nicky Florio's smiling face looked down at me through the fumes.

"Actually, global warming will usher in a new ice age," Charlie corrected me.

"I don't get it," I said, and not for the first time. "Global warming will melt the glaciers."

Charlie wagged his head from side to side. "Just the opposite. The Arctic doesn't get much snow because it's too cold and too dry, but global warming will cause a major increase in polar temperatures and humidity. That'll increase snowfall by perhaps forty percent, and the polar ice cap will reach Long Island."

Dandy, I thought. When it gets too hot, the earth freezes over. Makes sense, though. A perfect incongruous symmetry. If life is filled with ironies, why shouldn't nature be? Hard work leads to coronaries, love to heartbreak of another kind, life to death. As night follows day, sorrow follows joy. The affluent, many of whom labored mightily to get there, spawn indolent children. The kid from the ghetto gets an Ivy League scholarship, then is cut down in a gang fight at home. The rich get richer, the poor get poorer, and the meek shall inherit the shit.

A police siren wailed at the intersection of Tamiami and LeJeune Road, and we came to a halt again. "I remember one hot August day," Charlie said, gesturing toward the street with his pipe, "a fellow went to a convenience store not far from here to buy one of those South American sodas. Pony Malta."

"*Bebida de campeones*," I said.

"So they call it, but no champions could survive this bottle. The man fell into a coma after swigging half the drink. Brain-dead in an hour. They took him off life support, and I did the autopsy."

A van swerved in front of us from the left lane, and I laid on the horn. It played my favorite tune, "Fight On, State."

"A simple overdose," Charlie said. "The drink was fifty percent pure *cocaina*. Somewhere between Bogotá and Miami, the bad guys got their cartons mixed up. The contraband went to the convenience store, and the soda went to a smugglers' warehouse."

"I'm more concerned about a recent autopsy," I said.

It took Charlie only a second. "Oh my, Mr. Tupton. I nearly forgot. I've scoured the M.E.'s report, rechecked the findings. Acidosis due to hypoxemia in peripheral tissues. Ventricular fibrillation. Just as you said, nothing inconsistent with hypothermia."

"The prints, Charlie? What about the Super Glue?"

"Ah yes. The methyl-methacrylate test. A thumb and forefinger of sufficient clarity. Quite a nice double loop on the thumb and a tented arch on the forefinger, as I recall. Have you ever read the definitive text by the Argentinian Juan Vucetich? *Dactiloscopia Comparada*. Published a hundred years ago, but still valuable in assessing—"

"Charlie!"

He cleared his throat. "Sorry for the digression. The prints came from the right wrist of Mr. Tupton. Others on the left wrist were simply not usable."

"And?"

"Well, the ones we've got match up quite nicely with that of your client, Nicky Florio."

"I see."

Charlie was silent a moment. "Do you?"

"I'm not surprised, that's all."

"Why?" Charlie asked. "It proves nothing. When the paramedics arrived, the body was outside on the patio. Florio gave a statement saying he carried Tupton out there. Obviously, he may have grabbed the man by the wrists to hoist him up and carry him out."

"Or he may have dragged him into the wine cellar by the wrists when Tupton was still alive."

Charlie scowled at me. "Just whose side are you on, Jake?"

Again I was silent. At trial, I try not to ask a question when I don't know the answer. In real life, I don't like to respond to questions for the same reason.

An open Jeep with four Hispanic teenagers was crowding me on the left, its radio blaring *"Sopa de Caracol."* Again, I tapped the horn, which now blared a few notes of the Penn State alma mater.

The guy riding shotgun in the Jeep, a pimpled bodybuilder in a muscle T-shirt, reached under his seat and came up holding a nine-millimeter handgun. He didn't point it at me, just sort of waved it in the air with a smirk on his face. What is it our local humorist Dave Barry likes to say? *Miami is a place where homicide is a misdemeanor, and motorists use guns instead of turn signals.* Something like that. As if to prove the point, the Jeep pulled into the far left lane, cutting off a florist's delivery truck, then screeched around the corner without flashing a turn signal.

"I read somewhere that the homicide rate goes up when it gets hotter," I said.

"So? What does it mean?"

"That the heat makes us angrier, I suppose. People lose their temper, that sort of thing."

Charlie shook his head. *"Quot homines, tot sententiae.* So many men, so many opinions. There are a myriad of variables that could affect the homicide rate. Other factors may coincide with the summer months besides heat. Perhaps unemployment, heavier drinking. Do you follow me?"

"Like a duck behind its mother."

Charlie chewed on his cold pipe. "There's another study that shows that men's sperm count goes down during the summer. Would you say the heat causes that?"

I was getting too smart to jump to conclusions. "No, it probably has something to do with baseball."

"Just as likely," Charlie said with a laugh. "Men who live and work in air-conditioned surroundings also have reduced sperm counts in the summer, so the heat may be irrelevant."

Traffic thinned as we neared Sweetwater, a suburb of Nicaraguan émigrés on the western fringe of the city. "So what's my point, Jake?"

"Same as always, Charlie. Things are seldom what they seem."

"Correct! *Non semper ea sunt quae videntur*."

"You took the words right out of my mouth," I told him.

A handsome white ibis sat on the hood of a Dodge pickup. We pulled in next to the truck, and the bird flapped its black-tipped wings and took off, but not before leaving behind a memento on the windshield. Next to us, two charter buses from Wachula were disgorging their elderly passengers. I helped Charlie Riggs out of his shoulder harness, and we walked into the bingo hall, a gleaming white building the size of a convention hall.

Inside, the pot-of-gold and pull-tab video games blinked their red and green lights, dispensing coupons redeemable for cash. No jangle of coins here, but these were slot machines just the same. Slide a twenty-dollar bill into the slot, get twenty plays. If three oranges come up, you win. Three gold bars pay top prize of $5,592. Nearby, in a perimeter room, a game of thirty-number bingo was under way.

In the main hall, the crowd was still forming for the early-bird game. According to the signs, the games would continue until 4:00 A.M. Some of the old folks were ambling through the cafeteria line, bringing fried chicken and mashed potatoes with iced tea back to their seats. The Wachula retirees—white shoes and bright plaid outfits—were trooping toward the tables. Their voices, chirpy and expectant coming through the door, dropped into respectful murmurs as they entered the main hall, their cathedral of chance and providence.

In the center of the hall was a small motorboat on a trailer, one of the many prizes of the night. Television monitors blinked out the numbers before they were called. "B, five; O, sixty-four." The players, women in polyester slacks, men in bowling shirts, turned plastic ink bottles upside down and squooshed the sponge heads on their cards to record a number.

"Jake, come have a look at this."

Charlie was toddling toward a glass showcase behind the motorboat. Inside the case was what looked like a miniature town. Scale models of a main street of three-story buildings. Shops on the ground floor, offices and apartments above. Beige stucco walls, orange barrel-tile roofs, a faintly Spanish look. A few blocks away, a semicircle of twelve-story condos surrounded by a moat. An elementary school with tiny figures of children and even an Irish setter frolicking in a grassy yard. Gas stations and a bus depot and a familiar fast-food palace with golden arches. A golf course wended its way around bodies of water.

A tasteful green-on-white sign announced:

CYPRESS ESTATES
ANOTHER FLORIO ENTERPRISES COMMUNITY
Reservation Deposits Now Being Accepted

It could be anywhere, this generic white-bread community. You could stick it west of Boca Raton near the turnpike or down in Homestead by the old air force base. But it was intended to be built somewhere else entirely. Inside the glass playworld were adornments not usually seen in models of dream towns.

Plexiglas saw grass.

Miniature wood storks and flamingos and spoonbills, lazing in shallow water.

Cypress trees draped in cotton, spray-painted to resemble Spanish moss.

An airboat seemingly skimming across the saw grass.

A great blue heron—its wings swept high—in the sky above the man-made Glades, suspended in space by a single thread.

Alligators, green and scaly, in a moat surrounded by a concrete wall.

A restored Indian village, or at least a designer's idea of one, with dugout canoes, campfires, and natives dressed in loincloths pointing bow and arrow at a Lilliputian deer.

Charlie was thumbing through one of the brochures stacked by the display case. He read aloud: " 'Back to nature. Enjoy the beauty of the Everglades as no one ever has.' "

"Or will again," I said.

Charlie tapped his cold pipe against the glass case. "They don't show you the infrastructure, do they? You don't see the bulldozers destroying the egrets' nests. You don't see the fill turning the water to slime or the sewers or the dredging or the leaks from the gas station's tanks. You can't hear the infernal racket of the pile drivers or smell the fumes of the diesel engines. You don't see the Styrofoam cups or the plastic six-pack holders that strangle the fish and the birds."

"Easy, Charlie, you'll pop a blood vessel."

"Surely you don't approve of this, do you, Jake?"

"No. I just can't believe it will ever be built. Think of the permits required. County, state, Army Corps of Engineers, Department of Resource Management. Even with all Nicky's lawyers and lobbyists, I don't see the project getting the green light. It'll be just another developer's pipe dream, a model under glass."

"Let's hope you're right," Charlie said, "and if the government can't stop it, maybe the environmental groups can tie up Florio with a lawsuit. The way the courts work, it'd take years, and by then, he could lose his financing or be focused on other deals. It happens all the time."

That sounded familiar. "That's what Gina said Nicky was worried about, an environmental suit. Nicky must have been infuriated that somebody he considered a pipsqueak could wield such power. . . ."

"Motive," Charlie mused. "Would that be sufficient motive to kill a man, to keep him from suing?"

I didn't answer. My attention was diverted.

"Jake?"

Charlie's gaze followed mine. On a balcony above us, uniformed employees scanned the floor of the bingo hall. A man and a woman stood at the railing. He was in his thirties with thick sun-bleached hair tied back in a ponytail. He wore one of those shapeless black sport coats with the sleeves pushed up. Thick, veined forearms. Even from here, I could make out a diamond-stud earring sparkling in the glare of the overhead lights.

Pretty-boy looks with a bonecrusher jawline to keep from being too pretty. He wasn't smiling, but I imagined perfect pearly whites, one of those guys with a natural ease with women. I'd been around enough to recognize the type, an oily charm, all his brains in his bikini briefs.

The man said something to the woman, who touched his sleeve and laughed. She said something back to him, and it must have been hilarious, too. If this were the 1940s, you would say they were laughing gaily. I'd been right. The guy had a great grin.

Their eyes locking on each other, they didn't look our way. Or any other way. There is the cliché about lovers being alone in a crowd. But like a lot of clichés, it is based on truth. The rest of the world be damned. Sirens could be wailing, the building could be ablaze. No matter.

I had seen the look in a woman's eyes before. I had seen the look in *this* woman's eyes before.

Next to me, Charlie was stirring. "Say, Jake, isn't that Star . . . ?"

"Gina," I said.

"Whatever. Unless my old eyes deceive me, that ponytailed gentleman is not her husband."

"Rick Gondolier, and he's no gentleman," I said. "He handles Nicky's gambling business."

"Perhaps that's not all of Nicky's that he handles. Goodness, boy, do you know your neck and ears have turned quite red? Either you have a touch of dengue fever, or . . ."

Gondolier leaned close, and the two of them gently kissed. Not a passionate kiss. Only their lips touched. But the kiss lingered and seemed to reflect a silent affirmation of something more. I am not an expert on body language, but I know a thing or two about kissing. This one spoke of a comfort level between the two, of a naturalness. It clearly said that they were lovers.

"Jake, you're not involved with that woman again, are you?"

That woman sounded like a communicable disease. I didn't answer him.

Charlie sighed. "*Amantes sunt amentes.* Lovers are such lunatics."

They turned around, Gondolier's hand lightly falling across Gina's shoulder, guiding her. Then they stepped away from the railing and disappeared.

"Well, now," Charlie said, "isn't that the man you wanted to see, the one in charge of the gambling?"

"I've seen enough," I said, and started for the exit. I didn't stop to fill out a raffle ticket or try my luck at the electronic slots.

Charlie trundled after me, straining to keep up. "A bit huffy, are we?"

I didn't say a word.

"If you ask me—"

"No one has," I told him.

". . . Nicky's the one who should be jealous, not you. What's the legal term, Jake? You have no standing, isn't that it? You're not a party to the transaction."

I pushed through the door to the parking lot with Charlie on my heels. I stopped short, turned, and looked down at my old friend. "Charlie, do me a favor. Stick to the fingerprints and the bodily fluids, and the other stuff you know. You're out of your field now, so please lay off the personal relationships. I'm a big boy, and I can handle myself."

Charlie stared at his shoetops. He looked like an old mutt that had just been kicked. Which only made me feel worse. I knew what I was doing. Angry at Gina, angry at me, angry at the big, wide fickle world, I was taking it out on my dearest friend.

Damn, I'm stupid sometimes.

I tossed an arm around his shoulder and rumpled his gray wiry hair. "I'm sorry, Charlie."

"Instead of clamming up, why not talk about it?"

"It's painful."

"All the more reason to speak from your heart of hearts."

Around us, more plaid and polyester folks were streaming into the bingo hall. Why does everyone over seventy seem so short? We moved a few paces from the front door and stood on the edge of the parking lot.

"It hurt when she left the first time," I said. "And hurt more every time she came back, because she'd always leave again. I was a way station for her, a pit stop on the way to something better. It didn't matter if she was married at the time. I'd always be there for her."

"And now, Jake? What makes it painful to see her with another man? After all, she's married. What's another spoon in the soup?"

"It cheapens what we have. Or had. It reminds me what a fool I was. Or am."

The squeal of brakes. I stepped back as an armored truck, a tin can on wheels, pulled up. A set of double doors opened from inside the bingo hall, and a uniformed security guard wheeled a golf cart out and headed toward the truck. Attached to the golf cart was a wagon filled with leather bags three feet high. Two other guards, their guns drawn and pointed at the ground, followed the cart to the truck.

"What makes you a fool, Jake?"

"For feeling the way I do about Gina."

"How do you feel?"

"I don't know."

The rear door of the truck opened. Inside, a man with a shotgun scanned the parking lot. He looked at Charlie and seemed to decide he didn't pose a threat. He looked longer at me.

"Jake, you're blocking it out, sealing yourself off from your feelings."

"Didn't realize you did psychological counseling, too. You must have had some troubled corpses over at the county morgue."

"C'mon, Jake. No wisecracks. How do you feel where Gina is concerned?"

Analyzing feelings isn't my strong point. If I kept it up, I'd turn into a quiche-eating, wine-sipping semisensitive man of the nineties. "Weak. Wistful. Full of regrets."

Now I was looking at one of the security guards. He wore gray pants with a black stripe, a blue uniform shirt with epaulets, and a gold badge. He was chunky, short, and round-faced with a squashed nose. His eyes were hidden under the bill of his cap. In a pudgy hand, he held a .357 Magnum. It was pointed straight at the ground ever since the money came out of the bingo hall. He looked famliar, but in profile, and in that uniform, it just didn't compute.

"Jake," Charlie said, "are you telling me that you love the girl?"

"I don't know, Charlie. Maybe it's just always wanting what I can't have. Maybe it's not knowing what I want. There was a time when I could have had her, but I let her go. I didn't tell her how I . . ."

The guard was staring at me. He had turned and now faced me straight on. Then he smiled. "Ay, Counselor, never expected to see you here. Testing your luck at the tables?"

No, it couldn't be. But it was.

"Hello, Guillermo. I didn't recognize you. How'd you get a permit to carry the piece?"

"I got no felony convictions that haven't been overturned on appeal or pardoned. I always get the best lawyers, remember."

"Whoever represented you upstate must have known his stuff, or you'd be doing twenty-five years minimum mandatory at Raiford right now." Charlie nudged me and cleared his throat. "Doc Riggs, say hello to Guillermo Diaz, a former client."

Diaz ignored Charlie and laughed, though nothing seemed particularly funny. "From what I hear, Counselor," Diaz cackled, "you may do more time in that case than me. I got off clean. Speedy-trial rule."

"I didn't think the dockets were that crowded in Ocala."

Diaz laughed again, his belly bouncing. His colleague was tossing the moneybags into the back of the truck. "Didn't say they were. But what does the state do when its star witness is missing?"

"Gets a continuance."

"Four continuances. You gotta give those shitkickers credit, they kept trying. 'Yo Honor, we cain't find Mr. Ra-fa-ale Ray-mose anywhere. Jes' give us another thirty days.' "

"You do redneck real well," I allowed.

"Yeah, well, those country boys continued their asses right into the speedy-trial rule. Case dismissed." He turned toward Charlie. "Hey, Doc. Some shit-for-brains horse trainer doesn't know how to use a power saw, they charge me with murder."

"What happened to the missing witness?" Charlie asked, because I didn't. But then I already knew.

Diaz raised the gun and pointed it directly at my head. "Bang, bang," he said. "And bang." This was so funny he rumbled up another laugh. "I don't know. Maybe he committed suicide."

The shotgun-toting guard pulled the doors of the truck shut from inside. Diaz lowered his gun and holstered it.

"What are you doing here?" I asked.

"What's it look like? Working for Mr. Gondolier. I'm head of security. No more leg breaking. Just making sure there's no smoking in restricted areas and no wise guys trying to pull a heist."

"I don't believe it," I said, shaking my head.

"Ay, why not, Counselor? Don't you think I can do the job?"

"Sure you can, Guillermo. A fox can always guard the henhouse."

Chapter 6

Hello, Heartbreak

"WHAT PRICE HAPPINESS?" SHEILA SLUTSKY ASKED. "I INTRODUCE the *schlemiel* to a beautiful girl. All right, not so beautiful, but she's got a decent job plus all her own teeth. Not that he's so wonderful to look at, unless you like hairy ears. Anyway, I introduce them, she marries him, and now the *gonif* don't want to pay me. From this, you could die."

"Or sue," I said.

"Exactly." Sheila Slutsky smiled and fished a crumpled document out of a purse shaped like a hatbox. I had seen larger women, but none wearing a gold lamé jumpsuit with shoulder pads an offensive lineman would envy. Her hair was dyed candy-apple red and swept into what used to be called a beehive. Eyeglasses dangled from her neck on a chain of imitation pearls. She slid the document toward me and tapped her index finger, *thumpety-thump*, on my desk. "Read the fine print, *boychik*."

Actually, it was bold print, in a box lined with red: "The undersigned contracting party agrees to pay a bonus of $2500.00 to the Matchmaker within twenty days of the marriage of said party to any person introduced, directly or indirectly, to said party by the Matchmaker."

"My son-in-law Sheldon wrote that," Mrs. Slutsky announced. "A lawyer in Jersey. Not a fancy-schmancy office like this . . ."

She gestured toward the bayfront window. "But he makes a living, *kineahora.*"

I scanned the rest of the contract. Meyer Feinstein, D.D.S., with an office address in Lauderhill, paid a registration fee of a hundred dollars plus an additional fifty dollars for every woman introduced to him by Sheila Slutsky. In the event of marriage, according to the red-boxed clause, Meyer owed another twenty-five-hundred dollars.

"What's the problem?" I asked. "Why won't he pay?"

"*Feh!* So it's my fault she ran off?"

"Who, the bride?"

"With the Porsche yet."

"What? She stole his car?"

"Of course not. He gave it to her as a wedding present. Three days later, she was fed up with his *mishegoss,* tying her up with dental floss, who ever heard of such a thing, so she ran off. But they're married, right? If that *farshtinkener* son-in-law of mine had written the contract like I said, I would've been paid at the wedding."

Just then, Cindy buzzed me on the intercom. She reminded me that clients were lining up in the waiting room. There was a young man from Hialeah who wanted to sue the striptease joint for his injuries in an oil-wrestling bout with Brenda the Battling Banshee.

Mrs. Slutsky was still talking, mostly to herself. "Such a *nebbish,* that dentist."

Cindy was telling me that Alex Soto was waiting, too, arrested again for the Spanish Lotto con. He buys lottery tickets, choosing the number that won the week before. By carefully changing the date, he's left with what looks like a $7-million ticket. Then, claiming he's an illegal alien—the only part of the scam that's true—Soto convinces the mark to cash the ticket for him, asking for ten thousand dollars as good-faith money.

"Okay," I told Cindy. "No time to go out today. Better order me a cheeseburger and a shake."

Cindy made a sound like a cow in distress.

"Is the whole world crazy or what?" Mrs. Slutsky asked.

Summer had turned to fall, though you couldn't tell the difference. It still rained every afternoon, steam rising from the streets after each thunderstorm. Fall became winter, and still it stayed warm. Christmas Day was 83 and muggy, with just the slightest breath of a breeze. The first cold front passed through on New Year's Eve, and the natives welcomed it. Our tropical winter is ordinarily dry and pleasant, daytime temperatures in the 70s, the sky an azure blue. It is not a time to be locked inside conference rooms, studying documents and taking depositions, but H. T. Patterson was pushing the Tupton case to an early trial. We completed discovery in January, announced ready for trial at a calendar call on Valentine's Day, and were scheduled to begin picking a jury the first Monday in March. Now I was trying to clean off my desk and clear out my mind prior to the battle.

I was reading the morning paper and chomping a burger at my desk when Cindy walked in again. She'd recently gone blond, and I hadn't gotten used to it. She'd straightened her hair, too, and wore it in bangs in front and long down the sides. Sort of a sixties' look that made me think of Peter, Paul, and Mary, or at least of Mary. Today she wore a blue denim jacket with silver piping and matching jeans. Her earrings were Plexiglas squares. Embedded in each one was a condom still in its wrapper. A woman's group sold the earrings at fund-raisers as a visual reminder of safe sex. In case of need, the Plexiglas opened and the condom popped out.

My secretary may have looked ditzy to the world, but not to me. Everyone underestimated her. Cindy chewed gum, typed fast, and cracked wise, and I don't know what I'd do without her.

Today Cindy was busy organizing files for the upcoming trial. I was gobbling some french fries while reading the local section of the paper. Another judge was indicted for taking kickbacks from lawyers appointed to represent indigent defendants. As a bonus, the judge ate on the lawyer's tab at a fancy Italian restaurant in Coconut Grove. Fried calamari was the judge's entrée of choice, which prompted local columnist Carl Hiaasen to wonder if there were a *squid pro quo.*

I put down the paper and gestured to Cindy with my burger. "Want a bite?"

She made a face. "You know I'm a vegan."

"I thought you were from Sacramento, not Vegas."

"A vegan, silly. A vegetarian who doesn't eat animal products or use them in any way. No meat, milk, or fish. No wool, leather, or furs. No products that are the result of animal experiments."

"You don't know what you're missing," I told her, wiping a glob of oil from my chin.

Cindy looked as if she might blow lunch, if she ever had any. "The other day I was at the deli, and a man was eating a tongue sandwich. Can you imagine, eating an animal's tongue?"

"I've tried it. Not bad with mustard."

Cindy winced. "I can't imagine eating something that comes out of an animal's mouth."

"How 'bout some eggs?" I asked her.

"You are so gross. But if you want to keep loading yourself with nitrites and benzopyrene, pesticides and heavy metals, just keep snarfing your hamburgers."

I grunted my intention of doing just that.

"Speaking of poison," she said with a sly smile, "guess who's in the waiting room."

I was slurping my chocolate shake, so Cindy answered her own question. "*Missus* Florio."

Oh, her.

Cindy eyed me, looking for a reaction. When I gave her my poker face, she asked, "Why can't she make an appointment like everyone else, or does she have special privileges?"

"She has the past."

"If I were you, *jefe*, I'd keep it that way."

Gina wore a black cotton jersey dress with bare shoulders. There is something about an ivory-skinned blonde in black, a promise of heaven, a threat of hell. The dress was held together by a row of black buttons from the neck to the hem, which nearly reached her ankles. It would have been a demure look if she bothered to button up from midthigh down.

She waltzed around my office, inspecting the surroundings as if she'd never been there before. She picked up a deflated football with the score of a long-forgotten game painted on the side. She replaced the ball, studied a team photo from my college days, and remarked that I looked dorky with a mustache. She thumbed through an open volume of *Southern Reporter*, 2nd Series, skimming past a case where a prisoner sued the state for the right to be served decaffeinated coffee because real java made him jumpy. She looked out the window where an easterly was kicking up whitecaps on the bay. Then she turned and stood still, staring at the Dictaphone on my desk as if it were an object of beauty and wonder.

Something was bothering her, but what?

I hadn't hugged her, or kissed her, or shaken her delicate hand. Hell, I hadn't even stood up when she came in.

"We have to talk," she said finally.

Have to.

Which means the subject is painful. Okay, that could be a lot of things. She could confess that Nicky killed Peter Tupton. Or maybe she wanted to admit the affair with Rick Gondolier. Come clean with old Jake. He would understand. Maybe she . . .

"We can't see each other anymore," Gina blurted out.

I blinked. Then I shrugged. It was intended to say, So what? Inside, my stomach felt like the elevator suddenly dropped twenty floors.

She turned away and looked out the window again. Along the shoreline at Bayside, flags stiffened in the breeze. Across Government Cut, one of the cruise ships was easing out of the port, tugboats front and rear. "I guess it doesn't matter to you that much," she said.

"It stopped mattering a long time ago." I stared at her back, admiring the fine lines of her neck. She was facing east, toward Bimini. Good. My face might have given it away. For a lawyer, I am a lousy liar.

"That makes it easier. But, still, I'm sorry."

"Okay, if that's it, I've got work to do. Hey, you could have called or mailed it in."

She turned, walked toward my desk, and sat down in a client's straight-back chair, crossing her long legs. She fumbled in her purse for something. The purse was smooth leather, small and black. It probably cost a thousand bucks at a Coconut Grove boutique. She withdrew a pink envelope and handed it to me. "I wrote you a letter, but . . . ."

I turned it over in my hand, a dainty pink envelope carrying the scent of her perfume, bringing back a thousand memories. I resisted the urge to close my eyes and press the envelope to my nose. My name was written on the front in red ink. Girlish script. Straight up-and-down letters. The letter *J* looked like two fat balloons, one on top of the other.

A "Dear Jake" letter.

I opened it and withdrew a neatly folded piece of pink stationery. A rose on top and the initials *GMF*. It struck me that I didn't know her middle name. Of course, even if I did, it could have changed over the years.

It wasn't a "Dear Jake" letter after all. More like "Dearest Jake," written in the same up-and-down handwriting with very round O's and curlicues on the G's.

> *Dearest Jake,*
> *You are so very special and have been for so very long, and that only makes this more difficult. I know how you feel about me, even though you really don't say it. I have hurt you in the past, and I should not keep coming back to you. I care for you and hope for the best for you, but I will never leave Nicky. He loves me and is good to me, and I want to be just as good to him. So finally, dearest Jake, it is over.*
> *With deep affection,*
> *Gina*

Good-bye lover. Hello heartbreak.

I wondered if Rick Gondolier received a similar letter. And maybe a third and fourth guy, too. If Gina had a word processor, she could avoid writer's cramp. But something wasn't making sense. "I didn't ask you to leave Nicky."

"I know you, Jake. You always hoped—"

"Ah, you're a mind reader now, in addition to your other talents, most of which are accomplished on your back."

I don't know why I said that.

Petty.

Stupid.

Cruel.

If my words had stung, Gina didn't show it. She just studied me, her deep blue eyes betraying no emotion. "Go ahead and insult me, Jake, if it makes you feel better."

"Hey, what's the big deal? Easy come, easy go. Hey, it's like you always said to me: 'Maybe I'll see you later, and maybe I won't.' "

"Jake, why can't you grow up and express your feelings?"

"What feelings? Look, all of this was your idea. You're the one who always got the ball rolling. You're the one who showed up at my house, or here, or at the beach. My only mistake was not kicking you out of bed."

She reached into the black leather purse and grabbed a pack of Winstons. She tapped out one cigarette and placed it between her pursed lips. If she was waiting for me to light it, she had a long wait. She reached back into the purse, found a gold lighter, struck it, and craned her long neck as she inhaled. "Don't be like that, Jake. It always happens."

"*Always?* With all men? Or always with me?"

She exhaled a long plume of smoke that drifted to the ceiling. "With you, Jake. You either retreat into a shell or strike out. Show no pain, isn't that your motto?"

"Play with pain is the way the coach always put it."

"It would be better to acknowledge the pain, talk about it, deal with it."

"Now you're a therapist, too."

"I've been there, Jake. I've been hurt, and I've dealt with it."

"Forget it. I'm a big boy. I can take a hit."

Sure I can. I'm a former varsity member of the AFC Eastern Division All-Star Party Team. In the old days, I led the league in broken curfews and broken hearts. I could find an after-hours club in Buffalo during a power outage in December. Buffalo! But I retired. The stewardesses, secretaries, and models have come and gone. An endless variety of sameness. Names, faces, legs, all merge into a creamy blur. The same idle chatter, the same sweet deceptions, the same empty morning-afters.

"Do you understand why I'm doing this?" she asked me.

"Maybe you feel guilty, and you've decided to stay home afternoons and bake apple pies. Maybe you're joining a convent." I put an edge on my voice. "Maybe you found someone else."

Now I studied her.

"There's no one else, Jake."

She lies so much better than I do. Maybe all those marriages were good training.

"I'm doing it for Nicky," she said softly, "but I'm doing it for you, too."

"Gee, thanks, and on behalf of Nicky, double thanks."

What was in those eyes now? A touch of sadness. "This is better for you, Jake. Why do you suppose you've never gotten married, never even lived with anyone?"

"I lived with *you*, or you lived with me. Three months my last year in the league. You'd been evicted from your apartment for playing The Who at two hundred decibels."

"Okay, other than me, you've never lived with anyone. And when you and I are involved, you don't see anyone else, do you?"

"No. I'm not ambidextrous. I can't handle two women at once."

She smiled a sweet, soft smile. "You've been waiting for me all these years, and I've been letting you do it, encouraging you by coming back again and again."

"There are lots of women in my life," I said defensively.

"I know," Gina said, "but why isn't there one?"

Chapter 7

The Gods Make Their Own Rules

"Now, mrs. morales, do you agree that a host has a duty to protect his guests from harm?"

Gloria Morales eyed H. T. Patterson with suspicion. She was a stocky forty-one-year-old airline reservations clerk with two children in public school and a husband who repaired copying machines. Jurors didn't come any more typical than this. "If the judge says so, sure," she answered warily.

"Right, Mrs. Morales." H. T. Patterson looked in awe at the woman, as if she had just solved the mysteries of cold fusion. "One hundred percent cor-rect!" Bouncing on his toes, Patterson moved closer to the jury box rail. "And do you promise to follow the judge's instructions as to the law in this case?"

Now that was an easy one.

"Yes," Mrs. Morales said, "of course."

"All of you now," Patterson boomed, his gaze sweeping across the jury box, "will you all follow the judge's instructions as to the legal duty of a social host to his guests?"

Patterson stepped back and watched as eight heads nodded. After preaching to hundreds at his inner-city church, this couldn't be too hard. We needed six jurors and two alternates, and so far Patterson was skillfully indoctrinating the panel with his slant on the case. At the same time, he was working on a corollary of Festinger's

Dissonance Theory: Public commitment leads to behavior change. Get a juror to publicly commit to a position—the accused is presumed innocent, or injured persons deserve compensation, or the moon is made of green cheese—and the juror will pattern his or her behavior to the commitment in order to avoid dissonance. That's a fancy way of saying that most people feel bad about lying.

Outside the courthouse, the temperature had dipped into the forties. I liked the chill in the air, though I hoped it wouldn't remind the jurors of Peter Tupton's blue feet. A Canadian cold front had dipped through the Midwest, bringing snow as far south as Atlanta. Frightened central Florida citrus growers hauled out the smudge pots and put their faith in black smoke and midnight waterings. In Mia-muh, everyone turned off their A/C, except me, because I don't have any. Across the bay, the women in Bal Harbour retrieved their furs from storage, and the trendy types along Ocean Drive on South Beach dusted off their leather motorcycle jackets.

The winds had clocked around from southeast—the direction of the soggy Caribbean air—to northwest. As the temperature plummeted, the TV newsguys went gaga with shots of locals bundled up and tourists from Quebec sunning on the beach as if nothing were amiss. That morning, I could see my breath as I picked up the paper from under my poinciana tree. I read the usual assortment of Miami news—murders, mayhem, and the destruction of the Florida Keys coral reef—and had my usual breakfast of fresh winter strawberries and a high-protein shake of OJ, banana, and eggs. I foraged in my closet, found a wool herringbone suit that needed some fresh air, and headed for court.

My juror selection consultants—Marvin the Maven, Saul the Tailor, and Max (Just Plain) Seltzer—were kibitzing in the front row of the gallery. Altogether, they'd lived about 225 years, and I valued their experience more than the sheepskin of a newly minted Ph.D. Marvin, who owned a shoe store in Brooklyn for fifty years, was immaculate in a sharkskin suit and highly buffed black oxfords. Saul, who hand-sewed suits for Fiorello La Guardia, carried a straw hat that he always clutched in his lap during crucial testimony. Max, who claimed to have invented the egg cream, was balder than one of Peter Tupton's endangered eagles. Monday through Friday, they bused over from Miami Beach and wandered from courtroom to courtroom in search of the best action.

I explained the dissonance theory to Marvin one time, and he just waggled a liver-spotted hand at me. *"Dissonance-schmissonance. Just look at their shoes, boychik. If a man's heels are run-down and the shoes unpolished, he doesn't care about his appearance. He won't pay attention. If he's wearing expensive Italian loafers with tassels, all buffed up, he's too concerned about himself. No feeling for the other guy. With women, it's not so easy, but then, with women, what is?"*

H. T. Patterson was a pro, and he worked the jury venire carefully. He didn't ask whether the jurors believed a party host had to protect a slobbering drunk from himself. That was my angle. Patterson wanted to focus on the careless host, encouraging teetotalers like Peter Tupton to drown in a river of champagne.

It's all how you phrase the questions, and sometimes you can mislead without meaning to. In one case, I asked prospective jurors whether they believed bus drivers should exercise caution in rounding curves. The jurors naturally believed there'd been a crash. They were let down to learn during opening statement that the bus had merely swerved, and my client, an overweight woman, was tossed off the toilet, jamming her bare buttocks into the open emergency window. It took firemen an hour to free her and the jury ten minutes to award her two thousand dollars, which hardly seemed worth the trouble.

"Mrs. Morales, have you or any member of your family ever been injured due to the negligence of others?" Patterson asked.

He was touching all the bases. When we're not overbilling clients or having three-hour lunches, lawyers sit around reading articles titled "Constructivism and the Study of Human Communication." We learn the not-surprising fact that attitudes are the product of our backgrounds. A defense lawyer in a criminal case doesn't want a juror whose husband is a cop. She'll know how often bad guys go free, and even if the evidence is weak this time, the bum probably deserves to be sent away for Lord knows what. A plaintiff's lawyer in a P.I. case doesn't want an insurance adjustor on the jury because the verdict will be for pocket change. And so on.

Some lawyers claim cases are won in opening statement. Others say the best closing argument takes the prize. But trial maven Stuart Grossman, a bearded wizard of a plaintiff's lawyer, once told me it was voir dire. Picking jurors with the right background, or more appropriately, excluding jurors with the wrong background, is the key to the case. "They've got to like your client even more than you do," Grossman said.

With me, that was easy. I *dislike* most of the paying customers. Unlike friends, clients are seldom chosen. They simply walk through your paneled doors and into your life. A lawyer is a rocky isle in the middle of a swift-flowing river. Downstream are the treacherous falls. Clients are wretched, capsized souls frantically reaching for a handhold as they are carried to the precipice. If you save one, it is usually only temporary, for the river rages on.

"Now, Mrs. Morales, do you understand that this is not a criminal case?" H. T. Patterson asked.

Next to me at the defense table, Nicky Florio shuffled uncomfortably. From behind me, I heard Saul the Tailor. "That's a nice dress, but in this weather, she shouldn't be sleeveless. She'll catch a cold before the week is out."

Max (Just Plain) Seltzer responded, "She carries a sweater, she'll be fine."

Marvin the Maven said, "Navy-blue pumps, good arch support. An honest woman. Jacob's a *putz* if he don't take her."

Mrs. Morales gave the question some thought before nodding her agreement. "I understand. Nobody goes to jail here."

Not always true. I've been held in contempt in both criminal and civil cases. These days, I don't try a case without packing a toothbrush in my briefcase.

Patterson appeared pleased with her answer. "Cor-rect again, Mrs. Morales. The standard by which you ladies and gentlemen will judge this case is called pre-pon-der-ance of the evidence. . . ."

Patterson intoned the words as if he were speaking of the Holy Grail. "Not proof beyond a reasonable doubt," he continued. "In order to prevail, all I have to do is prove by the greater weight of the evidence that Nicholas Florio, the defendant, was negligent, and that his negligence caused the death of Peter Tupton. This is the reason you see a scale as the symbol of justice." Patterson stretched his arms, one to each side. "Our case is won by a slight tipping of the scales." He lowered his right hand and raised his left. "You don't need absolute moral certainty or proof beyond a reasonable doubt." Now his right hand was at his waist and his left at his shoulder. "You can have doubts! Doubts are acceptable. Doubts are the norm. But if there is the slightest tilt in the scales—"

"Objection, Your Honor!" I was on my feet. "This is supposed to be voir dire, not closing argument."

Judge Dixie Lee Boulton peered through her bifocals at H. T. Patterson, who stood, hands stretched out, a slight tilt to the right side, a look of childlike innocence on his handsome face. Dixie Lee was past retirement age, but no one had the heart to tell her. She was hard of hearing, absentminded, and hadn't read any law since the Magna Carta, but she was fair and honest, and I'll take that over a brilliant scoundrel any day. "Is there a question coming, Counselor?" she asked.

"Indeed there is, Your Honor." Patterson bowed to the judge, then returned his gaze to the jury box. "Do you understand that your job is to balance the scales of justice? Can your scales be as accurate as those which the old miners used in the Gold Rush days, the Forty-niners. . . ."

The only 49ers I knew played in windy Candlestick Park.

"Those old miners used to pay for their salt pork and beans with gold dust, and a single flake would tip the scales of the honest merchant—"

"Reminds me," Saul the Tailor whispered behind me, "I gotta pick up a quarter-pound corned beef on the way home."

"That's what this case is about," Patterson concluded, "a single flake of gold dust."

Melinda Tupton was a perfect widow. Not pretty, not plain. Not fat, not skinny. Not intimidating, not cowering. Brown hair, not long, not short. A blue calf-length dress with white buttons and a single strand of white pearls. A fine, strong nose, a steady voice, an ability to look the jurors straight in the eye.

"Tell us about your husband, your *late* husband, Mrs. Tupton." H. T. Patterson backed away from the witness stand. With a good witness, you get out of sight. Let the jurors focus on your star. Come into view only if you need to do a fast shuffle to distract them.

"He was a good man, the best I've ever known. . . ."

I've never met a dead husband who wasn't.

"We began dating at the University of Miami about ten years ago. He was getting his master's in marine biology. He'd done his undergrad work in petroleum engineering and had worked for one of the oil companies, until he got fed up. When I met him, he said he would spend his life protecting the environment. He said it was a calling to educate people and fight to save the planet."

He said, he said.

I could have objected, of course. Classic hearsay, and not an exception to the rule in sight. Or I could just take a two-by-four and hit the widow upside the head. It would have the same effect on the jury. They wanted to hear Peter Tupton's story, and the only one who could tell it was his widow. Young lawyers sometimes get carried away with the rules of evidence and challenge everything objectionable. They're on their feet the whole trial. As you get older, you rest your feet and hoard your objections. If the answer doesn't hurt, stay in your chair. Even if it does, sometimes you're better off being quiet. Don't highlight the weakness of your case by trying too hard to keep out answers or documents the jury is likely to hear or see anyway.

Melinda Tupton took us through the courtship and marriage, Peter's early jobs with the Department of Environmental Resources and the federal Environmental Protection Agency. Then came the opening with the Everglades Society, an executive, policy-making position with public exposure. He leaped at it. This was his destiny.

"He loved the natural beauty of the Glades, its incredible variety of plant and animal life. He studied its history. Sometimes he would use Indian terms or call it by the name the Spanish explorers used, *El Laguna del Espíritu Santo*, the Lagoon of the Holy Spirit."

This was getting a tad too mystical for my tastes. And was it my imagination, or did Melinda Tupton look straight at Gloria Morales when speaking Spanish with perfect intonation? Oh brother, this one was slick.

The widow told us how Tupton had prepared position papers for congressional investigative teams. He fought the sugarcane barons whose fertilizer drained into the great slough and who tampered with its water level through vast irrigation. He battled the developers and the froggers and the hunters and the macho off-road vehicle rednecks and everyone else whose vision was so crabbed they only saw the River of Grass as their own personal playground or cesspool.

"Peter discovered the source of the mercury pollution in the Glades," she said proudly. "It comes from local garbage incinerators and is carried to the west by the prevailing breezes, then dumped into the saw grass in afternoon thunderstorms. Peter wanted to preserve the natural habitat for all the animals and to preserve the water supply for the millions of us"—she turned toward the jury box—"for all of us who live here."

Then we learned about the wildlife her husband loved so much. Patterson had already played the television-interview tape, so the images of the hawksbill turtle and the seaside sparrow were fresh in the jurors' minds. Melinda Tupton droned on about nocturnal opossums and pink flamingos and tiny fiddler crabs. She described how to tell the difference between the American crocodile with its long, narrow snout and olive-green color and the alligator with its blunt nose and black back.

"Peter loved the animals so much. Even the mosquitoes . . ."

Oh give me a break, lady.

Patterson let her keep going for a while, then got down to business. "Referring to Plaintiff's Exhibit Twelve, Mrs. Tupton, can you identify this document?"

Patterson handed a one-page letter to the witness. "Yes, that's a letter from Mr. Florio to my husband, threatening to sue him if he didn't stop making trouble—that's what the letter says, 'making trouble'—for him with the Army Corps of Engineers and the Collier County Commission. It's called a SLAPP suit, Strategic Lawsuit Against Public Participation, and . . ."

Next to me, Nicky Florio's thick neck was threatening to burst out of his white-on-white shirt. I had to shoosh him, so I could hear the witness.

". . . it's what happens when a rich company files a frivolous suit to silence its opposition."

"Objection!" Sometimes, I don't heed my own advice. "Your Honor, the question was whether the witness could identify the document. That didn't call for her opinion of the character of an unfiled lawsuit."

"Sustained." Dixie Lee leaned toward the witness and gently admonished her, "Please just answer the question, Mrs. Tupton."

Score one for our side.

Patterson took the letter back and replaced it on the clerk's desk. He shuffled some note cards, found what he wanted, and asked, "Did there come a time when Mr. Tupton had a meeting with Mr. Florio?"

"Yes, they had lunch one day to discuss Peter's opposition to Mr. Florio's planned project in the Everglades."

"And when did this occur?"

"Sometime in July. About two weeks before Peter's death."

Oh brother. Here it comes, the stock option, or what Patterson will call a bribe, if he gets the chance. I was leaning forward in my heavy walnut chair.

"What transpired at this meet—"

"Objection!" I was on my feet in world-record time. "Unless it is established that Mrs. Tupton was present, the question is improper."

Judge Boulton didn't even look at Patterson before ruling. "Sustained."

Score two for our side.

"Did Mr. Florio offer your husband anything at this meeting?"

"Objection, leading." I was still standing, moving closer to the bench, as if my voice would reach the judge's ears quicker.

"Sustained."

On a roll now. Hey, I'm getting good at this.

"Did your husband tell you what transpired—"

"Objection, hearsay."

"Sustained."

Patterson paused and riffled through more of his note cards. There was no way he could get what he wanted into evidence. Apparently, there were no witnesses to the meeting, no documents that would reflect the conversation. Other than making me look a little frantic to keep out some evidence, Patterson had dug a dry well.

Patterson cleared his throat. "Now, Mrs. Tupton, did there come a time that your husband went to the Florio house for a party?"

"Yes, Sunday, August ninth."

"Did you go along?"

"No. I was volunteering at the hospital that day."

Ouch. She probably discovered a cure for cancer during her lunch break.

"Mrs. Tupton, do you miss your husband?"

I didn't need to hear the answers. Direct examination is preordained. I could write the script. *Every day. The house is so empty without him.*

Her eyes glistened. "So very much. Everywhere I look, in his study, in his workshop, there are so many reminders of him."

"Why did your husband go to the home of a man who was threatening to sue him?"

Because my husband was a saint. He'd try to talk the devil out of his pitchfork.

"Because Peter was always willing to talk. He believed that he could reason with Mr. Florio. He took along photographs and a videotape of the animal life in the Everglades. All the studies about the aquifer, the water table, everything."

"Was your husband a drinker?"

No, unless you count when he offered a toast to Mother Teresa at a charity dinner.

"No, sir. Once in a while, he'd have a glass of wine with dinner, that's all."

"When is the last time you spoke to your husband?"

Before he left for the party, and I left to scrub the floors of the ICU, he gave me a kiss and told me how much I meant to him.

"When he called me at the hospital from the Florios' house."

Huh?

I had taken her deposition, and she never mentioned a phone call. Of course, I hadn't asked. . . .

"And what did your husband say to you?"

"He—"

"Objection! Hearsay, Your Honor." No way I was going to get sandbagged.

With a look of pure tranquillity, H. T. Patterson turned to the judge. "May we approach the bench, Your Honor?"

Dixie Lee Boulton waved us up. The court reporter, a dazed-looking young woman who chewed gum relentlessly, brought her little machine to the side of the bench away from the jury. The judge leaned our way, both of us straining to get close. "What is it, Mr. Patterson?" the judge whispered. "Sure sounds like hearsay to me."

"Once the question's answered, Your Honor, it's going to fall right into the excited utterance exception of Section Ninety-point-eight-oh-three, subsection two." Patterson cocked his head toward me. "You're familiar with the statute, aren't you, Jake?"

"I've rubbed up against it once or twice," I said, turning toward the judge. "Anytime a lawyer's got some hearsay, he thinks he can put an exclamation point on the statement and get it in. Your Honor, the statute's only used for the truly exceptional statement made under stress—'He's got a gun!'—that sort of thing."

"Mr. Lassiter's right," Patterson conceded, "but we fit into the rule."

"Only one way to find out," the judge told us. "Bailiff, take out the jury."

When the jurors had filed into their little room, H. T. Patterson asked the question again. With the jury out of earshot, the judge, Marvin the Maven, and I all listened expectantly. At the defense table, Nicky Florio scowled.

"What did your husband say to you on the phone?"

"Peter was so excited. I could hear it in his voice. He was hyper, talking a mile a minute, saying he was in Mr. Florio's den, and he didn't have much time. Everybody else was at the pool. He had come into the house looking for a bathroom. At first, he was just looking around. Mr. Florio had all these alligator hides, mounted bonefish, boar heads, and other pretty disgusting trophies. Then Peter looked on Mr. Florio's desk. He said he knew he shouldn't, but couldn't help himself." Melinda Tupton cleared her throat and looked at the judge. "There was a document, he didn't say exactly what, but he'd read it quickly and then called me, more excited than I'd ever known him. 'The condos are a cover!' That's what he kept saying, shouting really. 'The condos, the shops, the town, it's all a cover!' He said it was a nightmare, worse than anything he had imagined. Those were his last words to me. 'It's a nightmare, worse than anything I had imagined.' "

I couldn't have picked up my jaw from the floor with both hands, so I made up for lack of poise with excessive volume. "Outrageous, Your Honor! It's still hearsay. I can't cross-examine *Mr.* Tupton, so we're left with this supposed excited utterance allegedly heard over the telephone about an unseen document not in evidence, a document obviously not related to the issue of my client's alleged negligence in serving alcohol to an intoxicated guest. So the statement is hearsay on hearsay, and further, the statement is not relevant or material. It's prejudicial and inflammatory. It's . . ."

"Overruled. Bring in the jury."

Story of my life. Little victories followed by a major squashing. So I got to listen to the story again. This time Mrs. Tupton dispensed a tear or two just as she said, "Those were his last words to me."

"Where's Gina?" I asked Nicky Florio while I packed my trial bags at the lunch recess. I wasn't taking them anywhere, but I didn't want to leave my notes on the defense table. Like newspaper reporters, lawyers can read upside down, and I didn't need H. T. Patterson scanning my papers.

"Why, you miss her?"

There was an edge to his voice, and I didn't like it. "I just like a wife to stand by her man. The old Tammy Wynette routine. It looks better for the jury. Besides, Gina makes a good appearance."

"Oh, you noticed."

We headed toward the elevators, fighting the crowd of lunchtime lawyers, hungry as a school of bluefish, pushy as . . . well, as a crowd of lawyers. "Hey, Nicky. What gives? Why you giving me grief?"

"Forget it. You know I hired you because Gina asked me to. Old times' sake. Some guys wouldn't have done it. They'd be jealous, threatened, that sort of thing. But a real man, Jake, a real man controls his emotions. You lose control, you make mistakes. You make mistakes, you get hurt. You with me?"

Or against me, my mind was asking.

"I think so," I said.

The elevator doors opened, and we elbowed our way in. "Good. I've gotta keep my mind on business. Gondo and I are trying to get Cypress Estates off the ground, and I'm stuck in court all day listening to that little jackrabbit bad-mouth me."

In the lobby, Marvin the Maven and his friends were standing under a mural of the Spanish explorers making nice with the Calusa Indians. It is only one of many lies to be found in the courthouse. "*Nu*, Jacob, how you doing, *boychik*?"

"I don't know, Marvin. I think Patterson scored some points this morning."

Marvin fingered the part on his toupee and seemed to think about it. "Window dressing. Just window dressing, Jacob. Nobody cares about the boids."

*   *   *

In the cool, dark confines of Paul Flanigan's Quarterdeck Lounge across the street from the courthouse, I munched a burger and drank three iced teas. No beer during trial. Florio sipped at his coffee, black. I can never understand guys who skip lunch. By noon, I could eat the animals mounted in Nicky Florio's den.

"What about her story?" I asked. "What'd Tupton see in your den?"

"The fuck should I know?" Nicky straightened the knot on his flowery silk tie. "It's the first time I heard about it."

"What'd he mean about the condos being a cover?"

"Who knows? The guy was three sheets to the wind. Besides, like you said, what's the relevance?"

"I'm not sure, yet. I just don't like surprises, so it would help if you'd tell me everything you've got planned for Cypress Estates."

"Look, Jake, I got certain business matters that are private, and I don't go around broadcasting them until the time is right. In business, timing is everything. *Capisce?*"

"I'm your lawyer."

He gave me a look. "Yeah, so what?"

"So I owe you certain duties, confidentiality for one."

"And loyalty, too. Isn't that right, Jake?"

"Sure. It's in the rules. A lawyer can't engage in conflicts of interest."

"Rules." Nicky Florio's smile was nearly a smirk.

"You don't believe in them."

"Only losers play by the rules, and you're not a loser, Jake."

"What are you saying?"

"The gods make their own rules. One of the old Romans said that."

"I'm not following you."

"Oh, I think you are. I don't play by anyone else's rules, Jake, and neither do you. If you did, you wouldn't have your dick on the chopping block with the Bar Association. And you wouldn't have conflicts of interest, would you?"

I stayed quiet. I thought I knew where he was going, but I wasn't going to help him get there.

"The fact is, Jake, you and I are a lot alike. Hope that doesn't insult you, Counselor, but it's the truth. You don't believe me, just ask Gina. A woman like Gina has great instincts. She knows men, Jake. She knows us better than we do."

Chapter 8

Swallowing Golf Balls

THERE ARE FEW SURPRISES IN TRIALS ANYMORE. THANKS TO THE discovery rules, a lawyer learns the other side's case before trial. Your opponent must provide you with a witness list and copies of all exhibits. You can ask written questions under oath and require production of documents. You cross-examine all your opponent's witnesses before ever setting foot in a courtrom. So, it's not like Perry Mason. I have yet to see a bombshell witness fly through the courtroom doors to save the day. Never have I even heard of a member of the gallery standing up and proclaiming, "All right, I admit it, I killed Norby Frebish, and I'd do it again!"

Still, you must be quick on your feet. You may think you are fully prepared—a sturdy ship maintaining a steady course—but it never works quite that way. At best, you're a rickety boat sliding down treacherous waves in a sea peppered with unseen mines. As in a stage play, you rehearse and rehearse. Unlike a play, in court, after the first act, you often tear up the script.

You need *strategy*, and that is different from preparation. Building your case is one thing. Changing it as you go is another. Imagine you are building a house. You dig the foundation and carefully follow the plans. You lay every block in line, drive every nail straight, and align every wall true.

That is the way most people live and work. But with generals,

coaches, and lawyers, it is different. Just when you get that two-
by-four in plumb, some joker with a sledgehammer whacks it out
of place. Lay in the wiring, and the same joker shreds it. As soon
as the windows are in place, you hear the sound of tinkling glass.

The lawyer, like the general, must have a plan, but must also
foresee the opponent's next move. And when the move is a surprise,
you'd better have plans A, B, and C ready. If war is endless boredom
interrupted by moments of sheer terror, trial work is deadening
preparation followed by panicky ad-libbing.

I didn't expect the excited utterance from Melinda Tupton, and
I was unsure how it would play, Tupton's fears about a document
so sinister as to evoke his worst nightmares. For once I didn't agree
with Marvin the Maven. I doubted that the intent was to provoke
sympathy for the Everglades animals. No wood storks died in the
Florio wine cellar. I thought Patterson was simply trying to create
animosity toward Nicky Florio. It even helped Patterson's case that
the document was unseen by the jury. What is more horrifying
than the unknown?

Maybe Patterson's strategy went like this:

First, convince the jury that Peter Tupton was a good man.

Second, suggest that something planned by Nicky Florio repulsed
and terrified Tupton.

Ergo, as Charlie Riggs would say, Nicky Florio is a bad man.

At the essence of every case is the attempt to get the jury to like
your client and hate the opposition. When liability is foggy, it makes
the hard evidence less important than raw emotion.

It was just after lunch when I finally figured out what Patterson
was doing. It became clear as I was thumbing through the plaintiff's
proposed jury instructions.

The instructions are the last words the jurors hear before retiring
to their little room. Each side prepares an independent set. The
introductory ones are innocuous. Jurors are told to test the believability of witnesses based on their experiences. They are instructed
not to base their verdict on sympathy, an important one for the
defense in a death case. They are told that negligence is the failure
to use due care and that they should also evaluate the comparative
negligence of the plaintiff, which can reduce a verdict.

I was standing at the clerk's table, skimming through Patterson's
requested instructions.

Ho hum.

The standard stuff. Believability of Witnesses, Prejudice and Sympathy, Definition of Negligence, Punitive Damages.

Whoops. What was that again?

Buried in the stapled stack of the plaintiff's instructions was one simply entitled Punitive Damages.

If you find for plaintiff Melinda Tupton, as Personal Representative of the Estate of Peter Tupton, and against defendant Nicholas Florio, you may consider whether in the circumstances of this case it is appropriate to award punitive damages, in addition to compensatory damages, as punishment and as a deterrent to others. Punitive damages may be awarded in your discretion if the conduct of defendant Florio was so gross and flagrant as to show a reckless disregard of human life or safety.

The jury-charge conference would come at the end of the case, but I couldn't wait. I buttonholed H. T. Patterson at the plaintiff's table. "What the hell's this?"

He shrugged. "The standard punie charge, right out of the book. You may recall we amended the complaint to include the claim."

"I recall, but that's a throwaway. There's no evidence to support—"

"No evidence! Jake my boy, were you listening this morning? It's quite obvious. Peter Tupton had discovered something so heinous that your client dispatched him."

"Are you out of your mind! You can't prove that."

"I'm not claiming it was a premeditated murder, and you're half-right. There's no way I could prove it, at least not in criminal court. But, Jake, we're downtown with the buzzards, who, strangely enough, only circle the civil courthouse. I've always wondered why they stayed away from the criminal-justice building, but—"

"What's your point?"

"Simple. I only need to prove my case by a preponderance of the evidence, and the way I figure it, the jury will conclude that Florio discovered Tupton in the den. They argued over the document. Nicky Florio's not the kind of guy to pull out a gun. He tries to smooth-talk Tupton, maybe even offers him a bribe again."

"What do you mean *again*? My objection was sustained. Your client never got to answer—"

"But there was the question, wasn't there, Jake? Come now. You know how jurors pick up the slant on things. You were sweating bullets to keep out the answer, and you did it, but the jurors saw it. They think your guy's dirty, and frankly, so do I." Patterson gave me his cat-to-the-canary smile. "You want to hear more?"

"I'm all ears."

"Whatever Florio tries, threat or bribe, it doesn't work. Tupton's too honest. Florio isn't used to this. He's been buying off zoning boards and county commissioners for so long, he doesn't know what to do. He needs time to think. Tupton's already had too much to drink. Florio wants him to drink some more. At first, I thought they probably went back out to the pool. But no, at this point, Tupton's getting loud and excited. You heard his wife's testimony. He was hyper, and there are politicians and journalists outside. Florio can't afford a scene. And if you recall, none of the guests can place Tupton outside again after he went inside to piss."

"Or to spy."

"Have it your way. But there's a wet bar in the den, did you know that?"

I didn't know, and I didn't answer.

"It's really quite a nice bar." Patterson smiled malevolently. "When we had the inspection of the house in discovery, we took photos. Polished teak, I believe. So perhaps Florio offered Tupton something a little stiffer than a mimosa. Just a couple of men in a dark, paneled den. A little scotch, perhaps. Tupton would be staggering by now. From the den, it's just a short walk down the hall to the wine cellar. No one would see them. There are two chairs in there, bleached wood to match the shelving. White pads for comfort. Maybe open a bottle of wine, or more champagne, the good stuff, showing his guest respect."

"I still haven't heard anything about murder."

"And you won't, not in this courtroom. Florio just wanted to keep Tupton on ice . . . sorry about that, keep him away from the crowd, buy some time. I figure he left him there with all the bottles and goes to get his partner, what's his name?"

"Rick Gondolier."

". . . who's making nice with the ladies out by the pool. Florio and Gondolier come back, and there's Tupton sprawled out on the floor, passed out, with some expensive champagne running down his chin. They just leave him there. It gives them time to figure out what to do when he wakes up. Except . . ."

Except he wakes up dead, I thought.

". . . he doesn't wake up. Are you following me, Jake? Florio doesn't figure Tupton's going to die, but he doesn't really give a shit. That's the essence of punitive damages, isn't it? Complete disregard for the well-being of another."

H.T. didn't have to say the rest. The damages are assessed in an amount sufficient to punish the defendant. The richer the defendant, the bigger the award. Biggest bummer of all, punitive damages are the equivalent of a criminal fine, and insurance won't cover them.

"So, Jake, I'm wondering if the blackboard is big enough to hold all the zeros I'm going to put up there in closing argument. How does ten million sound to you?"

Like a funeral dirge, I thought.

"Why tell me all this?" I asked. "Why lay out your case?"

"To give you a chance to save us all a lot of work. The trial, appeals, years of delays."

"How much?"

"Five million," he said with a shrug. "Think about it."

I thought about it. H. T. Patterson had succeeded in making a simple negligence case into a civil version of a murder trial. I hadn't been ready for it, and now I was beating myself over the head. I had deposed Melinda Tupton. What should I have asked? Did your husband call you and make an excited utterance? No, of course not. But a simple "When was the last time you spoke to your husband?" would have done quite nicely.

The case had turned from the negligence of a social host serving alcohol to a guest—a tricky case for a plaintiff because jurors expect people to take care of themselves—to something far different.

Gross negligence.

Willful and wanton misconduct.

Reckless disregard of human life.

Punitive damages.

Yeah, let old Jake handle the case. He can't fuck it up. And if he does, the insurance company will cover his ass. Not anymore, Nicky.

* * *

I stood up for cross-examination of Melinda Tupton and strode confidently toward the witness stand. Never let them see your fear. I buttoned my navy-blue suitcoat, proving I could walk and accomplish other rudimentary tasks simultaneously. My shirt was white, a tad too tight at the collar, which is what happens when you have an eighteen-and-a-half-inch neck. My tie was burgundy and didn't have any gravy stains, as far as I could tell. My face was tanned but felt overheated and flushed.

What to ask?

There was the stuff about Florio's threatened SLAPP suit. I could get her to admit that her husband's main tactic was doing the same thing, threatening suit. These days, it's sometimes a race to the courthouse to see who files first, the developer or the bird-watchers. But that was a double-edged sword. Tupton's threats could provide the motive for killing him—or letting him die—even without the mysterious document in the den.

The document.

Whatever it was, Nicky either didn't know or wouldn't tell me. I could ignore it, of course, and try to show the jury it didn't bother me. I could also hope that the tooth fairy would deposit silver dollars under my pillow. On the other hand, by getting into the phone call and the document, I might open the door to redirect examination that could go even further than the so-called excited utterances on whose petard I was now hoisted.

I opted for the low-key approach and hoped I would know what to do when the time came. My questions were so soft, the jury had to lean forward to hear them. You don't come out of the box swinging wildly at a widow lady. Not unless you want the jury to lynch you and bankrupt your client.

I asked about her education and her job as a public school teacher, gently implying that she was self-supporting and didn't need a fortune to sustain her. I asked her age, thirty-four, not to be impolite, but to let the jury know that there was still time for her to meet, to marry, and to procreate. I asked—because I knew the answers—whether she had been treated by a psychiatrist for depression after her husband's death, whether she had missed an excessive amount of work, and whether she needed sleeping pills or other medication.

No, no, and no.

Slowly, I asked one boring question after another, trying to build an impression that might chip away at the mental-anguish claim, the ominous intangible that lights up the scoreboard in wrongful-death cases. The conclusion I wanted the jury to reach was simple: This is a young, strong, intelligent, vital woman who will survive, and in time, prosper. So don't break the bank at Monte Carlo to help her out.

I established that her husband had been a workaholic who spent little time fixing things around the house, or repairing the cars, so as to reduce the lost-services claim. I purposely did not ask if she had started dating or planned to remarry because it angers jurors, and the answer wouldn't have helped my case. I made no gestures and accepted every answer kindly and tried to let the jury know that I am a decent-enough fellow who does not strangle kittens or malign widows.

I paused and walked back to the defense table. Nicky Florio looked up at me expectantly. His eyes seemed to be pleading for more. He couldn't believe I was finished.

Neither could I.

I put all my notes on the table, turned, and moved closer to the witness stand. "On direct examination," I began, "you testified about a phone call from your husband on August ninth."

She nodded, prompting the judge to remind her to keep the answers audible for the court reporter.

"During this phone call," I said, "your husband seemed excited, did he not?"

Melinda Tupton sat with her legs crossed, her hands folded in her lap. "Yes."

"Was his voice louder than usual?"

"Yes, somewhat."

"Was he speaking rapidly?"

"Yes."

"Some of his words slurred?"

"Not slurred, exactly. But he wasn't as articulate as usual. It's hard to explain."

"Did he say he'd been drinking?"

A pause. She was thinking about it. "Yes. He either told me

outright, or I asked him, I don't remember which. Either way, he said he'd been drinking champagne mixed with orange juice."

"And the reason you think you may have asked him is that he didn't sound quite like himself?"

"That's right."

"Mr. Tupton was not a heavy drinker, was he?"

"No, I already said that when Mr. Patterson asked."

I smiled my tolerant smile. "I understand, Mrs. Tupton, but this is cross-examination, and your answer may lead us to something else, so please bear with me. The few times you saw your husband drink, he became tipsy, didn't he?"

Bluffing her.

She couldn't know if I knew. . . .

Holding my breath now.

The book says you don't ask a question on cross-examination unless you know the answer. But instinct told me I was right and that Melinda Tupton was honest. The book also says that you try to frame the question to get admissions. You're allowed to lead the witness. The perfect cross-examination does not elicit a series of long-winded explanations. The answers should be a string of yes's and no's, depending how you phrase the questions.

"I'm not sure what you mean," Melinda Tupton said.

Not knowing where I was going, but figuring the truth would hurt her case. Still, not wanting to lie.

Take a risk, now. Chide her, let the jury see her reluctance to answer, but be careful not to offend. "Come now, Mrs. Tupton, you know the meaning of the word 'tipsy.' "

"Objection, argumentative!" H. T. Patterson was not going to imitate a potted plant.

"I'll rephrase," I offered before the judge could rule against me. "Could your husband hold his liquor?"

This time the answer came quickly. "No."

Heaven praise an honest woman.

"So it took only a couple of drinks to make him inebriated?"

"Yes."

"People respond differently to alcohol, don't they, Mrs. Tupton?"

"Objection!" Patterson was on his feet again. "Calls for an opinion. Outside the witness's expertise. No predicate. And irrelevant."

"Anything else?" Judge Boulton asked.

"It's a silly question," Patterson said.

"Overruled. It's a matter of common observation."

"I suppose they do," the witness said.

"Some people get loud and obnoxious. You've seen that, haven't you?"

"Yes." Her voice barely a whisper.

"Some people get sleepy and quiet."

"Yes." Softer still.

"And your husband would become excited and hyper, would speak rapidly, wouldn't sound quite like himself."

"Yes."

Though her voice was faint, I heard the answer, and so did the jurors. But I wanted them to hear it again, so I fibbed. "I'm sorry, Mrs. Tupton. I couldn't quite hear you. When your husband became inebriated, he would become excited and wouldn't quite sound like himself, correct?"

"Yes, that's correct."

"And when you spoke to him on the phone on August ninth, you knew he'd been drinking, didn't you?"

"I thought so, yes."

Time for a quick change of pace. Keep her off-balance. "Your husband wasn't the kind of man to snoop through someone else's desk, was he?"

Whack! Patterson slapped the top of the plaintiff's table. "Objection! Mischaracterizes the evidence. No one *snooped* through—"

"Denied," Judge Boulton declared. "The jury heard your direct exam and can make up its own mind."

I turned back to the witness, my eyes asking her to answer.

"No," Mrs. Tupton said. "He wasn't like that."

"But he changed when he became inebriated, didn't he?"

"I suppose we all do, to an extent."

"He became less inhibited?"

"I guess."

"Did you ask him what it was he had found in Mr. Florio's den?"

"Yes."

I walked back to my table and picked up my trusty yellow notepad. I thumbed past my *X*'s and *O*'s diagram of a sprint draw play and found my notes of the direct examination. "But he 'didn't say exactly what it was.' Weren't those your words?"

"I believe so."

"Just as a drunk driver doesn't hear the train whistle or see the Stop sign, he may not have even heard you, correct?"

"Objection! Calls for a conclusion." Patterson had stayed on his feet. No slipping a fastball by him now.

"Sustained," the judge said.

"At any rate, it was apparently hard for him to concentrate on your end of the conversation, wasn't it?"

"I don't know." Not as good as a yes, but the jury could still get the point.

"And despite your request, he never told you what he allegedly saw."

"That's right."

"And you have no way of knowing what it was, do you?"

"No."

"It could have been something that had nothing to do with Cypress Estates, something of no concern to the Everglades Society."

"Well, I doubt that."

"But you don't *know*, do you, ma'am?"

"No."

"And you have no way of knowing whether he understood what he allegedly saw?"

"He was a very bright man."

"When he was sober," I added gratuitously. "How about when he was drunk?"

"He was so seldom . . . I just don't know."

"Did your husband tell you that anyone at the party had forced him to consume alcohol?"

"No, of course not."

"Did he say anyone treated him badly?"

"No. He said he'd been eating and drinking. . . ."

"So, at a party at which he was drinking champagne and being treated as an honored guest, he exceeded his tolerance for alcohol, and thereafter sneaked into a private room and snooped through a desk . . ."

I shot a little look at Patterson, needling him.

". . . where he found something that excited him," I continued, "though you have no idea if he understood it, and as you sit here today, you couldn't begin to describe it, correct?"

"I don't think he sneaked—"

"No further questions," I said.

That night in my little coral-rock house in Coconut Grove, I listened to the sounds of the neighborhood possum banging over garbage cans and the occasional whine of a police siren. When Nicky Florio called to reject Patterson's settlement demand, I asked if he had a counteroffer.

"Yeah, tell him I offer to punch his lights out."

In the morning, I would inform Patterson that, after due deliberation, we must regretfully decline his thoughtful proposal for settlement.

After grilling some hog snapper over hot coals for my supper, I opened the Florio file and thumbed through a stack of folders until I found what I wanted. In discovery, we had given Patterson a list of the party guests. Like a lot of lawyers, when it came to filing a witness list, Patterson listed everyone who ever passed within ten miles of the *locus delicti*. He didn't really intend to call all of them. It's just a safety net. Rick Gondolier's name was there, but Patterson had never taken his deposition. When I filed my witness list, I named everyone on Patterson's list plus some of my own. I had planned to interview Gondolier at the bingo hall but never did it.

I found Gondolier's number and was ready to call him when my phone rang.

Rick Gondolier.

Funny how things happen that way. Maybe some electromagnetic force in the universe, who knows? Gondolier was in his office at the bingo hall. For some reason, I expected to hear the announcer calling out "B-thirteen" in the background, but it was quiet on the other end.

"I got two subpoenas here," Rick Gondolier said. "One from you and one from . . ." He paused, and I heard papers shuffling. "Henry Thackery Patterson." Calm voice. Deep and resonant. I pictured him. Thick, sun-bleached hair swept back, a hand toying with his little diamond earring. Las Vegas slick.

"You're a popular guy," I said. "Patterson is Tupton's lawyer. He may call you to testify, though I doubt it. He knows he can't get you to say what he wants."

"Which is what?"

"That Florio caught Tupton reading an incriminating document in the den and then got him drunk and waltzed him into the cooler. That Nicky either intended to kill him or didn't care if he died or not. And that maybe you helped him."

He didn't take a deep breath or curse or laugh. "Pretty far-fetched, don't you think so, Mr. Lassiter?"

Unruffled. Maybe that's the way Gina liked them.

"Yeah. And damn hard to prove. But I may want to put you on the stand, so I have to ask you some questions. Did you see Tupton at the party?"

"Of course. Nicky introduced us out at the pool by the buffet table. Tupton was hitting the mimosas pretty good, trying to be sociable, talking up a storm. Told me how Everglades mosquitoes could kill a horse with enough stings around the eyes. Some anecdotes about how to tell alligator shit from crocodile shit. A real raconteur."

"What did you say to him?"

"I told him to watch the mimosas, they sneak up on you. He giggled, stumbled around, and grabbed another drink from a tray. Is that useful?"

"Very. What else? I don't suppose you know anything about a document Tupton saw on Nicky's desk."

"Sure I do."

"What!"

"It was late in the afternoon, but not yet dark. I was talking to Tupton out by the seawall. Like I said, he'd been drinking a lot. His face was flushed and sweaty. Anyway, he excused himself to find a bathroom. I didn't see him for maybe twenty minutes or so. Then he came back out to the pool—"

"He came back out?"

"Yeah, what of it?"

"Nobody else at the pool saw him once he went into the house."

"Maybe nobody was looking. He was a pretty nondescript guy. Anyway, he came back out, flapping his jaw about the golf course."

"What golf course?"

"At Cypress Estates. A championship course."

"I didn't know there was one. I didn't see it in the model."

" 'Course not. It was under wraps. We knew there'd be a blowup from the Everglades Society. Not that there's anything wrong with it. It'll be a real showpiece, completely in sync with nature. Nothing else like it in history. The water hazards will be the natural slough, the roughs will be saw grass. Ponds and streams everywhere. Every imaginable bird would inhabit the place. 'Course, we'd have to regulate the water levels. Can you imagine the development potential for the town houses and condos if we got a PGA event out there on national TV?"

"How did Tupton know about it?"

"He'd found the architect's drawings on Nicky's desk. The schematics, the cost estimates, impact studies, and he was running off at the mouth, going ape shit."

"What'd he say?"

"The usual environmental crap about the dredging and the filling, the canals and locks disturbing the natural water flow, the effect of the pesticides and the fertilizers. I made a joke about a golfer reaching for his lost Titleist in a gator hole, and he went bananas. Whining about gators swallowing golf balls and shitting tees, that kind of thing."

"That's all he found, a document about the golf course?"

"Yeah, that's all he was carrying on about."

"Anybody else overhear this?"

"I don't know. When he got started, I sort of steered him back along the seawall toward the bay. Like I said, we're not publicizing the golf course. We don't plan to announce it until all the financing is in place and we're ready to go."

Something wasn't ringing true, but what?

"Why didn't Nicky mention this to me?"

"Guess 'cause I didn't mention it to him."

"Tupton dies at the house, your partner gets sued, and you don't mention this conversation?"

"Yeah, it didn't seem important. Is it?"

Later, sometime after midnight, I was lying in the hammock between my live oak trees, listening to the warble of a mockingbird calling its mate, or at least looking for a one-night stand. I wondered what Clarence Darrow would do. He once said there was no such thing as justice, in or out of court. That didn't help any, so I had a beer. A sixteen-ounce Grolsch with the porcelain stopper. That didn't help either, so I had another.

I thought of Melinda Tupton, a good woman by any standard. I thought of Gina and tried to pretend I didn't miss her. What was the hold she had on me?

I thought of Rick Gondolier. I wouldn't trust him as far as I could throw Hulk Hogan. What kind of guy sleeps with his partner's wife?

Probably the same kind of guy who sleeps with his client's wife.

And I thought of Nicky Florio. He clams up, but his partner talks. What could be so secret about the golf course? And what was so terrible about it? If they're going to bulldoze the marshy hammocks and mangroves for the condos and the shops, what difference does a golf course make?

Not much, except as a symbol of man's callousness. Destroying nature for a manicured playground of the rich.

A nightmare. That's what Tupton told his wife about it. *Worse than anything I had imagined.*

It didn't fit. Way too strong. He already knew about the proposed development. It was a whole town, for crying out loud.

The condos, the shops, the town, it's all a cover.

But the town can't be a cover for a golf course. Maybe for something else, but not that. Sorry, Gondo, but I think you're making it up. Maybe there was a golf course planned, but in my heart, I know that's not what Tupton saw. But is that my job? Don't I have to present the evidence as it rolls in the door?

And what a piece of evidence. Two pieces, really. First, Gondolier told Tupton to watch how much he drank, and Tupton ignored the advice. Talk about a plaintiff's comparative negligence. Second, Gondolier witnessed Tupton's drunken overreaction to the golf-course plans. No wonder the guy ended up unconscious in the wine cellar. He was out of control.

Hey, Gondo, you're a real gamesaver. That phone call to me. How timely. Wonder who called *you* earlier in the evening. Nicky probably figured I wouldn't use evidence if I thought it was phony, so the two of you cooked up this little charade.

I had another beer and began thinking abstract thoughts, something that's not my strong point. Words like ethics and perjury and conflicts of interest fluttered across the beer-soaked landscape of my mind. I like to win, but I like to win fair and square. A lawyer isn't supposed to use perjured testimony. You can look it up. But who made me a mind reader? I could put Rick Gondolier on the stand, and if the jury didn't believe him, we would lose.

Justice would be done. Take that, Clarence Darrow.

But the jury might believe him. And we would win. But then, we deserved to, because if the jury believed him, we must be right. Isn't that the way the system works, or is that circular reasoning?

I needed another beer to answer the question. I crawled out of the hammock to get one, then slipped a Jimmy Buffet disc into the machine. I sang along, not more than half an octave off-key, and twanged an imaginary guitar, and by the time Jimmy got to "Why Don't We Get Drunk and Screw?" a quiniela I found to be physically improbable, I was drifting off toward a restless sleep.

Chapter 9

The Brain Trust

GRANNY LASSITER WAS CHOPPING FLORIDA LOBSTER WITH A SAW-tooth diver's knife and tossing the white morsels into a frying pan with slices of onion and green pepper. The cooking oil sizzled and popped, and her small kitchen was redolent with piquant aromas. I was barefoot because it's against the law, or ought to be, to wear shoes south of Key Largo. The rest of me was covered by denim cutoffs and a faded Penn State T-shirt. My job was to whack a coconut in two with a machete and grate the meat. Charlie Riggs's job was to sip Granny's home brew and kibitz.

Granny wasn't my grandmother, but there was some relationship, maybe a great-aunt on my father's side. Everyone in the Keys called her Granny Lassiter, and most of the natives drank her moonshine. She raised me after my father was killed and my mother ran off. Granny was a small, wiry woman with high cheekbones and a pugnacious chin, and her black hair was streaked with white. Today she wore canvas shorts with button pockets and a tank top from a Key West oyster bar that advised its patrons to "Eat 'em raw." Under the tank top, it was just Granny. No bra and, sure as heck, no silken camisole. She lived just outside Islamorada in a four-room wooden house with a front porch and a rocking chair and a kitchen window that caught the breezes from the Gulf of Mexico.

Granny poured some sherry into the frying pan with the lobster, then took a swig from the bottle. I shredded the coconut into the sizzling mixture. Charlie was into one of his soliloquies, rambling on about determining time of death based on the amount of maggot growth in the corpse. It was one of his favorite mealtime topics.

When the lobster was golden brown, Granny added tomato paste, curry powder, and turmeric, then put the whole shebang into a casserole that she slid into the oven. Then she ordered me to cook some wild rice, so she could sit down with Charlie at the kitchen table to have a drink and rest her dogs, which is what Granny called her feet. I followed her instructions, boiling the rice, all the time inhaling the pungent fragrance of the spices and the cooking lobster.

"Speared those suckers myself," Granny said, gesturing toward the oven or maybe toward the Gulf. "Don't have time to trap 'em."

"Marine Patrol could confiscate your boat," I told her. "Lobster poaching's a crime."

"So's larceny," she said, "but that don't stop you shysters."

"*Panulirus argus,*" Charlie mumbled. "The spiny lobster is actually a crawfish." He took a sip of home brew from a jelly jar. "Now, where was I? . . ."

"Something about maggots," Granny suggested, though I don't know why she encourages him.

"Right. These days, a good coroner has to know the lifestyles of flies and lice," Charlie said. "Jake, have I ever told you about the case I handled a few years back in Lacoochee?"

"Not recently," I allowed.

"A body was found in a swamp in July, some drug runner. No one knew how long the body had been there. There was a suspect who had an alibi for the previous week, but that was it. If the body had been there longer, he couldn't account for his whereabouts."

"So?" Granny prompted him.

"The body was infested with fly maggots. Based on the time the flies took for feeding, laying eggs, and the development of the maggots, it was clear the body was more than a week old. That blew the alibi."

"Keep it up, I'm going to blow lunch," I said.

Granny dismissed me with a wave of her nut-brown arm. "Boy's a tad squeamish. Never wanted to eat catfish if I cooked 'em with the head still on."

"Granny!"

"Then, I remember the time we were snorkeling off Matecumbe Key, and a moray eel bit clean through his fins. The boy wouldn't go back in the water for a week."

"Granny, please. No old stories. Let's talk about anything but me."

That only provoked her. "You married yet, boy?" She'd taken off her sandals, and her feet were propped in Charlie Riggs's lap.

"You know I'm not."

"Good. I never married, and I never regretted it. Not that I ain't been asked. If I recollect correctly, five fellows proposed, a couple of 'em sober at the time. But who needs a man, and who needs rug rats? You were enough to handle, and you were what, eight or nine, when you started bunking with me." She turned to Charlie, who was munching his appetizer, some of Granny's deep-fried hush puppies. "Lord, that boy could eat. Pork barbecue, yellowtail snapper, six-egg omelets, you name it. And raise a ruckus, whoooee. He used to hit the walls. Hit 'em with his shoulders, shake the whole house. I figured he was just going through puberty, but he kept it up so long, I made him go out for the football team."

"These days, he usually hits the walls with his head," Charlie said, between crackly bites.

"C'mon, I asked for help, not abuse. You two are my brain trust."

Granny cackled at me. "Then you're in trouble, boy. Charlie's half-potted on white lightning, and I never did understand your business. Just talky-talk."

"Really, Granny, I need help. I've got the weekend to figure out what to do, and then it's back to court Monday."

Charlie poured himself a refill. Beads of sweat appeared on his forehead. "I don't see the problem, Jake. You're ethically bound to use Gondolier's testimony. You're not in a position to judge his veracity." *Ver-ashity.*

"Charlie, admit it. Whatever Tupton found, it wasn't a plan for a golf course. It's something far worse. His reaction was way over the top."

"You're assuming Tupton's reaction was rational, even though he'd been drinking heavily." Charlie paused long enough to burp. "And you have no proof that Gondolier is lying."

"But I *know* he is."

"How? Do you have documentary evidence? Contradictory witnesses? Have you caught him in inconsistencies?"

"No, dammit, I just know. I do this for a living, remember. It's my job to know."

Outside the kitchen window, the Gulf breeze sent shivers through the bell-shaped flowers of a violet jacaranda tree.

"It's your job to give your client the best representation you can." Charlie cleared his throat. It sounded like a train leaving the station. "It's *not* your job to cloud your judgment with conflicts of interest."

"The boy in Dutch again?" Granny asked. "I'd bet my new spinning rod it's a woman. He's been fooled by more than one."

Charlie patted his lips dry with a dish towel Granny used for a napkin. "As Virgil asked, *'Quis fallere possit amantem?'* Who can deceive a lover?"

"Easy," I answered. "The lover's lover."

"Ah, the cynic in you speaks."

"The voice of experience," I said.

"Just so you haven't taken up with that cheerleader again," Granny said, sipping at her drink. "Son, that girl was nothing but trouble."

I had been promoted from "boy." "She was a dancer, Granny."

"And she married that fellow who builds those crappy condos on stilts from Hialeah to Marathon. I read the society pages, just to remind myself how much I hate evening gowns, tuxes, and the people who wear 'em."

"She's got nothing to do with this," I said defensively.

They both looked at me as if I'd spent too long in the midday sun.

"Don't you believe me?" I asked.

Charlie was massaging Granny's feet under the table, and Granny wasn't complaining. He looked at me with a headmaster's stare. "What do you believe, Jake? Why is this case different for you from just another insurance-company defense?"

"Do you know you have an irritating habit of answering a question with a question?"

"What's wrong with that?" Charlie replied.

I was trying to wash down Granny's mango cheesecake with a cup of coffee the color of crankcase oil that had gone more than its allotted miles. "If only I knew what Tupton really found in Nicky Florio's den . . ."

"Why don't you ask Gina?" Charlie asked.

We were sitting on Granny's front porch. A redwinged blackbird was making *chucking* sounds as it circled the jacaranda trees. I was in the old wicker rocking chair, my brain trust in the love seat. Granny was snoring peacefully, her head on Charlie's shoulder. Charlie poured himself a second cup of coffee. If that didn't clear the fog, nothing would.

"Ask her what? To go through her husband's desk? To tell me if her husband's planning anything illegal, unethical, or particularly nasty?"

"She is your paramour, is she not?"

"I hate to tell you this, Charlie, but people don't use words like 'paramour' anymore."

"Para-mour any-more," he mused putting a little tune to it.

"Besides, what makes you think Gina would help me?"

"Since we know Gina is not loyal to her husband in matters of the heart, perhaps the same would be true in business affairs. I am assuming, of course, that you have already violated your attorney-client relationship against my advice."

"Forget it, Charlie. It wouldn't work, anyway. It's over with Gina."

"Why, because of Gondolier? You couldn't handle her dancing in two discos at once. Is that lingo more with it?"

I ignored his jab. "I'd like to tell you I dropped Gina, but the fact is, she lowered the boom on me. She wants to work on her marriage."

He shrugged and downed the rest of his sludge. "Odd way to work on the marriage, don't you think, with her husband's partner?"

"I really don't care."

Charlie raised a bushy eyebrow at me. Granny stirred in her sleep and grunted.

"Really, Charlie. I'm more interested in what Florio and Gondolier are up to."

"Or is that simply the pretext for maintaining connection with Gina? Is your suspicion of her husband and his partner rational, or is it a subconscious attempt to facilitate your obsession with the woman?"

"Obsession's a little strong, Charlie."

"Oh, I don't know. Do thoughts of Gina intrude on your consciousness despite your attempts not to think of her?"

"Maybe."

"Jake, I'm trying to help you."

"Okay, okay, I think about her a lot. You happy now?"

"Are your thoughts repetitive and distracting? Do they interfere with your work?"

"I guess so."

"Have you been especially ruminative, your thinking unspontaneous? Do these thoughts seem to come from somewhere other than yourself?"

"Now that you mention it, yeah."

"Classic obsessional neurosis," Charlie declared. "As a child, your personality development probably was hindered because of alienation due to losses suffered very young, but that, dear lad, is another story." Charlie cleared his throat, perhaps signaling that our forty-five minutes was up. I was expecting him to hand me a bill, but instead he changed the subject. "And what do you think Peter Tupton found?"

"I don't know, but whatever it was, it killed him."

"As usual, you assume without knowing sufficient facts. You leap to conclusions."

"Wrong, Charlie. I don't assume anything, not even a seven percent mortgage. I listen. And what I hear is that Nicky Florio is a totally amoral, dangerous man who would do anything to achieve his goals. You know what he said to me?"

Charlie looked the question at me.

" 'The gods make their own rules.' Is that arrogant or what?"

"Ovid."

"Come again."

"Publius Ovidius Naso, or as we call him, Ovid. The line comes from *Metamorphoses*. 'Sunt superis sua iura.' " Charlie scratched at his beard and smiled to himself, doubtless remembering another pithy Latin verse. "Does Mr. Florio consider himself a god?"

"He thinks he's untouchable."

"Money and power do that to a man," Charlie said.

I stood up and did a couple of spinal twists, picking up a splinter in my foot from a wooden plank. I couldn't stop thinking about dead Peter Tupton and rich Nicky Florio. And because I generally say what I'm thinking, except in court, where I usually say the opposite, I asked Charlie, "What's Florio up to? What the hell is it that could be even worse than the damn town in the middle of the Everglades?"

"Figure it out."

"How?"

"Thank big, Jake."

"What do you mean?"

"Think like a god," Charlie Riggs said.

Chapter 10

Lord of the Sky

Every jury trial has a pace of its own. some crawl along with countless interruptions and delays. Judges who like to start late and quit early prolong cases. So do blabbermouth lawyers and tardy witnesses. Repetitive testimony and excessive use of exhibits—lawyers overtrying the case—can stretch out the proceedings.

Then there are the trials with the quick heartbeat. A skillful plaintiff's lawyer, and H. T. Patterson was certainly that, makes the courtroom crackle. The lawyer starts strong in opening statement, witnesses provide details in the middle, and the lawyer ends with a bang in closing argument.

Pacing.

Timing.

Ka-boom!

Patterson was doing his usual job. Crisp and focused, not letting the jurors get bored. In arguments with counsel, he could be a windbag, but he knew how to handle a jury. Lawyers who keep up with the times realize that jurors' attention spans are shaped by television. On *L.A. Law*, the crew at McKenzie, Brackman wraps up three trials and two love affairs every sixty minutes, including commercials. So keep your questions short and your arguments cogent. If you don't, the jurors will doze off and wonder why Judge Wapner doesn't move things along.

I was in a daze when we started up again Monday. I half listened as Patterson ran through his case, calling the paramedics and an assistant medical examiner in the morning and an expert on alcohol-related deaths in the afternoon. There wasn't much cross-examining to do. So I sat, chewing a pencil, staring at the sign above the judge's bench: WE WHO LABOR HERE SEEK ONLY THE TRUTH. If that were true, and not even a first-year law student believes it, most of our labor goes for naught.

The next hour, I sat, half listening to the witnesses, half thinking about Nicky Florio and Rick Gondolier. At lunchtime, I let myself fret about the brown manila envelope marked "Personal and Confidential" that reached the office in Saturday's mail while I was lazing with Charlie and Granny in Islamorada. Judge Herman Gold used all of eleven pages to find that one Jacob Lassiter, Esq., had illegally tape-recorded a client, and in so doing, had engaged in conduct prejudicial to the administration of justice. Further, by threatening his client with exposure to the state attorney, and subsequently doing so, the same miscreant mouthpiece breached the attorney-client privilege in acts "akin to extortion." That's what the old buzzard wrote.

Cindy, my trusty secretary, brought the order to the courthouse Monday morning. I read it the first time while a female paramedic who's also a champion bodybuilder was recounting the efforts to revive Peter Tupton.

I read it again.

Akin to extortion.

Funny, as I recall it, I was trying to prevent a murder by putting my own life in jeopardy, and the law considered my action "akin to extortion."

Granny Lassiter was right. I was in the wrong profession. I should have done something useful like sell Weed Whackers door-to-door.

"It's only a ninety-day suspension, plus a public reprimand," Cindy whispered, striving for encouragement. On the witness stand, the paramedic was saying something about Tupton's skin being colder than a well-digger's ass, and Judge Boulton scowled. Cindy leaned close to my ear. "And you can still appeal to the Florida Supreme Court, so don't get all bent out of shape."

I sent her back to the office, where she could use the time-honored (and occasionally true) dodge of telling clients that I was in trial and would return their calls upon my victorious return.

The assistant medical examiner, a lanky Harvard-educated pathologist with half-glasses perched on his nose, took the stand and told us what we already knew. Peter Tupton died of ventricular fibrillation brought about by hypothermia, an abnormal lowering of the body temperature. Next came an air force physician who studied the effects of cold on volunteers in Greenland. He testified that alcohol consumption contributed to the hypothermia. Throughout the day, Nicky Florio sat next to me, looking bored, occasionally opening his appointment book and making notes to himself.

Just after the midafternoon recess, we had a visitor. I felt a tap on my shoulder as yet another physician was testifying, attesting to Peter Tupton's robust health prior to being chilled out. I swiveled around in my chair.

The long, sallow face of Abe Socolow was smiling down at me. Smiling? Abe Socolow?

Then he gave me a teammate's friendly slug on the back, moved a step toward Nicky Florio, and mumbled something in his ear. Facing the jury box, Socolow smiled, clasped Florio as if they were blood brothers, nodded to the judge, and left.

H. T. Patterson watched the choreography, a pained expression on his face. The jurors saw it, every last one of them, their heads swinging away from the witness and toward us. They must have recognized Socolow from television. He was always announcing indictments, crowing over guilty verdicts, whining about acquittals. Now here he was, dispensing his blessings to a defendant in a civil case. Even I was impressed with Nicky Florio's clout.

Two hours later, half the jurors were yawning, so Judge Boulton sent them home with the usual admonitions not to discuss the case with their friends and families. The grateful conscripts responded with the usual pleasant lies.

On Tuesday, Patterson called to the stand one of Tupton's colleagues from the environmental movement. Harrison Baker was a patrician Bostonian who had brought his trust fund to Florida forty years earlier and hadn't worn a suit and tie since. He was tall and thin with a white mustache and a John Kennedy accent. He wore khaki pants, a bush jacket, and mud-stained boots. His specialty was the endangered Florida panther, and he testified how he mended the broken bones of the tawny cats run down by cement trucks on Alligator Alley. Patterson's strategy was clear. Tupton and his friends are the guys in the white hats. The builders and real estate developers are reincarnations of Satan himself. Baker said the expected, praising Tupton's dedication, his many good works, bemoaning the lost glories that could have been.

An economist took the stand and plastered numbers on a blackboard—lost earnings and net accumulations—reduced to present money value based on Tupton's life expectancy had he lived. I couldn't follow the math, and neither could the jurors, but surely the number $2.37 million stuck in their minds.

Wednesday morning, Patterson called Nicky Florio as an adverse witness. After the usual preliminaries, Nicky admitted that he and Tupton were adversaries in the dispute over development in the Everglades. He admitted that champagne was flowing freely at the party. He admitted that he saw Tupton around the pool, and that he seemed tipsy. He denied having any arguments with Tupton at the party and professed not to know what Tupton might have found in his study. "I'm surprised that a man of good character would pry into another man's private papers," Florio said, somewhat indignantly.

"And what private papers would those be?" Patterson asked.

"I don't know what Mr. Tupton saw, or if he was having delusions. As a gentleman, it's the principle that concerns me."

I tried swallowing my tongue to keep from laughing, wondering where more lies are told, courtrooms or bedrooms.

After lunch, Patterson rested the plaintiff's case, and I went to work. I called various guests from the party, both to draw attention to the distinguished crowd in attendance and for the testimony that nothing out of the ordinary was going on. No riproaring drunks, no drinking games or other tomfoolery. This was a Gables Estates soiree, not a fraternity party.

I called a pathologist who, for three hundred bucks an hour, testified that Tupton might have died from hypothermia even without the booze in his system, but on cross-examination, he admitted that Tupton wouldn't have passed out in the wine cellar if he hadn't been drinking and therefore wouldn't have been subjected to the cold. I put a psychiatrist on the stand to testify about the conflicting signals party guests send out and a drug counselor who discussed the difficulty of ascertaining a person's tolerance to alcohol. That sent Patterson scrambling to prepare *his* psychiatrist for rebuttal. These days trials are battles of highly paid witnesses. You can get a doctor to say anything you want if the price is right. Expert witnesses, we call them in court. There's an acronym we use on the street:

Witness
Having
Other
Reasonable
Explanation

On Thursday, I called Nicky Florio to testify. He marched to the stand as if he owned it. I let him talk about himself, and he was good at it. In five minutes, we had established he was a prominent figure in the community, a contributor to charities of every denomination, and a hell of a party giver. I had cautioned him to be humble, or at least to put a lid on the arrogance, and he carried it off well. We polished up the speech from his deposition, and it worked.

"I'm truly sorry about Mr. Tupton, a man I admired," Florio said, looking the jury straight on. "But what could I have done? I had a house and patio full of guests, a hundred people to attend to. The way I see it, and I don't mean to be disrespectful, a man's simply got to take responsibility for his own actions."

Florio wore his sincerity like a vestment, and the jury seemed to buy it. Two of the men nodded, or were they falling asleep?

I asked Nicky how much champagne was served at the party. We totaled up the bottles on a blackboard, figured the number of ounces consumed and divided by the number of guests, allowing some for spillage and half-empty glasses. It worked out to only nine ounces per guest. Jurors like numbers and hard data, and I was trying to reinforce the concept that most guests voluntarily limited their intake, and who's to blame if Tupton didn't? That had H. T. Patterson yelling up a storm of objections. "The average consumption of champagne at the party is irrelevant! What matters is how much they served to one guest, the late Peter Tupton."

"The statistics are relevant to show the basic air of normalcy at the party," I responded.

Judge Boulton shrugged and denied the objection. I asked how much champagne had been purchased for the party and established that two-and-a-half cases were left over when the party ended about 8:00 P.M. and the catering crew cleaned up. Hardly a scene of wild, drunken debauchery.

And then it hit me.

The leftover champagne.

The question that gnawed at me, but that I couldn't ask.

I wondered if Patterson figured it out, too. My questioning had led him to a wide-open door. If he went through it, he could destroy Florio's credibility and blow us out of the water. He could prove, or at least support by inference, just what he'd been beating his breast about the other day, the reckless, even willful, conduct that caused Peter Tupton's death. I sneaked a peek at the plaintiff's table. No sign of recognition. No furious taking of notes.

I sat down, holding my breath, waiting for Patterson to sink us on cross-examination. Patterson stood up, buttoned his white linen suitcoat, and approached the witness stand. Then he simply repeated much of what he had elicited from Florio during the plaintiff's presentation. I started breathing again. I leaned back and watched Nicky Florio. It made me wonder. Does every murderer look so good in a custom-made suit?

I like to try my cases in a reasonable order, liability first, damages last. But with experts, it doesn't always work that way. My economist had to catch a plane, so I put him on in the middle of my liability case. In contrast to the plaintiff's expert, mine predicted that, had Tupton lived, not only wouldn't he have accumulated a couple million bucks, he'd probably be in hock to his bank and the credit card companies.

The trial was spinning along, but I felt as if I were swimming in Jell-O. I asked my questions but didn't listen to the answers, a cardinal sin for trial lawyers. I still hadn't decided what to do with Rick Gondolier until he strode into the courtroom after lunch. He wore a black silk suit with padded shoulders, a white-on-white shirt and black silk tie with turquoise flowers. The thick blond hair was combed straight back and flipped up just above his shoulders. The diamond earring faced the jury box, causing Gloria Morales to nudge her neighbor, point at Gondolier, and discreetly tug at her own ear.

All in all, my witness looked like *Miami Vice*'s version of a major drug dealer with soap-opera good looks. If I were on the jury, I wouldn't believe anything after his name and occupation, and maybe not even that much. Or was I projecting my own jealousy? Damn, Charlie, you were right. I can't be objective. I can't help my client because I'm thinking of me, not him. I believe Nicky Florio is guilty of far worse than serving too much champagne to a tipsy, wimpy guest. But why do I think that? Because of the evidence or my own tangled emotions?

Gondolier promised to tell the truth, the whole truth, and nothing but the truth, and lightning didn't strike him dead. He smiled his pearly whites at the jury, and they smiled back. I hitched up my pants and decided to see if this Las Vegas slickster could tote the mail.

I took him through his background, trying to make a casino operator seem like a priest. I let him talk about the hundreds of thousands of dollars won by housewives and retired folks at the bingo hall, then I asked him about the party.

"Did there come a time that you saw Peter Tupton?"

"Several times," he said. "Nicky introduced me to him by the buffet table near the pool." Gondolier gestured toward the defense table, where Florio nodded his approval. "That was early afternoon."

"Can you describe that first meeting?"

"Nothing remarkable. I told Mr. Tupton I knew of his work and that I was a proud member of the Audubon Society and the Sierra Club. He told me he had visited the bingo hall. It was very pleasant."

"What was Mr. Tupton's physical condition at the time?"

Gondolier seemed to think about it. "Nothing unusual. It was very hot outside, and all of us were in swim trunks. The buffet table was in the shade, and there was a slight breeze from the water, but it was still hot. Mr. Tupton was drinking a mimosa. More than one, actually. I wandered off to say hello to Mrs. Florio and some of the guests, Mr. de La Torre from National Sugar, the mayor, a few others."

"Did there come a second time you saw Mr. Tupton?"

"Yes."

"And when was that?"

"Perhaps an hour later."

"And what transpired then?"

"It was still brutally hot, and I saw Mr. Tupton by the seawall. He was alone and seemed to be talking to himself. He was wobbling . . ."

Oh boy. Where did this come from? Gilding the lily, Gondo?

". . . so I told him to watch the mimosas, they sneak up on you. As I recall it, he giggled and grabbed another drink from a waiter who was passing with a tray on his way to the pool. Then he said he had to relieve himself and headed toward the house."

"Did there come another time that you encountered Mr. Tupton?"

Out of the corner of my eye, I was watching Patterson. Alert but not alarmed. He didn't know what was coming, and with this witness, neither did I.

"Maybe twenty minutes later," Gondolier said, "he came back, all in a lather."

"Could you be more specific?"

"He'd been in the house, and apparently he'd seen some papers in Nicky's den. He was ranting and raving . . ."

Patterson was wide awake. He couldn't believe we were shooting ourselves in the foot like this. Gondolier was eliminating any chance I could claim that it never happened. Just wait, H.T. This witness has been sucker-punching guys since the sixth grade.

". . . about our golf course."

"Your golf course?"

"Yeah. Apparently, he'd seen the plans for the course at Cypress Estates, and he was very unhappy about it. He was saying something about golfers yelling 'fore' and scaring off the birds, something like that. At first I thought he was joking, the way some people do when they drink too much. But he kept up, carrying on about the threats to the animals."

"Objection!" Patterson called out, glaring at me.

"Grounds?" the judge asked.

Patterson's eyes darted back and forth. "Violates the dead man's statute."

For once I was ready. "Not so, Your Honor. Section 90.602 only applies to probate proceedings where the witness has a financial stake in the estate. These statements are party admissions that are exceptions to the hearsay rule and not covered by the dead man's statute."

"Overruled," Judge Boulton declared.

So Gondolier told the story his way: A party guest who was a drunken lout raised a ruckus over nothing, a golf course, for crying out loud. I looked at Patterson. He was doing his best to keep the jury from seeing his dismay. He hadn't wanted the mystery of the den solved. It destroyed the insidious implication that Nicky Florio wanted Peter Tupton dead to cover up some horrible secret.

Rick Gondolier's yarn sounded just fine. Much like Florio, he was a good witness. So good, in fact, I almost believed him.

After Rick Gondolier left the stand, I took a deep breath and rested the defendant's case. I hadn't even had time to consider whether I had violated my own ethical rules. I hadn't lied to the court, but I was pretty sure my witness had. I shoved the thought to the deepest recesses of my mind. There would be time for self-analysis later.

The judge told us we'd give closing arguments at nine the next morning, so I had to prepare something to say. I did this the usual way. I headed to Coconut Grove in my ancient but amiable convertible and changed from my uniform—Lane's men's store off-the-rack blue suit, 46 long, white shirt, burgundy tie—into cutoffs and sneakers. I was shirtless. That can get you arrested in Palm Beach, but thankfully, Miami doesn't try to emulate the snob mob to the north.

It was an unusually humid day for March. The cold front was a distant memory. As thunderheads gathered in the western sky over the Everglades, I jogged the vita course in the park along Bayshore Drive. I did pull-ups, first palm-out for the triceps, then palm-in for the biceps. I jogged some more and was nearly sideswiped by two Rollerblading teenage girls in satin shorts and bikini tops. A coed volleyball game was under way on the grass. Bicyclists and speed walkers and mothers with strollers shared the asphalt paths that cut through the park to the shore of Biscayne Bay.

I stopped alongside an inclined plank, dropped to the ground, and did elevated push-ups. While I worked on my body, I was folding, spindling, and collating my thoughts. Later, at home, I'd bang out some notes on my old Royal typewriter. I like it because it works even during a power outage.

The wind was picking up, shifting direction from the bay to the Everglades. The white clouds turned an angry gray, and fat rain-drops started plopping, wet and cold, on my bare back. A bolt of lightning cracked, followed by a thunderclap. When I looked up, there was an open patch of sky, the darkness parting just where the land ended and the bay began. Something caught my eye. A billowy cloud on the landward side resembled the face of a bearded, hatchet-jawed man. In the sky—or was it in my mind—the cloud took on a wrathful countenance. I studied it as another lightning bolt creased the air, flashing across the face, which then appeared to glower directly at me from on high. As it moved across the sky, the cloud took shape, the face darkening into a shadowy silver-black furious glare.

It looked familar. I remembered an old musty text I had read, or at least skimmed, in college. *Introduction to Mythology*. I had needed a three-credit elective, and it sounded easier than quantum chromodynamics.

And there he was. A familiar face.

Zeus, lord of the sky, chief deity of the pantheon.

So why was he so pissed off at me?

Chapter 11

A Bird in the Hand

"I DON'T WANT TO BECOME EXCITED," H. T. PATTERSON WAS SAY ING, his voice rising to fever pitch. "I don't want to get emotional." His eyes filled with a reservoir of tears. "I simply wish to address your attention, ladies and gentlemen, to the circumstances under which this man died. Needlessly died. Died deprived of comfort and dignity. This was an unnecessary death caused by the negligence of the defendant. And when you consider compensation for that needless, wrongful act, do not strip the last vestiges of dignity from his memory. No, let your verdict stand as a recognition by you of Peter Tupton's humanity and dignity."

Dignity seemed to be the key word here, I thought. Patterson had already run through the liability portion of his closing argument, and now he was sharpening his tools to ask for umpteen million dollars. But he wasn't as confident as he had been after the widow's testimony. Rick Gondolier had taken some of the wind out of his sails.

"The jury, ladies and gentlemen, is our watchman, or watchwoman, as the case may be," Patterson said, nodding to Gloria Morales. "The jury is the keeper of the lighthouse. The jury is the seaman, or seawoman, in the bird's nest. The jury keeps a close eye, a protective lookout, just as Peter Tupton was our watchdog over the Everglades."

Or watch cat, I thought, my mind tumbling into a void of the absurd as I tried to pay attention.

"You have to understand and keep clear that this is not the death of a man, this is the death of a husband, a special person. This was Melinda's spouse and soul mate, and she is without him, for now and forever. And remember this, marriage is God's greatest invention."

Greater than football?

"But now, instead of facing a future of togetherness, she has only black hours of loneliness. Her husband was taken from her, and not by the will of God, but by the negligence of man. Now, instead of a future filled with love, there is a future filled with fear. The fear of waking up at night alone, the fear of hearing noises in the dark, the fear of . . ."

Having to listen to lawyers babble on.

". . . eternal loneliness, the fear of not having the security of her husband. Who is there to share her life? There is nobody who wants to see the scrapbooks or the home movies. There is nobody with whom to share the memories, because the only person who would have cared is gone."

Patterson paused and turned toward the widow. As if on cue, the jurors followed his gaze. Melinda Tupton wore a navy-blue pleated skirt and a matching double-breasted jacket over a white silk blouse. No makeup, no earrings. Her eyes were moist and red. With the jury still transfixed, Patterson asked, "How do you put a monetary figure on that loss?"

If the jurors didn't know, H. T. Patterson could tell them. Very generously. But before scribbling numbers on the blackboard, he had another question for the panel. "When Mr. Lassiter stands up, what's the first thing he's going to do?"

Ask the judge for a five-minute recess so he can take a piss.

"He's going to remind you of something he said in voir dire and something the judge will say in his instructions. The judge will tell you that your verdict is not to be based on sympathy. Fine with us. We don't want sympathy. Melinda Tupton has had all the sympathy she'll ever need. She had a funeral. She had tears. She had notes and cards and flowers. Today, she's here for what she's entitled, money damages. So let us now talk about the items of damages which the law provides. Let us talk of loss of comfort, society, and consortium. Mental anguish and suffering. Lost support, lost . . ."

And talk he did. More about her empty world. A couple of old saws about the value of human life, and how much money we spend protecting the lives of our astronauts and pilots or searching for one capsized boater in the Gulf Stream. Lawyers are great at making non sequiturs sound like eternal verities. When he finally built to a crescendo, Patterson asked the jury for $6.5 million. Nobody winced or gasped. Not even me.

Before I stood up, Nicky Florio clasped me on the shoulder. It was as close to a display of affection and goodwill as I would get. I walked toward the jury box, being careful not to knock over the lectern. It is unpleasant having jurors laugh at you. When I was a public defender, just out of night law school, I was snakebit. I originally attracted Marvin the Maven's crowd because they thought I was better than a stand-up act in the Borscht Belt. In one of my first criminal trials, I tried to discredit a prosecution witness by asking, "You're not an unbiased witness, are you, sir? Isn't it true that you, too, were shot in the fracas?"

"No, sir," he answered. "I was shot midway between the fracas and the navel."

Now I planted myself in front of the box and thanked all the good folks who gave up their normal routine to come downtown and risk being mugged. Briefly, I agreed that Peter Tupton was a fine fellow, and it was a shame for him to die before his appointed three score and ten. Then I hammered away at liability. I told the jurors that not every accident ought to lead to a lawsuit. I talked about personal responsibility as one of the great American character traits. Ruling for the plaintiff, I implied, was somehow unpatriotic.

"There were more than a hundred people at the party, and only one got falling-down drunk. How can that be the host's fault? In this country of self-sufficiency and freedom of action, we take care of ourselves."

As I spoke, I watched myself. Our brains let us do that. We raise a camera, look down, and listen and judge ourselves. On the surface, I was doing fine. A B+ in trial tactics, a solid B in performance. But there are other subjects in my personal report card, and another part of my brain was computing the moral responsibility of my actions. Lawyers aren't supposed to do that. We *really* are hired guns. Give us the targets and the ammo, and we'll blast away. But here I was, grading the culpability of my own actions, just as I was saying. . . .

"You heard a grieving widow, and it is right and proper that she grieve. What is not right is that my client be made to pay for her grief. You heard the testimony from Mr. Gondolier. He sees a wobbly Peter Tupton and warns him, 'Watch it, those mimosas can sneak up on you.' Mr. Tupton should have known that he couldn't handle his liquor. He's drinking in the hot sun, and he's warned, but he goes on drinking. He wanders into the house and snoops around the host's desk. I'm not here to cast aspersions, but it wasn't very polite. No sir, that's not the kind of conduct you expect from a guest.

"Then he goes back outside and drinks some more and becomes belligerent for no reason, except one. His judgment was clouded. He was intoxicated. He harangues Mr. Gondolier over the proposed golf course. He's behaving badly, rudely. Then he goes back into the house and ends up in the wine cellar, where he continues to drink his host's champagne, but not by invitation. There is but one conclusion, ladies and gentlemen, and that is that the harm which befell Peter Tupton was of his own making. Nicholas Florio was not the proximate cause of Peter Tupton's death. Peter Tupton was."

So my personal report card had me failing the course in basic decency and morality, even though I did everything by the book. I had an ethical obligation to use Gondlier's testimony because I did not *know* it to be false. When I surreptitiously taped Guillermo Diaz, I broke the rules but did the right thing. Now, I followed the rules, but what I did was unalterably wrong.

After I sat down, H. T. Patterson got his last chance. It's the plaintiff's great advantage in a civil case, the government's in a criminal trial. Rebuttal. The last word.

He pointed out that we had no corroboration for the testimony of Rick Gondolier, an associate and dear friend of Nicholas Florio. He harked on the animosity between Florio, a filthy-rich developer, and the saintly Peter Tupton. He hinted at a vague conspiracy and the bizarre nature of his client's death. Finally, he told a little story.

"There once was a smart-aleck young boy who wanted to fool a wise old man," Patterson said. "The boy captured a small bird and asked, 'Wise old man, what do I have in my hand?' And the wise old man said, 'You have a bird, my son.' 'But is the bird alive or dead?' the boy asked. And the old man smiled a sad smile and answered, 'The bird is in your hands, my son.' "

Patterson turned to look at me, though I didn't hold any birds. "The old man knew that if he answered that the bird was dead, the boy would open his hand, and the bird would fly free. If he answered that the bird was alive, the boy would squeeze the life out of it. So it is with Mr. Lassiter, who controls the premises, the party guests, the testimony of Nicholas Florio and Rick Gondolier. We introduce evidence of a shocking revelation made by Peter Tupton in the Florio home, and Mr. Lassiter has a ready explanation. A golf course! Really, now. The party guests were friends of Mr. Florio and Mr. Gondolier. They don't contradict their friends' testimony. Peter Tupton didn't have any friends at the party, so Mr. Lassiter holds all the marbles. He holds the bird in his hand. We present the evidence of excessive drinking at the party, and Mr. Lassiter presents his statistics that we are not in a position to refute. Nine ounces per person. Do you believe that? We weren't there, and you weren't there, but you can use your common sense. An answer for everything, that's their defense. They say they even had champagne left over, so how much drinking was going on . . . ?"

Then it came to him.

I saw the emotions cross his face. One after the other.

Confusion, then delight, then terror.

Because he hadn't asked the question of Nicky Florio when he could have. And now it was gone, though he gave it a shot, anyway.

"And what happened to that leftover champagne?" Patterson asked. "Where did it go after—"

"Objection, Your Honor." I was calm, quiet. No need for alarm. "There's been no testimony about the disposition of the champagne. Rank speculation is not comment on the evidence."

"Sustained."

Patterson licked his lips, tried to remember where he was, and closed up with a plea to award just compensation for Melinda Tupton's sorrow.

*   *   *

The judge gave his instructions and sent the jurors into their room, telling them to first pick a foreman. For a while, the county had switched the language to "foreperson" but switched back again after one verdict form came back to the judge all bollixed up. Below the signature line for the foreperson, four jurors signed their names.

The knock from inside the jury room came seventy-eight minutes later. Fast. Figure ten minutes to pick the foreman, fifteen for everyone to use the bathroom, and another ten to order dinner. Which left less than forty minutes to decide that Nicholas Florio was not liable for either compensatory or punitive damages and "shall go hence without day." That's what it says on the form, and I've never known what it means.

Nicky Florio laughed, then cuffed me twice on the shoulder and told me I was a better lawyer than he thought.

Thanks a lot, I told him.

He said I'd have to come play poker with him some night; we'd drink beer and swap lies. He was nearly skipping down the lime-stone steps on the way out of the courthouse when he asked something else. "What was that stuff about the leftover champagne?"

I didn't want to go into it. I really didn't want to know. Still, I answered him, Charlie Riggs style, with a question. "The party ended about eight o'clock, right?"

"Yeah. It was supposed to go until six. But you know how it is, some hit you for dinner as well as lunch. The last people left around eight."

"And nobody saw Tupton after what, three or four o'clock?"

"I guess."

We crossed Flagler Street, avoiding a Miami policeman on horse-back and a clutch of South American tourists wheeling microwave ovens in shopping carts.

"The champagne. Did the caterers provide it?"

"Hell no, not at a hundred percent markup. I buy in bulk. It came from my wine cellar."

"That's what I figured. Patterson figured it, too, but not quickly enough."

"I don't follow you."

"Who took care of the leftover champagne?" I asked.

"I don't know, the bartenders, some of my workers. Why?"

"When did they do it?"

"Right after the party. They wanted to clean up and get home. I'd say they were finished no later than nine."

"And what did they do with the leftover champagne?"

"They put it back in the wine . . ."

A bus horn bleated at us as we jaywalked across First Street, heading for the parking lot. Nicky Florio wasn't going to do it, so I finished his answer for him. "They put it back in the wine cellar, of course. That's where it had come from. If Peter Tupton had been there, they would have stumbled over him. He would have been alive, and they would have saved him. But, of course, they never found him. You're the one who found him, right in front of the champagne racks the next morning, right?"

We stopped in front of a hot-dog vendor. Nicky Florio didn't look hungry. "So Peter Tupton wasn't there, Nicky. He was someplace else from the middle of the afternoon until he was dumped in the wine cellar sometime after nine o'clock. Dumped there by party or parties unknown, as the police like to say."

"There's no evidence—"

"Don't talk like a lawyer, Nicky. And don't look so worried. I'm your lawyer. I did my job, and I won. I owe you the duty of loyalty and confidentiality. You bought it fair and square."

Chapter 12

Story of My Life

I SELDOM DRINK.

Really drink.

Sure, I'll have a beer or two with a burger or a steak. But sit at a bar and down the hard stuff? Not for me.

Usually.

If I've lost a case or a woman, I'll head to the Gaslight Lounge downtown and watch Mickey Cumello make a martini. Plymouth gin, two and a half ounces give or take a drop, four ice cubes, and a splash of dry vermouth. He stirs with a glass swizzle because shaking clouds the drink. Then Mickey strains the potent concoction into a chilled glass. Finally, he squeezes a lemon peel above a burning match, letting the oil pass through the flame and into the drink. The perfect martini—sharp as a polished blade—with just a hint of burnt lemon.

Okay, so I don't just *watch* him make the martini. But I seldom drink more than two.

Sometimes, I tell Mickey Cumello my problems. He's a good listener. Quiet, attentive, thoughtful. I've never seen Mickey in the light of day and probably wouldn't recognize him if he came out from behind the scarred teak bar. In the dark, windowless lounge, he's a stocky man of indeterminate age wearing a short-sleeve white shirt and black bow tie, his gray hair combed straight back, revealing a lot of forehead and a widow's peak.

"A woman or a trial?" Mickey asked.

"I lost the woman and won the trial," I told him, "but I wish it was the other way around."

From behind me, a woman's voice: "You were always a romantic, Jake."

I turned on the barstool and didn't fall off. She was holding a tray full of empty cocktail glasses and soggy napkins. Wanda had red hair she hadn't been born with, long legs, and the practiced smile of a woman who depended on tips to pay the rent. She was wearing one of those outfits that makes a waitress look like a French maid in a porno flick, a black mini with a deep-V top, bare shoulders, stockings with meandering black seams, and black shoes with stiletto heels. If she had a tail, she could have been a bunny, if they still had bunnies. She'd been in the chorus line in a couple of Broadway musicals, but that had been twenty years and three husbands ago. "I always told Mickey you were a romantic," Wanda said, winking at me. "Just like what's-his-name tilting at windmills."

"Wanda, how long have we known each other?" I asked.

"Jeez, Jake, forever. You handled my last divorce, remember?"

"Do you think I'm a good man?"

"The best. You're practically the only guy who comes in here who doesn't hit on me. Except for the choreographer types, I mean."

"But do you think I'm essentially moral? When faced with questions of good versus evil, which path would I choose?"

"I dunno, Jake. Good, I suppose."

"What if evil is an easier path, paved with milk and honey?"

"Sounds sticky."

"While the good path is a potholed son of a bitch."

"Just like Bird Road," she agreed, emptying her tray onto the bar. "Hey, Mickey, how 'bout a frozen 'rita, hold the salt, a Campari and soda with a slice, one Pellegrino, and one Calistoga."

Mickey tried not to wince, but I caught him, anyway. He was from the old school. Bourbon, rye, scotch, and gin, maybe something fizzy for the ladies.

"Good is always the harder path," I said.

"I know what you mean," Wanda whispered to me, leaning close. There were freckles at the top of her cleavage. "Like should I declare all my tips to Uncle Sam, right?"

"Something like that."

"Yeah, and like last weekend, this gentleman—at least I thought he was a gentleman—asked me to cruise the bay on his new Bertram. Wouldn't you know it, we're halfway to Bimini, and it's the same old story. Suck or swim. Spread or tread."

"A real Hobson's choice."

"Huh? This guy's name was Kornblum. He sells insurance."

Mickey loaded Wanda's tray with a green slushy drink, a watery red one, and two bottles of expensive water. Wanda turned and high-heeled it to a corner table where two young men had stripped off their suit coats to reveal suspenders and custom-made shirts with shiny cuff links. I would have known they were lawyers even if they weren't loudly boasting of recent courtroom triumphs, real or imagined, ridiculing judges and their vanquished opponents. With them were two women dressed for success in designer suits— one blue, one peach—that were probably designer labels from Bal Harbour Shops. I analyzed the two couples in my detached, objective, nonjudgmental way and concluded they were Republican-voting, squash-playing, Volvo-driving Yuppie scum.

I caught Mickey's eye and made a stirring motion with my index finger. He nodded and reached for the bottle of Plymouth gin.

I thought about it some more, the ethical morass I had wandered into. Hell, had *created*, if we're being honest. I thought about taking the easy way out. The case was over, so forget it. Gina was out of my life, so forget her. Whatever Nicky Florio and Rick Gondolier had done was none of my business. I did my job, won the case. But I kept wondering. What had Peter Tupton seen on Florio's desk? What were Florio and Gondolier up to? I waited for the cool drink to erase the thoughts, to clear the mind by muddling it.

Just walk away.

It would be so easy.

Get back to the old routine, a reception room full of clients, a beach full of women. Meaningless work, meaningless play.

Mickey delivered another martini. The first sip seared my throat with its icy heat. The second sent a shiver through me. I felt Wanda's presence behind me. Actually, I felt her breasts pushed against my back. "I get off at one," she whispered.

I tried to say something, but my lips were numb. I felt myself nodding, my head too heavy a load for my shoulders to support.

Wanda ran a hand through my hair and pulled hard. "Don't fall asleep on me, big guy." She let go and raised her voice a couple of notches. "Hey, Mick, give Jake a cup of coffee, will ya, hon?"

Wanda had a town house in one of those clusters on Kendall Drive west of the Turnpike. All asphalt parking lots and wedge-shaped buildings. Not a blade of grass in sight, even if I could see. The place was furnished in fifties' ultrafeminine. Fluffy pink pillows, fluffy cream drapes, fluffy white cat. Stuffed animals on the sofa, reproductions of Degas nudes on the living-room wall, a wooden wine rack on the kitchen counter. She slid a CD into the player, and Natalie Cole sang "Unforgettable." Her dad joined in, thanks to some electronic wizardry.

Wanda cooed sweet things at me and undid my tie with swift, sure fingers. My awesome powers of deductive reasoning told me she had done this before. I got my shirt off without any help, but she intervened when I tried to take off my pants before my shoes.

In her bedroom, I leaned forward to kiss her but missed, my nose ending up in a sweep of red hair that smelled of cigarettes. She turned toward the bed, steadied me with one hand and used the other to pull back a thick white comforter. Then she effortlessly stepped out of her waitress mini, took me by the hand, and pulled me on top of her. My head touched down between her large, freckled breasts. I was aware of the white smooth expanse of her, the womanly scents. From somewhere, she produced a stack of foiled condoms, connected along perforated lines. There must have been a dozen. Either we were going to make party balloons, or she had confused me with somebody else. I fumbled with one of the foil wrappers, before she took it away and expertly opened it. The latex kind. White and cold and sexy as a surgical glove. Prevents disease, pregnancy, and nearly all pleasure. Like having sex through galoshes.

Wanda was one of the sighers and moaners, the omigod-I-never-dreamed-it-could-be-like-this types. I took a few bows, but if you've been around the track a few times, you don't take your press notices seriously. When she wasn't purring with cinematic sincerity, she was a warm and giving bedmate with the full complement of womanly slopes and curves and warm, tender places.

Sometime around dawn, she told me I looked like Harrison Ford. Or was it Henry Ford?

I drifted in and out of sleep. I dreamed I was blitzing a quarterback on a rainy day on a field covered with knee-high mud. I moved in slow motion. An offensive lineman stood on sturdy ground and laughed at me. I tried the swim move, a high-arm maneuver, but he got underneath and pancaked me into the cold mud, which filled my nose and mouth. Just before I sank below the surface, I saw his face: Nicky Florio.

I was alone and shivering in a bank vault. Lots of money and no way to spend it, no way to get out. It was hard to breathe. Then it got colder still. I was naked. The vault became a meat locker. Beef carcasses hung from shiny hooks, blackened blood puddling on the icy floor. I fought my way through fat-streaked slabs of meat, desperately trying to escape, my feet slipping out from under me. I raced crazily down an endless row, my hands raised in front of my face, fighting through the carcasses, slick with gristle and bone, smacking against me. Suddenly, I was hit hard and knocked to the floor. A shadow swung back and forth over me. Filled with dread, I looked up. Suspended from a grappling hook, rocking crazily from side to side, was the corpse of Peter Tupton, a ghastly smile frozen on his face.

Laughing at me.

I awoke to find myself alone, the sheet and comforter kicked to the floor. The air-conditioning vent was right above the bed, louvers pointed down. My bare body was a forest of goose bumps.

I lay there staring at the ceiling, listening to kitchen noises—cabinet doors closing, silverware clattering, the beep-beep of a microwave. I got up and pried my eyes open. In the bathroom, I realized I wasn't home when I found the toilet seat down. In the kitchen, I found Wanda singing to herself as she made breakfast. An old Diana Ross song, "All Night Lover." Wanda squeezed fresh orange juice, sizzled three eggs sunny-side up, topped by half a dozen strips of bacon, toasted some cinnamon bread, then watched me eat, explaining how it's a woman's pleasure to see a man enjoy himself. She allowed as how I had been pretty wonderful, considering my condition.

While we ate, she was moved to ponder how strange it was that we were drawn together after all these years as friends, or at least acquaintances, and isn't life weird, and what does it all mean, and will I call her later, and maybe we could go to the antique show in Boca Raton next weekend, and would I like it if she cut her hair short.

Antique show?

That old feeling. Total displacement. What have I done? Who is this person, and why am I here? It had been years since I had a one-night stand. Sad then, sadder now. The total futility of the random joining of persons unconnected in any other way.

By the time I headed the old convertible east, the sun glared angrily in my face. I felt pasty, bloated, out of sorts. My mouth was parched. I wanted to run on the beach and swim in the sea. I wanted to cleanse my body and my mind and my soul, if I had any.

I thought about my dreams. Charlie Riggs once told me that Freud was all wet. "Dreams as repressed wishes, what hogwash! A pity Freud didn't have the benefit of research into brain chemistry."

I had waited for him to go on. As usual, he didn't disappoint me. "Dreams let us work on unsolved problems or unfinished business from the day and allow brain cells to recharge their transmitter chemicals."

Unsolved problems.

Unfinished business.

Story of my life.

Maybe it was time to finish something and not be stuck somewhere between the dreamscape of a muddy football field and a meat locker.

And that's just what I wanted to do now.

I wanted to play poker with Nicky Florio.

Chapter 13

Heaven on Earth

IF I HAD BEEN JIMMY STEWART PLAYING A COUNTRY LAWYER IN *Anatomy of a Murder*, I just would have hung out a GONE FISHIN' sign. But I toil on the thirty-second floor of a high rise on Biscayne Bay where my time is billed at $250 an hour, and going fishing is an expensive avocation. So first I had to dictate the usual dilatory motions, bill customers for time spent ruminating on their problems while showering, return important phone calls from Granny and Charlie and the guy who's shaping a new sailboard for me.

I skimmed a lawyers' magazine with tips on how to get clients to pay for your word-processing system without their knowing it. I answered interrogatories in a lawsuit between two Ocala cattle ranchers over contraband bull semen. I interviewed a man with a mustache and goatee who said he was Carlos Manuel de Cespedes y del Castillo, the great-grandson of the man who proclaimed Cuba's independence from Spain in 1868. He wanted to sue an imposter who was giving speeches to the Little Havana Kiwanis Club claiming to be a descendant of *el padre de la patria*.

I listened to a man whose eyes darted furiously around my office as he explained why he wanted to bring a class action against a brewer that claimed to make its beer with "Rocky Mountain spring water." The beer actually contained poisonous gases from Neptune, he revealed, brought by aliens in cigar-shaped spacecraft that land on the Continental Divide.

"Neptune?" I asked him.

"Neptune," he repeated, his eyes seeming to cross as they jumped back and forth.

"You're sure it's not Uranus?" I asked him.

I returned a phone call from a plastic surgeon in trouble with the Department of Professional Regulation for failing to warn patients of the dangers of silicone breast implants.

"A frame-up," he told me. "The medical association's out to get me because I advertise on TV."

"What's wrong with advertising?" I asked.

"They got a hard-on for me because of my toll-free number. I got the idea from a dermatologist friend, '444-ACNE.' "

"I still don't see what's wrong, unless . . . no, you didn't . . ."

"Yeah, 444-TITS. Hey, business is business."

The last appointment was with a guy arrested for slashing the bark off red mangrove trees, cooking it, and selling the foul-tasting potion to local *botánicas*. The tannin in the bark either cures diarrhea or causes cancer, depending whether you believe witch doctors from Little Havana or scientists from Harvard. I turned down the case, preferring murderers, con artists, and quack physicians to tree killers.

Then I told Cindy I was going fishing.

It was a top-down, partly cloudy March day. A trifle too humid, a trifle too warm for this time of year. The weather guys were calling for rain, maybe thunderstorms tonight. I had changed into jeans, deck shoes, and an old aqua-and-orange jersey, number 58, that the Dolphins had forgotten to retire. The ride on Tamiami Trail was smooth and straight. I found the dirt road just west of the Miccosukee Restaurant—fried catfish and frogs' legs—and turned north. The narrow road bumped and twisted through wet prairie. Occasional cypress strands sprouted out of the saw grass, towering trees dominating the flatlands. I slowed and let two river otters cross the road, then heard a rumble, a mechanical growl somewhere in front of me. I came to a dead stop, and the noise grew louder against the silent landscape.

Then, from around a bend, it bore down on me. At first sight, the truck was all high bumper and huge tires. It braked and kicked up dust as it came to a halt just a few feet from the grill of my old convertible. It was about the size of a cement truck, but where the rotating cylinder would have been was a series of antennae and what looked like satellite dishes. There were two men in the cab, both wearing sunglasses and black baseball caps. They looked at me. I looked at them. Nobody said a word.

The sidewalk wasn't big enough for both kids, and I was the smaller kid, so I flinched. I backed up and edged onto the gravel berm, trying not to get entangled in vicious mangrove roots. The guy on the passenger side got out, came to the front of the truck, and hand-signaled the driver to turn the wheel a hair to the right to get past me on the narrow road. A slight man in his thirties with narrow shoulders, he wore rubberized boots and white coveralls stained with mud up to the knees. The name "Tucker" was stitched across the chest of his coveralls.

"Don't see many people out here," I said pleasantly. "Or trucks like that."

He mumbled something in agreement.

"What the heck is all that equipment?" I asked, like the good-natured rube I am.

The truck edged by me, threatening my classic canary-yellow paint job, but just missing. On the side of the cab in black letters was the name ENVIRONMENTAL SYSTEMS, INC. No address, no phone number, no cute slogan.

Without answering me, the guy in coveralls climbed back into the cab, and the truck rumbled off. I let out the clutch, eased back onto the road, and kept heading north. In ten minutes, I came to a Y and bore to the right, just as I'd been told, and in less than a mile, I ran out of road. I was on a rocky teardrop peninsula. Some bushes, some scraggly pine trees. Wet prairie surrounded me on three sides. A muddy green airboat sat in the shallow water, and a dark-complexioned man in the traditional Micanopy Indian jacket of turquoise, black, red, and half a dozen other colors stood silently on the shore. Maybe five nine, he had a brush cut of thick dark hair, broad shoulders, and short legs. In the Indian jacket, he resembled a colorful fireplug.

I turned off the ignition, put up the top, and locked the doors out of habit, probably thinking an alligator might steal the car. I walked over to the man by the airboat. "Jim Tiger?" I asked him.

He nodded and motioned me in. There were two molded-plastic chairs high on a platform above the flat-bottomed boat. He hit the starter, and the airplane engine coughed to life. The old wooden propeller jerked once, twice, then fired into a whirlwind spin. Tiger didn't seem talkative, and just as well. Over the roar of the engine, I couldn't hear a thing. We skimmed along the top of the water, sawing off shoots of grass, flying past pinelands and palms, flushing herons and egrets out of the shallows. From the position of the sun, we seemed to be heading north, but after two or three sweeping turns, I lost my sense of direction. There was no land, just occasional islands called hammocks, a few cypress domes where wood storks waded, looking for lunch, and the endless river of saw grass.

We think of the Everglades as a vast swamp, but it is actually a shallow river fifty miles wide, flowing southwest for over a hundred miles to the Gulf of Mexico. Two thousand square miles of the Everglades are part of a national park, but that is only a seventh of its total area. Depending on the time of year and the location within the Glades, it can resemble a vast African savanna, dense forests, blue-water bays, rocky beaches, or even the swamp of our imagination.

Time travels slowly in the Glades. The roar of the engine, at first jarring, had a narcotizing effect, the drone making me sleepy after a few minutes. My eyes were growing heavy by the time the engine slowed, the throaty roar diminishing. We swung past a sandy outcropping into deeper water, then headed straight for a hardwood hammock. Trees had been cleared along the shore, and a towering house built of pine stood on stilts where the tree line ended. The rear stilts were on the ground, the front stilts in the water. A porch surrounded the house on three sides, wooden staircases leading from the rear down to the island, and from the front down to a small dock. A gasoline-powered generator sat behind the house, three feet above the ground, on its own stilted platform. In the summer, I imagined, the hammock was partly submerged. The slanted roof of the house was shiny corrugated metal. Drain spouts emptied into a cistern. Two satellite dishes and a microwave antenna were planted on the southwest corner of the roof.

Jim Tiger cut the engine, and we drifted toward the dock, where he hopped out, carrying a bowline. He tied the airboat to a dockside cleat, and I followed him, stretching my legs, before heading up the stairs to the porch, thirty feet above the waterline. On the way up, I caught sight of half a dozen gray-black gators snoozing on the muddy bank below. I hadn't seen them from the water level, as they blended in with the muck and were partially hidden by the pickerelweed and swamp ferns.

Nicky Florio was sitting in a rocking chair of dark wood, a fishing rod dangling lazily in his hand. He wore chinos and a matching shirt with epaulets and too many pockets. His olive complexion had turned a darker, richer shade from the sun. His black hair was freshly washed, still wet, and combed straight back. Black sunglasses shielded his eyes. On a table of the same dark wood as the chair sat a half-empty champagne glass. A bottle of Perrier-Jouët rested in an ice bucket. Nicky gestured to an adjoining chair. "Welcome to my humble home-away-from-home."

"Not so humble," I said, easing into the rocker. The chair was carved from reddish-brown mahogany, with a firm, close grain. The armrests were graceful curves, the legs beveled and smoothly finished. "Not what I pictured when you told me a fishing cabin." Below us, perched on a fallen branch, a roseate spoonbill fluttered its pink wings and swung its flat bill side to side, sifting through the water. "How'd you ever get the permits to clear the hammock and build in the water?"

"Permits?" The word seemed amusing to him, like "platypus" to a comedian. "This is Injun country, Jake. Seventy thousand acres, and the state and federal government got no rights out here. No Army Corps of Engineers, no Environmental Protection Agency, no Department of Natural Resources. Not even a building inspector to bribe with a case of scotch. You get it, Jake? To a builder, this is heaven on earth."

Nicky laughed, pleased with himself. Another dark-complexioned man in an Indian jacket appeared from the house. He was carrying a tray that held a chilled mug and a bottle of Grolsch. "You're welcome to the champagne," Nicky offered, "but my sources tell me beer's your drink."

His sources were right.

In a moment, the same man reappeared carrying a spinning rod.

He handed it to me, then disappeared around the side of the porch.

"What, no one to bait my hook? What kind of host are you?"

Florio used his foot to shove a bucket toward me. I took a look inside, expecting to see shiners or night crawlers, not live finger mullet. "Thought we were fishing for black bass."

"You kidding? Bass in the Glades been showing up with mercury. Tupton was right, you know. Goddamn garbage plants ruining the environment."

"Tupton was right?" I asked. I was glad he brought up the name. It saved me the trouble.

"He was right about a lot of things. The phosphorous runoff from the farmlands, the pollution from the sugarcane fields, the scarring of the flats with off-road vehicles."

I put a mullet on the hook and dropped my line into the water. "Right about everything except your projects."

"Let's say he was overzealous when it came to Florio Enterprises. I tried to talk sense to the bastard. I told him we could be allies, I'd fund his favorite causes. Keep the poachers and the three-wheelers out of the Glades."

"The penny-ante stuff. Meanwhile, developers like you and Gondolier dredge waterways, drain swamps, pave over wetlands, and plan the biggest project the Glades have seen since Tamiami Trail was built sixty years ago."

He kept his eyes on the water. "Believe me, what we're going to do will make the Trail seem like . . ."

"A two-lane road," I said.

"Exactly."

Below us, the snouts and humped backs of two manatees appeared above the waterline. Gentle homely mammals related to elephants, this pair probably ran close to a thousand pounds each. I watched the manatees without saying a word, still trying to figure out how to move the conversation in the right direction. Finally, I decided to wade into the murky water. "What'd Tupton find in your den?" I asked.

Florio didn't blink. "You heard Gondo. The golf course plans."

"Bullshit. Where was Peter Tupton between six and nine o'clock? He sure wasn't in the wine cellar, or he would have been found."

"I give up. You tell me, Counselor."

I let my line drift with the current. Fishing wasn't my highest priority just now. "Tupton was with you, probably in the den. Maybe Gondolier was there, too. The two of you were trying to bargain with him, but he wouldn't listen. He wouldn't take your bribes or your grants, or whatever you called them. But he'd drink your champagne, even though he couldn't hold it. He passed out, and you carried him into the wine cellar. Maybe you just wanted time to talk it over with Gondolier. Maybe you even made a little joke. 'Let's put the bastard on ice for a while.' Later, the bastard is dead."

Florio growled and reeled in his line. His bait was gone. "Wild talk like that could upset people."

"People?"

"Gondolier isn't as fond of you as I am. Of course, he doesn't have the common bond we share, right, Jake?"

For a second, I didn't know what he meant.

Then I did.

"Or does he, Jake? Maybe we both should be pissed at that grease-ball ladies' man."

I tried to look confused. It isn't hard for me. Florio seemed to buy it. He dipped his hand into the bucket of mullet and brought out some fresh bait. "I hired you because of Gina. She'd be very unhappy to hear that you were causing trouble, making crazy accusations you couldn't prove."

"Even if I could prove every word, I wouldn't. I can't use something I learned while representing you in a way that would harm you."

"Ethics, Jake?"

"That's right."

"Just like with Guillermo Diaz?"

Below us, two pink flamingos were flapping their wings and long-legging it across the top of the water. They came to a stop, folded their legs underneath their bodies, and floated close to some swamp lilies. "Diaz was threatening to kill someone. I thought I could stop him."

"You found a loophole, right? A technicality. You guys who deal in words, you so-called professionals got an excuse for everything. You understand words but not bricks and mortar. Guys like you and Tupton don't *build* anything. You *stop* people from building."

Tupton and me, I thought. A couple of guys who get in the way. And only one of us dead.

"Progress, Jake. People need homes. Florida's growing like a son of a bitch. We're the fourth-largest state now. A thousand people a week move here. Do you know what that means to somebody in my business?"

"Heaven on earth," I said.

"You got it." His laugh was like a dog's bark.

Below us, on the muddy bank, one of the alligators, a nine-foot bull, slipped quietly into the water and disappeared under the surface. "It's a damn shame," Florio said, "but people get a distorted view of builders from the news media and zealots like Tupton. We're not predators." With the tip of his rod, Florio pointed toward the sky where six white birds flew in formation. "The snowy egret. Nearly became extinct because women wanted feathers in their hats a hundred years ago. What kind of bullshit is that? I'm as sensitive to the environment as the next guy, but I'm here to deliver what the country needs and wants."

"Who decides what the country needs and wants? You?"

"No, the consumer decides. I just fill the need, me and guys just like me. Businessmen. Who'd you rather have doing it? Congress, state agencies, local mayors?" He looked back toward the sky, but the birds were gone. "You think developers are money-hungry sleazebags, don't you, Jake?"

"Well put," I agreed.

"Then wake up and smell the money, friend. Who's been convicted lately? The mayors of Miami Beach and Hialeah, commissioners in Sweetwater, city and county cops, bankers and lawyers and judges you probably have lunch with. Bribery and extortion and what have you. It's all a game. Money and power. Whoever's got the biggest dick wins. It's all around us, Jake. It's the way of doing business down here. Always has been and always will be."

All the talk of criminals reminded me of somebody. "I was surprised to see Diaz working for Gondolier," I said.

"For Gondolier? Diaz works for me. *Everybody* works for me, including that pretty boy Gondolier, though he tends to forget it."

The manatees cruised back under the house, and Florio dragged his line away from them. Like a lot of people, I figured, he didn't want to hurt a living creature he could see up close.

"You think it matters to me that you fucked over Diaz?" Florio said. "I couldn't care less. If anything, it just proved something I suspected."

My look shot him the question.

"I don't play by anyone's rules but my own, and neither do you, Jake."

"What are you saying, that deep down, we're blood brothers because we do things our own way? You can't reduce a man to one character trait."

"Maybe not, but we're more alike than you might think." Florio cranked at his reel. "Just ask Gina."

I wasn't going near that one. Florio looked back at the water. "C'mon, now, let's have some fun. You want to catch some snook?"

"Snook?"

"Yeah, ever hear of them?"

"I don't have a saltwater license or a snook stamp. Besides, they're out of season."

"Ay, Counselor, you don't listen real well. You don't need a license. You don't need a stamp. This is God's country."

And the gods make their own rules.

Florio dragged his line across the top of the water and began telling snook stories. Hard to find, much less catch, the fish detects movement on the water with that black lateral line along its body.

A thunderous splash from below jarred me.

The bull gator surfaced, its tail smacking the water, its jaws wide. One of the pink flamingos disappeared into the gator's huge mouth. One chomp, no more flamingo. The other bird squawked and flew away before it could become the second course.

"Survival of the fittest, Jake, in the wild and in the boardroom. Some animals survive with toughness, some with cunning. With men, it's best to have both."

"How about a measure of decency?"

"In small doses, like a dash of sherry in a bowl of conch chowder." He jiggled his rod. No bait, no snook. "We come up empty, I might get Jim Tiger to help. You're not opposed to a little gigging and netting, are you?"

I gave him a look.

"Now don't go and tell me that's illegal, Jake. Remember, we're—"

"In Florio country," I interrupted.

"Right. You're catching on, partner. C'mon, put some mullet on your line. I pulled out a thirty-pounder last week on eight-pound test line." He paused to remember the fight. "You ever taste snook, Jake?"

I had. Last summer, Charlie had caught a pair, the daily limit, and asked me to drive over. You can't get snook in restaurants. Against the law to sell them. A rare, sweet-tasting fish of firm white meat.

"We have any luck," Florio said, "Jim will cook us up some fillets. Afterward, we'll see just how much alike we really are."

Chapter 14

Six-to-Five Against

IT WAS NEARLY DARK WHEN A SECOND AIRBOAT MANEUVERED TO-
ward the dock. I heard it from inside the house, just as Nicky was
showing me where all the mahogany trees from the hammock had
gone. Reddish-brown paneling, custom-made furniture, hardwood
floors. Windows were open on either end of the house, and what
had been a gentle breeze earlier in the day was whipping up into
gusts from the west.

The screen door opened, and Rick Gondolier walked in followed
by Guillermo Diaz. Gondolier was wearing baggy black pants,
black loafers without socks, and a black silk shirt. More South
Beach than Tamiami Trail. Diaz wore jeans and sneakers, a blue
shirt and a blue nylon jacket. A gun in a shoulder holster protruded
from under the jacket.

"Ay, my favorite *abogado*," Diaz greeted me.

Gondolier shook hands with me, but not as if it were the highlight
of his day.

Jim Tiger grilled the snook over an oak fire. A thirty-incher I
caught and a whopper, a twenty-two-pounder, brought in by Florio. Basted with butter, seasoned with a little celery salt and basil,
some paprika for color. There was also a salad of cabbage palm,
some boiled corn, and a dessert of pumpkin pie sweetened with
Everglades sugarcane. We ate at a knotty-pine picnic table on the

porch, then sat on rockers drinking whiskey and talking sports and politics and weather and nothing at all.

By nine o'clock, raindrops were tap-dancing across the metal roof and we were back inside. Jim Tiger closed the shutters on the western side to keep out the wind-driven rain, and we sat in straight-backed wicker chairs at a table covered with green felt. A shaded lamp hung directly over the table. I faced Florio with Gondolier to my left and Diaz to my right. I don't know why I thought of it, but Diaz's gun hand was on the side away from me. "Seven-card stud?" Florio asked. "Ten-dollar, twenty-dollar?"

"They're your cards, Nicky," Gondolier replied.

"Right, and don't forget it."

Diaz divided the chips among the four of us, five hundred dollars to a man.

Florio shuffled the deck, which he offered to me. I cut, and he began dealing. Three cards, the first two facedown, the third face-up. "Jake, you know anything about the Indians in Florida?"

"Not much."

Florio showed a king, Gondolier a seven, and Diaz a deuce. I had a ten up and a pair of eights down, a good start. The first three cards are called Third Street, with the high card showing opening the betting. Florio slid a ten-dollar chip into the center of the table, and everyone called him. Jim Tiger delivered a tray of fresh drinks to the table and took a chair behind his boss to watch the game.

"It's a damn sorry history," Florio said, as he dealt a card faceup to each of us. "First you have the Calusa and the Tequestas. They fought old Ponce de León back in the 1500s. That was just the beginning of what turned out to be hundreds of years of bullshit by the whites. Now fast-forward a bit, and there's Andy Jackson's soldiers chasing the Creeks south from Alabama and Georgia. White men called them the Seminoles."

Florio showed a king and a nine, Gondolier a pair of sevens, and Diaz added a king to his deuce. My ten was joined by a three, while my pair of eights grew warmer underneath. Fourth Street. Gondolier opened with ten dollars.

"By now, Jackson becomes president and begins removing Indians from east of the Mississippi to what was called Indian territory. It was a useless desert we now call Oklahoma. Do I have that right, Jim?"

"The Trail of Tears," Jim Tiger said. "Your government violated the Treaty of Moultrie Creek."

"Right," Florio agreed. "Rule number one, Jake. Never trust the government."

Florio slid a ten-dollar chip into the pot, calling Gondolier, and Diaz folded. "Of course, not all the Indians left for the west. Chief Osceola led a band of underarmed, underfed warriors against the U.S. Army. Eventually, of course, he was overpowered, and his people retreated into the Everglades. The army pursued them, using maps the Spaniards made in the 1500s. The poor bastards had Lake Okeechobee in downtown Miami. What's the joke about army intelligence, Jake?"

"It's the classic oxymoron."

"Right. Hey, you and I make a good team."

I matched the ten dollars and raised another twenty. Gondolier and Florio called the bet without hesitation. The wind made a whistling sound off the corrugated roof. Jim Tiger stood up and closed some shutters that were banging against the house.

"So there they were," Florio continued, "a proud, independent people living off the land and water, sleeping in little chickee huts built on hardwood hammocks. They ate the fish and grew corn and cane and had about a hundred uses for alligator hides and meat, and meanwhile the U.S. troops kept dying of malaria or gangrene or an occasional bullet, and the war got so expensive, the government just called it off."

"Sounds like Vietnam," I said.

Florio dealt us into Fifth Street, another card faceup. I latched on to a third eight and tried not to smile or yell *hoo-boy*. As far as anyone could see, I had a bunch of scattered cards.

"Good analogy," Florio said. "And what's the lesson?"

Gondolier drew a three, and Florio showed a second king, the king of hearts, holding a sword in his left hand. But did he have a third one? Realizing he had the highest hand, Florio frowned and checked. No third king lurking facedown. If he had it, he would have anted up ten lousy dollars. By checking, he forfeited the right to raise when it got back to him. But Florio's second king was enough to scare off Gondolier and his pair of sevens, and he tossed his cards away in disgust.

I dropped a ten-dollar chip into the pot and said, "Lots of lessons. Some about the morality of dispossessing a people, another about the strategy—"

"Fuck the morality!" Florio thundered. "Immoral battles are fought every day. Immoral wars are won by the meanest sons of bitches who ever lived. The lesson, Jake, is that you can't fight if you don't know the territory. It's rule number two. If you're on somebody else's turf, you gotta co-opt the enemy. Infiltrate, buy 'em off, make 'em your partners. You can't just ride your horses into their swamps, blowing your bugles, or you'll disappear in the mud."

Florio slapped a chip down, staying in the game, and dealt us into Sixth Street. Just the two of us. A six for me, a deuce for him, faceup. Again, he checked. I was getting confident. I put in my ten bucks, and he called. He dealt the last card, facedown to each of us. He had his two kings, a nine, and a deuce showing. Four different suits. I had an eight, a six, a ten, and a three up, and my two eights underneath, now joined by the king of clubs facedown.

A king!

Diaz had drawn the king of diamonds way back on Fourth Street. Nick had the king of spades and hearts showing. I was right all along. Unless this was a deck with five kings, Nicky Florio had a lousy pair of kings, or maybe two pair, kings high, if he had a second nine or deuce underneath. No difference to me. My three eights take the pot.

Nicky opened with the required ten. I slid in my matching ten and raised him twenty. He did the same, and I did again.

And again.

And again.

And again.

And then I simply called, feeling good.

Which is when he showed me the ten, jack, and queen that were facedown. Which he combined with his nine and king, giving him a king-high straight.

Oh.

Nicky swept in the chips. About three hundred bucks' worth,

give or take a twenty. "Sorry, Jake, some days three of a kind is just a loser."

"I wasn't thinking straight," I admitted. Then I laughed. "That's funny, isn't it? I mean I was afraid you'd draw a third king, and not thinking about you filling a straight."

"Happens to the best of us," Florio said. He signaled Jim Tiger to bring another round of drinks. Florio had switched to scotch on the rocks. Two with dinner, two after, another one when he started dealing.

We played another couple of hours as the storm built, lightning glinting off the black water below the windows, the thunder rattling the roof. I won a few hands, lost a few more, and was still behind maybe two hundred bucks when Florio looked me straight on. "I need some legal advice, Jake."

"Shoot."

"You have a way with words, Counselor." His face was smiling, but I wasn't sure about his mind. A bolt of lightning crackled outside, and the room brightened with its reflection. "It's a criminal law question."

Diaz was dealing the first two cards. Jim Tiger returned to his chair behind Florio. He was using a machete to cut slivers of sweet sugarcane from a stalk.

The third card arrived faceup, but Florio didn't look at his or anyone else's. "What's it called when somebody kills someone else, but he's got a reason for doing it, a reason that'll get him off?"

"A lawful excuse," I answered, "like justifiable homicide. If somebody's threatening your life or breaks into your home trying to rob you, you're justified in killing him in the heat of the moment."

He seemed to think about it. "Very interesting, Counselor. Now, how about if somebody you know has been fucking your wife?"

I had a jack showing. Spades. The jack seemed to be laughing. Jim Tiger was sucking on a chunk of sugarcane. Diaz and Gondolier were studying their cards.

"What do you mean, Nicky?"

My voice sounded weak.

Tinny.

Guilty.

Florio was tapping his face card with an index finger. The ace of spades. "Like a husband knows someone's fucking his wife, maybe has been for a long time. The husband gets the proof. Dead-solid perfect proof, and it enrages him. Rocks him to the core. So in the heat of the moment, he kills the bastard. Think he'd get off?"

I felt my face heat up. "Depends on the circumstances. If he caught them *in flagrante delicto*," I heard myself saying, sounding like old Charlie, "it wouldn't be Murder One or Two, but it'd still be Murder Three or Manslaughter."

"What would a guy get, eight years, out in three?"

"Maybe. But if it was planned," I added, quickly, "an assassination, it could be Murder One."

"But what if there's no body recovered? Think the guy would ever be charged?"

I looked at Gondolier and Diaz. They were both staring at me as if horns had sprouted from my forehead.

Florio waited for an answer. Jim Tiger stood and moved to a position behind me. The machete hung straight down from his right hand.

I hate a blade.

Guillermo Diaz slipped his hand inside his nylon jacket. I was frozen. "What's this all about?"

"I think you know. C'mon, Jake, talk. Were you billing me for the time spent screwing my wife? Or was that part of the overhead?"

"Nicky, I'm your lawyer. I—"

"And a half-assed one at that. I had to get Rick here to make up a story just to win a lousy civil case. And who do you think sweet-talked Abe Socolow into that little courtroom visit? I did, pal, not you. You see, Jake, we might be alike in some things, but not in others. I play to win! That's the name of the game."

"You warp the system, Nicky, and I don't."

"Listen to him!" Florio turned toward his buddies, then back to me. "Don't give me that Boy Scout bullshit, you hypocrite. You don't know the meaning of the word 'loyalty.' A man who won't lie, cheat, and steal for a friend is worthless to me. And one who stabs his friend is gonna get it back in spades."

"Look, if you're implying that Gina and I . . ."

"Implying! Want to listen to the tapes of your phone calls? How about a little letter?" He reached into one of the buttoned pockets on his shirt and took out several sheets of monogrammed pink stationery and slid them across the table.

Dearest Jake . . .

Five or six of them. All starting the same way.

You are so very special. . . .

A different word here or there, the paper crumpled. Her rough drafts. Poor Gina. She wrote the letter a bunch of times to get it right. She must have tossed them in the garbage, where Nicky or one of his helpers salvaged them.

"There's nothing in that letter that admits a sexual relationship," I said. Ever the lawyer, making a fine point, not really lying but ignoring reality.

"Don't insult my intelligence, Jake. We both know the truth. Gina's a beautiful woman. You've had a thing for her for years. A husband and a wife have problems. They drift apart. A woman is weak. She likes a shoulder to cry on, someone to listen. But you do more than listen, don't you, you bird-dogging son of a bitch? You fucked your client's wife. It's a mortal sin, Jake, a goddamn mortal sin. You had free will, and you abused it. You've fallen from grace, and you'll go straight to hell without collecting your two hundred dollars."

Outside, thunder rolled across the Everglades, and the stilted house shook. No one said a word. I could hear the soft, creaking sounds of the house groaning in the wind. I seemed to have stopped breathing.

"Of course, there is repentance," Florio said, "and there is absolution. So, Jake, do the right thing and tell me about it."

"Tell you about what?"

Stalling.

Thinking.

Sweating.

What's worse, I wondered, the shame of being caught or the fear of inflicted pain? Perspiration tracked down my back, chilling me. I counted my options. They kept coming down to Diaz with a gun and Tiger with a machete. "Look, Nicky. I'm not going to lie to you. I've known Gina a long time."

"I know all about that. I know what's bullshit and what's not. Just answer my questions. What'd Gina tell you about me?"

"Nothing really. That she loves you, but she's not in love with you, whatever that means. That you're good to her, that she and I could have had something, but our timing was always off."

"And what'd she tell you about the Everglades project?"

"Cypress Estates? Nothing I remember."

"Not Cypress Estates. The other one . . ."

"The other? Look, Nicky, I don't know what you're talking about."

He studied me. "If you're a liar, Jake, you're a good one, and judging from the way you play poker, you couldn't bluff your way out of a speeding ticket."

He was smiling now, if that's what it's called when a shark shows its teeth. "I'm going to deal with you later." Then he turned toward Gondolier. "At least the shyster tells the truth, which is more than I can say for you."

Gondolier's handsome face lost two shades of its suntan. He shot a look at Diaz, who sat motionless, his hand still inside his nylon jacket. "Whaddaya mean?" Gondolier asked, his voice straining to sound casual.

Diaz looked toward Nicky. "You want I should do him, Mr. Florio?"

Whoa. A changing of the guard.

Gondolier's eyes shot back and forth between the two men. Florio shook his head sadly. "Rick, Rick, Rick. We could have made each other very wealthy. All the pussy in this town, but you gotta come sniffing after my wife."

"No. It's not true, Nicky. I swear on the life of my mother."

"Your mother's a guinea whore, and you're a greaseball with a phony name."

"Nicky, please. C'mon. You need me. We've got our plans."

"Need *you*? I could replace you with a gold-plated croupier in a rented tux. I could buy and sell a hundred of you."

Florio's mouth curled into a sneer. He reached over and grabbed Gondolier's dimpled cheek and twisted. "Now why don't you do like the lawyer and fess up? Maybe you'll be forgiven." Florio let go. "Why'd you fuck my wife?"

Gondolier sobbed, his shoulders heaving.

"Gondo, you're lower than gator shit, which you just might be by morning. Tell me, you want to be a turd at the bottom of the swamp?"

Tears streamed down Gondolier's face. Nicky kept talking. "Now the mouthpiece has an excuse. He's known her a long time. He's got seniority." Florio allowed himself a bitter laugh. "What the fuck's your excuse? You couldn't skim enough money from the bingo, you thieving scumbag? You had to humiliate me at home, too, you two-bit, pretty-boy dickhead. What the fuck's *your* excuse?"

"I don't know," Rick Gondolier whimpered. "She was . . . just . . . there."

"That ain't good enough. That's not a lawful excuse, right, Jake?"

I didn't make a sound.

"That's not justifiable screwing," Florio added, answering his own question. "Goddamn you, Gondo, it's a capital offense, fucking your partner's wife."

Florio turned to me. "Hey, Jake, what are the odds that hard-on here is gonna live long enough to take a morning piss?"

"I wouldn't know."

"C'mon, Jake, you're good at beating the odds. I'm giving you a chance to set 'em. You know me, and you know Gina. You know what Gondo has done with my Gina." Again, his smile bared his teeth. "*Our* Gina."

"Six-to-five," I said.

"How's that?"

"Some writer once said all life is six-to-five against, just enough of a chance to make it interesting."

Florio leaned back in his chair, thinking it over. "I like that. The lawyer called it. Anybody want a piece of the action, six-to-five against Gondo making it through the night?"

Gondolier was whimpering. A vein was throbbing in Florio's forehead, and he was breathing hard in short, raspy breaths. "No takers, Jake. Even Gondo recognizes a sucker bet, and tonight, he's the biggest sucker in the swamp."

Florio nodded to Jim Tiger. Suddenly, there was movement all around, Gondolier trying to back away from the table, the shadow of Tiger behind me, moving to my left, Diaz pulling his gun, pointing it at a startled Rick Gondolier, who froze to his chair.

It might have been in slow motion, my mind snapping dozens of stills, the cards still on the table, a king of hearts—the same one Nicky used to win the first pot—staring at me, piles of blue and red chips stacked against the green felt background, the ice cubes melting into the caramel liquid of Florio's scotch glass.

The machete made a *whoosh* as Tiger swung, two-handed, like a baseball bat. He was a lefty, and the swing had a slight uppercut, like Willie McCovey going for the fence in Candlestick Park. The blade caught Gondolier in the back of the neck, chopping off the ends of his long blond hair. The machete bit through skin and muscles, through blood vessels and spinal canal, and stopped dead with a sickening crack as it lodged in Gondolier's cervical vertebrae. The impact jolted his body forward, his face stopping just a few inches from the table. Tiger yanked back on the machete, straightening Gondolier, trying to pull the machete free, but it was stuck there. Gondolier's mouth was open, frozen in disbelief. His eyes screamed with horror.

Tiger yanked again, but bone and blade seemed fused. He lifted his left leg from the floor and planted a snakeskin cowboy boot in the middle of Gondolier's back. Pushing away with his foot, Tiger used the leverage to wiggle backward on the machete handle, finally yanking the blade free. Gondolier teetered in his chair, his hands still holding the tabletop. Tiger went into his backswing, this time grunting with effort as he brought the machete forward, keeping his head down and motionless like a major leaguer, squarely hitting the same mark, crunching cleanly through tissue and bone with an explosive *pop*.

Blood gushed straight into the air, and Gondolier's head plopped onto the green felt table, rolling into Diaz's chips, where it came to rest, straight up, mouth and eyes still open. A series of trembles shook Gondolier's body, but it stayed in the chair, headless, his hands gripping the table. The blood spurted in two distinct streams. Gondolier's vertebral and carotid arteries were cleanly severed, but the heart was still pumping, and the stream of blood now splashed against the ceiling and drizzled down on the table. I looked up and was splattered, a red sticky shower closing my eyes, a warm, sweet mist covering my lips. In front of Florio, blood puddled on the king of hearts. Diaz shifted the gun to me.

I hate a gun just as much as a blade.

My eyes were on Diaz. The room was silent except for the dripping of blood, from ceiling onto table, from table onto floor. Then I heard the sound of a chair scraping against the floor.

"Rule number three, Jake," Florio said evenly, sliding away from the table as blood made islands of his towers of chips. "Never fuck another man's wife, unless you got a real good excuse."

Chapter 15

Partners

The rain eased into a gentle tapping against the roof, and the thunder diminished to a distant echo. I lost track of the time and place. Sometime after midnight, somewhere near hell.

Nicky Florio hadn't stopped talking. About progress and loyalty, friendship and women, politicians and bribery, money and power. The sight of the blood, of Rick Gondolier's twitching body, must have opened the spigots on his adrenaline flow. It did the opposite to me. I was a 223-pound slug. Florio's words were a sticky blob, a recording played at half speed. Time flowed like a languid river, the Everglades itself.

I thought of Jim Tiger, his shirt soaked with blood, as he hoisted the headless body of Rick Gondolier over his shoulder and carried it to the porch. Florio motioned for me to follow. Diaz stayed half a step behind, watching me. Tiger put the body down by the rail.

"Help him," Florio ordered me.

I didn't understand.

"Take his arms, Tiger'll take his legs. Swing him over the rail."

Jim Tiger could have done it himself. He was thick through the neck and shoulders with powerful wrists. But Nicky told me to do it, and like an obedient dog standing in the gentle, cooling rain, I obeyed, grabbing Gondolier's lifeless arms. I had been spared, and something made me want to please Nicky Florio, to thank him for his benevolence. If I had a tail, I would have wagged it.

Below us, the outdoor spotlights cut narrow shafts toward the black water. "Hey, Jake, look at this." Florio was pointing with a three-foot Kel-Lite, the kind the cops use to peer into cars or beat you over the head. "You can't even see those beautiful bastards; they blend into the mud." He gestured toward the soggy bank. "There, look for the eyes."

I followed the shaft of light.

At first I didn't see a thing. I was concentrating on holding on to Gondolier, conscious of the still-warm blood, tacky on his arms.

Then I saw them, staring up at us, half a dozen sets of greenish-yellow eyes. "You see any red ones?" Florio asked. "They're the bull gators. Don't know why, but the mamas and the children have yellow eyes, the males red." He stopped the beam and moved it back a few feet. "There! Can't tell his size, but look at those eyes, like the Devil himself. Five'll get you ten, he'll be the first one there. Okay, let 'em rip. On three."

Florio counted, and we swung the body, letting it fly on the count of three. It hung in the air at the top of its arc, then dropped straight into the inky water where it hit with a smack, submerged, then popped up again. On the bank, the red eyes, glowing like the fires of the bottomless pit, moved toward the water, the bull gator slipping below the surface, swimming powerfully but silently toward the splash. Only the fearsome eyes and the tip of the snout were visible in the beam of the flashlight.

It crossed fifty yards of water in a matter of seconds, striking first at the legs. The first chomp snapped the femur, maybe both of them, with a clearly audible crack. The body seemed to break in two, and in a moment a second gator was there, seizing the top half and dragging it under the water. Now the water was alive with the animals, thrashing about, scavenging for torn flesh, a meaty bone, an overlooked morsel.

I leaned on the railing, the rain pelting me. From behind me, there was movement, and for a split second I thought Tiger was going to push me over. I whirled and saw a blur of motion. Rick Gondolier's head. It fell to the surface and plopped off the back of one of the gators before sliding into the water, faceup. A distant flash of lightning illuminated the sky. Gondolier's face was frozen in a death mask, his eyes black holes. A second later, his head disappeared into the maw of one of the yellow-eyed females, which swallowed it in one gulp.

Back inside the house, I was cold and shivering, the fatigue crushing me. I was vaguely aware of sounds and smells. The swish of a mop across the floor, the sharp sting of disinfectant, the crackling oak logs in the fireplace where bloody rags went up in smoke.

Nicky Florio poured scotch into a fancy Scandinavian glass that seemed to be made of icicles. I held the glass in my hand and swirled the bronze whiskey into a whirlpool. I sank into a soft-cushioned sofa of Haitian cotton near the fireplace. Florio grabbed a straight-backed chair, swung a leg over it, and leaned on its back, facing me, like a cowboy in a western saloon. Tiger was still cleaning up. Diaz stood to the side, two feet behind his boss, the gun back in its holster under his jacket. He had an unobstructed view of me, as he had ever since Gondolier was killed.

"I confronted Gina," Florio said, "and she swore she didn't tell you anything about the project, but I didn't know whether to believe her. I still don't. But it doesn't matter anymore, because you'll know soon enough."

I tossed down the scotch. It burned my throat and closed my eyes. "Know what?"

"I'm going to be honest with you. I told Gina I was going to kill either you or Gondolier. It didn't make any difference to me just so it was one of you."

"Why only one?"

"One guy disappears, no big deal. Happens all the time. Two guys with connections to me disappear, it gets a little hairy. Besides, I wanted to find something out from her."

He looked at me to see if I caught on. It took a second. "You gave Gina the choice . . ."

He smiled at me. He approved. I was a good student.

". . . and she chose to let me live."

Florio poured me another scotch, shook his head, and said, "No, she told me to spare Gondolier. Kill the lawyer, she said. Just like Shakespeare, huh, Jake?"

The wind went out of me. Maybe it was the accumulation of tension and exhaustion, horror and fear. Maybe it was a lot of things I'd seen and heard and done and had done to me. Maybe it was the image of Rick Gondolier's floating head disappearing into the mouth of a yellow-eyed dragon.

Peter Tupton was dead, and unless I was wrong, the murderer was sitting three feet away, pouring me booze. I had used perjured testimony to help him win a lousy civil case. I was close to being tossed out of my profession, and I didn't seem to care. A few hours ago, I nearly pissed my pants when a poker table turned into a butcher's block. I watched a man decapitated, then helped dispose of the body, then watched as prehistoric beasts disposed of his carcass. And now this . . .

I fought through the numbness and looked Florio in the eyes. "She told you to kill *me* and to spare Gondolier."

I sounded lame, feeble.

"That's what she said, Counselor. What do you think of that?"

Nothing.

Emptiness.

Loss.

"Don't look so damn sorry for yourself. How long have you known Gina?"

"Forever," I said.

"And what mistake do people always make with her? I mean, when they see her. All blond, all boobs. What do they think?"

"They think she's a bimbo. They think she's stupid."

"Right. Is she stupid, Jake?"

"No. She has great instincts. She can read people."

"Damn right! She thought if she told me to kill you, I'd do just the opposite. I'd spare you and kill Gondolier. And she was right. Until I thought it over. Like I said before, Jake, you and I have something in common. We both know Gina, and lucky for you, I know her better than you do. I knew that if I killed you, I'd lose her, because I would have killed a piece of her. You're part of her history, you're part of her. Why do you think she broke off with you?"

"I don't know. It's happened before."

"Because she was in conflict. She cared for you. You made her life more difficult, and what does Gina do when life gets difficult?"

"She runs away. Always has."

"Right. Now Gondolier was another story. She had no feelings for him, so she could screw him without messing up her head, and at the same time, she could hurt me, because he was my partner."

I took a long hit on the scotch. My eyes watered, and beads of sweat appeared on my forehead. "Why should she want to hurt you?"

"Good question. Why has she fooled around on every man she's married? I didn't know, so I asked her to see a shrink. She goes, and after twenty grand or so, the shrink says she has low self-esteem. Doesn't feel she deserves the big house and the boat and the servants, and a man who adores her. So she tries to sabotage it every time, and she does a damn good job. As for Jake Lassiter, you're her safe harbor. You don't try to buy her—you're just a regular guy from the old days who shared some good times with her. So she starts to develop intimacy with you, which frightens her, and she bolts again."

"Why are you telling me all this?"

"Because I don't want to lose her. If you're dead, she'll mourn for you. She'll blame me, but even worse, she'll blame herself, lowering her esteem even more, fulfilling the prophecy—that's what the shrink called it—that she doesn't deserve happiness. So she'll fall into bed with the next guy, or maybe even leave me."

"And if I'm alive, what then?"

"You tell me, Counselor."

"Gina will come back to me. She always does."

He nodded thoughtfully. "Right. If you're happy and healthy and doing your own thing, sooner or later she'll run back to her safe harbor. On the other hand, after tonight's little show, you might be inclined to turn the lady down."

My head was spinning off course. I imagined Nicky Florio asking a psychiatrist whether killing me would be therapeutic for his wife. I imagined a bearded, pipe-smoking shrink in a cardigan telling him to bond with me first, discuss our common ground, then consider whether his desire to kill me stemmed from his unorganized, primitive id or a desire to help his wife.

"So, bottom line, Jake, we're competitors, enemies where Gina is concerned. She's my wife, but you knew her first. You've got history, but you're playing on my territory, so I make the rules. Are you with me?"

The gods make their own rules, I thought, the phrase still rattling around in my head. "I'm not sure."

"Think about it, Jake. What have you learned tonight?"

"A straight beats three of a kind."

Florio was shaking his head. "You always made her laugh. She told me that. But I don't think you're that funny. I think you use the wise-guy stuff to avoid reality, and, Jake, my friend, reality is staring you in the face."

I sensed Diaz shifting his feet. Maybe he was tired of standing there, or maybe he was getting ready to put bullet holes in the white cotton sofa, a goodly portion of which was covered by me.

"I spent all this time with you," Florio said, "trying to teach you a lesson. I wanted you to see Gondolier get it. It was important for you to understand your situation, your lack of options. I wanted you to know what happens with just one fuckup."

I polished off the rest of the scotch. It was suddenly very warm in the house on stilts built without permits. "Message received, loud and clear."

"Good. Because I want to give you a chance. I'm offering you the benefit of my wisdom and experience, and you sit here and crack wise. Don't you see what I'm trying to teach—"

"Rule number two," I said. "Co-opt the enemy. Infiltrate, buy 'em off."

His smile seemed genuine. "You got it right. I want to keep you where I can see you."

"Which is where?"

He stood up, swinging a leg over the back of the chair and spinning it away. He walked over to the sofa and looked down at me. "Stand up, Jake."

Now what?

Diaz moved a little to his left, getting Florio out of his line of sight. Or was it his line of fire?

I stood. I had become so obedient so quickly.

Florio extended a hand. I reached out, tentatively, and he shook it firmly. "Welcome aboard, Jake." He turned toward Diaz. "Hey, Guillermo, let go of your gun and shake hands with my new partner."

Chapter 16

The Loophole

Dawn was an orange glow to the east, a chattering of birds, a succession of splashes and ripples in the water below. In the distance, I heard what sounded like thunderclaps, but after a moment they seemed to be a series of dull, thudding explosions. The morning light cut across a table in what could have been a bedroom in the southeast corner of the house. But there was no room for a bed. A table took up most of the entire room. It held a larger version of the scale model of Cypress Estates that Charlie and I had seen at the bingo hall. The same shops and apartments, burger palaces and gas stations, the lagoons and wood storks. But other things, too.

The golf course.

Parking garages.

Miniature buses. Dozens of them.

And a huge building on stilts, a cream-colored flying saucer of a building that looked like a domed stadium. Next to it, connected by a shaded catwalk over the water, was a miniature version of the same building.

"Know what you're looking at, Jake?"

"Looks like a modern sports complex, a football stadium next to a basketball arena. Kind of like the Vet and the Forum, except your stadium is domed."

"This ain't Philadelphia, Jake. The small building will be the Living Everglades Museum. The roof is retractable, lets the sun shine in. Rain, too. It'll have a zoo, a herbarium, a living garden, an aviary, an electronically controlled habitat of every species of life found in the Everglades. We're going to grow the plants and raise the animals and make it all accessible. I'm the guy who's going to preserve the Everglades. I was going to make Tupton the executive director of the museum and living habitat. I'd fund everything. Now look at this." He pointed to a remote section of the model, a hardwood hammock with several airboats pulled up to a dock. Models of dark-skinned men and women sat around campfires near miniature chickee huts. "Our authentic Indian village. No alligator wrestling, no T-shirt stands. The real thing. Indians living and fishing and cooking for everyone to see the old ways."

He saw the look I was giving him. "You didn't think this stuff was important to me, did you, Jake? You thought it was all about money. Well, you're wrong. You and Tupton and all the do-gooders think in clichés and stereotypes. A man's a developer, he must be a robber baron who doesn't give a shit about the birds. Damn, it's not that simple. I grew up hunting in the forest near Ocala. I used to fish for bass in Lake Okeechobee. Don't you understand I *agreed* with Tupton on the goals? It's his methods that sucked. Lawsuits against developers, a freeze on building permits in Monroe County. Double the impact fees in Collier County. Lying down in front of the bulldozers for the TV cameras. That's all crap."

"I don't get it. If you were going to do all this, why was Tupton fighting you?"

"He wasn't, not at first. I needed his support for the project, and in the beginning he was receptive. At least, he said he'd listen."

"Until he saw the golf course . . ."

"Fuck the golf course! The golf course is diddly-squat. Until he saw the *casino*."

Florio pointed to what I thought was the domed stadium. "Look at it, Jake. Forget bingo. Say hello to blackjack, roulette, craps, slots, keno, poker, the whole works. And look what else. Unlike Vegas, it's got windows, a walkway three hundred sixty degrees around the building and into the museum. Bring the kids for a nature walk. You can look out over the slough, commune with nature, watch snowy egrets soar . . ."

"Draw to an inside straight," I said.

"It's not funny, Jake. I had everything lined up, but Tupton blows it."

Nicky Florio sat there thinking about it, and I waited for him to tell me the story. It didn't take long.

"At the party, Tupton wanders into my den and sees the plans for the casino. When he came across the estimates of the number of visitors, he nearly fainted. I had told him we were going to bring gambling to the project, but maybe he didn't comprehend what that meant. He wanted the museum and the habitat so much, maybe he closed his eyes to the rest. But now he sees the ten-year projections, and they stagger him. Widening Tamiami Trail, two thousand buses a day, Phase Two of the housing plan, high-rise condos, apartments, town houses. It blew his mind, but what could he expect? How did he think I was going to pay for the museum?"

"Selling alligator wallets at the souvenir stand," I suggested.

"We're talking forty-five million for construction and other capital expenditures, another fifteen in start-up costs, and ten to twelve million in shortfall revenue per year. I couldn't pay for it with greens fees."

"So you killed him."

Florio shook his head. "Wrong! Christ, don't you know I told you the truth about Tupton? The guy was drunk. He wandered into the wine cellar, popped a few corks, and passed out."

"We've been over this," I said. "Why didn't the caterers find his body?"

"Damned if I know. Maybe he wandered off and came back after the caterers left, who knows? Maybe somebody moved him, but it wasn't me. Jake, I liked the guy, I really did. I tried to tell him we could have it all. In addition to everything else, I promised him fifteen percent of the casino profits for preservation of endangered species. Do you know how much money we're talking about? Shit, they could create *new* species with the cash flow. We're talking ten million visitors a year."

"Which is what he objected to."

Florio nodded. "Not even willing to listen. He was going to run to the papers with news about the casino. It would've blown sky-high."

"Sooner or later, it'll happen anyway," I said.

"But I'll choose when and where. It's the only way to keep the media from screwing everything up. There was a headline the other day that the Florida Keys coral reef is dying, and who do they blame? Builders, because everyone wants simple answers, and we're the guys who bulldoze the mangroves, dredge up the sediment. It doesn't occur to these smart guys that hurricanes, cold fronts, black-band disease, and a bunch of other natural causes can kill the coral. Why the fuck shouldn't the coral die? Everything in nature dies. Maybe a hundred years from now, another coral reef will form somewhere off Australia, but they don't consider that. We're so damned intent on preserving nature that we don't let nature take its course."

"You're saying the alligator kills the wood stork, so why shouldn't you?"

"I'm saying nature is deadly. In the Glades, some Australian pine trees are so toxic their falling leaves will kill other plants along the canals. That's Mother Nature, pal. Lightning hits a hammock of slash pines and turns the shrubbery into kindling. But once the shrubs are burned up, the sunlight reaches the ground where the pine seedlings are just taking root."

"So you're just another lightning bolt?"

"As usual, Jake, you're missing my point, which is that developers are easy targets. We're as despised as . . ."

"Lawyers."

"Yeah, almost. We make better villains than the farmers. Why don't they take on Big Sugar? You know how much of the Everglades is planted with cane? I'll tell you, five hundred thousand acres. You can't even imagine it until you see the fields. The runoff of phosphorous has done more damage to the ecosystem than all the condos ever built." Florio stared out into space. "Fucking De La Torre." He turned to me. "You know him?"

"President of National Sugar, but I always thought his first name was Carlos."

"The prick fucking owns Tallahassee. Between government price supports and paying slave wages, he's gotten filthy rich."

"You sound jealous."

"Yeah, well, I gotta pay union wages and bid on jobs. But it ain't all sweet with sugar. The new free-trade treaty with Mexico, the imports from Cuba when Castro falls, the GATT treaty, they all keep De La Torre awake at night. So he wants a sideline, some extra security for the future."

"What's that have to do with you?"

"De La Torre's the only one who could have stopped us. He held me up like a highway robber, but I greased his palm, so he's on board, just like the Indians. Christ, I had everybody in my pocket except Tupton."

Something was gnawing at me. "What about the legislature? You can't buy 'em all, and I don't see how you'll get a gaming bill passed. You'll be up against the unholy alliance of racetrack and jai alai interests plus the fundamentalist Christians. The hotel industry's been trying to pass a casino law for thirty years and has never come close."

"That's the beauty of it, Jake. We don't need a law."

"Of course you do. Casinos are illegal in Florida."

"You still don't get it, do you? We don't need permits. We don't need impact statements. We don't need zoning variances or business licenses or special laws."

"You don't?"

"Jake, why the fuck don't you listen? We ain't in Florida. This is Injun country."

Nicky Florio explained it to me. By the numbers.

One: In 1962, the United States secretary of the interior approved the constitution of the Micanopy Tribe. Seventy thousand acres of land were now under the exclusive jurisdiction of the tribe's general council. Tax-exempt land with some soggy farms and lots of alligators and not much the white man wanted.

Two: Florio began doing business with the Indians in the seventies. He built low-cost housing for them in hard-to-reach areas. He fished with the Tiger family and became friendly with council leaders.

Three: Florio purchased an option for a ninety-nine-year lease on ten thousand acres for the housing, commercial, and recreation ventures. The lease is boilerplate and all-inclusive, granting everything from construction and air rights to mineral rights. The tribe will get 10 percent of pretax profits. He smiled a pickpocket's smile.

Ten percent of Florio Enterprises' profits, Florio emphasized. But that company assigned the long-term lease to a holding company, which assigned its rights to a Cayman Islands Trust. Florio Enterprises only gets a management fee from the holding company. The real profits, hundreds of millions, will be passed through, and the Indians don't get a cent of them.

A red cent, Florio said.

Four: The mixed residential-commercial town went off without a hitch. No permits needed, except from the tribe's general council.

Five: the law.

"You ever hear of the Federal Indian Regulatory Gaming Act of 1988?" Florio asked.

"I don't pay attention to statutes unless they have something to do with fender benders or burglaries."

"The Act allows Indians to run the same gambling allowed by the state."

"Fine. Open a racetrack or a fronton. Florida law doesn't allow casinos."

"Sure it does, Counselor. The churches hold Vegas night for charity all the time. It's right in the law. How do you think we operate a bingo hall with cash awards? Because churches are allowed to. It's the same principle."

I thought about it. A loophole, Nicky would call it. But that's what lawyering is all about, drawing parallels between your client's quirky facts and those from a case that goes your way. Making analogies, sidestepping distinctions, taking exceptions and making them the rules, and in general patching holes in the water bucket that is your case.

"You'll still face a court challenge," I said. "The state attorney general or the racetrack folks or someone will want to keep you out."

"I expect that. So be my lawyer. Give me an opinion. Who'll win, and no bullshit about needing time to research it. Rely on your instincts."

My instincts hadn't been very good lately, but I gave it a shot. "You'll argue that the state can't allow a church to operate a casino, even one night a year, without letting the Indians do it full time under the federal statute. It would be discriminatory to bar equivalent gambling games on Indian land. The law is just one side of the equation, of course. Politically, the strength would be with the opposition. On your side, you've got a few thousand Indians who live in a swamp and want to lease you land for a casino. On the other, some big moneyed interests in horse racing, jai alai, and dogs will fight you every step of the way. Even the teachers' unions will be against you, since the state lottery benefits education. I'd be willing to bet that you'd have a drastic effect on lottery revenues."

"A forty to fifty percent decrease, according to our studies," Florio said, "plus we'd cripple racing and jai alai within three years. Hell, we'll hurt Vegas and Atlantic City, too. With no state or federal taxes to pay, our slots can increase the payoff and give a higher rate of return than anything there. On the games that have some room, we'll give better odds."

"That's why you'd be such a threat," I agreed, "and I don't have to tell you that the courts are moved by political realities. If the attorney general decides to sue, you could be tied up for years. The state could argue that you're the real operator of the casino, not the Indians, so the whole setup is a sham. Your response is that the state has no legitimate concern how the profits are divided or who runs the gambling. In fact, the judicial inquiry must be limited to the narrow question of whether casino gambling is permitted under state law. If so, no state or federal court has the power to inquire further. The Indians can allow casino gambling on their land, and it's simply none of the government's business."

Florio was beaming at me. "Gina was right about you. You're smarter than you look. Anything else? Anything you need to know?"

"I don't understand what Carlos de La Torre and the sugar industry have to do with this."

Florio showed a sour smile. "The Indians foolishly gave up a piece of their sovereignty to the Water Management Board. They signed a damned compact. No new development in land covered by the board's jurisdiction without board approval. Part of the move was to help the tribe's image after the big-game fiasco."

My look told him I didn't understand.

"The Indians were going to bring in lions, tigers, elephants, and let the yahoos blast them out of the saw grass for five thousand bucks a pop. No way the state could stop them, but the public furor made 'em back down. Then the tribal council agreed to submit all plans that will affect the environment to the Water Board, and to abide by its decisions. It's a binding compact. The board doesn't do anything without the sugar industry's approval, and that means Carlos de La Torre. All he cares about is water for the cane and money for his pockets. But I've got him covered, and a damn good thing, too. The board meets next Tuesday, and that's when we submit our proposal."

"You're going to make the casino plan public?"

"It has to be done, sooner or later, but that's what I meant about timing. The papers won't have anything about it beforehand. Most meetings, it's just some tomato farmers feuding with the cane growers and your usual assortment of fruitcakes from the Audubon Society. The board meets in a school gym up in Belle Glade on the edge of a cane field, in case the commissioners forget who pays the freight. There's an agenda item that simply says, 'Micanopy land-use plan.' We'll have the vote recorded before the newspapers go to print. So I'm not worried about Big Sugar or the Water Management Board. But you tell me, Jake. What about the state cabinet?"

"The governor will ask for an AGO, an attorney-general opinion, as to the legality of the planned casino. The attorney general is Don Russo, but he hasn't read a law book in thirty-five years. Either he's on the golf course, or he's taking his secretary to Sanibel Island at taxpayer's expense. He'll turn to Abe Socolow as the local state attorney."

"Socolow's a friend of yours, isn't he, Jake?"

" 'Friend' is maybe too strong a word. We're adversaries, have been for years. Let's just say we have a healthy respect for each other."

"C'mon, Jake, you're too modest. You've been involved in his election campaign."

"I've endorsed him. That's all. Me and a thousand other lawyers."

Florio helped himself to the scotch bottle. "I'm a supporter of his, too. Contributions strictly legit. All reported, none above the legal limit. The guy's a straight arrow."

Florio was right. Abe Socolow had been appointed acting state attorney when Nick Wolf was indicted for playing footsie with major drug dealers. Before then, Socolow had been chief of the major-crimes division in the office. A working prosecutor, not a paper pusher or a politician, Socolow had a messianic drive to rid the streets of murderers and other hoodlums. He looked like an undertaker but was seldom as cheerful. He was long and lean, sallow and mean. And honest.

"Look, Nicky, if you're thinking of bribing Abe Socolow, you've been out in the sun too long. The guy's untouchable. He'll indict you. He'll set you up and sting you with TV cameras popping out of the ceiling."

"I wouldn't even consider bribing Mr. Socolow," Florio said, solemnly.

"Good. For a moment, I was afraid you—"

"That's *your* job, partner."

Chapter 17

Shades of Gray

"HE GAVE YOU A MILLION DOLLARS?" CHARLIE RIGGS ASKED, HIS bushy eyebrows arched in disbelief.

"Cash. In fifties."

"Goodness gracious!" Charlie's hand trembled and he slurped conch chowder through his mustache. "And where have you stashed the loot?"

When he gets excited, Charlie tends to talk like a B movie. "I stashed it in an old Dolphins' equipment bag that I liberated from the locker room about a thousand years ago. The bag is sitting in the trunk of my antique Oldsmobile about thirty yards yonder."

Charlie shot a glance into the parking lot and back to me again. When he tries to act inconspicuous, Charlie looks like a man trying to act inconspicuous. Beneath the bushy beard, his face was beginning to color. Either he was holding his breath or they put too much Tabasco in the chowder. We were sitting on the front porch of Tugboat Willie's, a ramshackle fish joint behind the Marine Stadium on the Rickenbacker Causeway. With the February boat show on Miami Beach and the art show in Coconut Grove, it was just about the only place you could eat outdoors that wasn't mobbed with tourists in Bermuda shorts and Hooters' tank tops. "More than a mouthful," according to the slogan on the back.

Charlie looked from side to side, then lowered his voice. "You should sequester the, *ah-chem*, cookies in your safe-deposit box."

"Huh?"

"A million cookies."

"Oh, I get it. You afraid I'll eat them?"

"No, lose them."

"Can't put them in the box," I said. "My safe-deposit box is about as thick as a goal-line stripe. You know how much room a million in cash takes?"

Charlie made a *shushing* sound with a finger to his lips.

"To give you an idea, my old equipment bag used to hold all the shoulder pads for the offensive line, and it's jammed full. We're talking twenty thousand fifty-dollar bills."

"Okay, okay," Charlie whispered hoarsely, glancing nervously at two boaters at the next table. The men were chomping dolphin sandwiches—fried fillets with mayo and onions on white bread—oblivious to our discussion, though Charlie doubtless imagined them fugitives from Interpol.

I was scooping smoked fish spread onto saltines and nursing a beer. "Sometimes in the movies, a guy opens a briefcase, one of those three-inch Samsonites, and there's supposed to be a couple million bucks inside. No way."

A pouting waiter in a Florida State T-shirt, a kid with a ponytail and one earring, brought Charlie's yellowtail snapper, broiled well done, and dropped a plate of stone crabs in front of me. Maybe I'm just getting old, but the young today seem to slouch and sulk more than we did.

When the waiter retreated to the kitchen, Charlie whispered, "You've got to go to Abe Socolow at once. Take the money to him."

"That's exactly what Nicky Florio wants me to do."

"You know what I mean. Tell Socolow everything. Testify in front of the grand jury."

"What for?"

"To indict Nicky Florio, of course."

"For what, or did I just say that?"

"Jake, what's wrong with you? For murder and attempted bribery."

Charlie's fish was getting cold. A breeze was blowing from the bay, and the palm fronds clattered against each other. At least we weren't getting a whiff of the sewage plant from nearby Virginia Key. "As for murder," I said, "Socolow's got no jurisdiction. It didn't happen in Dade County. Hell, it didn't happen in any county. It's Micanopy territory."

"The *locus delicti*," Charlie muttered.

"The tribal police have investigatory powers, and the federal courts have ultimate jurisdiction if there's a case. But there's a big problem, Charlie. No body."

"No *corpus delicti*," Charlie said.

"Now I could go under oath and tell Abe I witnessed this murder, and then helped dispose of the body. . . ."

"Accessory *post facto*."

"But there are three witnesses who'll claim I'm lying or hallucinating. . . ."

"Ah, the *dramatis personae*."

"Charlie, do you think you could stop that?"

"*Deo volente*, God willing."

"Even if the feds can find the place, and some sophisticated canoemaker like you can find a splotch of blood or a tooth at the bottom of the slough, my word won't be good enough."

"Why not?"

I dived into the stone crabs. The claws hadn't been thoroughly cracked, and I was using a cocktail fork like an ice pick to dig out the meat. "For the same reason I can't blow the whistle on the bribery. The million bucks came from Rick Gondolier's safe. He skimmed it from the bingo hall. At least that's what Florio says. Now I show up, blabbing that Florio's trying to bribe Abe Socolow, but if Abe is dirty, he's already in Florio's pocket, and he'll tip Florio that I've pulled a double-cross. If Abe's honest and looks into my charges, Florio will claim that Gondolier and I stole the money, then had a falling-out, after which I killed him, and to save my own hide I—"

"Tried to frame Florio," Charlie said. He stabbed a fried plantain with his fork and toyed with it. "So just give the money back to Florio. Just say no."

"I can't do that, either."

Charlie raised the plantain to his mouth and stopped just short. He was going to lose weight if this kept up much longer.

I gave a helpless shrug. "Nicky told me he still reserved his first option."

Charlie's look asked the question.

"To kill me. He'd justify it to Gina. 'Hey, I gave the guy a chance, and he screwed up.' "

"So what are you going to do?"

I polished off the beer and signaled the waiter for one of its cousins. The kid looked right through me, his optic nerve apparently not connected to his brain.

"The bull rush," I told Charlie.

"Bull . . ."

"No spin moves, no snatch and go, just a frontal assault. Hit 'em high, take a shot, hit 'em again. Somebody falls on his ass."

"Jake, speak English, please."

"You're one to talk. Ouch!" My cocktail fork had slipped, and I pierced my thumb on a jagged piece of shell. I sucked a pinprick of blood from the meaty tissue just below my thumbnail. An infinitesimal spot of red, but it made me think of Rick Gondolier, his neck spurting blood, his life gone in seconds.

"What I'm going to do, Charlie, is real simple. I'm going to do my job. I'm going to bribe Abe Socolow."

In law school, they teach us ethics.

They teach us not to steal from our clients and not to lie to the court. They teach us not to suborn perjury and not to obstruct justice. They teach us to put the client's interest ahead of our own. They teach us right from wrong, black from white. But they don't teach us shades of gray.

A long time ago, Charlie Riggs told me there was only so much to be learned from books. *Doctus cum libro*, he called it, numbered rules and tidy paragraphs intended to guide our conduct. But life is messy. B doesn't always follow A. The system doesn't work if you make up the rules as you go along, and the rules work only if the players follow them.

The books don't describe the icicle shivers down the spine when a man with a machete stands within arm's reach, measuring the distance with hard eyes. The books don't describe the taste of bile and the clenching fear. The books don't prepare you for life, or death.

In the end, we march along a path drawn by our own moral compass. The sum total of our life experiences guides us in a way our conscious minds could never decipher. We make choices without realizing why and trigger events we never foresee. And always we rationalize who we are and why we act the way we do.

Our instinct for self-preservation is accompanied by a hearty dose of self-delusion. Nicky Florio is a lover of nature and a creator of jobs, not a robber baron and a killer. Abe Socolow is a dedicated prosecutor, not just another hack politician on the take. And I am a hardworking professional who dedicates himself to the diaphanous concept of justice, not a shyster who illegally wiretaps, sleeps with another man's wife, helps cover up a murder, and bribes public officials.

Knowledge of self is acquired through a shattered mirror. But we can always close our eyes.

My friends know the doorbell doesn't work. Hasn't for years. Someone who tries the knob will think the door is locked. It doesn't budge. But friends know the door is humidity-swollen, and one good whack with a shoulder will squeak it open. So I keep it unlocked.

The little house is two stories, made of coral rock, and sits on a Coconut Grove lot ninety-five feet wide. There are poinciana and chinaberry trees in front and a rope hammock strung between live oaks in the weedy backyard. Inside are several ceiling fans, stacks of newspapers and windsurfing magazines, a bowl of star fruit on the kitchen counter, last night's spaghetti in the fridge, a coffee table made of a sailboard propped on concrete blocks, and other designer touches that never won an award in *Architectural Digest*.

It was a fine late afternoon in March. I was wearing cutoff jeans with stringy holes and nothing else when somebody knocked on the door. It was a dainty knock.

A process server would bang harder.

A former teammate would simply barge in.

Charlie would mutter ancient Roman sayings as he tried to sweet-talk the door.

And Granny would curse up a blue streak.

At first, I didn't know whose fist belonged to the delicate knock.

I must have forgotten, must have banished memories of afternoon visits.

I yanked the door open.

"I had to see you," Gina said.

She was wearing a pink leotard, white high-top sneakers with pink laces, white tights, and pink wristbands. The manicured nails were perfect and pink. Her long blond hair was pulled back from her forehead by a pink sweatband. She looked like strawberry-swirl ice cream in a sugar cone. Her face was flushed, and a fine line of perspiration trickled down her neck. What was it someone said? Men sweat, women get dewy.

"I just came from the gym. I must look like an old sweathog."

Sure. And Venus de Milo is an old chunk of rock.

I stood there, staring dumbly at her.

"May I come in?" She brush-kissed me and slid inside, her steamy fragrance bringing back memories, and not of jogging or aerobics.

"I had to see you," she repeated, in case I missed it the first time.

She didn't sit down. She wandered around what passes for a living room, running a finger over furniture the Salvation Army couldn't give away, avoiding a barbell loaded with 315 pounds of steel plates, tapping her fingers on the keys of an old manual type-writer. Finally, she turned to me. "Where's Rick?" she asked.

"Rick? Rick Gondolier? You came to ask me about him?"

I didn't like my tone. Whiny, petulant. How could she still affect me like this?

"Do you know where he is? Nobody has heard from him."

"You mean he hasn't called you. Why don't you ask your husband about good old Rick?" Whiny had become mean.

"I did."

I just looked at her.

"He said, 'Ask Jake.' "

"So here you are."

"Well?"

"Your husband is a dangerous man, but you probably know that."

"I think he's gone off the deep end. This new project in the Everglades, the . . ."

"The casino."

She stopped wandering and looked at me. "He told you about that?"

"Right down to the last crap table and the charter buses from Punta Gorda."

"And the rest of it?"

"The rest?"

"Besides the gambling."

"The town, of course. The expanded condos, the golf course, the complete resort."

"Anything else?"

I tried to read the look on her face. "The museum," I said. "Nicky told me about the museum and the living habitat."

She stayed quiet. A thought was bouncing back and forth behind her black-rimmed blue eyes.

"What else is there, Gina?"

She wasn't talking. Whatever she was thinking, whatever else Nicky was up to, was locked inside. She came to me, looked up from under her dark lashes, closed her eyes, parted her pouty lips, and said, "There's this, just like always."

Then she kissed me with open, salty lips. I knew it was intended as a distraction. So it shouldn't have worked. I should have pressed her, cross-examined her, used all my skills to figure it out.

But just then, our tongues were dancing soft and slow, and while part of me wanted to toss her out the front door, if I could get it open, the rest of me, the part descended from the primordial soup, wanted something else entirely. I dipped a hand under her thighs and scooped her into my arms. She put her arms around my neck and giggled girlishly, then nuzzled my neck, as I carried her up the stairs.

"I should shower," she said, but I shook my head. I wanted her overheated, flushed, and pungent. In the bedroom, she took off her sneakers and peeled down her socks. She stripped off the pink leotard and white tights, without any help from me. She fell backward into the bed and waved me aboard. I dropped my cutoffs to the floor and did a perfect swan dive that ended with my head between her breasts.

"Nicky knows about us," she breathed into my ear.

I knew that.

"I promised I wouldn't see you anymore."

I knew that, too. Nicky had told me.

"He'd kill you. . . ."

I figured that out all by myself.

A new lover is anticipation tinged with tension. The promise of unknown thrills, the possibility of disappointment. A familiar but occasional lover is comfort enhanced by exhilaration. And now it was intensified, the thrill heightened by the risk, the risk as real as a razor-sharp blade. We carried into bed the past and our own lost innocence. Together, apart, together again. Physical pleasure plus a depth of feeling that can never exist in a one-night stand. We carried, too, the present, a high-wire balancing act, the sense that this time could be the last, the next breath the final one.

After a while, there was no sense of time or place. Just an awareness of rhythmic movement, a dizzying trail of lips and fingers, breasts and loins, electric sensations, gentle pulsations, and firm pressures of two lovers who know themselves and each other. The pace increased, breaths chugging faster. Our bodies joined in a fury of urgency, conscious thoughts lost in the roar of each other's engine, a syncopated meshing of gears, turning faster, thrusting deeper, clenching harder. In one explosive moment, the vise of her legs tightened, and she bit down hard on my lower lip, and her body and mine flowed into one.

I lay there on top of her, a drop of blood falling from my lip onto her breast. I kissed the spot, salty and sweet from the sweat and blood.

"My legs are shaking, Jake. I couldn't stand up if I had to."

"You don't have to."

"Does that mean I can stay?"

"As long as you want, or until you have to make dinner for your husband, whichever comes first."

"I don't make him dinner. That's what servants are for."

Ah, how quickly they learn. "But Nicky will want his lovely wife at the table."

She squiggled out from under me and gave me a shove. "Jerk! You can't let it be, can you? I'm here with you in the afterglow of the deepest emotional experience I've maybe ever had, and you take a cheap shot like that."

I rolled onto my back and locked my hands behind my head. Above me, the paddle fan *whompety-whomped* through its turns. I tried to keep my eye on one of the blades. It made me think of a machete. "Just thought it might be nice to welcome you back to the planet Earth after the talk about staying."

She propped herself up on an elbow and looked me in the eyes. "You mean you don't want me?"

"In a court of law, my actions would give rise to a contrary inference. A pretty big rise, as it were."

"I mean it, Jake. If I left Nicky, would you want me?"

"What do you mean?"

"Like permanently."

"Gina, with you, nothing is 'like permanently.' "

"Except you, Jake."

"If I'm so permanent, why do you keep leaving?"

"I told you before. Because you never asked me to stay."

"Look, Gina, it's a little late in the game for soap-opera dialogue. 'All this time it was you, Jake.' Too many years, too many Rick Gondoliers. It's too late to turn back the clock."

She ran a pink fingernail over my chest. "I didn't come here to ask about Rick. I came to see if you still cared."

"Why do you need reassurance? You know I do."

"Do you love me?"

The paddle fan kept making its circles. The fingernail kept making its figure eights. My mouth kept closed.

"Jake?"

I was sucking my swollen lower lip. "What difference does it make?"

"You do love me. Why can't you say it?"

"Okay, let's say, hypothetically, I loved you as much as Tristan loved Iseult."

"Who?"

"From mythology . . ."

"Naturally. Love is pure myth to the blockhead, Jake Lassiter."

"Tristan was a great knight whose job was to fetch the beautiful Iseult from Ireland and bring her back to King Mark in Cornwall who wanted to marry her. On the ship, Tristan and Iseult unwittingly drank a love potion and fell hopelessly in love."

"Same thing used to happen to me with Chardonnay."

"Hush now and listen. Tristan becomes a knight at the Round Table and has a passionate affair with Iseult, who now is married to the king."

"Sounds like us. Are you making this up?"

"No, when I wasn't banging heads on the practice field, I took Mythology 101 in college. One day Tristan is wounded by a poison spear. Iseult has great healing powers, so he sends for her. He desperately tries to hang on, and she sets sail to reach him. But he is falsely told that she is not aboard the ship, and, alas, he gives up hope and dies before she reaches him."

"Alas?"

"On finding his body, she kisses him and dies of grief, falling beside her lover."

"Is there a moral to this story, Jake?"

"Sure. Tristan was a true romantic. He yearned for this woman he could not have, except for stolen kisses in brief, secret moments. He lived a life of loneliness without her. No other woman ever measured up to his idealized view of his love goddess. Eventually, the notion that she would not come to his side killed him."

"I get it," Gina said. "You don't want to be like Tristan, right?"

"Yeah, and I'd also like to avoid poison spears."

"But you do live a lonely life, Jake. You reject other women because you're waiting for me. You're living like Tristan, but you don't have to. You could have me, but you're afraid to ask."

It had gotten dark outside the windows. The neighborhood mockingbird began *troo-loop, troo-looping*. The fan still made its endless droning circles. "Okay, I've spent half my life waiting for you to come back and the other half afraid that you would."

She smiled down at me. "How big are your closets, anyway?"

"Closets?"

"For my clothes, silly. You wouldn't believe how much room I need. I'd get rid of most of the gowns, the opening-night outfits. I'd never get you to take me to the opera, anyway, though it might do you some good. I can keep the furs and ski stuff in storage. I'd have to, since it's always so sticky in here. You're going to have to get air-conditioning sooner or later. No more of that stuff about how coral-rock walls keep out the heat, and . . ."

Some long-forgotten lyrics about letting a woman in your life popped into my head, something about her redecorating your home from the cellar to the dome.

". . . Jake, maybe it's time to think about moving. There's a new high rise on Waterway Drive where each apartment has its own elevator."

Did she say high rise?

"A condo? You want me to go to meetings where they decide how many pounds your poodle can weigh and what time you have to turn off the stereo?"

"It's time you became domesticated."

"Like you?"

"Are you being sarcastic?"

"Does Joe Paterno know football?"

"Why do you get like this just when we're getting close?"

"Because if I don't, I'll end up getting stung. Sooner or later, you'll leave. And if you didn't, I would. We're like those little magnetic chips the kids use in science experiments. Once the chips get too close, they peel off in different directions."

She rolled out of bed and stood up. "What is it you lawyers say in court? 'Let the record reflect . . .' "

"Yeah, what about it?"

"Well, let the record reflect I offered to stay, to come to you, to be with you, now and forever. Let—"

"Forever? Gina, with you, forever lasts as long as this season's hemlines."

"See, Jake? You can't take it. You always thought you wanted me, but I knew that once I was available, you'd run. I'm going to tell you anyway. Let the record reflect that I love you. I always have. And maybe you think it sounds like a soap opera, but that's the way it is. It's always been you, Jake."

She dressed hurriedly, heading down the stairs carrying her sneakers. "So long, Jake," she called back, over her shoulder. "Maybe I'll see you later. And maybe I won't."

Chapter 18

Buzzards' Peak

DURING THE NIGHT, THE WIND PICKED UP. SWHIRLING GUSTS FROM the northwest, humming and whistling and trilling a wintertime song. The trees moaned in protest. Twigs snapped and were pulled away from their mothers. Lids of garbage cans rolled down Kumquat Street. Green coconuts thumped to the ground and careened like bowling balls against picket fences. In my neighbor's yard, a gate with a broken latch blew open and banged shut.

Our second cold front of the season. Arctic air moving down from Canada, a deep freeze in the Midwest. This was the mother of all cold fronts as far as Florida was concerned, dipping far south, freezing the citrus groves hard, bringing snow flurries to Orlando, and giving us a nighttime frost as far south as Key Largo.

By morning, the wind was due north and holding strong, not even suggesting that it would begin clocking toward the east and warmer air. The sky was a brittle blue and cloudless, and Miamians were agog with the novelty of it all. The graphics guys at the *Miami Journal* had icicles dripping from the masthead. The weather gal on the morning TV show gave frostbite advice, and a crop specialist fretted about the winter tomato and strawberry crop.

In my Coconut Grove neighborhood of small, older houses, a different smell was in the air. The fragrance of hibiscus was replaced by the smoke from fireplaces. Inside, my old coral-rock house was

warm and comfy; only a layer of frost on the windows revealed just
how cold it was. I dug out my wool suit, the conservative gray
herringbone, and polished my black wing tips. I chose a white shirt
and a gray tie with a rose-colored pattern.

I made a breakfast of shredded wheat with slices of yellow star
fruit, fresh-squeezed orange juice, and a cup of coffee, black. I
skimmed the headlines in the *Journal*—more Rolex robbers mugging
drivers at gas stations for their watches, the head of Planned Par-
enthood quitting because she became unexpectedly pregnant—then
grabbed my bag and took off.

The upholstery in my antiquated chariot was cold and stiff, cracking when I sat down. The engine coughed and hacked and sputtered
and said to hell with it a couple of times until I coaxed her into
life. I let the old gal warm up, whispering sweet nothings about a
new wax job while the defroster blew noxious air at the windshield.
The clutch rebelled when I put her in gear and tried to bounce my
left knee into my jaw.

With the frost melting and the engine backing off, I took my
usual shortcut through the south Grove, from Poinciana up Doug-
las, passing Royal Palm, Palmetto, Avocado, and Loquat, hanging
a right on Thomas by the old Negro Cemetery, then scooting over
to Hibiscus, and north a block to Grand. Morning rush hour was
building with rich white folks from Old Cutler Drive, Cocoplum,
and Gables Estates cutting through the black Grove to get downtown, so I swung left on Matilda, and then right on Oak, which
becomes Tigertail, and takes me right to the entrance of I-95 just
north of Seventeenth Avenue. Of course, I could have headed north
on U.S. 1 to get to the same place, but I never take the straight
path when a serpentine route will get me there thirty seconds faster.
Besides, I was running late, and Abe Socolow hates to be kept
waiting.

There are three courthouses in Miami, to the utter confusion of
citizens called to jury duty. Our town is the venue of choice for
international drug dealers, as well as a convenient place to bring to
trial various savings-and-loan scoundrels and notorious presidents
of banana republics. This prompted the federal government to add
a bunch of judges and build a new courthouse connected to the
FDR-era post office that housed the old one. Sometimes, prospec-

tive jurors summoned to hear fender benders in state court inexplicably end up there. Baffled, they watch busloads of shackled Latino cocaine cowboys hustled into the building for their arraignments, the good citizens wondering if they've been transported to some Central American principality.

For big trials, the feds still use the old Central Courtroom, a spacious two-story affair with coffered ceilings, dark wainscoting, red velvet draperies, and a hand-carved witness box. On the wall, dating from the early forties, is a twenty-six-foot-long pastel mural depicting our state's past. Indians, fishermen, farm laborers, beauty queens, fruit growers—a joyous rainbow of different-colored Floridians living and working together. Like many of the symbols foisted on us by government, the mural is a pleasant deception.

Twenty-five blocks away, in the civic center complex, an above-ground walkway connects the county jail to the Justice Building, a misnomer to be sure. Inside, state judges process an endless stream of traffic, misdemeanor, and felony cases, shoveling defendants into and out of our overcrowded prisons. The building houses a slice of Miami's underbelly, hustlers and losers, drifters and grifters. The voices inside speak in a polyglot of languages from the Caribbean, Central and South America. The corridors teem with store robbers, home burglars, small-time crack dealers, wife-beaters, drunk drivers, and an occasional murderer.

The state attorney's office is in the building, and usually Abe Socolow can be found there, either trying capital cases or conferring with his major-crimes prosecutors. But for reasons related to history and custom, the grand jury meets downtown in the civil courthouse. It is there that evidence of corruption is heard, prosecutors unveiling their major investigations for twenty-three citizens chosen to determine who shall be indicted.

The county courthouse dates from the 1920s. It is a limestone tower, a wedding cake of rectangular floors growing smaller from bottom to top. Back before there was a Justice Building, both criminal and civil cases were heard in the county courthouse. The jail was at the top, then the highest point in the city. The state attorney still maintains a small office in what used to be the jail, and it is there that Abe Socolow spends much of his time when the grand jury is in session.

Socolow's office is small but has the illusion of size because of windows where bars used to be on three sides, windows twenty-six floors above Flagler Street. A parapet with gargoyles surrounds the windows, and in a surreal fusion of life and art, black vultures perch there. The vultures arrive each winter and depart each spring, just like the tourists. And every year, the jokes downtown are the same.

I see the courthouse buzzards are out in force today.

The birds?

No, the lawyers.

A lone receptionist, unsmiling and bored, sat at a desk in the anteroom on the top floor. If I brightened her day, she did her best to hide it. She eyed my oversize duffel bag, buzzed her boss, then waved me in.

Abe Socolow sat behind his battleship-gray desk made of the finest alloys the state could buy secondhand. The desk was covered with files. Each file had a colorful sticker identifying the case by number. Socolow didn't stand up, shake my hand, or whistle "Dixie." "I've been expecting you, Jake."

Now what did that mean? Of course he'd been expecting me. I'd called him. Or did Nicky Florio call him too? Maybe I was paranoid, but was Socolow giving me an odd look? Sizing me up, like he'd never seen me before. Gee, I'd been there when he won his first capital case. I'd been too close, in fact, sitting first chair at the defense table.

"Welcome to buzzards' peak," he greeted me. His voice grated, always had, the sound of metal shearing metal. He shot a look toward the windows. Outside, three vultures were balanced on the parapet, watching half a dozen buddies soar in the thermal air currents around the building. The black birds had white down-turned beaks and bald, scaly red heads like wild turkeys. A couple of the bigger fellows had six-foot wingspans. "Sit down, Jake. That's quite a load you're toting."

Was that a smile or a sneer?

Socolow's suit was the same color as the vultures' feathers but didn't fit as well. He always looked skinny in his full-cut Brooks Brothers attire. His shirt was white, the tie black with the usual pattern of silver handcuffs. Until recently, he wore rimless eyeglasses. A campaign consultant must have suggested contacts, and now I noticed the dark pouches the glasses had kept hidden. His dark thinning hair revealed a high, furrowed forehead. He was tall and narrow, with slightly hunched shoulders. Not a photogenic politician, just a hardworking career prosecutor who finally got a shot at the brass ring when his boss took a spill.

I slung the duffel bag to the floor and sat down in a state-issued lumbar-busting chair. "I wanted to thank you for stopping by during the Tupton trial."

"Nicky asked me to do it, so I showed the colors. A little moral support for a friend."

Nicky. Friend. I measured his words and mannerisms.

"I didn't realize the two of you were close."

"Never were, but you know how it is in politics, strange bedfellows and all that. The reality is you can't run for office without a sizable war chest. Do you know what thirty-second TV spots cost in Miami these days?"

"Must be difficult," I said, "with the thousand-dollar limit on campaign contributions."

"The law's supposed to prevent undue influence, right, but what's the effect of it? Only the wealthy or those with established political machines can run. Look, if a guy's worth ten million dollars, he can spend two of it on his campaign, and it's perfectly legal. But if I have two friends who want to give me a million each to run, I'm violating the law."

"Life's unfair," I agreed.

"Everybody knows the campaign laws are bullshit. There hasn't been a candidate the last twenty years who hasn't taken unreported cash, services, whatever. It's a fact of life."

I took a deep breath and tried to say it. I had wanted him to make it easier for me, and he had, but still, I couldn't get the words out.

"You all right, Jake?"

"Sure, why?"

"I don't know. You look a little tired, run-down maybe. Been working too hard?"

"Maybe. Doing a lot of work for Florio Enterprises," I said.

Hint, hint. C'mon, Abe, ask for the money.

"That's what I hear," he said.

"Yeah, a lot of work for Florio Enterprises," I repeated.

He leaned forward over his desk, and on cue, I leaned forward in my chair. I thought he was going to whisper something, but his voice was still the familiar rasp, loud and irritating. "How long have we known each other, Jake?"

"Long time. I'd just sneaked through night law school, barely passed the Bar, and the P.D.'s Office gave me a job because they needed some heft on the touch football team. You were young, but already a hotshot."

"You remember the first case we had against each other?"

"*State* v. *Fonseca*. What'd you charge him with, extortion or obstruction of justice?"

"Both. You were highly creative. Of course, you had to be. Here's your client facing trial in a fencing scam, and he mails a five-pound cow's tongue to the informant."

"He was *accused* of mailing it."

Socolow's laugh was a horse's whinny. "Yeah, after we learned his brother-in-law owns a wholesale meat business . . ."

"Which you got into evidence."

". . . along with the fact that the tongue arrives at the informant's house in an L.L. Bean carton that was originally addressed to your client."

"He'd ordered some waders for trout fishing," I explained.

"You remember your closing argument?"

In a moment, it came back to me, and I raised my voice in lawyerly indignation. " 'No one is that stupid! Obviously, my client has been framed. An enemy may well have gone through his garbage, retrieved the incriminating carton, and sent the meat.' "

"That was it," Socolow said, "the last-ditch effort of a desperate lawyer."

"What else could I do? I was just trying to stir up some reasonable doubt."

"You must have done it, because Fonseca walked."

"I remember. He sent me a smoked turkey that Christmas."

Socolow nearly smiled. It didn't seem to break his face. We shared a quiet moment of unspoken reminiscence. Finally, Socolow said, "We're just dancing around it here, aren't we, Jake?"

"Like Fred and Ginger," I agreed.

"So, you have something for me, or not?"

"Yeah, I guess so."

Outside the south window, two vultures soared high in the updrafts, huge wings spread wide, then came to rest on the little balcony that surrounded the top floor. The birds seemed to like Socolow's office. Maybe it was the view. Maybe it was the company.

"I'm waiting, Jake."

"Like having sex the first time, I know what goes where, I'm just not sure about the preliminaries."

Socolow leaned back and laced his fingers behind his head. "Let me help you out. You don't have to kiss me first."

"Okay, Abe. I've got something for you. Something from Nicky Florio, but I guess you know that."

"From Nicky? Why did I think it was from you, personally?"

"Don't know."

"And this something, I take it, is in the canvas bag at your feet, the one which conspicuously says in large print that it's the property of the Miami Dolphins."

"That's it."

"And whatever is in this bag, Jake, is it a gift?"

"A gift?"

"Yes, what is the purpose of your delivering this rather dilapidated old bag and its contents?"

"To help you in the campaign, of course. To put your face on billboards and buy TV spots where you promise to execute murderers within thirty days of trial, or even before trial, if opinion polls favor it."

"Ah yes." Abe nodded, contentedly. "Are there any strings attached?"

"I didn't think we would get into that."

Socolow rapped his fingers on his metallic desk, *rat-a-tat-tat*. Why did it sound like the drumroll of a funeral dirge? Again, he looked out the windows, then back to me. He was watching a lone black bird, its wings swept back, as it circled the courthouse. "A Cuban fortune-teller once told me that the vultures are the souls of lawyers doing endless penance."

"Doubt it. Lawyers never repent."

He turned back to me. "You and I share the same cynicism, Jake."

There was a thought behind those dark eyes, but what was it? "The birds have their own predators. When threatened, do you know what a vulture does?"

"Gets a lawyer bird to write a nasty letter," I guessed.

"Vomits on its enemy and spoils its appetite."

"Same thing," I said.

Socolow studied me a moment before speaking. A wind gust rattled the window on the north side. "To accept this token of your client's friendship, I must know if a quid pro quo is expected."

"You mean is this just an illegal campaign contribution or outright bribery?"

He raised a hand and wrinkled his forehead. "Jake, Jake, Jake. Please."

I stood and walked to the window facing east. Even with the newer, taller downtown skyscrapers, I could see a slice of the bay, crystalline blue, topped with whitecaps. "You don't want to dance, Abe, so here it is. You take the gift, and when the state cabinet turns to you for an opinion on a certain matter involving Cypress Estates, you come down on Nicky Florio's side."

I couldn't see his face, so I took the silence to mean he was thinking about it.

"And if I take the gift and don't go Nicky's way?"

"The governor will have to pick someone to fill your unexpired term."

He looked puzzled.

"Knowing Florio, you'd be harder to find than Judge Crater."

Might as well add extortion to bribery.

"I see," Socolow said. He left his chair and joined me at the window. On the bay, a sailboat slid across the whitecaps on a close reach. I wanted to be on deck, bundled up against the cold wind. I wanted to be anywhere but here. Magically, the boat disappeared behind one of the skyscrapers.

I turned and looked at Socolow, barely a foot away. He put a hand on my shoulder, an unusual gesture for a guy who'd have to warm up to be called a cold fish. There was a hint of sorrow in his eyes.

Then the screeching sound.

A high-pitched electronic wail.

Coming from him.

And me.

"You're wired!"

He said it. And so did I.

The door to the reception room swung open and banged off the wall. Two men in suits flew through the door. One of them, a barrel-chested guy in brown plaid with a brush cut, looked familiar. I'd seen him around the Justice Building. County detective or F.D.L.E., maybe. He got to me the first. "Jacob Lassiter, you are under arrest for the attempted bribery of a public official and other charges to be later specified. You have the right to remain silent. Anything you say may be used against you in a court of law. You have the right to an attorney, and if you cannot afford an attorney, one will be provided to you." He turned to the smaller man. "Hank, frisk him." Brush Cut turned back to me and smiled malevolently. "Okay, asshole, assume the position."

I spread my legs and leaned against one of the windows, my palms pressed to the glass. A black buzzard on the parapet swung its long neck around and gave me a beady-eyed look. Lucky bird. Nobody was smacking his private parts.

"Hey!" Hank yelled. "What the hell's this?"

"Can't tell you," I answered, over my shoulder, still watching the bird. "I'm remaining silent."

Hank was under my herringbone suit coat, now pulling out my shirt. I felt a ripping as he yanked the tape off, taking some of the skin of my back with it.

"He's wired!" Hank announced.

Socolow leaned against the window. "What gives, Jake?" Now the vulture was looking at Socolow.

"Oh shit!" It was Brush Cut. I sneaked another peak. He stood next to Socolow's desk, dumping the contents of the duffel bag onto the floor. "Hey, asshole, what the hell is this?"

Apparently, as far as Brush Cut was concerned, I had a new name. Even worse, I was responding to it. "Laundry," I answered. He kicked some tattered Penn State sweatpants across the room. "Hey, careful," I warned him. "Those have sentimental value."

Brush Cut was cursing, and Hank was muttering to himself, but he didn't tell me to turn around or put my hands down, so I stayed put. I'd seen enough angry cops to do what I was told and not do anything else until I was told to do that, too. Socolow was still next to me, waiting. I said, "Abe, I had to find out if you were dirty. Nicky Florio wanted to buy you. At least, that's what he told me. I was supposed to be the bagman. He wants your vote on something very big."

"Cypress Estates?"

"Yeah."

Socolow shook his head. "Doesn't wash. He's got my vote on that, and he doesn't have to pay for it."

"You don't understand. Not just the housing and the resort." I took a deep breath. "Casino gambling, too."

"I know."

"You do?" I was floored. "How do you know?"

"Florio took me into his confidence. He'd given me some support, drummed up contributions in the building industry, all reported, all aboveboard. I researched the issue to see if I could support him. Look, a decent lawyer can argue either side, we both know that. But here, it's really clear. His leases are in order, and the federal law favors his position. I don't think the state can stop casino gambling on Indian land. I told him I'd support him with the cabinet, no sweat, and it won't cost him a dime. As far as I'm concerned, he can move Las Vegas out there."

Now I turned around without asking anybody for permission. Brush Cut was tossing my T-shirts across the room and peering into the duffel bag, hoping to find something more incriminating than a sweat-stained jockstrap.

"I don't get it, Abe," I said. "Why would Nicky want me to bribe you to do something you're going to do anyway?"

"Well, that's not the way Nicky sees it. He told me you were coming to offer me a bribe all right, but not on his behalf."

I waited.

"For yourself, Jake."

"I still don't get it."

He seemed to be thinking about how much to tell me. I watched Brush Cut take a pair of scissors from Socolow's desk and begin cutting the lining out of the duffel bag. "You're wasting your time," I told him.

He scowled at me. "Really, asshole?" He picked up the phone and dialed a number. After a moment, he said, "Gunther here, what'd you find?" He listened a moment. "How much?" He paused again, then smiled. I was hoping he wouldn't smile at me like that. He hung up the phone and walked over to the window, squaring his shoulders and looking me in the eye. We were the same height. He was ten years older, but in good shape. Square shoulders, flat gut.

He reached into his suit pocket and pulled out a blue-backed piece of paper. "Do you own a motor vehicle, a 1968 Oldsmobile 442, license plate J-U-S-T-I-C-E with a question mark at the end? Is that right, *JUSTICE*?"

"Yeah, why?"

"What a shitty plate. Like the dickheads who used to wear the American flag on their jeans." He handed me the paper. "I'm serving you with a copy of the search warrant obtained for your motor vehicle. The search was carried out in the parking lot across the street just a few minutes ago. In the wheel well in the trunk, instead of a spare tire, there was found a substantial quantity of fifty-dollar bills. It's being inventoried now, but apparently it's in the range of a million bucks."

I turned to Socolow. "See, Abe, that corroborates what I've been telling you."

Socolow was thinking about it. He seemed profoundly unhappy. "Not the way I see it. Nicky Florio gave us a sworn statement saying you and somebody named . . ."

"Gondolier," Gunther helped out.

"Yeah, you and Gondolier skimmed a million dollars from the bingo hall. You were supposed to be the company's lawyer and Gondolier the manager of the hall, but the two of you ran your own little scam with the cash."

I was shaking my head, as it was becoming clear how Nicky Florio had framed me.

"Gondolier's missing," Socolow said, "and here you are with the money in the trunk of your car. According to Florio, you planned to offer me a piece of the action to buy some protection when he blew the whistle on you."

"And you believed that?"

"I told him I'd known you a long time, and I couldn't believe you were a thief, but that I'd follow through. When you called to see me, I set up the sting. But the way it looks to me, you changed your mind."

"I did?"

"You show up without the money but wired, trying to incriminate me on tape. You didn't know I'd already given my blessing to the gambling, so you want me to agree to a bribe. If I had, you'd have dirt on me, and that was your protection. You wanted to compromise me, not pay me."

"Abe! You can't believe . . ."

Socolow left me by the window and walked to his desk, his shoulders slouching. "You got greedy. You're dirty, Jake, and you thought you could buy me."

"That's so stupid. Everybody knows you can't be bought."

"Then what were you doing with the bag and the wire? What the fuck were you trying to do to me, Jake?"

"Like I said, Florio told me you were for sale. I didn't believe it, but I just had to know. I had to know if I could trust you, or if you already belonged to Nicky Florio."

"And if I had turned it down cold?"

"I would have told you the truth. Everything. Including what happened to Gondolier."

"I'm listening."

But I was finished blabbing. I'd already said too much. In a minute, they could add accessory to murder to the charges, or maybe worse. "I think I'd like to talk to a lawyer now."

Gunter was in my face again. He called me a familiar two-syllable name to get my attention, then got down to business. "Additionally, Mr. Lassiter, you're under arrest for the crime of grand larceny. You have the right to remain silent. You have—"

"Oh shut up!"

Gunther's face lost most of his expression, and there hadn't been much to start with. I started past him toward Socolow. I never saw the short right. Gunther threw it from his hip and caught me squarely in the solar plexus. A sucker punch. I folded in half and dropped to a knee, gasping. I couldn't get a breath in. My stomach heaved.

I heard Socolow's voice. "Gunther, Jesus Christ, was that necessary?"

"Hate the asshole's license plate," he answered.

The wave of nausea hit me quick and hard. Two heaves, then I let it go, soiling Gunther's black brogans like a spooked vulture.

"Goddamn it!" Gunther backed away, shaking his shoes, leaving a trail across the state of Florida's gray industrial carpeting. "Cuff him, Hank."

I was still on one knee.

"Jesus, let him clean up first," Socolow said.

My old buddy. He thought I was a thief, but he didn't want to deprive me of my dignity. Once I got out of this jam, I would thank him, take him out for steaks and beer. I would also kick Gunther's ass from here to Sopchoppy.

Socolow took me by the arm and helped me up. He pointed to a door leading to his private bathroom. I nodded, walked unsteadily to the door, went in, and closed the door. I turned on the water and washed out my mouth. I threw what passes for cold water on my face. There was an old-fashioned eight-paned window that had been painted shut, probably during the Eisenhower administration.

I wanted some fresh air.

That's all.

I wasn't going to escape. After all, where was there to go?

I strained to push the window up. It didn't budge. I flexed my knees and got my center of gravity lower. The window frame began to creak, or was that my knee?

"Hey, Lassiter, hurry the hell up." Gunther's impatient voice.

I flushed the toilet, and while the water was rushing, flipped the lock on the door, hoping they didn't hear the click. Back at the window, I tried again, and this time, the dried paint cracked away from the window frame, and it shuddered open. A blast of cold air smacked me in the face. I took several drags.

I bent over and stuck my head out. The south side of the building. A splendid view of the elevated Metrorail tracks, the high-rises of Brickell Avenue running along the bay, and farther south, heavily wooded Coconut Grove, where only this morning I was cozy and safe.

There was an impatient *knock-knock* at the rest room door.

"Be right out," I hollered.

And I was, stepping right out onto an old balcony three hundred feet above Flagler Street, stepping out into knee-deep birdshit, stepping out among my feathered friends, who eyed me warily, spreading their wings and hopping a safe distance away along the parapet, probably all thinking the same thought: What's the asshole up to now?

Chapter 19

Death of the Dinosaurs

It was a vulture's-eye view, looking down at the tops of buildings, Biscayne Bay peeking from behind the modern sky-scrapers. Above me, a jumbo jet roared, its gear down, on final approach to the airport. I imagined the passengers, foreheads pressed to windows, expectant with new adventures.

I took two steps along the balcony and heard a cracking under my feet. The old building was nearly as fragile as Nicky Florio's new condos. Gingerly, I approached the parapet and leaned over.

Whoa. A long way down. But the first few floors would be easy. The balconies jutted out with each succeeding lower floor. I took another crunching step, this time because I was in the deep doo-doo, as George Bush might say, but here, it was literally true. I swung a leg over the rail, and then a second one. I grabbed a gargoyle covered with bird droppings and hung there a moment. Maybe it was the wind, but I thought I heard the gargoyle laugh at me. As my herringbone suit coat flapped in the breeze, I dropped to the balcony below.

And then did it again, and again.

I heard shouts from above.

I shimmied along the wall and jumped through open space—only about four feet—to an adjoining balcony. The next few floors had no balconies, but there were ledges, maybe eighteen inches wide, and the limestone blocks of the building itself were ridged, and if I didn't look down, I could grab the ledge, put a foot on the ridge, and keep on going, hand over hand.

My hands were calloused from windsurfing and twenty years of bench presses, but they were still getting roughed up. By the time I had gotten halfway down, I had reached another full balcony. I was winded and stopped to rest. I put my hands on my knees and bent over, sucking in air. I was nearly ready to go over the side again when I noticed the floor-to-ceiling double window facing the balcony. Streaked with years of grime, it was latched from the inside by a simple brass hook. I jiggled the window. Once, twice, three times, and the hook fell away.

The windows opened to the outside. I stepped inside and was enveloped in a set of drapes that must have weighed a ton, half of which was dust. I heard someone talking, fought to stifle a sneeze, found the opening between the drapes, and peered out.

A courtroom.

A few street people snoozing in the gallery.

Some exhibits plastered to a blackboard, maps of streets, some plastic overlays.

A lawyer I didn't recognize standing near the bench, and a middle-aged man in a suit sitting on the witness stand, droning on about the value per square foot of commercial property along Arthur Godfrey Road.

Judge Dixie Lee Boulton on the bench, pretending to pay attention as she read the morning paper, occasionally grimacing at something the witness said, or was that a facial tic?

A condemnation trial, the owners of property trying to get more money from the county than it wanted to pay when it took slivers of their land to widen a street. Even more boring than a slip-and-fall, probably a dead heat with a dog-bite case.

That was it, except for the folks sitting in the jury box, which backed up against the heavy, dusty drapes where I now stood. No way I could get out of here. I turned around, pushed the window open again, and peeked outside.

Whoops.

A uniformed Metro officer stood on the neighboring balcony. He faced the other way, looked up, looked down, then turned my way just as I ducked back inside and closed the window. I found the opening in the drapes again and slid into an empty chair in the back row of the jury box.

"Sorry I'm late," I whispered to the middle-aged woman next to me. "I'm the new alternate."

She patted me on the arm. "You didn't miss a thing."

I listened attentively to the morning's testimony, fighting the urge, first, to object to leading questions, and then to doze off. When Judge Boulton called the noon recess, I marched along with the others behind a bailiff who was older than the courthouse. We all piled into an elevator and headed to the Quarterdeck Lounge. Why not? After what I'd been through, I figured the county should buy me lunch.

My mind listed the places I couldn't go. It was longer than where I could.

I couldn't go to my office. There'd be two deputies sitting in the reception room. I couldn't go home. Or to Granny's or Charlie's. And I couldn't drive anywhere because the cops had my car. But I could use the phone.

At the Quarterdeck, I changed a five-dollar bill into a handful of quarters and began making some calls. I started with Cindy, my loyal secretary.

"Jeez, where are you, *jefe?* Did you kill somebody or what? You wouldn't believe what's going on over here."

I told her I believed it, and tell whoever asked that I was headed to Cancún.

I called Granny in the Keys. She had a retired merchant seaman waiting for her in a skiff, and in a shallow bay thereabouts was a bonefish calling her name, and maybe she was going to get a tattoo later today, and by the way, how come the police called, asking about her ne'er-do-well kin?

I called Charlie, and his recorded voice told me he was dissecting brains over at the morgue, hoping to find some causal link to cerebral hemorrhages.

I called Gina, who yelped, "Omigod, Jake, did you really steal all that money, and even if you didn't, Nicky is angry as a bull with its balls in a cinch," an expression I figured she picked up when she was engaged to a rodeo star.

Then I called Nicky Florio, because I didn't have anybody else to call. I caught him in the trailer at a construction site in Kendall. Ticky-tacky town houses all in a row.

"You set me up, Florio," I said when he picked up the phone. "Maybe you can't kill me because of Gina, but you could sure as hell frame me and let Socolow send me away."

I heard him breathe into the phone. "Who says I can't kill you?" And then he was gone.

I walked across the street into the government-center complex. Just another suit hanging around the County Commission Building. Probably only one of a dozen guys who had bribery on his mind that morning. I took the escalator to the Metrorail station, slipped some more quarters into the slot, and headed to the next level. A security guard looked right past me.

A gleaming train was tooting its horn as it pulled in.

Northbound.

It really didn't make any difference.

I got aboard. Nearly empty. A family of European tourists, Germans maybe, the husband in those open sandals with thin brown socks, a wife and two boys in shorts, Mickey Mouse T-shirts, and instant sunburns. The man had a camera bag slung over a shoulder, his passport sticking halfway out of his pants pocket. If they got out of town with their traveler's checks, they'd be lucky.

I liked Metrorail, a clean, smooth billion-dollar elevated train that was hurting for business. I rode it now to the northwest, skimming the tops of the trees through Overtown, cutting by the Justice Building, where I imagined a warrant for my arrest was being typed by a bleary-eyed secretary. I stayed on the train all the way to Hialeah and the grand old racetrack, which had come back from near-bankruptcy.

I bought grandstand admission, buried my face in a *Racing Form*, and bet the number-three horse the first four races, losing eight dollars. I ate a hot dog with chili and sat there in the seedy charm of the place where bougainvillea crept along crumbling balustrades.

There were still a few hundred pink flamingos on the island in the center of the turf. Even though they feed the birds a mixture of rice, shrimp, and dog biscuits, the rascals tend to fly away, preferring the wilds of the Everglades and what's left of the Keys.

So after a while, the bird handlers began clipping the pink feathers, grounding the flamingos, or at least keeping them on the racetrack grounds. A fancy prison.

It took me half the afternoon and two more nags out of the money to figure out what to do. I rode Metrorail south, getting off this time at the hospital complex. It was a short walk to Bob Hope Road and the morgue.

I went in the back way, pounding on the metal doors until a young assistant medical examiner came by, his gloved hands bloody. I told him I wanted to see Charlie Riggs, and he pointed to the lab. I walked in, adjusting to the smell—part formaldehyde, part rotting tissue—and found Charlie sitting on a high stool, huddled over a counter, using a scalpel to slice tiny slivers of brain tissue and examine them under a microscope. In a rubber bucket next to him, a dozen brains, resembling a bushel of cauliflower, waited their turn.

I told him where I'd been and what I'd done, skipping only the part where I hurled chunks onto the big cop's shoes, and he took the brain he'd been working on and gently placed it back in the bucket. He listened and occasionally asked a question. As we talked, several assistant medical examiners stopped by to pay their respects. Though retired, Charlie was still a legend among canoemakers in the red-brick death house.

A mustachioed man in a lab coat asked Charlie to examine thirty-three stab wounds on a murdered prostitute. We stepped over to a chrome tray that held what had been an overweight woman in her thirties. Her torso and thighs bore multiple puncture wounds. Her arms were sliced where she had tried to defend herself. Chunks of her flesh were missing where the M.E. had taken dissections to follow the track of the blades. No weapon had been found. The young M.E. was confused by the different-shaped tracks and thought there had to be three weapons. That would be unusual and would probably indicate at least two assailants.

After a moment, Charlie said, "Two weapons only. A long-bladed vegetable knife, mistakenly called a butcher's knife by most policemen. That'd cover the large wounds. The small ones were likely made by an ice pick." Charlie examined a slide of the wound. "This one from her abdomen is the vegetable knife again. It just went in the same wound twice. The first time, the assailant pushed the blade down, the second time up. That's what gives it the saberlike appearance, but it's just a vegetable knife."

The young doc thanked the old doc, who turned back to me. "What are you going to do now?"

"Bring down Nicky Florio before he brings me down."

"How?"

We were interrupted by an Oriental woman in a white lab coat with an I.D. badge on a chain around her neck. She held a skull that resembled a coconut bashed by a sledgehammer. "Dr. Ling," Charlie said, with a slight bow.

"I'm having trouble determining which perforating gunshot wound was the initial one," she said.

Together, they examined the cracks in the eggshell-like fissures in the skull. From their conversation, I gathered that the victim was struck by two bullets from different guns. The victim was an innocent bystander in a shoot-out with police, and the good folks in the state attorney's office wanted to know if a cop or a robber pulled the trigger on the fatal shot. "It's the windowpane effect," Charlie said. "Imagine that you strike a pane of glass and get a fracture line. Hit the glass again in a different place, and the second fracture will stop where it meets the first fracture." Charlie traced an index finger over the longer crack. "Here's your trail of death."

Dr. Ling expressed her thanks, tucked the skull under her arm, and cheerfully headed back to her lab table.

"Now where were we?" Charlie asked, turning back to me.

"I was about to tell you how I was going to get Florio. First, by lining up some allies. The Micanopy Tribal Council won't be too pleased with Florio when they learn how he hoodwinked them out of their full ten percent."

"You're going to violate your client's confidence."

"Hey, I've done it before. Besides, we weren't in an attorney-client relationship at the time. More like murderer and accessory."

He chewed that over and didn't seem to disagree. "Okay, so what can the Micanopies do to help?"

"They can get me back to Florio's house in the Glades. No way I could find it otherwise. I'll take you along to sift and scrape, and maybe we'll find some speck of Rick Gondolier that can be used as evidence. Maybe the tribe can give me some manpower, help bring in Tiger and Diaz. If we've got the physical evidence, and if Diaz would roll over, I could nail both Tiger and Florio for the murder of Gondolier."

Charlie was cleaning his fingernails with a scalpel as he thought about it. "Too many 'ifs' and 'maybes.' "

"But that's not all. There's something else Florio is up to. He kept pressing me on what Gina had told me about his project in the Glades. Then she asked if Nicky told me about 'the rest of it.' There's something else Florio is hiding, something big." My eyes roamed around the lab. "I don't know what it is, but it's out there somewhere."

"Then go find it," Charlie said.

"I intend to, but I don't mind telling you that I'm more than a little worried."

"Worried?"

"Okay, scared. I had a nightmare last night that a head rolled across a table into my lap. When I looked down, it was *my* head."

"The dinosaurs may be back, Jake."

"Huh?"

"And we may be gone."

For a moment, I thought Charlie might have sliced too many brains, including his own. He produced a pipe from a pocket in his lab coat and sucked on the cold stem. "An asteroid may have led to the extinction of the dinosaurs, but it was an earlier one that led to their emergence."

"What does that have to do with Nicky Florio and—"

"Hush, now." Charlie removed his pipe and gestured toward space. "About two hundred million years ago, an asteroid hit a forest in Canada, creating a fireball fourteen hundred miles wide. Billions of tons of soot poured into the atmosphere. Years of darkness followed. The animals starved or froze when the temperatures plunged. Then the enormous amounts of carbon dioxide led to global warming, and in some untold thousands of years, the plants returned and dinosaurs developed. Millions of years go by, and another giant asteroid hits, and again much of life is wiped out, including the dinosaurs."

"Is there a point to this, Charlie?"

"Same as always. We're all going to die. Our species will un-doubtedly be wiped out when the next huge asteroid hits, if we don't do it to ourselves first. The end may come next year or a thousand years from now. Our individual lives are puny, meaning-less. So do the right thing. Seek the truth, *quaere verum*, and don't be afraid."

He gave me the keys to his pickup truck and wished me Godspeed. I told him I'd see him tomorrow, or if not, when the dinosaurs came home.

Chapter 20

A Drop in the Bucket

CHARLIE'S OLD DODGE PICKUP HAD MUDDY FENDERS, A JOUNCY ride, and squeaky shocks. It hadn't had a wheel alignment since Zsa Zsa Gabor was an ingenue. The radio was set on a big-band AM station, and the front seat was littered with week-old newspapers and a couple of paperback books. I threw the papers in a trash can, tossed a dog-eared copy of *The Corpse Had a Familiar Face* by Edna Buchanan into the glove compartment, and headed west on Tamiami Trail, playing tug-of-war with the steering wheel, which kept pulling right toward a muddy canal.

I fell in behind an eighteen-wheeler, which soon chugged ahead of me. I let a kid in a Trans Am zoom by me on the two-lane road. Going fifty in Charlie's truck on a straightaway was exciting enough. It also gave me time to figure what I was going to say to the chief.

The stiff breeze was rattling the thatched fronds of the chickee huts in the Micanopy village. The doll-making and basket-weaving booths were empty. Precious few tourists had paid their five dollars to observe Indian women sew their patchwork quilts or watch a husky young man wrestle a bored gator. It looked as if cobwebs were growing on the eight-passenger airboat—half-hour ride, seven dollars—and the restaurant wasn't dishing out much Indian fry bread.

Inside the information center, a one-story concrete-block building, I asked a dark-haired, heavyset girl in a turquoise skirt where to find the chief. She smiled, told me I meant the chairman of the tribe, and pointed down the corridor. I followed her directions, knocked on the thin, paneled door, and he coughed me inside.

Henry Osceola sat in his windowless office sucking on a cigarette. The office was decorated in no-frills clutter. Metal filing cabinets, mica desk, the walls bare except for a calendar from a Naples bank and a faded print of a marshy hammock at sunset.

He was a lanky man with a seamed, lived-in face and white hair pulled back in a ponytail. He could have been fifty or seventy or anywhere in between. He wore a blue knit shirt with a green crocodile on the breast, faded jeans with a beaded belt, and the same high-top basketball shoes favored by a guy with a shaved head in Chicago. His forearms were heavily veined and the color of Nicky Florio's mahogany furniture. The cigarette dangled from the corner of his mouth, and an ashtray on the desk held butts of a dozen more. No filters. He coughed at me a second time, hacked, then used a metal waste can as a spittoon.

Osceola looked at my herringboned self and informed me in a raspy voice that the tribe had all the insurance it was going to need for the next twenty years. I told him I was a lawyer, and he let me know that the airboat passengers all sign waivers, so I could go chase ambulances somewhere else, he had work to do. Then he opened a folder and began going through what looked like a stack of bills. He was writing checks, muttering to himself, oblivious to me. The nails of his thumb and index finger on his right hand were stained a deep yellow.

"I'm here about something else," I said. "Your dealings with Nicky Florio."

"You Florio's lawyer?"

"Yes. No. Well, I was."

"Not too sure of yourself, are you?" He looked up at me through a haze of cigarette smoke. "I don't remember you from the negotiations."

"I wasn't there. I want to talk to you about the ninety-nine-year lease."

There was the hint of a smile. "White man want to break treaty?"

I didn't know what to say.

He barked out a laugh. "That was a joke, Mr. Lawyer. Like the comedians on the cable." He pointed over his shoulder. "I installed the satellite dish for the village. One hundred twenty-three stations. Soccer games from Hungary. Parliament from London. Nude commercials from Scandinavia. Comedians on the pay channels, but of course we don't pay. The air is free, and if HBO sued us, we would say that the Great White Father in Washington granted us domain over the land, both to the core of the earth and to the stars in the sky."

He looked at me but didn't get a reaction. "That was a joke too. An Indian in an old Western might say, 'Great White Father.' So, I am being self-deprecating and sarcastic at the same time. Am I going too fast for you?"

I told him he had a better sense of humor than most CEOs I deal with, so it would take me a while to keep pace.

"Do you watch the comedians?" he asked.

I told him I liked Dennis Miller and Robin Williams, George Carlin and Richard Pryor. He nodded judiciously, as a chief, or tribal chairman, should.

"The African-American ones are my favorites," he said, after thinking about it. "Pryor especially. He expresses the pain. Eddie Murphy, too, but like a young man, all he thinks about is . . ." He made a motion of running his right thumb through a circle made of his left thumb and index finger. "Bill Cosby is too soft. No pain. As for his television program . . ." He shook his head sadly. "You are probably thinking that Native Americans have a natural affinity for African Americans."

"Certainly, both groups have been victimized."

"Victimized is such a sugarcoated euphemism for genocide, don't you think? Did you know that my tribe gave refuge to runaway slaves in the early 1800s?"

I shook my head.

"That, of course, led to attacks by the American troops. Neither the first nor the last." He took a deep drag on his cigarette, leaving him with a quarter-inch butt that disappeared between his thumb and finger. "What is your interest in the lease?"

"It's not my interest, really. It's yours. And your tribe's. And all the people of Florida."

He regarded me skeptically.

I regarded me skeptically.

Without taking his eyes from mine, Henry Osceola ground out the butt in the ashtray and pulled a fresh Camel from a pack on the desk. "Are you here on behalf of Mr. Florio?"

"No. He doesn't know I'm here. He wouldn't like it if he knew I wanted to help you."

Osceola ignored a plastic lighter on the desk and reached into his desk drawer for a six-inch-long wooden match. He struck his thumbnail to the phosporous tip and let the match burn for a moment before lighting his cigarette in the orange flame. Why did I get the feeling he was putting on a show for me?

"Ah," Henry Osceola said, "a turncoat. Like Kevin Costner in the movie with the wolves, you have abandoned the ways of the white man to help the Native American."

I couldn't help feeling that he was mocking me.

"Now what is it you have come to say, that the great white builder of condominiums is not to be trusted?"

"Yes, but more than that. If what I've been told is true, the lease is unconscionable. Is there a clause that allows Florio Enterprises to assign the lease without the tribe's consent?"

Henry Osceola spun around in his chair, bent over, and opened a file drawer in a green metal cabinet. He fiddled around for a moment, then withdrew a blue-backed document. He handed it to me, dropping a thin line of ash on the cover page. I thumbed to the back. Forty-seven pages in total. I went to the front.

Whereas the Micanopy Tribe of Indians is the owner in fee simple of certain realty more particularly described as follows . . .

I looked at the Terms and Conditions clause. Florio paid a lousy fifty thousand for the option to lease the land. The lease wouldn't become effective until the option was exercised with a payment of $1 million when construction began on Cypress Estates, described in the lease as a "residential-commercial" venture. A separate clause described in general terms the "cultural-tourism" phase of the project, a smokescreen for the casino. No money up front. Just as Florio had told me, a provision giving the tribe 10 percent of Florio Enterprises' gross receipts.

I skimmed quickly through the rest. The assignability clause would be near the back along with the boilerplate—the choice-of-law, arbitration, and severability provisions—that nobody but a

Philadelphia lawyer ever reads. And there it was, on page 45, innocuous as could be.

The Lessee may freely assign all or portions of this Agreement in its discretion, whether to third parties, or to affiliated entities, without the consent of the Lessor.

I pushed the lease back across the desk toward Osceola. "Did you understand this clause?"

He coughed, exhaling a puff of smoke in my direction, looked quickly at the page, and said, "You probably think we're just a bunch of dumb Indians. We had a lawyer, you know. A real estate man from Collier County. He read all the fine print. He told us we were getting a good deal because we were in for a percentage of the gross receipts. 'Stay away from the net,' he kept saying. 'If it's net profits, they'll load up all their expenses on you, and you'll never see a dime.' That's what we focused on."

"Well, he lost sight of something else. Florio Enterprises can assign its contract for one dollar to another of Nicky Florio's companies. Then you'll get ten percent of whatever that other company decides to pay to Florio Enterprises as a management fee. It doesn't matter if they're making a hundred million a year in profit, they can give the management company anything they want."

Henry Osceola turned toward his wastebucket and hacked up a wad of phlegm.

"What Florio's paying you is a drop in the bucket," I said, immediately regretting my choice of words. "This lease is going to make Nicky Florio one of the richest men in the country. See, there's something Florio didn't tell you. The so-called cultural-tourism phase isn't just a museum and Indian village. It's gambling, and I don't mean bingo."

I wanted to let the curiosity build. There is a look a man gets when he knows he's been taken but doesn't know quite how. He's desperate for the knowledge but doesn't want to show it. I hoped to see that look on Henry Osceola's face but didn't get it. He cocked his head and waited. If anything, he looked puzzled by me, not curious at what I was saying.

"Blackjack," I said.

I let it soak in. He stubbed out his cigarette and didn't reach for another.

"Craps," I said. "Poker, keno, slots, roulette."

I told him everything I knew, leaving out only the decapitation of Rick Gondolier. While I spoke, Henry Osceola didn't smoke, spit, or talk. His creased face took it all in and didn't let any of it out. I told him the projections on traffic and population and visitors. I told him how this information probably got Peter Tupton killed. I told him I couldn't represent the tribe, but I could get him a lawyer to challenge the lease. Get some publicity on how the slick developer cheated the Native Americans. Turn it all around. Invalidate the lease, maybe get the federal government to investigate.

He studied me for a while. Outside the windowless office, a scratchy public-address system was announcing a special cooking demonstration.

Finally, he said, "We know all about the gambling."

"You do?"

"It was disclosed by Mr. Florio. Not in the documents, of course. They become public records, and we understood the need for confidentiality until the time is right."

"I don't understand. Why would you let him do this? You're being shortchanged, taken advantage of. You're selling Manhattan Island for twenty-four bucks."

"The gambling is secondary. Surely you know that."

"Secondary!" The rest of it, I thought. Just as Gina said. But what was the rest of it? "Secondary to what?"

He leaned back in his chair, his hand automatically reaching for the Camels. The pack was empty. His fingers crushed the paper and tossed it into the stained waste can. "The other contract, of course. As Mr. Florio's lawyer, you must know . . ."

My face had given it away.

"You don't know, do you?"

I could have tried to bluff it—*oh that contract*—but I wouldn't have known what to say. Maybe I wasn't a good enough actor to be a lawyer. Maybe I was just a lousy liar. I shook my head. "No, I don't know, but you could tell me."

"Your concern for our welfare is heartening," Henry Osceola said, "though I wonder about your loyalty to your client. Rest assured that we are quite aware of what we have given and what we shall receive in our dealings with Mr. Florio." He made a point of looking at his watch, an old Timex on an alligator band. "Now, if you'll excuse me, I need to pay the bills of the froggers and crabbers and other thieves who supply the restaurant, to say nothing of the fuel and electrical bills for the village." He smiled pleasantly at me. "And at five o'clock, the classics channel is showing *Fort Apache* with John Wayne. I never miss it."

I didn't know whether that was a joke, but I know when I'm being asked to leave. As I let the door close behind me, I peeked over my shoulder and took one last look at Henry Osceola.

The smile was gone. With the telephone cradled to his ear, he punched out a number he must have known by heart.

Chapter 21

Zapped

THE WIND WHIPPED ALONG TAMIAMI TRAIL, TUGGING AT CHAR-lie's top-heavy pickup, which shimmied and shook, rattled and rolled. It was cold enough to fire up the heater, but the knob was missing. I twisted the threaded screw and was hit in the face with a blast of fumes that would have shut down Three Mile Island. Ahead of me, a full moon hung over Miami. I headed due east, the saw grass waving in the wind on each side of the road.

I was still thirty miles east of town when I saw the blue light in the rearview mirror. I checked my speedometer. The needle was jumping between 50 and 55. I slowed to make sure the police car meant me. It pulled to within a few feet, and a voice over its loudspeaker politely asked me to please bring my vehicle to a safe stop.

When I pumped the brakes and clunked to a halt on the berm, the same voice told me to please exit my vehicle, step to the rear, and bring my license and registration with me. I got out and did most of what I was told. The police car had its high beams on, and the blue light kept flashing. I squinted at the officer who approached me, one hand on the butt of his still-holstered revolver, just the way they teach them. He was dark-complexioned with long, straight black hair and, like so many cops these days, he had the overblown trapezius muscles that sloped from shoulders to neck and revealed the serious weight lifter.

The uniform was unfamiliar to me. Then I read the arm patch. MICANOPY TRIBAL POLICE. The nameplate identified him as "G. Alachua." I handed him my license, explained that I'd borrowed the truck and didn't have the registration unless it was in the glove compartment with some fishing lures and road maps that predated Ponce de León. He didn't crack a smile. They teach them that, too.

G. Alachua studied my license for a moment. "Please wait here, Mr. Lassiter."

He returned to the police car, this time approaching the passenger side. For the first time, I noticed another cop. They spoke to each other through the open window. Then the door opened, and both officers walked toward me. In the glare of the headlights, I couldn't make out the features of the second one, who was shorter than his partner. This one was carrying a nightstick, and somehow his walk seemed familiar. I recognize people that way sometimes. On the football field, even if the number was obscured and the face hidden beneath a face mask or behind another player, I identified teammates and foes alike by the way they carried themselves.

Alachua spoke first, drawing my attention to him. "Mr. Lassiter, we must ask you to take a roadside sobriety test."

"What for? Was I driving erratically? Was I speeding? Why was I stopped?"

Lawyers are trained to ask questions.

With amazing agility, the other cop turned away and spun around, his back facing us as he unleashed his right foot in an explosive kick that shattered the right rear brake light on the old Dodge. The *ushiro mawashi-geri*, the back roundhouse kick in karate, impressive because it's delivered blind. "Faulty equipment," he answered.

Then he faced me directly and smiled, and a chill went through me. The same short dark hair, the same broad shoulders, the same short, powerful legs.

"Jim Tiger! You're a policeman?"

"Captain Tiger," he responded calmly, the smile gone, replaced by the familiar taciturn expression of the guy with few words but a sharp machete. "Now, are you going to voluntarily submit to the sobriety test, or do we take you in?"

"In where? Where's your station?"

"Back at the village, though sometimes we take a short cut through the saw-grass prairie."

"That wouldn't be a short cut," I said. "The village is a straight shot west on the Trail."

Tiger turned toward Alachua. "Mr. Lassiter wants to teach us geography."

"Okay," I said. "You've made your point. I'm not welcome in your territory. Fine. I'll head home." I started to move toward the cab of the pickup, but Alachua grabbed my shoulder. I could have shaken him off. I could have pivoted with my left foot and caught him in the gut with a hook. I could have done a lot of things, but I just stopped and looked at Jim Tiger. I was big and strong, but he was cruel and vicious. I could hit hard, but he could kill and do it without blinking, do it calmly and dispassionately. "I'll take the sobriety test," I said.

Tiger reached into his back pocket and smiled again. That made two in one night. He pulled out a silver flask that glittered in the headlights, blue sparks flying from the metal with each revolution of the police car's light. He unscrewed the cap and offered me a drink.

"No, thanks. I never drink when my constitutional rights are being violated."

"Drink it!"

I took the flask and sniffed at it. Cheap bourbon or something like it. "Who you saving the good stuff for, José Canseco?"

I considered the alternatives. Alachua still had his hand on his gun. Tiger still held his nightstick. In the movies, the hero would toss the whiskey in one bad guy's face and kick the other one in the balls. But in the movies, they choreograph it. The second bad guy has the reflexes of a mollusk. He stands by and allows the hero to take out the first bad guy before being surprised himself. In real life, two against one is just a shitty bet. I took a short swig, letting a little of the warm liquid into my mouth but plugging the bottle's opening with my tongue.

"More!" Tiger ordered. "Drink it all."

Again, I sipped at the flask. "*Hmmm*, good. Firewater strong medicine." It was a line I thought Henry Osceola would like.

Jim Tiger didn't share the chairman's sense of humor. "Do you think Native Americans are funny?"

On the road, a pair of eighteen-wheelers rumbled past, kicking up dust clouds in the glare of the headlights.

"No. I just make bad jokes when I'm scared."

"Mr. Florio was wrong about you. He said you were smarter than you looked."

"Thank you," I said.

"Is there anything you want to tell us before we get on with this?"

"Did you hear the one about the bosomy blonde who was trying on dresses with plunging necklines?" I asked, stalling for time. They both stared at me as if I'd lost my mind. "She asks the saleswoman if the dress she had on was too low-cut. 'Do you have hair on your chest?' the saleswoman says. 'No, of course not,' the woman responds. 'Then it's too low-cut.' "

"That's enough!" Tiger shouted. "Drink it. Drink the whole thing. Now!"

I leaned my head back and let it flow. The whiskey was warm and raw in my throat. It was still gurgling down when I sensed movement in front of me.

A blur.

Oomph.

Tiger's left fist plunged deep into my gut, and I spit whiskey all over my herringbone suit. I dropped to a knee, gasping. It wasn't the hardest I'd ever been hit. It wasn't the hardest I'd been hit today, but I wasn't going to tell Tiger that.

I was sucking in air, and Tiger was talking. "Faulty equipment, driving under the influence, and resisting arrest. Get to your feet."

I pulled myself up, using the rear gate of the pickup for leverage. I was huffing and puffing, but part of it was an act. Playing possum. Enough of the scaredy-cat.

"Cuff him," Tiger ordered. He had backed up a step.

Alachua took his hand off his gun and reached behind his back to find the handcuffs. I needed a step to get to Tiger, but I didn't want to leave my feet by lunging at him. I didn't know how much quick I had left after having the wind knocked out of me, but I didn't have a choice. I took the stutter-step on wobbly knees, feinted with the left, hoping to bring the nightstick in that direction, so I could have a clear shot with a short right at his jaw.

I didn't get within two feet. Tiger saw me coming and lifted the nightstick toward my chest. It never touched me, but a green explosion caught me square in the sternum, a fluorescent flash that knocked my feet out from under me and sat me on my ass.

I didn't see stars.

Stars would have been better.

My legs were noodles, my arms paralyzed. My teeth felt loose. My tongue was swollen, and my ears were playing Mozart's Turkish March. I felt wet and clammy. I looked down. I had pissed my pants.

"Whoa, baby!"

It was Alachua. He was cackling. "Whoa, baby!" Over and over, or was it just bonging back and forth in my brain?

He cackled again. "Never saw the Zap Stick used before on a person. Holy shit."

"Twenty thousand volts will do that," Tiger said.

I was aware of the noise. A droning whir.

It made me want to sleep. Maybe I was in bed. But my head seemed to be bouncing off a metal floor. Cold metal. And that noise. It made my jaw ache. Or was that the cold?

I felt myself shiver. Trying to sit up now. Jerked back down again, my right arm refusing to follow the rest of me. Shaking my arm. A rattling. My wrist cuffed to a cold, rusted railing.

Above me, the moon. The sensation of movement. Fast. I listened to the droning whir. I propped myself up on one elbow and looked over a low railing. I was right. We were moving. Flying through a wheat field.

No, not a wheat field. A jungle, maybe. I'd been here before, but when? I couldn't remember. A splash of water came over the rail and smacked me in the face. I tried sitting up. In a chair above me, a shadowy figure with his hand on what looked like a rudder. I started to say something. With his other hand, he picked up what looked like . . . no, not that again. I remember that.

The world exploded into green fluorescence.

Somebody said something. What was it?

"He smells boozy and pissy. Like my old *abuelo*."

I wasn't flying anymore. No more water. I cracked my eyes open. I was lying facedown on a smooth wooden floor. It smelled of clean, fresh varnish. I wanted to lie there awhile.

"Are we going to wait for the boss?"

A different voice. Familiar. I'd have to roll over to see who. The last time I rolled over, somebody put me back to sleep.

"*El jefe*'s busy making money. He gave me the papers, but he should be here in time for the closing."

A chuckle. "The closing. I like that."

I didn't.

I turned my head an inch and peeked. One alligator cowboy boot. One shiny black shoe. My astute powers of reasoning—inductive or deductive or whatever—told me the same man wasn't wearing both. In all probability, there were four feet altogether, divided by two equals two men, one belonging to each voice. Very good, Lassiter, go to the head of the class.

Another peek across the room. Dark furniture, shuttered windows. I knew this place. I'd been here before. Nicky Florio's humble fishing cabin.

Heaven on earth.

I rolled my head just enough so I could look up. The ugly face of Guillermo Diaz was staring down at me. "*¡Hola, abogado!* Ey, Sleeping Beauty is up."

The pudgy creep was wearing low-slung pants, a western shirt, and cowboy boots to make him taller. Another head appeared. My old pal Captain Tiger of the tribal police. It was his strong dark hand that reached down and grabbed me by the scruff of the neck. I still had on my suit coat and felt overdressed for the occasion. I helped him get me up, swinging my feet underneath me and standing on rickety legs. He guided me to a chair at a card table. A table with a green felt top. Hey, I remember the table, too. But there weren't any stains. The table was new. I looked toward the ceiling. No dark spots. Then at the floor. It had been sanded and refinished. Not a trace of Rick Gondolier's spurting blood.

Diaz and Tiger took seats on either side of me.

"No thanks, boys," I said. "The last time I played poker here, I lost my shirt, and somebody else lost his . . ."

A thin leather briefcase sat on the table in front of Diaz. He reached inside and withdrew a file. Inside the file was a document he pulled out and shoved in front of me. It had my name on top, how flattering: *Statement of Jacob Lassiter*. But the typing was haphazard.

"Read it!" Tiger ordered.

" 'Drink it, read it.' That's all I get from you. Nag, nag, nag."

"Okay, shithead, just sign it."

"No, I think I'll read it. Hey, you don't see many manual type-writers anymore. That floating *e* makes it look like it was typed on my . . ."

Diaz smiled his lowlife's smile. "Ey, how come you don't lock your door? Not that it would matter. I could break into Fort Knox if the price was right." He allowed himself an egg-sucking laugh. "You like my typing?"

I started reading to see what I decided to say. "To Whom It May Concern." Ah, the personal touch.

I kept reading: "I'm sorry for everything I've done. I'm sorry it had to come to this." The words seemed to be floating all over the page, and not just because the old Royal was one step from the scrap yard. My head was swimming. I put a finger on a line of type and traced along as I read.

"I'm sorry that I lost sight of right and wrong."

I seemed to be sorry about a lot of things. I'd let down my partners and my friends and my Granny. That was a nice touch, throwing Granny in there. How about Coach Paterno and Coach Shula?

I'd gotten greedy, too. A lot of greed and sorrow, it seemed to me.

I'd lost sight of ethics. Well, that was certainly believable.

Greed's the reason I stole the money from the bingo hall.

And killed my buddy and co-conspirator Rick Gondolier.

And tried to bribe Abe Socolow.

"What, nothing else, fellows? Wasn't I on the grassy knoll in Dallas?"

I kept reading. It looked like something I might have typed. Lots of typos, a few words misspelled.

"If you two think Nicky Florio can get away with this, you're crazier than he is," I said. "This confession is worthless. I'll disown it in a minute. It won't be admissible. It isn't worth the paper it's—"

"Keep reading, shithead," Tiger said.

I did.

Oh. There it was in the last paragraph. The statement wasn't a confession, at least not one I'd have a chance to repudiate.

It was a suicide note.

Chapter 22

Die Easy, Die Hard

Nᴉᴄᴋʏ Fʟᴏʀɪᴏ ɢᴇɴᴛʟʏ sᴡɪʀʟᴇᴅ ᴛʜᴇ ᴅᴇʟɪᴄᴀᴛᴇ Fɪɴɴɪsʜ ɢᴏʙʟᴇᴛ by the stem, smiling to himself as he *sniff-sniff-sniffed* the crimson liquid. "Full-bodied," he proclaimed after a moment. "A hint of violets, ginger, and tobacco." He turned toward me. "Care to sample France's finest?"

I shook my head, and various hinges and latches groaned where they fastened my neck and shoulder muscles to my bones. "You want to slip me a Mickey, why not just bash me over the head?"

Florio showed his patient, tolerant look. "In due time, if it is your desire. But I think we can be more creative than that, don't you?"

"You gonna get me drunk and freeze me to death? You have a wine cellar here, too?"

"Not necessary. Just an air-conditioned room to keep the Bordeaux at sixty-eight degrees." He picked up another goblet. "Château Carbonnieux from the Graves area. It's a Bordeaux 1961." He gestured toward the table full of bottles. "They all are. The greatest year ever, even finer than 1945." He poured a glass for me. "Let it sit for a while. It's not as delicate as the Château Cantemerle, which I allow to breathe for a full hour, but no more."

I stared at the wine, wondering how long Nicky Florio would let me breathe. We were sitting at the knotty-pine picnic table on the porch of the high-stilted cabin. The slough was alive with sounds of birds tuning up their voices and unseen animals rippling the water just before dawn. Was it only two days ago that I sat at this table, eating snook with cabbage palm, boiled corn, and pumpkin pie? Jim Tiger had been the cook, Rick Gondolier a guest. Tiger wasn't doing any cooking today. Still in his cop's clothes, he was hauling bottles of wine from a back room as Nicky Florio shouted instructions. A Latour and a Pétrus, two Lafite-Rothschilds.

Florio sat across from me at the table in his safari khakis, his dark face brooding at his wine. A cool breeze stirred through the slough, the air ripe with the pungent aroma of fermentation, of growth and death and renewal of life. Tiger silently poured from half a dozen bottles into two sets of glasses.

"Lassiter, do you understand what I'm doing?" Florio asked.

"Sure, you're showing me just how much savoir-faire you've got. You want me to know you're something I'm not. It all goes back to Gina, doesn't it?"

"Does it?"

"Look, Nicky, she chose you. She's your wife. You won. You don't have to prove anything to me."

"Quite right, quite right." The French wine was making him sound like a phony European count. Florio sniffed again, then took a sip from one of the goblets. "Complex and opulent," he opined, putting the glass down and savoring the taste, his eyes closed. "Tell me, Lassiter, how would you describe the Lynch-Bages?"

I studied the contents of a freshly poured goblet. "Red. It's definitely red." I took a dainty sip, then polished it off in a second try. "I don't know how opulent it is, but it tastes damn good."

"Let's compare the Mouton, another Pauillac wine."

Tiger, the homicidal sommelier, poured me a fresh one.

"By the way," Florio said, "you may want to savor the wine a bit more and not . . . chug it."

I stuck my nose into the goblet and sniffed with the earnest diligence of a Labrador retriever. "Rich," I intoned judiciously. "And, of course, red, still red."

He nodded. Maybe I was a natural at this. I drank up, finishing it off, letting him frown at my lack of couth.

"Next, perhaps a Château Pétrus from the Pomerol region."

I tried it and found a new word. "Fruity," I told him.

Again, he nodded judiciously. "Spicy and fruity, to be sure.

Today it would go for twenty-five hundred dollars a bottle—if you could find it."

I nearly squirted him with about a hundred bucks' of the stuff. When I finished coughing, he was pouring more wine. We sipped along with each other for a while, running through a Lafite, which I agreed was delicate, a powerful Pichon-Lalande, and a sturdy, somewhat acidic Figeac. Over yet another bottle, we debated whether a Montrose was drying from age, but we agreed that some of the wines from Saint-Julien were past their peaks.

And so was I.

In the last sixty hours, I had watched a man decapitated, then helped dispose of the evidence. I got hooked into a bribery scheme and was framed for a million-dollar heist. I had been punched by two cops, one of them apparently honest, which is about the average in these parts. I had been zapped twice by a stun gun and shanghaied aboard an airboat. I'd read my own suicide note, insulted the guy who wanted to kill me, then drunk enough wine to drown a cat. I wanted to ponder the cosmic significance of these events, but at the moment my head was throbbing, my temples were in a vise, and my eyes were pressed shut. Somebody was saying something, but I wasn't interested.

I felt a hand on my shoulder, shaking me. Apparently, I had found a comfortable spot to sleep, my face resting on the tabletop. I jolted to attention.

"Up and at 'em, Jake. We've got business to discuss."

I pried my eyes open and ran my tongue across my teeth. I don't care how much the wine cost. My mouth tasted like it had been stuffed with rags soaked in 10W-40 Quaker State. Nicky Florio still had his hand on my shoulder. Jim Tiger stood at the railing, watching us both, a pistol on his hip, the stun gun in his hand. "More vino," I said. "Bring on the grapes."

"I didn't know you had an appreciation of the finer things in life," Florio said.

"Oh, but I do. Wine, women, and . . ."

"Song," Florio helped out.

With that, I broke into "Fight On, State," giving the arms-up touchdown sign when I got to the part about rolling up the score, fighting on to victory ev-er-more.

"Have you enjoyed our little tasting?" Nicky Florio asked.

"Sure have. Now where are the women?"

"There are wine experts who would have killed to taste the 1961 French Bordeaux you've been guzzling."

"But not you, Nicky. You wouldn't kill for wine. Or for a woman, for that matter. You didn't murder Gondolier because of Gina. If you had, I'd be dead, too. You kill for money. Maybe Gondolier cheated you, or maybe you didn't want to share the casino with him. Either way, it was just for the dollars. Peter Tupton was going to cost you a bundle, so you aced him. And now, there's me. . . ."

My little speech had made me thirsty. I picked up a bottle of Châteaux Latour and put it to my lips. Hey, it tasted good this way, too. "Powerful yet still youthful," I said, licking my lips. "And red. Red as blood."

"Why do you think I invited you to join me in this special event?" He gestured across the table at the half-empty bottles. My gaze followed his hand, but my eyes were unfocused. My head was swimming in an ocean of wine.

"You're trying to impress me, but I'm not impressed. Next, you're going to tell me about some trip to France where you bought all the wine from Château LaDouche at double what it's worth. That's your style. You married Gina because she looks good on your arm, so people would say, 'Oh, that Nicky Florio's got great taste.' But what Nicky Florio's got is a major case of self-deception. Or do you really know? Maybe deep inside, you know that you're a chicken-enshit small-timer who hasn't done anything straight since the sixth grade."

"I see that wine loosens your tongue."

Actually, it was my brain that seemed loose. I looked at Nicky Florio, and there were two of him.

"Sure, Lassiter, I bought the wine in France. But I didn't pay double. I paid next to nothing, because I recognized early just how special the 1961 Bordeaux was. I have always been able to recognize quality. It is why I am where I am today, and why you are . . ."

He held up both hands as if to indicate the utter insignificance of me. I took a healthy swig of the Latour.

"At any rate, it is time to discuss our business," Nicky Florio said. "We have a matter to conclude."

"I'm not shin-ing any note," I slurred. "Wait a she-cond." I tested my numb lips with my tongue. Was that wine or Novocain?

"You probably wonder why I haven't had you killed already," Nicky Florio said, matter-of-factly.

From somewhere in the darkened swamp, a bird cawed, and another one ca-cawed right back. I looked at my watch. The big hand was on the nine, and the little hand was spinning around. "Yesh. You've been tardy, naughty boy. And what kind of a host are you, anyway? Wine, wine, wine, but no munchies. Where are the chips and onion dip?"

I grabbed another bottle. Something from Saint-Julien.

"Like it says in the Bible, Lassiter, it all comes around. Ashes to ashes . . ."

I took a gulp from the bottle.

". . . dust to dust," he said.

I gagged. "Wine to vinegar!"

Nicky Florio tugged the bottle from my hand and sniffed. He-wrinkled his nose with displeasure. "It happens," he said, almost apologetically. "A defect in the cork, improper storage. Pity."

"Ah, what one has to put up with," I said sympathetically.

"All right, that's enough." Florio's mood had changed. "I want to know some things."

"Me, too. What really happened to the dinosaurs? Charlie Riggs says it was a big asteroid, but some people think it was a bunch of volcanoes. And how does Dan Marino release the ball so quickly?"

"Who have you told?"

"Told what?"

"What you know."

I squinted at him. "*I* don't know. What you know?"

"No, what *you* know!"

"I know plenty. What you know?"

He tilted his head and looked at me, trying to figure out if I was drunk or just jerking him around. Even I wasn't sure. My eyelids were as heavy as theater curtains.

"Look, Lassiter, I know you told Socolow, and I know you told Osceola. Who else did you tell about the casino?"

"Mike Wal-lash. That is, Mike Wallace. There'll be a camera crew here soon."

"Did you tell Doc Riggs?"

"If I say yes, are you going to give him some of the vino, too?"

"You did, didn't you?"

"It isn't just the casino, though, is it Nicky? The casino's secondary. That's what Osceola said. There's something even bigger, right?"

"What would that be?"

"I know, but I'm not telling. I've got a secret."

He looked skeptical. "Osceola says you don't know anything about it."

I sang it out. "That's because it's my seeeeee-cret! And I told only people I trust."

"You're trying too hard, Jake. It isn't going to work. You don't know shit. There's no way you could know."

In the slough, the blackness began to fade to gray, and pink slivers of light appeared at the eastern horizon. Florio stood and headed toward the front door of the cabin. With a shrug of his head, he motioned to Jim Tiger, who was leaning against the rail.

"Gina told me," I said. "Gina knows a seeeeee-cret."

Nicky Florio stopped in his tracks. He turned to face me. "Either you're lying, or you're trying to get her killed. Which is it?"

He had pushed the right button. I looked at his face, dark with concern. He was dead serious. I had underestimated Florio. He knew me better than I knew me. He knew I cared more about Gina than he did.

"I was lying," I said.

"Were you, or are you lying now to protect her?" He thought about it a moment. "Either way, you're through." Florio turned back to Tiger. "Close the transaction."

Florio went into the house, letting the door bang behind him. A moment later, Guillermo Diaz came out the door, carrying the briefcase to the picnic table. Tiger opened the latch and pulled out the same paper I had looked at last night, or was it a thousand years ago? "Sign it, shithead."

"Whatever you say."

He handed me a fat Mont Blanc fountain pen. I made a couple of exaggerated arm motions, found the signature line, and wrote a single word.

Tiger picked up the document and drew it close to his face. He may have been nearsighted. "What the fuck! What the fuck is this?"

"You said to sign it 'Shithead,' " I explained calmly.

"Why don't we just feed him to the gators?" Guillermo Diaz suggested. His chubby face was pinched in a frown. Maybe his cowboy boots hurt his feet.

"Look," Tiger said, "let me tell you where you're at. In a few hours, you're going to be hanging by the neck from the ceiling fan in your living room. Somebody will find you the first day that's hot enough to carry your stink to the neighbors' yard. Now we can do this easy or hard, it's up to you. You want to spare yourself some pain, just sign the paper."

Die easy or die hard. I was hoping for a third alternative.

Tiger reached into the briefcase and pulled out another copy and slammed it down in front of me. Then he lifted the stun gun and tapped me on the side of the head with it, just above the ear. "Sign!"

I held the expensive pen, and this time, in my best penmanship, wrote three words:

Jacob Lassiter, not!

Tiger bent close to look at it, his index finger tracing under the words. I shifted the pen from my fingers into my fist, fourteen-karat gold tip pointed toward the sky.

He squinted at the words. "The fuck is this?"

When his face was a foot above the table, I brought the fist up. Straight and hard.

The dagger-sharp tip sank into his right eye, and I jammed it home. I pushed it through lens and iris and cornea and the orbital bones and the optic nerve, and judging from the gush of blood that spurted like a garden hose, I'd pushed it straight through the internal carotid artery, too. Then, with a final shove with the palm of my hand, I rammed it straight into the frontal lobe of the brain.

The scream was the wail of a dying beast. Blood gushed from his eye socket over his face, down onto the table and over the papers. The lens and iris popped out and hung, suspended from his face, dripping a jellylike fluid. Tiger staggered backward, his hands groping for the pen, which had vanished inside his eye socket. He whipped his head back and forth like a horse trying to toss its bit, spraying blood in every direction. He opened the other eye, then screamed that he was blind, which he would have been from the severed nerves. Finally, he fell, his body twitching, his screams silenced.

Jim Tiger was stone-cold dead, and I was stone-cold sober.

Guillermo Diaz stood, frozen. By the time he reached inside his nylon jacket, I had picked up the stun gun and aimed it at his chest. The first electric zap buckled his knees and opened his mouth. The second sat him down. The third drove a palsy through his arms and legs.

I heard the door bang open behind me and turned in time to see Florio, a twelve-gauge shotgun cradled in his arms, coming toward me. I dived to the deck and rolled just as a blast tore out a chunk of the railing, the noise ringing in my ears. The shotgun barrel followed me to the floor, and I kept moving, scrambling hand over hand. I looked over my shoulder to see Florio pump and raise the gun once more. I took two steps and dived over the railing, a blast of pellets tearing at my coattail.

Into the blackness.

The fall took forever.

I expected to be shot out of the air, like a clay pigeon.

And then the splash.

It was something between a belly flop and an Olympic medal, closer to the former. I went under, not knowing how deep it was but thankful for once that Nicky Florio had dredged, with or without permits.

I heard another blast and felt the ping of pellets in the water above me. I stayed under as long as I could.

I surfaced and took a breath, my lungs exploding with pain. My breathing sounded like a locomotive in my ears. I tried not to splash. The sun was sizzling on the horizon, the black water glinting with morning light. I wondered what Nicky could see from the high-stilted porch.

I listened to the sounds of the swamp. Birds chirping, frogs burping, the screech of an animal I had never heard before. I floated on my back, my legs weighted down by my wing tips. I discarded the shoes and kicked gently, moving away from the house.

Another roar from the shotgun, but farther away.

Still moving backward, I bumped into something rough and scaly.

A log?

I whirled around, searching for yellow-green eyes, or worse, red ones. . . .

It was a large branch of a lignum vitae tree.

I resumed my easy backstroke, tearing off my suit coat and letting it float away. I maneuvered around the hardwood hammock, putting more distance between the house and myself. Five minutes later, I could barely see the light from the windows through the tops of the mahogany trees.

I was trying to conserve my energy, floating, swimming, floating again, when I heard it.

A heavy breath beside me. I rolled to the side and was sprayed by a fine mist from two nostrils just above the water's surface. The rest of the animal was hidden below the surface.

From diving, I remembered what to do when you encounter a shark. Don't panic; don't splash; don't strike out. I wondered if the advice applied to alligators. No matter. I was too scared to do anything. I just floated there while it moved closer and breathed its hot breath on me and finally nuzzled me with its snout.

Chapter 23

Siren of the Sea

I TREADED WATER AND THE ANIMAL RAISED ITS HEAD.

Dull gray, the color of an elephant, with a blunt-nosed face. It reminded me of a hippo.

Then it squeaked and nuzzled me.

A big, lumpy manatee. A sea cow with bad breath. It squeaked again. I treaded water some more, backpedaling. Lumpy moved its armlike front flippers and came close enough to kiss me. This guy, or gal, must have weighed half a ton.

I didn't know what to do, so I imitated its sound. Mine was more of a squawk, a little off key. I hoped it was the manatee version of hello, and not a war whoop. Or a mating call.

The manatees are essentially harmless and friendly. They eat grass and drift through life not bothering anybody. Man is a much greater danger to the manatee than the other way around. The big lugs float just below the surface in our waterways and canals, where power boaters frequently slice them up with their propellers.

Sirens of the sea, they are the sea maids from *A Midsummer Night's Dream*. Five hundred years ago, Columbus saw manatees floating by as he approached the New World. His log revealed he thought they were mermaids. Columbus had been at sea too long.

Another squeak from Lumpy, another squawk from me.

Then it did a pirouette, slowly spinning 180 degrees, showing me its wrinkled gray back. I tentatively stroked its head, provoking a *squeak-squeak.*

I stopped stroking, and it turned and faced me again.

The sun was an orange fireball just above the horizon. A heron croaked as it flew overhead. There was the splash of feeding fish nearby.

I was tired of treading water. "What do you want, pal?"

Another squeak. Then another pirouette.

It just floated there, its back to me.

Waiting. It expected me to do something. But what?

Growing even more tired, I put my arms around its neck and held on. Lumpy started swimming. So that was it. The manatee was a cabbie, and I was the fare. We would not break Mark Spitz's records, but we were moving. Judging from the position of the rising sun, we were headed north and maybe a little east. Not that it made much difference, since I didn't know how to get out of here anyway, but we were going deeper into the Glades and away from Tamiami Trail. Keep it up, and we might hit Lake Okeechobee.

We passed dozens of hardwood hammocks, staying in the deep water well offshore. Live oak and royal palm trees were outlined as silhouettes against the brightening sky. I heard a woodpecker *rat-a-tat-tatting* and watched a black-and-white wood stork wading in the shallow water near shore. We swam through patches of green water lettuce and lilies and kept on going.

I saw an osprey dive-bomb the water and come up with a fish in its talons, then head back toward a hammock and what I imagined was its nest filled with young birds. A black-and-yellow snake slithered by, and I told myself it wasn't a diamondback rattler.

By the time we approached a strand of bald cypress trees, my arms were starting to cramp. In the distance I heard two thudding explosions, the same sounds I thought had been thunderclaps the morning after Gondolier was killed. A heavy mist hung over the water, and the air was cooler here. This time of year, the trees were bare of their needles but were cloaked with ethereal tapestries of Spanish moss. I was trying to figure it out. We had headed north, farther from the national park, farther from the Trail, deeper into Micanopy territory.

Of course. We were in the Big Cypress, the part of the Glades that truly looks like a prehistoric swamp. The water, stained by tannin, was the color of richly brewed tea. The rising sun was shimmering behind the Spanish moss. Air plants and red bromeliads and white orchids grew out of the cypress trees, which, in turn, grew out of the dark water.

Figuring the water was shallow, I let go of Lumpy and tried to stand. The water closed over my head, and I never did touch bottom. I came up and found my friend waiting, squeaking, then turning around for me. I felt unworthy of such tender care but climbed on anyway.

I lost track of time. The sun was high overhead, and my throat was constricted with thirst when I saw the hardwood hammock in front of us. It seemed larger than the others, and there was another difference, too. At the shoreline, covered by gumbo limbo trees, was a wooden dock that even Lumpy knew was the sign of man.

I figured the manatee brought me here thinking I wanted to be with my own kind. You're wrong, Lumpy. I'd had enough of Nick Florio and his buddies to prefer the company of a thousand-pound creature with halitosis. But maybe this place had a fishing cabin where the thoughtful owner left a six-pack of beer behind.

Lumpy stopped about twenty yards from shore. I let go, swam three strokes, and was able to wade the rest of the way on the rough limestone shelf. I heard the manatee squeak again, then watched it turn and drift away in the current.

My knees buckled, and I collapsed on the beach. Total exhaustion. I lay there a few minutes, then began shivering as a breeze rattled through the cabbage palms and chilled me. I remembered from my windsurfing days just how easy it was to suffer hypothermia. And die from exposure. Which made me think of Peter Tupton all over again.

I was determined to get warm. The air was cooler than the water had been. I stripped off what was left of my sopping-wet suit and stood there, stark naked, trying to figure out what to do. I walked along the beach. A great blue heron eyed me from the shallow water, then began wading. From the underbrush near the shore, I heard a rustling and saw an oppossum scurrying for cover.

Then I found what I needed. A depression in the beach maybe two feet deep and five feet long. A gator hole. During the dry winter months, the alligators make their own swampy condos. It was filled with mud warmed by the midday sun. I stepped into the hole and started slathering the mud on my chest and arms, then legs. I reached around and did my back, finally applying a thin layer to my face. Hey, women pay big bucks for something like this at a Bal Harbour spa.

Finally, I was warm. But thirsty.

The water of the swamp was brackish. I headed away from the beach and into the trees. On the trunk of a gumbo limbo, I saw several pine airplants, looking like pineapples with their leaves curling up and out toward the sky. I climbed the tree and found rainwater in the cup of the plant. I had to chase a tree frog from one, but I leaned down and slurped out the moisture from each of them. Two black vultures circled overhead, drifting in the air currents. Best I could tell, neither was a member of the Bar. I figured they had spotted a dying bobcat, maybe a raccoon, or even a white-tailed deer. I hoped it wasn't a scared, exhausted lawyer.

I went back to the beach and began walking the circumference of the hammock. I tried to count my steps but lost track after 1,232. I found the remnants of a campfire that couldn't have been more than a few days old, and on the far side of the hammock, another wooden dock, this one larger. What seemed to be a path led into the woods, and I wanted to follow it, but I promised myself I'd finish the trek around the island first. I did, but there were no other signs of man. No boats, no cabins, no Styrofoam cups from 7-Eleven.

It was already afternoon by the time I got back to my starting point. I had stopped to drink from more wild pine plants, but it did nothing to alleviate my hunger. How long had it been since I had eaten?

I knew from my secretary, Cindy the Vegan, that lots of grasses and seeds were edible. I just didn't know which ones. She had a book with pictures. Some of the plants were gourmet delights; others were toxic one-way tickets to the emergency room.

A few hundred yards from the shoreline was marshy ground surrounded by dark green bulrushes with stems eight feet tall.

Brown bristly spiked flowers hung from the ends of the stems. Unless Domino's delivered out here, I really didn't have a choice. I broke off some shoots and sprouts and tried them. Not bad. Sort of like a health-food cereal with lots of crunch and zero taste. Nearby were greenbrier vines with woody, prickly stems. For some reason, the long leaves reminded me of a twelve-dollar salad at a trendy South Beach restaurant. I sampled the heavily veined leaves. Leathery but tasty. Some virgin olive oil and fresh garlic would have helped.

I kept moving toward the interior of the hammock. The tree trunks were covered with colorful snails. Escargots anyone? I passed. I came upon a strand of pine trees, bursting with male pollen antlers. Maybe a burger would have tasted better, but the pollen probably had as much protein. I ate a few, then picked some cones from the tree, cracked them open, and swallowed the seeds.

I was scurrying through the woods, sniffing leaves and flowers, nibbling this and that, when I saw the glint of sunlight off glass. It didn't register at first. I just squinted at the glare.

Sunlight off glass!

I dropped a handful of acorns and padded through the brush toward the light.

A gleaming white truck with a series of antennae and satellite dishes. On the side of the cab in black letters, ENVIRONMENTAL SYSTEMS, INC. It was either the same truck I saw the first day I headed to Florio's cabin or one of its brothers. But no guys in ball caps and coveralls.

A blur of questions.

What was it doing here, half-hidden in the trees?

How did it get here?

Where were the men?

And what the heck was it anyway, this space-age machine so out of place deep in the swamp?

I climbed to the cab. Doors locked, windows up tight. Hey, what were they expecting out here? In the underbrush, I found a decent-sized log of a live oak tree. So decent-sized, I could barely hoist it with two hands. The ship called *Old Ironsides* was made from this wood, and the history books say it could repel cannonballs.

My first try, I toppled over backward and dropped the log, then sat down and laughed. There I was, naked and alone and covered with a layer of dried mud, attacking this steel-and-glass monster with a stick. The second try, I got under the log, using my legs and back for leverage, and tossed it from my shoulder squarely into the driver-side window. The glass shattered with a startling noise.

I reached in, avoiding the jagged fragments, and opened the door. Being careful not to cut my feet, I climbed into the cab, brushed the broken glass from the seat, and sat down. A few added touches not usually found in your everyday truck. A computer keyboard, a printer, sets of dials and gauges that made no sense to me. A stack of computer paper was piled up in the printer's receptacle. I looked at it. Sharp lines, forming peaks and valleys, like an electrocardiogram. Next to the keyboard was a map, neatly folded. I opened it. The northern part of the Everglades, including the Big Cypress Swamp.

The hammocks were numbered. A red X on each of thirty or so hammocks, a date written in ink alongside. One of the dates was yesterday. That had to be this hammock. At least I knew where I was. Next to each date were letters and numbers that were meaningless to me.

I got out of the cab and looked around. A canoe with two flotation devices and two paddles was stashed under some big-leafed ferns. So far, that was the best news of the day.

And that was it. No tents, no shovels, no six-packs of beer. I followed the tire tracks through the woods to the shore. It was no more than five hundred yards. I emerged near the larger dock on the far side of the hammock from where I first set foot. But the tracks stopped where the path from the woods hit the beach. I bent down and looked closer at the sandy soil. The ground had been whisked clean by palm fronds. I had missed it my first walk around the hammock.

Okay, smart guy, what do you know?

Somebody hauled the truck here, either on a barge or on the back of a very large manatee. The workers were here yesterday and would likely be back soon. That was good for me, or was it? Who did they work for, and what were they doing, and why did they hide the truck like that?

More questions than answers. I kept thinking, turning it over. The workers don't stay overnight. They either travel by boat or helicopter. You could easily land a chopper on the beach, away from the trees. They sometimes travel offshore but not far; otherwise they'd have a powerboat and not just a canoe. They take some effort to disguise the fact they're here. Maybe they just want to protect the truck from vandalism by fishermen or froggers or the other iconoclastic types who hang out in the Everglades. But the way the truck was jammed into the trees seemed to suggest that they didn't want to be seen from the air, either.

It didn't compute. I thought of Nicky Florio. We were probably ten miles from his fishing cabin and thirty miles from his planned Las Vegas in the Swamp. This was something else, but I couldn't shake the feeling that Nicky Florio's grimy paws were all over that truck.

I went back into the woods and committed a little gentle larceny. Climbing into the truck, I took the map, then hauled the canoe out of the brush. It was an old wooden model, painted green. Wooden paddles, too.

I started out in midafternoon, watching the position of the sun and heading south. I took long, deep strokes with the paddle, counting out, "left, right, left, right." I sang as many Nat King Cole songs as I could remember and replayed an AFC championship game in my mind. I passed through the mist of the cypress strands and what seemed to be open lakes. I paddled until just before dark, then decided to look for a Holiday Inn.

I chose a hardwood hammock with a fine line of pine trees to spend the night. I slept on a bed of soft grasses and awoke at dawn, famished and dreaming of room service: fresh-squeezed orange juice, blueberry muffins, and eggs Benedict with a steaming pot of coffee. I had wrapped the map in my discarded shirt, which dried out in the sun. Now I used the shirt to wipe the dew from the plants, squeezing it out and drinking the fresh water. More pinecone seeds and pollen for breakfast.

I paddled and drifted, paddled and drifted, the slow, easy current from north to south helping me out, but not much. I used the map to navigate south toward Tamiami Trail. Sometime before noon, I heard a thunderous explosion and looked toward a hammock to the west. A cloud of dust rose from a clump of mahogany trees, and a dozen herons croaked in protest.

By midday, I saw airboats at a distance, lazing in the water, with fishing poles sketched against the sky. A barge went by, two more of the gleaming white trucks perched on the deck. A short time later, the water became less, and the land became more. A ragged shoreline was strung with the hated melaleuca tree. Introduced from Australia in a misguided effort to dry up the swamps, it was doing just that, squeezing out native trees and plants, sucking the water from the slough, depleting our aquifer. Now, years later, we're importing a sawfly from Australia that likes to eat the melaleuca and Lord knows what else.

Just before sunset, not more than a mile from Tamiami Trail, I heard the roar of an engine ahead of me. A touring airboat with perhaps a dozen tourists was headed for me. It slowed, politely, I thought, so as not to swamp me. Then it idled, and I heard the tour guide as he pointed, not so politely, at me. He was a young guy with a mustache who exuded the counterfeit charm of a used-car salesman.

"Ladies and gentlemen," he announced, his eyes hidden under a New York Yankees cap, "coming up is an excellent photo opportunity. Here we have an authentic Micanopy brave in full . . . ah . . . war paint."

"War paint, my ass!" The skeptical customer was a pudgy man in plaid shorts and a Budweiser T-shirt. He had creamy sunblock on his nose and sat next to a middle-aged woman in a straw hat. "Looks like dirt to me," the man added.

I kept paddling and was close enough to hear the *click-clicks* of the cameras.

"Yes, indeed," the guide sang out, studying me as I got closer. "Quite right. War mud. One of the little-known practices of the remnants of the Creek Confederation."

When in trouble, a savvy tour guide, like a quick-witted lawyer, improvises, trying to turn shit into gold. I always appreciated the talent.

"The mud ritual is also part of the ceremonial rain dance," the guide continued, still winging it.

"Bullshit," the tourist said. "Don't waste your film, Martha."

"Harold!" The middle-aged woman shushed him with a stern glare.

"It is one of many festivals of the Seminole and Micanopy. There is the harvest dance, the high-tide ceremony, the full-moon chant. . . ."

"The harvest dance?" The tourist snickered and shook his head. "Sounds like Friday night at the country club."

I was directly alongside now. It was time to stretch anyway, so I stood up slowly, taking care not to tip the canoe. As I did, I displayed the one part of me not covered by ceremonial mud.

Drifting by, I heard the woman gasp. "I'll get a picture of that for the bridge club."

The guide didn't miss a beat. ". . . and, of course, the ceremonial fertility rites."

Then he gunned the motor, revved up, and was gone.

Chapter 24

Let It Die

I PULLED THE CANOE ONTO A GRASSY BANK, WADED BACK INTO THE water, and dived under, trying to get clean. It was futile. Caked into mortar by the sun, the mud had become my suit of armor. Soaking wet, I climbed the bank to a wooden dock, wrapped my T-shirt around my waist to provide a modicum of modesty, and headed off, leaving a trail of grimy footprints.

I was in the parking lot of a small marina just off Tamiami Trail. I walked to the highway, pointed myself east toward Miami, and held up my thumb. I didn't look any more threatening than, say, Charles Manson if he'd just escaped from prison through a sewage canal.

A Jaguar zoomed by. So did a Mercedes and a Lexus. So did two eighteen-wheelers, a tour bus, a couple of Winnebagos, and assorted other cars, motorcycles, and vans.

I did get plenty of looks, some catcalls, and a full can of Colt 45 that just missed my head. But it was a pig farmer from Frog City who stopped.

He was a big man with gnarled hands on the wheel of a Chevy pickup with worn shocks and squeaky brakes. His two nephews shared the cab. In the back were a dozen pigs, a carpet of straw, and odoriferous reminders of last night's swine feast.

I could ride along if I didn't mind the company of the squealers.

If they didn't mind me, I didn't mind them. Somewhere under the straw, the farmer told me, was an old pair of overalls that Rufus liked to sleep on. I didn't know if Rufus was one of his nephews or two hundred pounds of pork chops, so I just hopped into the back, rooted around until I found what had once been blue-denim bib overalls. I shook straw and pig droppings out of the creases, stepped into the overalls, and fastened the snaps. The farmer popped the clutch, and I toppled over into a pink-skinned, short-haired oinker as we clanked into gear and headed toward the city.

I dozed off a couple of times, my head flopping toward my chest before snapping up again. I told myself it didn't really smell so bad back here, what with the breeze blowing and all. From time to time, a pig sniffed me, didn't like what it smelled, then backed away.

I tried to let the wind sharpen my senses. When the cobwebs cleared, I thought about Nicky Florio. How I tried to bring him down and how I had failed so miserably. I tried to enlist an ally in the tribal chairman, but he was in Florio's pocket. I still needed an ally, but who?

The farmer was headed to a slaughterhouse in Hialeah. Gables Estates was twenty miles—and several social strata removed—but he took me there anyway. It was just after noon on a Monday, if I'd been keeping track of time correctly. Nicky Florio should be at a construction site or in his office. Gina would either be sleeping late or shopping.

A dozen royal palms stood at attention on the perimeter of the circular cobblestone driveway that had a pleasant up-slope thanks to fifty tons of fill. I climbed the driveway to the four-car garage, crouched down, and peeked in through the air vents. Gina's red Porsche was there; Nicky's Bentley wasn't.

I circled behind the house, dodging the rotating water sprinklers and wending my way through six figures' worth of landscaping. I tiptoed past a bed of birds of paradise, their orange leaves like the feathers of a parrot. I avoided the cocoplum and sea grapes and stopped to survey the scene from behind a copperleaf acalypha shrub. The back lawn, which fronted a canal that led to the sea, was framed by twin hibiscus hedges blooming with red flowers. A blue jay eyed me from the safety of the sea grapes, then flew away.

I crawled forward toward the pool deck, which was surrounded by purple azaleas. The pool gleamed turquoise in the afternoon sun. Lying on a chaise longue, wearing the bottom of a string bikini and nothing else, was Gina Florio. Her eyes were closed, her body glistening with oil.

I fought my way through the azaleas and padded quietly along the keystone pool deck. I passed a whirlpool large enough to accommodate an all-pro offensive line, his-and-her cabanas, a redbrick barbecue grill that looked as if it had never been used, and a bar accented with green marble inlays. I stood at the foot of the chaise longue, barefoot and befouled, wearing Rufus's overalls. I watched a bead of sweat trickle south between Gina's suntanned breasts.

Either she sensed me or she smelled me. Her eyes opened, took a second to focus, and then she gasped. Her hands tried to cover her breasts. Hands won't do the job.

"One step and I'll scream!" she shouted, her voice struggling for control. "My husband's in the kitchen, and he's got a high-powered rifle."

"A rifle in the kitchen?" I asked. "What, next to the Cuisinart?"

Her mouth dropped open. She studied me. "Jake? Is that you?"

"I'll bet he's no better with a rifle than he is with a shotgun."

"Jake! What's happened? Why are you so . . . so stinky?"

"Is Nicky here?"

"No. I was making that up. I didn't know what to say." She took her hands away from her breasts and now arched her back toward me. Old habits die hard.

Then she laughed. "Jake, if only you could see yourself. Wait here." She ran into the cabana with little bouncy steps and came out carrying a Polaroid camera. She made me pose while she clicked off a shot of a profoundly odd-looking ex-football player, ex–public defender, ex-a-lot-of-things, including, possibly, ex-lawyer.

"The creature from the black lagoon," she announced, examining the photograph. "Come inside and get cleaned up. Then tell me what's going on."

The house was shaped like a croissant, the architecture nuevo-Mediterranean. Cast-stone columns, terra cotta barrel-tile roof, and patinaed window frames gave the place a look of graceful aging, which was a good trick because it was three years old. Inside, the fabrics and wall coverings were eggplant, aqua, and green. The floors were rough-hewn stone. A staircase to the second floor was made of travertine marble with a sweeping iron-and-mahogany rail. Weathered woods throughout let us know we were close to the sea.

Gina led me to a downstairs bathroom that was all rock: slate, limestone, and granite. The shower opened onto a lanai blooming with purple orchids and white jasmine. A couple of whiffs could make you dizzy. She brought me some industrial-strength soap the gardener uses and some fluffy black towels. Then she left me alone.

For about two minutes.

She came into the shower carrying a loofah sponge and wearing a smile and nothing else. The brush stung my skin, but the only other choice was a chisel. She scrubbed me hard and rinsed me soft. The hot water rose in billows of steam. I was clean and wet and warm when she kissed me with open lips. She pressed herself to me, our bodies squishing under the tumbling spray. She was sleek from the suntan oil, her body warm and catlike. I felt sleepy and soothed, but strangely, not aroused. The fear gone, fatigue was setting in.

She kissed me again, and we traded tongues for a long minute. Still no reaction.

She rested her head on my chest and looked down. "Where's the Jake I know so well?"

"Somewhere in the Big Cypress," I said, my words drowned out by the blast of water on tile. "Somewhere on the back of a manatee or on a hardwood hammock. I don't know, Gina. Too much has happened, and it's not over yet."

"Hush. You think too much, and you talk too much." Keeping her breasts pressed against me, she slithered lower, her tongue cleaning a path down my neck, my chest, my abdomen, and lower still. She stayed crouched there, like a catcher behind the plate, the water bouncing off the top of her downturned head.

After a moment, she looked up, smiling. "Ah, there we are, darling. There's the Jake I know."

*   *   *

The master suite had a fine view of the canal and the bay beyond. I was on my back on soft pink sheets in a canopied bed. Gina was curled next to me, her head resting on my chest.

"What did you mean about the shotgun?" Gina whispered.

I told her.

I told her everything I had left out before and added what had happened since. She listened, wincing when I got to the part about a machete and Rick Gondolier, but she didn't act surprised, and if she grieved, she kept it to herself. I told her how Nicky framed me, and how I misjudged Henry Osceola, and how, when it came down to Jim Tiger or me, I'm the one who got lucky. I told her about diving into the water with shotgun pellets spraying an arc above my head, and I told her about a hardwood hammock with a shiny truck. Then I asked her a question.

"What's the missing piece of the puzzle? What's 'the rest of it'?"

I had the sensation that she was shaking her head, the long butterscotched hair tickling my chest. "I can't, Jake. Nicky's still my husband."

"And you're loyal to him? After everything I've told you? After all you know? After this?" My gesture encompassed the bed. It was a little clumsy, but she knew what I meant.

"It's too dangerous," she whispered. "None of this would have happened if you had backed off after the trial. You should have let it die."

"Nice choice of words."

"You know what I mean. Why are you stirring everything up?"

"It's my fault? Is that the way you see it?"

"It's too big for you, Jake. You think in little bits and pieces, always asking if something is right or wrong. Nicky's on a different scale entirely. With him, it's a question of power. Is everything lined up? Can it get done?" She sat up on an elbow and looked at me. "You don't understand him."

"You're wrong. I understand he's completely immoral."

"That's what I mean. You're judgmental, and as long as you see things in moral terms, you'll never beat him. You'll never play by his rules."

The gods make their own rules. There it was again.

"If it's being judgmental to determine that murder is wrong, that's what I am. Your husband killed Tupton and had Gondolier butchered and tried to blast a hole in me that you could toss a bowling ball through."

"He didn't kill Tupton," she said.

"Okay, so two out of three. Time off for good behavior."

Outside the bedroom window, a cuckoo was singing—brisk *cuck-cuck-cucks* without the *ooo*—sounding like rapid-fire laughter.

"Tupton wasn't murdered, Jake. Really."

"So tell me."

She sat up and looked at the clock on the bedstand. "Uh-oh. I've got to get moving. I'm meeting Nicky at the club for an early dinner with Mr. Sugar."

My look told her I didn't understand.

"Carlos de La Torre. There's some hearing tomorrow, and Nicky needs to know everything's set."

"The Water Management Board," I said.

"Yeah, that's the one."

"I thought it was a done deal. Big Sugar won't oppose the casino plan."

"Right, but with Nicky, even after the nail's driven into the board, he gives it one more whack."

"Does De La Torre know about the rest of it, Gina?"

"He knows a lot, but not that." She smiled. "Carlos would not be happy about that, not at all."

"*Carlos*," I said.

She cocked her head at me. "A very handsome man in a very Latino way." Then she laughed. "Jealous?"

"No, curious."

"Really, Jake, I've got to get going, and I've said too much already." She bounded out of the bed and headed into the master-bath suite, disappearing into a maze of showers, tubs, and makeup mirrors suitable for a Hollywood star. When I heard the water gushing, I got up and went through some dresser drawers. I found a pair of silk pajamas, turquoise and white, with Nicky's initials embroidered on the breast pocket. In his closet, I pulled out a jaunty sailor's hat. A nice ensemble, I thought, as I got dressed.

I ran quickly downstairs to the kitchen, grabbed the newspaper from the breakfast nook table, and dashed back up to the bedroom. I snatched the Polaroid camera Gina had brought in from the cabana, found a spot on the dresser that had a clear view of the bed, and pushed the ten-second delay shutter.

I hopped into the bed, showed my best shit-eating grin, held up the newspaper like a hostage in the Middle East, gave the thumbs-up sign, and blinked when the flash lit up the room. I waited the prescribed time and looked at the photo. The pajamas and hat were unmistakable, the canopied bed distinctive in its own right. The newspaper had a headline, HOMICIDE RATE UP. They didn't know the half of it.

I took off the cap and pajamas and put them back where they belonged. I found a pair of Nicky's shorts that were too big and a polo shirt that was too small, and got dressed. I borrowed fifty dollars from Gina's purse, scooped up the photo of the sewer rat taken on the pool deck and the one of the satisfied lover from the bedroom—a bizarre before and after—called a cab, and tiptoed down the stairs.

I left the house without giving Gina the chance to set the odds on seeing me again.

The apartment building once had been seafoam green with sunny-yellow racing stripes darting through the stucco. Now the two colors blended into one pale pastel. Cantilevered sunshades hung over the windows like eyebrows. Despite the building's Art Deco origins, this one hadn't been restored for trendy yuppies with Volvos. It was still home to the geriatrics, who watched life from lawn chairs on the front porch.

Marvin the Maven was having afternoon tea when I rapped on the hollow door of his apartment. Afternoon tea was not freshly brewed West Bengal Darjeeling with a silver platter of scones and brandy snaps. For Marvin, it was a twice-used bag of Lipton dipped in a cup of steaming water, a prune Danish on the side.

Marvin cracked the door, leaving the chain attached. I didn't recognize him at first without the gray toupee. He looked up at me, squinting. "Jacob, *boychik*, what are you doing here?"

"I need to use the phone."

"What, you cross the causeway for that?"

I told him I couldn't go home or to my Granny's or to Charlie's or to my office. He led me to the kitchen table and offered me a Danish, prune or poppy seed, take my choice. The open second-floor window overlooked Flamingo Park. I could hear the shouts of the handball players.

Marvin the Maven slurped his tea, wrinkled his puss at me, and asked what kind of *mishegoss* I'd gotten into now, and why were my shorts so loose, my shirt so tight, and what's with the bare feet?

"I'm in a little trouble," I said.

Marvin offered me a another Danish, and I accepted. Then I asked him for a small favor. Could he go out and buy me some clothes?

His high, creased forehead added a few furrows. "Clothes?"

"You know, pants, shoes, a shirt. I'll tell you my sizes."

"Where do I get these clothes?"

"I don't know. Wherever you shop. I'll pay you back."

"Shop? I shop at the deli and the bakery, once in a while the fruit stand. Clothes I haven't bought since Harry Truman ran a haberdashery."

I told him some new stores had opened on Ocean Drive, but stay away from the ones where the clerks are going through their Carmen Miranda stage.

When he was gone, I started dialing the phone, which is what you do on an old-fashioned black rotary number. I called Abe Socolow, who asked where the hell I was, and before I had time not to answer, he pleaded with me to surrender.

"Come on in, Jake. I'm worried about you. This has really gotten serious. Gunther and half of Metro are combing the streets for you. So are the federal marshals, and one of Florio's hired hands has been snooping around the courthouse, your office, your house, the bars you frequent. . . ."

"Let me guess, Guillermo Diaz."

"Right. I've seen his rap sheet, and I know all about that business with a horse trainer upstate. I want to find you before he does, old buddy. We can protect you, and you'll get a fair trial, I promise you that."

"Trial? Abe, listen. Nicky Florio's pulling off some gigantic scam involving Micanopy land. He's got a hearing tomorrow in front of the Water Management Board, and if—"

"Screw water management! You listen to me, Jake. The grand jury handed up two indictments for first-degree murder, and your name is on the front page of each one."

"Two?"

"Yeah. One Ricardo Galliano aka Rick Gondolier and one James White Feather Tiger."

"I didn't kill Gondolier."

"Jesus Christ, Jake. What are you saying? You have the right to remain silent. You have the right—"

"I know my rights. Look, Tiger killed Gondolier. Nicky Florio ordered it. I was there. I killed Tiger, but it was self-defense."

"He was attacking you?"

"Not at the time. He was trying to coerce me into signing a confession."

"So you *killed* him? He was a cop, for Christ's sake. He was doing his job."

"He was framing me for a murder he committed, and then he and Diaz were going to kill me and make it look like a suicide. He was doing Nicky Florio's dirty work. I did what I had to do."

Through the line, I heard a bitter laugh. "I've seen the autopsy report, Jake. You rammed a pen into his brain, then blew off both his legs with shotgun blasts. It looks like an assassination, and the pictures aren't pretty. Two grand jurors blew their lunch."

"Florio must have used the shotgun."

"Why?"

"Who knows? Because he was angry, because he wanted to make it look worse for me."

"Florio told the grand jury that you and Gondolier stole a million bucks from the bingo hall. He says you killed Gondolier in some dispute between thieves and then killed Tiger, who was investigating the murder."

"Then Florio's guilty of perjury besides everything else."

"Look, Jake, my sources tell me Tiger was dirty, but that stuff tends to get overlooked when a guy with a badge gets blown away. What we're looking at here is a twenty-one-gun salute, a funeral with uniforms from all over the state, and a half-assed lawyer branded as a cop-killer. All hell will break loose when the indictments get unsealed. Even now, we got some trigger-happy guys on Metro who might take you out if this Diaz creep doesn't find you first. Jake, I figure you got about twenty-four hours to live if you don't get your ass in here where I can protect you."

We both listened to the buzzing on the line for a moment.

"You're not coming in, are you?" he asked finally.

"No. If I do, I'll never get what I need on Florio. I can't clear myself sitting in the can."

I heard him sigh.

"Okay, what's this shit about the Water Management Board? Anything illegal, anything I can pull Florio's chain about?"

"I don't know. Just show up. The hearing's in Belle Glade. If I can't nail Nicky there, you can bring me in, but leave Gunther home. Next time I see him, I'm going to put him on his ass."

Socolow was telling me to stop threatening state officers, I was already in enough trouble, but I hung up halfway through his speech and laboriously dialed another number. Mike Goldberg answered the phone in his red Ferrari. He was a private investigator who specialized in divorce work and once did ninety days for wiretapping the lusty wife of a bank executive. I asked him about some technical equipment, and he said he could have it ready and working in thirty minutes.

Then I called Sam Terilli, who used to run a cockfighting racket in Sweetwater. I walked him on animal cruelty and gambling charges when the roosters refused to testify, and now he took bets on pro football when he wasn't seating the beautiful people at the Ocean Club. I asked him if he knew Nicky Florio, and he told me that everybody knew Nicky Florio. I asked if he was seating Nicky's party at a particular table this evening, and he took a moment looking at his reservations book. In about an hour, Sam said, Nicky would be at his usual table. It overlooks the marina, and he can see his Bertram through the window. I looked at the clock on Marvin's old stove and told Sam I'd see him in forty-five minutes.

Chapter 25

Water Flows Uphill

The lobby of the Ocean Club was dim. On the wall of the reading room was a faded mural of three pink flamingoes. The building was aging gracefully, if that's what you call it when the stucco walls might have been used for mortar practice. To demonstrate a blasé attitude about appearances, the upper crust relishes a gentle seediness that distinguishes its playpens from those shining chrome palaces of the nouveau riche. Still, in hard times, old money makes compromises, like admitting into membership a contentious real estate developer named Nicky Florio.

The club was 1930s Miami, complete with portholes for windows and wooden decks for balconies. On the roof were soaring towers resembling the smokestacks of a ship. It looked like a cardboard set for a Fred Astaire–Ginger Rogers movie. Critics who worship the period would call it theatrical, romantic, and imbued with a sense of fantasy and animation. To me, it was just a dank old place with peeling paint, a society joint that discriminated against minorities and gave shelter to politicians and businessman who hatched quiet deals out of view of the public and press.

There was a dining room that fronted on a marina, an adjoining bar, and forty-five hotel rooms on three upper floors. I passed under an ornate chandelier with hanging crystal doodads, and went straight to room 212, the desk clerk studying me as I breezed past him. I was wearing a blousy black silk shirt with enough material for a parachute. The pants were black leather and crackled with each step. My feet hurt from the high-heeled boots, black again, with silver piping. I looked like a reject from a Harley-Davidson convention, but Marvin the Maven told me it was either this or rayon pants with pink roses, so I thanked him and vowed never to shop on South Beach.

Sam Terilli said I would be directly over the dining room. The door was open, just as he had promised. Mike Goldberg had already installed the equipment. The small console was turned on, the red light glowing, the volume adjusted. I picked up the earphones. Just the faraway clatter of a busy dining room.

The telephone rang.

Terilli told me the Florios had arrived and were in the bar. They were waiting for Mr. de La Torre.

The bar.

I hadn't counted on that. They could sit there and drink half the evening away, and I wouldn't hear a thing. I drummed my fingers on a cigarette-scarred dresser, studying a print on the wall, a still life of avocadoes and mangoes.

The telephone rang again.

Mr. de La Torre had joined the Florios in the bar. Everyone ordered drinks. Nicky and Carlos were doing the talking, but when Terilli tried to move close, they clammed up.

Five minutes later, another ring. "Pick up the earphones. I just seated them."

Another round of drinks. Jack Daniel's straight up for Nicky, Absolut on the rocks for Carlos, and white wine for Gina.

Small talk and the gentle clinking of glasses.

What a lovely dress you're wearing, Mrs. Florio. Hasn't it been a dry winter? Are you going to Aspen for spring skiing, or have they ruined the place? The ambience in Idaho is so much better. The discount rate dropped half a point, maybe construction will pick up. The audio was decent, but the *cloppity-clop* of footsteps on the old tile floor kept interfering. The microphone must be under the table. Carlos de La Torre had a faint Cuban accent and the loudest voice. He complained about the damn do-gooders pushing for better working conditions for his Jamaican sugarcane cutters.

He complained about having to pay $4 million in fines for dumping carcinogenic chemicals into the water waste at his sugar mills. He complained a lot.

They ordered appetizers. Melon and prosciutto for Gina, an eggplant crepe filled with mozzarella and covered with tomato sauce for Carlos and a good old shrimp cocktail for Nicky.

"Well, tomorrow's the day," Nicky said, after the waiter took the order.

"*¿Todo en orden?*" Carlos asked.

"No problems at my end. I'm counting on you, of course."

"I will be there personally. It is better than sending the lawyers. If necessary, I will remind the board members of a wonderful weekend they spent on my ranch hunting quail."

There seemed to be some chuckling at that one.

The waiter returned, and Nicky ordered another bourbon. Mineral water for Carlos and Gina this time.

"I am very grateful for your help," Nicky said. His tone was respectful, his manner formal. I wasn't used to him that way. But Carlos de La Torre had more money than Nicky Florio, and maybe that was how the pecking order was determined. "I couldn't do it without—" *Cloppity-clop.*

"*Correcto!*" De La Torre boomed. "*Totalmente correcto!* It's worth ten percent of the gross, right? And we're not—"

At a nearby table, someone barked instructions at the waiter. Trying to follow the conversation was like listening to overlapping dialogue in a Robert Altman movie. It took all my concentration.

". . . the management company's gross." Carlos de La Torre again. "You're not dealing with the Indians here, Nick. I want a dime of every dollar from every slot machine, craps, and blackjack table in the place. Not to mention the roulette and poker and whatever other legalized thievery you're planning."

"It's a lot of money," Florio said.

"Yes, for a . . . what did you call me in the contract?"

"A consultant."

Laughter, Gina joining in.

"My friends on the water board must not know—" *Cloppity-clop-clop.*

"No, of course not," Florio responded. A piece of silverware banged against a plate. I pictured Nicky Florio gesturing with a fork. "The bastards would *each* demand ten percent, and what would I have left?"

More laughing all around. What a hilarious group.

They resumed their small talk, Carlos drawing Gina into the conversation. Then a discussion of diets, and which friends had stopped eating red meat. The waiter returned, and they ordered. Angel hair pasta with fresh tomatoes for Gina, a whole fried snapper in ginger sauce for Carlos, and a Porterhouse steak, medium rare, for Nicky. Caesar salads all around, hold the anchovies.

"One more thing," Nicky said, his voice a shade lower. I pictured him leaning closer to De La Torre. "We've got more soil tests to do out there, and I'd love to drop the water level another foot."

"So?"

"I can't tell the board members because they don't want the Big Cypress any drier, and I don't want to send the water south through the park because the rangers will scream we're flooding the gator holes. So, Carlos, can you use a few billion cubic feet of water?"

"Water," De La Torre mused. "What is it the Bible says? 'If thine enemy be thirsty, give him water to drink.' "

"Carlos, what are you saying? We are friends."

"*Verdad*, and the very best kind, friends of convenience. Our friendship floats on a river of water. Is there another commodity so precious? In a drought, my company would pay anything for water, but we don't have to because the Water Management Board would drain the Big Cypress for us. In my business, we have a saying, 'Water flows uphill, toward the money.' "

There were the sounds of utensils clicking against plates, some mumbled words, feet shuffling under the table.

"We don't need the water now," De La Torre continued, "but to help a friend, we'll take some for the fields and dispose of the rest through canals. It'll be in the Gulf before anyone knows. But not a word—" *cloppity-clop* "—or there'll be hell to pay."

"Thank you, Carlos. You and I understand each other perfectly." Then Nicky excused himself. Too much bourbon, he said, provoking another laugh.

At first, Gina's voice was so soft I could barely hear her. But I knew it was her. I had heard that tone before. And the words, too. So many times over so many years. "I've missed you, Carlos."

"And I have missed you, *chiquita*." His voice a whisper now.

"I thought tomorrow . . ."

"No, business first. Besides, I promised your husband I'd be there."

"Business, business, business. The two of you are so much alike."

A soft chuckle. "That is not what you whispered to me when . . ."

Cloppity-clop.

"I should never have gotten involved with you. That first time, it was such a close call, we shouldn't—"

"That's why you did it! Don't you know that? It is the risk you enjoy. In your husband's home, a hundred people around, it turns you on."

"We were nearly caught."

"Nearly! We were . . ."

A throat cleared. "Would you care for coffee now, or are you waiting for the gentleman to return?"

Damn. Like a policeman, you can never get a waiter when you need one. But when you'd rather be alone . . .

"Espresso now would be fine," Carlos said. Here was a man who didn't wait for anybody.

"Two," Gina said.

Silence except for the background noise. I wanted to hear more. Come on, Gina.

A mumble. ". . . comes now."

The scraping of a chair against the floor. Straining to listen through the earphones was giving me a headache.

"So what were you two talking about?" Nicky Florio asked.

"Price supports for the sugar industry and its effect on the international trade of commodities," Carlos de La Torre said, and everybody had a good laugh.

My mind was buzzing as I raced down the staircase of threadbare carpeting to the main floor. There was so much I didn't understand about Gina. What made her tick, anyway? Did boredom make her a thrill-seeker? Was it for the sex, or the power she could wield over men? I had never understood her.

Passing by the dining room and the bar, I headed toward the lobby, aiming for the front door and the parking lot. Etched into the glass wall of the bar was a schooner under full sail. It made me think of open seas and steady winds. I chased the thought away and tried to concentrate on what I had just heard. The door to the bar opened, emitting sounds of happy chatter. A man came out, but I never looked his way. I was still thinking about water and roulette wheels, bribes and sugarcane, Carlos and Gina. Always Gina.

"Lassiter? Lassiter, that you?"

A smart guy would have kept going, head down. A guy in control wouldn't have jerked around and gaped, a puzzled look on his all-too-visible face. But that's what I did.

"Jesus H. Christ, Lassiter." Gunther wore a golf shirt under a brown plaid sport coat. His thick cop neck filled the open-collar shirt. "What the fuck are you doing here?"

It wasn't so much a question as an accusation.

I stared dumbly at him.

He reached inside his sport coat, patting for the shoulder holster that wasn't there. His mouth formed the word "shit."

"Hey, Gunther, you're out of uniform."

"But you're not," he said, examining my leather pants. "Looks like you're trolling for queers. You'll have plenty to choose from where I'm taking you."

"Where's that, the Policemen's Ball?"

He growled at me. "What's that supposed to mean?"

"Think about it. It'll come to you."

"I'm taking you in, asshole." He reached behind his back and came up with a pair of handcuffs. I took a step backward and raised my hands.

"Look, Gunther. Try to get this through your thick skull. We're on the same side. Nicky Florio is the guy you want. He's a con man, a murderer, and probably cheats at poker."

Gunther took a step toward me, so I took another step back. I was pressed against the wall of the corridor. The front door was twenty paces away. I saw Sam Terilli, the felonious maître d', standing in the service entrance to the kitchen, thirty paces the other way. He made a slight gesture with his head, telling me to come that way. Okay, Sam, I'm trying.

Next to me was a glass trophy case filled with tarnished silver bowls, dusty plaques, and antique golf clubs. I was aware of men in brightly colored slacks surrounding us. Most were gray-haired businessman types in their fifties. A man in a teal pullover sweater tried to step between us. "What's the trouble here?" he asked.

"I wouldn't let this mug play through on fifteen," I said.

"Shut up, Lassiter!" Gunther's face was reddening. "I'm a police officer, and if you'll all kindly back away, I'll place this man under arrest."

Gunther took a sideways step as if to reach behind me, but I moved the same direction. Sort of a fox-trot. Then a familiar voice. "I see you have encountered the fugitive," Nicky Florio said. "Be careful, he's quite dangerous, Officer."

This caused a stir in the golf-slacks-and-sweater crowd. A bald man, about sixty, approached Gunther, seemingly to offer help. I'll bet this was the most excitement they'd had at the club since women were allowed in the Men's Grill.

"Jake, you look like a Times Square cowboy," Florio said.

"And you look like a cold-blooded killer."

"Do I now? Well, I ask you who has been charged with murder? Who is a respected businessman, and who is under indictment?"

I was aware of two dozen eyes staring at me as if I were a cockroach on the pantry floor.

"Officer, I believe the man is quite deranged," Florio said. "I have testified before the grand jury as to his deeds." He looked at me with a self-satisfied smirk. Now I saw Gina half a step behind him, biting her lip. I felt my neck redden, embarrassed for her to see me this way, cornered and defenseless. A handsome man with a black mustache—Carlos de La Torre—was gently holding her arm, as if to protect her.

Gunther nodded in their direction. "No problem, Mr. Florio." He looked back at the posse of duffers. "But one of you gentlemen might just call nine-one-one and ask for some backup."

Two sweaters disappeared into the crowd. Not much time now. I stepped to my right and banged into the trophy case. Gunther moved toward me, his broad shoulders blocking my path. "Okay, Lassiter, it's over." He extended his right hand as if to grab me above the elbow. His left hand still held the handcuffs.

I let my body sag. "You win," I told him. "I know when I'm beaten."

Gunther smiled and stepped forward. I pivoted my left hip and threw a jab a tad too high. It bounced off his sloping forehead, but not without snapping his head back. His eyes closed, then opened wide. He roared like a wounded elephant, from anger, not pain, dropped the handcuffs, and charged me. He missed with a looping roundhouse right that I ducked. I feinted with a left, tapped his skull with a glancing right, tried to dig a hook into his kidneys, but he blocked me. As he backed up, I did my best imitation of a place-kicker. My pants rustled as I brought up a black boot aimed at his crotch. But the pants were too tight and the kick too slow. He caught me by the heel of my cowboy boot and slammed me backward into the trophy case. The door shattered, and shards of glass cascaded over me. My feet were slipping, and my right hand reached reflexively toward the wall to gain my balance. Instead, it went into the trophy case. I knocked over a couple of bowls and then felt my hand wrap itself around the wooden shaft of an ancient golf club that might have been a six iron.

I was shoving Gunther away with my left hand, but he was clawing at my face, trying to get both hands around my neck. I bent my knees, got leverage, and pushed him off, at the same time tearing the golf club out of the case.

Gunther stood three feet away, facing me, and I jammed the iron under his nose.

"No!" cried a man in a peach sweater and mauve polyester slacks. "That's Ben Hogan's mashie niblick."

"Gunther, nothing would give me greater pleasure than to knock your teeth from here to Augusta. Now back off!"

I jabbed at his chest with the old iron, and he backed up. So did everybody else. I moved forward three steps, and everyone backed up some more. I kept going, and so did they. This was more like it. Outside, I heard the wail of a police siren. Then another. Damn, no use heading for the front door.

"Jake, it's useless to run," Nicky Florio said, his voice soothing. "Turn yourself in. Let them get you some professional help." Now he was my friend, trying to steer me away from my life of crime and depravity.

I was under the crystal chandelier. I raised Ben Hogan's old stick over my head and took a giant swipe at it. The crystal broke, bulbs popped, sparks flew, and everyone ducked and scurried out of the way. Gunther covered his head with his hands but came at me anyway. I dropped him with a solid whack to the knee. Not a bad stroke, though I didn't have enough hip in it. He yelped and fell, cursing at me, clutching his knee, and rolling onto his side. The sirens shrieked closer.

I moved twenty paces toward the service entrance to the kitchen, neither running nor walking, just moving at a good clip. Florio broke from the crowd and followed me. I turned toward him, and he stopped. "You can run, Jake, but you can't hide," he said, taunting me in a voice just above a whisper. "If the cops don't get you, I will. You'd better hope they find you first."

I left him standing there and pushed through the door where Sam Terilli was waiting. He grabbed me by an arm, guided me past a stove brimming with pots of soup, around the freezers, and then hustled me out the back door. By a smelly Dumpster, two kitchen workers were speaking in Creole and smoking a reefer as big as a cigar. Terilli pushed me into a waiting taxi. I thanked him, and he said don't mention it, but forget about applying for membership at the club anytime soon.

Charlie Riggs was sitting on a stool at the counter of a Cuban sandwich shop on Calle Ocho. He sipped at a café Cubano. A tired waitress with dyed red hair took my order: a beer and a bowl of black bean soup, heavy on the onions. It was just before midnight, or just after, I couldn't tell which. My shoulders ached from two days of rowing a canoe. My back was stiff, and I pulled my hamstrings while launching the kick toward the balls of the loudmouthed detective. I hadn't had a decent night's sleep in days, or was it weeks, and my head was spinning because I still didn't know what was going on.

So I told everything I knew to Charlie. He asked me to go over it again, and I did. I showed him the map I had taken from the shiny truck on the woody hammock. He asked me to describe the truck in as much detail as I could, and I did that, too.

What else did Nicky say to De La Torre about lowering the water level? he wanted to know.

Nothing.

What kind of soil tests?

I didn't know. Nicky hadn't said.

Hmmm. Charlie ordered another syrupy café Cubano and poured enough sugar into it to make Carlos de La Torre even richer. "Anything else? See anything unusual out there?" He cocked his head to the west.

"*Nada.*"

"You're sure?"

"It was the Everglades, Charlie. Peaceful, except when I had to use a pen as a dagger, or I was ducking shotgun pellets. Quiet, except for the birds squawking and an occasional explosion."

He looked up at me from under bushy eyebrows. "What sort of explosions?"

"I don't know. The loud kind."

"Where?"

"Out there somewhere. Who knows where? I heard them first at Nicky's house the morning after Gondolier was killed. For a while, I thought it was thunder. Then, when I was paddling the canoe, I heard some more." I watched Charlie digest the information. "Why do you ask?"

Charlie harrumphed and thought it over. I had finished the soup and just realized how hungry I was. When the waitress came by, I ordered a *media noche* and an order of sweet plantains.

"The computer printout in the truck," Charlie said. "Describe it, please."

"Just a bunch of squiggly lines, like an EKG."

He scowled at me. "You might have thought to bring it with you."

"Hey, Charlie. I was traveling light. I didn't even have pants."

"Sorry. Let's have a look at where you found the truck."

The sandwich arrived, but I slid my plate away and spread the map over the counter. Charlie studied it, then tapped a pudgy finger on what looked like a tiny island among hundreds of others. "A-653-G2," he said, reading the handwritten notation. "That's where you were. Notice anything different about A-653-G1?"

I looked at a hammock maybe a mile away. "It's underlined. That's all."

"How about A-653-G3?"

It took me a while to find it. "Not underlined."

"Which means what?"

"I don't know, Charlie. C'mon. I got bored with the Socratic method my first semester in night law school."

"Not only does the numbering system identify the islands, it's the order they're being examined." His finger stayed on A-653-G3. "You were on G2. So were the workers, maybe a day or two before you got there. Next, your boys are headed to G3. Think you could find it?"

I looked at the map. A hammock like all the others. Teardrop-shaped, with the fatter end toward the north. The southerly water flow tended to erode the hammocks in that direction. "Not quickly, I couldn't. You get out there, they all look alike. It'd take a week."

"What about from the air?"

"Yeah, maybe. But so what? Do you know what's going on out there?"

"I think so."

"What! What is it?"

"*Sapiens nihil affirmat quod non probat.* A wise man states as true nothing he cannot prove."

"Then what am I supposed to do? What am I going to do when I find the hammock?"

Charlie smiled at me. It was the sad smile of the patient teacher to the slow student. "You're a lawyer, Jake. What is it that you do?"

"Breach confidences, commit malpractice, sleep with my client's wife. Why do you ask?"

Charlie frowned with disapproval. "As I understand what you've told me, there's a hearing tomorrow. . . ." He looked at his watch. "Dear me, look at the time. There's a Water Management Board hearing *today* at two P.M. in Belle Glade. The press will be there. The public will be there. Environmental groups will be out in force. You've got to find your witnesses, Jake. You've got to present your testimony. You've got to win your case."

Chapter 26

Dredge and Drain

SHRIMP BOATS WERE CHUGGING DOWN THE MIAMI RIVER INTO THE bay, heading out on their predawn runs. Across the black water, the high-rises on Miami Beach blinked in the darkness. I sat in the isolation of my thirty-second-floor office, thinking and waiting.

One chance. A long shot. Even if Charlie was right, I didn't know if I could bring it off. Like a double reverse to the wideout coming around, the timing had to be perfect. I needed a witness who would talk, a public forum to hear what he had to say, and enough people around to keep me from getting a machete in the back. And I needed it all by two o'clock this afternoon.

Cindy arrived at 3:00 A.M., bleary-eyed and curly-haired. Copper-colored curls, tight against her skull, like a 1920s flapper. She wore white jeans and a red T-shirt emblazoned SOME GIRLS DON'T, BUT I JUST MIGHT.

"What happened to the blond look?" I asked.

"What happened to nine-to-five? What happened to a boss who shows up for work, who still has his ticket to practice law, who isn't being chased by—"

"You fall out the wrong side of someone's bed?"

"*My* bed, and it didn't please Miguel one bit."

"Miguel? The firm messenger?"

"He can tote the mail. Now what's so urgent?"

"You still take shorthand?"

"With my eyes closed, which they're gonna be if you don't—"

"Okay, take a lawsuit. A class-action suit, Jane Lassiter and all others similarly situated versus Environmental Systems, Inc., Florio Enterprises, Inc., Nicholas Florio, and a few others I'll make up as I go along. Are you taking this down?"

She picked up a pad and pencil. "Did you say *Jane?*"

"Sounds better than Granny in a formal pleading, don't you think?"

So I dictated, and she scribbled. A suit for violation of every federal, state, and county environmental law I could find, plus some that ought to be on the books but aren't. By dawn, crisp double-spaced sheets were flowing from the laser printer, and when the clerk's office opened at 8:00 A.M., we'd have a pending suit and officially issued subpoenas.

In the partners' lounge, I splashed water on my face and changed into a dark blue suit, white shirt, and burgundy tie that always hang in my office closet for emergencies. After Cindy collated and stapled all the copies of the lawsuit, we drove in her car to the courthouse, where she paid the filing fees in cash. I dropped her off at the Metromover station with instructions to deliver copies to the newspaper and have Miguel do the same for the television stations, assuming he could still walk. Then I headed toward Tamiami Airport.

Hank Scourby flew F-4 Phantom II fighter-bombers in Vietnam. He survived a dose of the clap, a botched carrier landing that cost the taxpayers an aircraft, and the bombing of a Saigon brothel that broke both his eardrums. He came home a skilled pilot and a paranoid schizophrenic with a drug problem.

Scourby retired to Homestead, thirty miles south of Miami, tended a garden for a few years, then took up piloting 727s for East Coast Airlines. In those days, he drove a red Corvette that had a habit of bashing into parked cars in back of late-night saloons. I helped him keep his FAA license by beating three DUI charges. Just another public service by your neighborhood lawyer.

When the airline sank into the morass of bankruptcy, Scourby began flying charter helicopters for one of the few companies that didn't bring drugs in from the islands. I tossed some business his way, usually when I needed aerial photographs for a case.

Today, Scourby wore a U.S. Navy jumpsuit and tied his shoulder-length gray hair into a ponytail under his helmet. His bloodshot eyes tended to dart back and forth when he was excited and to glaze over when he was not.

I showed him the map. "Can you find this little island? A-653-G3."

"Find it? I could fucking napalm it."

Hank did a visual check of a four-seat helicopter, told me to climb aboard, chanted a Buddhist prayer to bless our journey, then got in next to me. He chattered to the tower, revved up the engine, then, in that up-up-and-away sweep peculiar to helicopters, we were airborne. We headed west, passing over town houses and tract homes of the suburban sprawl. Below us were strip shopping centers with empty parking lots and mounting vacancies. What used to be the eastern edge of the Everglades was a tangle of curving streets, barrel-tiled roofs, and turquoise swimming pools.

In a few minutes, the endless concrete and asphalt disappeared. Patches of saw grass, a wet prairie unfolded, the morning sun bursting off the water. From five hundred feet, the tracks of swamp buggies were clearly visible, scars in the tawny pelt of grass. A flash of movement, and a small white-tailed deer splashed through the water.

We soared over the national park, the water deeper and darker in the Shark River Slough. Turning north, we crossed Tamiami Trail and headed for the Big Cypress Swamp. We passed over mudflats and marshy hammocks, sparse trees, and thick forests. We watched the terrain change from pine rockland to mangrove swamps to cypress heads. We flew through morning mist and emerged into brilliant sunlight, watching the shadow of the helicopter skirt across the dark water below.

Hank took an occasional look at the map, subtly changed directions two or three times, and kept flying. I looked at my watch. Noon already. We would never make it.

At one point, he seemed to be lost. We flew in a circle, then reversed field and did it the other way around. Finally, he tapped me on the shoulder and pointed wordlessly ahead. I squinted into the sun. It was a hardwood hammock like hundreds of others. He dipped the helicopter a little quicker than I thought was absolutely necessary and headed for a clearing on the beach.

I saw the truck when the sun glinted off its window. It was pulled halfway into a strand of mahogany trees, gleaming white as we drew closer. By the time we touched down, sending up swirls of sand, two men in white coveralls and rubberized boots were walking out of the woods toward us.

I was out of the copter first, ducking under the rotor, wincing against the noise of the engine. I remembered another chopper blade, and how it ended the life of Matsuo Yagamata and saved mine. One of the men, the larger of the two, carried a clipboard. The other had a pair of calipers in his right hand. Both were clean-shaven, short-haired, and respectable-looking. Neither seemed alarmed or particularly surprised to see us. I was wearing my suit, carrying a briefcase, and doing my best to look like a working lawyer instead of a fleeing felon.

When the engine roar died, the larger man pointed to my brief-case. "Unless they're making 'em smaller than I remember, you're not carrying a seismograph in there."

"Afraid not," I told him.

"Shee-it." Texas dripped from his voice. "Twenty-four hours we've been waiting. Our graph's deader than communism." He studied me a moment. "So why'd they send you out here?"

I opened the briefcase and pulled out a file. "Which one of you is in charge?"

The other man stepped forward. Close up, he had a receding hairline and narrow shoulders, the slightly nerdy look of the grad student who never escaped from the lab or library. I had seen him before, climbing out of the cab of the truck on a narrow dirt road. "I am," he said.

I looked at my file as if something important were there. "Let's see, you're Mr. . . ."

"Wakefield. Tucker Wakefield."

"Yes, of course." I pulled out a pen and took the subpoena that had been issued two hours earlier in the name of John Doe, Ge-ologist. I wrote in "Tucker Wakefield." "You a geologist?"

"Of course. What else would I—"

I handed him the subpoena.

"What's this?"

The larger man looked over his shoulder and scowled. "Who the hell do you think you are?"

I ignored him and put on my formal, grown-up voice. "Mr. Wakefield, I'm taking your deposition this afternoon at two o'clock in Belle Glade. Your testimony is needed in the lawsuit of Granny Lassiter—that is, Jane Lassiter—versus Environmental Systems, Inc., et al. We'll take you there." I pointed toward the helicopter. "Now, if you'll just climb aboard."

Wakefield took a step backward. "I'll have to consult with the company lawyers, of course. And a deposition today is just out of the question. I've been deposed many times as an expert witness, and I've always been provided ample notice. Really, this is quite unprecedented. . . ."

The big guy glared at me. "This is bullshit!"

Wakefield thumbed quickly through the lawsuit, stopping at the signature block on the last page. "I assume you're Mr. Lassiter."

"Guilty," I said.

"According to this, your office is in Miami. Why would you want to take my testimony in Belle Glade?"

"I like an audience when I perform."

That puzzled him. Meanwhile, the big guy started walking toward their truck. "I'm gonna radio in, find out what the fuck's going on."

"Hold on, cowboy." It was Hank Scourby, and he pointed a .44 Magnum in the general direction of the big guy's kneecaps. "I blow a hole in your leg, you'll bleed to death before we get to the hospital."

I've had aggressive process servers before, but this was ridiculous. "Hey, Hank, let me handle this, okay?"

"You're not doing so well, Jake." He turned toward Wakefield. "Okay, egghead, we're going for a ride. Your pal can stay here, but let me have a look at that radio first. I think it may need a new part."

Wakefield did as he was told, and Hank Scourby added two pieces of steel-jacketed lead to the radio.

It was 1:15. We flew north and then east, and soon the saw grass gave way to sugarcane. Endless fields of brown stalks, poking toward the sky. Below us, huge mechanical harvesters rolled between rows of cane, invisible blades chopping the stalks. In other fields, cutters from Jamaica, bent at the waist, swung machetes in a rhythmic motion, doing the same job. On the horizon, black smoke rose from other fields as the leaves were burned away prior to harvesting. A huge mill on the edge of the fields exhaled white puffs of steam into the blue sky.

Over the noise of the engine, Tucker Wakefield asked me the subject matter of his testimony.

The truth, I told him. Just tell the board what you're doing out there.

He shrugged as if to say, no big deal.

Maybe he was right. Maybe no one would care. It might even be humorous to them, the dog-and-pony show I was planning. Maybe they knew the truth and didn't give a damn. As I listened to the *chucka-chucka* of the rotor, I closed my eyes, yawned, and envisioned it. The truth spilling out in front of the board, and Nicky Florio guffawing at me. *That's your case, Lassiter? You think you can stop Nicky Florio with that?* Then the commissioners, their pockets bursting with De La Torre's cash, would cackle with laughter. After a town and a casino, what's one more surprise? The only one not smiling would be Abe Socolow as he fastened the cuffs on me.

I kept looking at my watch.

Five minutes before two o'clock. We would be late. But there would be preliminary matters. Other voices to be heard. Below us the fields disappeared, and the town crept into view.

It took several more minutes to find the school. We made two passes over the football field; then, checking for power lines, Hank Scourby put the copter down on the asphalt parking lot behind the gym.

Two Micanopy tribal policemen leaned against their car, watching us, as the rotors whined to a halt and we got out. Friends or foes, I didn't know which. I waved to them, as if we were pals, and one waved back. Maybe they figured we were the environmental boys from Tallahassee. After a moment, they turned back and resumed talking. I didn't feel like towing Tucker Wakefield past them, so we slipped around the building to a side entrance, where there was another Micanopy police car with its distinctive emblem of alligator, saw grass, and colorful ceremonial jacket. Two more cops loitered there, chatting with a rangy man in sunglasses who wore jeans and a blue windbreaker with FLORIO ENTERPRISES printed on the back.

What were the cops doing here? This wasn't Micanopy territory. It was a small town practically owned by sugarcane baron Carlos de La Torre. Why did I think the tribal police had become Nicky Florio's private security force?

We hustled Wakefield past the cops and into the side door that led to a locker room. Signs were plastered on the walls for the young athletes. THE FOURTH QUARTER IS OURS. WHEN THE GOING GETS TOUGH, THE TOUGH GET GOING.

We took a stairwell to a balcony over the gym, home of the Fighting Sugarcanes, according to a banner. We crossed the empty balcony and took another set of stairs down to the gym floor, working our way to the front row of a section of bleachers pulled down for the hearing.

"Phosphorus and mercury levels are already appalling," a voice said through an amplified sound system.

Half a dozen tables, doubtless borrowed from the cafeteria, were drawn together at half-court. The chairman of the board sat in the middle, two fellow commissioners on each side. A stenographer took notes. The suits sat at another table, three board lawyers, an assistant attorney general, and Abe Socolow.

Nicky Florio and Carlos de La Torre were at their own table. Guillermo Diaz sat behind Florio, covering his back, as a good bodyguard should. The model of the Cypress Estates project—museum, casino, and all—was placed on a platform in front of the board. There were perhaps three hundred spectators scattered throughout the bleachers.

To one side was a press table. I recognized a couple of the reporters. Britt Montero was there from the *Miami Daily News*. We were supposed to go out for stone crabs once, but she stood me up for a three-alarm fire. Two television reporters were lounging around a table of sodas and coffee. Photographers from both newspapers and television sat cross-legged on the floor.

"When will this board ever stop the dredging and draining?" Hunched over a microphone at a lectern was a tall, thin man with a white mustache and a creased face. He wore muddy hiking boots, khaki pants, and a bush jacket and looked close to eighty. Harrison Baker, founder of the Everglades Society. He had briefly testified at the Tupton trial.

"First a town. Now a casino! What next?"

I knew the answer, but it wasn't my turn.

"We request a postponement of all board action until studies can be made," Baker said. "Why, we don't even know if it's legal."

"Hold on, Harrison. The state attorney's here on that point." Clyde Thornton, the board chairman, was a pudgy, balding, ruddy-faced retired tomato grower from Sarasota. He wore a beige suit with shoulder piping and a string tie.

Abe Socolow got to his feet and cleared his throat. "In the state's opinion, the proposal of Florio Enterprises, as endorsed by the Micanopy Tribal Council, conforms to the provisions of the Indian Regulatory Gaming Act of 1988," Socolow said, in perfect legalese.

"So there you have it," Thornton said triumphantly, playing to the audience, most of whom looked like farmers, some the gentleman-conglomerate variety. "The only amendment to the proposal is the addition of gambling to what was already a substantial commercial and residential development. Frankly, I cannot see a practical difference."

"Then you're blind as a bat," Baker muttered, half to himself.

"You've made your point," Thornton said, his eyes narrowing. "But we have also heard from the Micanopy tribe and from National Sugar, both of which endorse the plan. I'm afraid your group, as usual, stands alone. Now, unless you have anything new to add—"

"It's the same damn thing!" Baker shouted. "You boot-licking toadies would pave over Lake Okeechobee if the sugar industry wanted a parking lot."

"That's it!" Thornton hit a switch, and Harrison Baker's mike went dead. As if on cue, two burly men in Florio Enterprises windbreakers materialized from behind the bleachers. In a moment, they had gathered up the old man, one grabbing each arm, and were politely but firmly taking him back to his seat.

I had been right. This was Nicky Florio's show.

Thornton scanned the audience. "That concludes the formal agenda. Before we vote on the proposal, is there anyone in the gallery who wishes to address these issues?"

No one stood up.

Except me.

A split second later, Tucker Wakefield popped off the bleachers, nudged by Hank Scourby's elbow.

"May it please the board, my name is Jacob Lassiter, and I have a witness to present." I approached the lectern, Wakefield reluctantly following.

Nicky Florio wheeled, half rising from his chair, eyes aflame. His face flashed through a series of emotions, first surprise, then volcanic anger, and finally zealous determination. "Hold on! This man is a disbarred lawyer and a lunatic."

"I'm not disbarred," I said in my own semidefense.

Thornton nodded deferentially toward Florio, consulted with the commissioner on his left, a man with what appeared to be a cancerous lesion on his nose, and turned back to me. "Under our rules, anyone can speak. Let's get on with it, Mr. Lassiter, and please be brief."

I nodded my thanks and guided Tucker Wakefield to a chair that doubled as a witness stand. I ran through his credentials, a bachelor's degree in petroleum engineering from the University of Texas and a master's degree from the Colorado School of Mines.

Behind me, I heard a chair scraping the gymnasium floor. I sneaked a peek at Guillermo Diaz backing away from the table.

"How are you employed?" I asked.

"I'm a geologist for Environmental Systems, Inc., of Houston."

"What are you doing in Florida?"

"Seismic tests."

"How do you perform these tests?"

"We set off small dynamite explosions to send shock waves into the earth. Our equipment—when it's working—records the pattern of sound waves and helps us to determine what structures exist underground."

I watched Diaz take quick, choppy steps toward the side exit, then disappear through the door.

"And why do you do this?"

"It's my job."

Thornton snickered into the microphone.

"I understand that," I said. "What is the purpose of seismic tests?"

"To find oil, of course."

I shot a look at Nicky Florio. He shook his head and looked back over his shoulder. Diaz emerged from the side door, two Micanopy policemen with him, two men in the blue windbreakers a step behind.

"Have you found oil?"

"Yes."

"Where?"

Before Wakefield could answer, Thornton interrupted. "Mr. Lassiter, what's the point of this? The oil companies have held leases in the Everglades for years, but there's a state and federal ban on drilling. So that's got nothing to do with our proceedings. Now, if you have anything to say about—"

"Your ruling today is all about drilling for oil," I said emphatically. "You just don't know it yet." There was a stirring at the press table. One of the television cameras came on, its light forcing me to squint. Another camera focused on Nicky Florio. "Now, if I may proceed."

Thornton shrugged. I caught sight of Hank Scourby being escorted toward the locker room door by a tribal policeman with two of the men in blue windbreakers right behind.

"Where did you discover oil?" I asked.

At the front exit, several more Micanopy police appeared. I scanned the gym, waiting for the answer. The rangy man in sunglasses from outside was climbing the stairs to the balcony. He carried a long canvas bag. It contained either a fishing pole or a rifle.

"Well, several places, really," Tucker Wakefield said. "There's the Sunniland trend in the southwestern part of the state. It's about twelve thousand feet deep and runs in a line from Collier up into Lee and Hendry counties. Historically, it may have been—"

"But that's not where you've been testing lately, is it?" I wanted to speed him up.

"No, we've been in the Big Cypress Swamp."

"Which is in the Everglades considerably east of the earlier finds."

"Yes."

"And did you locate . . . ?"

Suddenly, I felt a presence next to me. I half turned. Guillermo Diaz was on his tippy-toes, whispering in my ear. "You stop now, you live. Keep going, you die." He shrank back to the table, behind

Nicky Florio, whose eyes burned with hate as he glared at me.

I stared back, gaping at him. Not here. He wouldn't try it here. Nicky Florio was a killer, but not crazy. Or was he?

"Mr. Lassiter," Thornton prompted me.

I turned back to the witness.

"Did you find oil in the swamp?" I asked.

"Yes. We located substantial reserves in the Big Cypress. It's really the South Florida Basin, which is a deep geologic bowl running under the Gulf of Mexico eastward toward—"

"Substantial?" I repeated, in case anyone missed it.

"Yes, a very rich oil field."

There was a murmur in the crowd behind him. I unfolded my purloined map and showed it to the witness. "Could you point out the precise locations?"

He studied it for a moment, then pointed to several of the numbered islands.

"Now, Mr. Wakefield, I notice that every place you have indicated is located within the boundaries of the Micanopy Indian Reservation, is it not?"

"Yes."

"Did you perform any tests on land outside of tribal land?"

"No."

"Why not?"

"Those weren't the orders form the client."

"And who is your client?"

I heard Nicky Florio cough. When I half-turned to look at him, he was watching the balcony.

"Florio Enterprises."

"Why were your instructions so limited?"

"I don't know."

"But Mr. Florio knows." I turned to Clyde Thornton, who was staring importantly at the witness, now that the TV lights were on. "Mr. Chairman, I wish to ask Nicholas Florio a few questions."

Two television cameras shone on Nicky's face, their lights harsh and hot. Florio squinted and scowled. "I don't have to answer this maniac's questions. He can't compel it."

"Mr. Florio's right," Thornton said. "This has been very interesting, but I fail to see the connection . . ."

I looked toward Socolow. He gave me a shrug. Like he wanted to help but couldn't.

"May I leave now?" Wakefield asked.

"Yes, indeed," Thornton proclaimed.

Tucker Wakefield headed for the exit. Two policemen blocking the door parted to let him pass. I didn't think they would do the same for me. In a gymnasium with three hundred people, I felt desperately alone. I needed time. I was trying to prove a case with circumstantial evidence, and I couldn't get all the circumstances into evidence. Besides, my fears had been right. They didn't care. They didn't understand. So Nicky Florio wants to drill for oil. Big deal. So do the oil companies. The law didn't allow it. But there was one difference in their situation and his. Nicky knew it, and so did I.

"Anything else, Mr. Lassiter?" Thornton asked impatiently.

Sure there was, but how could I prove it?

"The contract," I said finally. "Has the Florio Enterprises contract with the tribe been presented to the board?"

"It's here somewhere," Thornton said. One of the clerks began rummaging through a cardboard box of exhibits. While he was looking, I scanned the audience. "I'd like to ask Harrison Baker a question or two."

"Go ahead," Thornton said. "But, Harrison, no more speeches."

Hunched at the shoulders, the old man made his way back to the lectern.

"Mr. Baker, assuming that there were oil rigs in the Big Cypress and a spill took place—"

Florio was on his feet. "Damn it, this isn't about oil! It's about building a town and a casino. How much longer do we have to listen to this crap?"

Thornton's tone was respectful. "Now, Mr. Florio, let the lawyer say his piece, and we'll all go home."

"In the event of a spill, where would the oil go?" I asked.

"Well, the water flow would carry it south."

"To the national park?"

"Yes, and it would seep into the Biscayne Aquifer, which supplies South Florida with its drinking water. On the surface, it would reach Florida Bay and eventually the Gulf of Mexico. It would also pollute the sugarcane and vegetable fields."

That made Carlos de La Torre fidget in his chair.

"What would the effects of a spill be?"

"Devastating to both plants and animals. The birds and the reptiles are dependent on a fragile ecosystem. The beaches, the slough, the estuaries, would be a killing ground. Millions of animals would die. The wood stork and the Florida panther would likely be rendered extinct."

"And the effect to the farmers?"

"If polluted water is released to the fields, well, obviously, oil and sugarcane don't mix."

"And if it isn't released?"

"Death by drought or death by oil, take your choice."

Harrison Baker was no fan of the growers, and there seemed to be a perverse delight in his voice. I took a quick look at Carlos de La Torre. He had turned a dark crimson and was angrily poking an index finger at Nicky Florio, who was shaking his head.

From the bleachers, I heard a buzzing. The Everglades Society folks were nodding and speaking excitedly to each other. I'd convinced *them*, but that was preaching to the converted. What about the board? They knew oil was deadly, but there was still a missing link in the evidence. I still hadn't proved Nicky could drill for it.

The adrenaline flow seemed to have kicked in for the somnolent reporters and photographers. They knew something was coming but didn't know what. Neither did I. A still photographer was kneeling at my feet, clicking pictures. A radio interviewer stuck the microphone of a portable recorder under Harrison Baker's nose. Two reporters were trying to get Florio's attention, but he ignored them. He looked ready to kill someone, and I had a pretty solid idea of the number one candidate.

Thornton banged his gavel to quiet the audience. Finally, the clerk found the contract and handed it to me along with the resolution before the board. I let Baker head back to the bleachers and reviewed the contract I had seen once before in Henry Osceola's office. But then I'd been looking for something entirely different. Now I turned to the paragraph entitled "Grant of Rights."

"Mr. Chairman, under this lease, not only has the Micanopy tribe granted Florio Enterprises the right to build commercial property, it also granted "all earth and mineral rights of whatever kind, without any limitation whatsoever, and for no additional compensation to the lessor, for a period of years coextensive with the term of this lease."

I let that sink in for a moment and caught sight of Guillermo Diaz staring at me, drawing a line with his index finger across his throat. I added, "This clause allows the extraction of all oil and gas from the leased land, and if there were gold, diamonds, and uranium, that, too. It doesn't cost Florio a dime. The tribe doesn't get a cent. The state of Florida and the feds don't get a cent, but Florio gets the oil, at least he gets every drop that he doesn't spill. The rest of us will get that."

The audience was humming now. Again, Thornton pounded his gavel. I looked up into the darkened balcony. Maybe it was my imagination, but I thought I saw a shadow move. Was it a shadow or the barrel of a rifle propped on the metal railing in the front row? I walked right, and the shadow followed. I walked left, same thing. So I did the only sane thing. I moved in front of Florio's table and crouched down on my haunches, putting him in the line of fire.

"Now let's look at the resolution you're about to vote on," I said, thumbing through the copy, Thornton watching me curiously. "It calls for approval of the ninety-nine-year lease 'in every respect.' Just as the government can't prohibit the Micanopy tribe from running gambling on its land, it can't prohibit drilling for oil. The tribe seeks to assign that right, but it gave up its sovereignty to this board, at least where environmental matters are concerned. If it hadn't, there'd be oil rigs in the Big Cypress right now. In other words, Mr. Chairman, what you're voting on is whether Florio Enterprises can drill for oil in the Everglades."

Clyde Thornton was staring at his copy of the resolution, eyes wide. The buzz of the crowd turned into a dull roar.

"If I'm wrong about that," I said, "let Mr. Florio tell you."

With that, I peeked up over the table and dropped the lease in front of Nicky Florio. Then I reached into my suit pocket, pulled out a snapshot, and slid it in front of him. "Here, Nicky," I said. "I've marked the clause. Why not give us your interpretation?"

Florio didn't care about the lease. His attention was focused on a Polaroid photo of his favorite lawyer in a pair of borrowed pajamas.

"What about it, Nicky? I've looked this baby up and down, inside and out. I'll bet you have, too."

A rumble started in Florio's throat.

"I've given her my best shot," I continued, "and my input has been well received."

He continued staring at the photo. He turned it over in his hand, his face reddening, and tore the photo in two. He stood up, wagging a finger at me. "You bastard! You prick! You sneaky, bird-dogging son of a bitch, I'm gonna kill you!" He jumped to his feet.

"Mr. Florio!" Thornton didn't approve, but the TV guys were delighted. Florio swatted away one camera lens that was about six inches from his nose.

"No!" It was a thunderous exclamation, and Carlos de La Torre was on his feet, a perfectly furious look on his face. "National Sugar must reconsider its position in view of this development. We could not tolerate the risk to the wildlife in the Everglades, and our obligation to our shareholders requires our eternal vigilance to protect our investment in the cane fields. So, we must withdraw our support and urge the board to turn down the application."

He looked at Nicky Florio with disgust, but Florio only had eyes for me. His cheeks were flushed, and a vein throbbed in his forehead. His hands were clenched into fists. He turned to the balcony. "Now!" he screamed. "Now!"

I moved even closer to Nicky. He didn't know whether to strangle me or back away. Instead, he stood frozen in his tracks, then shot a look at the balcony.

Thornton whispered something to the commissioner on one side, then to the commissioner on the other. "If that's all, it would seem to be an appropriate time for our vote." They called the roll, and the board voted unanimously to reject approval of the Florio lease.

No town.

No casino.

No oil.

The clamor of applause. People stormed from the audience. A din of voices. Bedlam. That's when I turned to find Abe Socolow. He was surrounded by two cameras and three reporters.

I never heard the rifle shot.

The wooden floor splintered at my feet.

I dived under the display table, just as a second shot shattered the model of the casino. A third bullet *ka-pinged* off the metal supports of the table.

Screams from the audience. Bodies pushed into each other. Chairs overturned. Thornton was yelling for calm, but the microphone screeched with feedback.

"Kill the bastard!" Nicky was screaming somewhere in the mob.

I rolled out from under the table and scurried toward the side entrance, trying to blend in with the panicking crowd. I tucked my head down, bent at the knees to appear shorter, and smacked right into Abe Socolow, who grabbed me. "This way," he screamed in my ear. I didn't know if he was rescuing me or arresting me, but I followed him toward the exit until I paused to let a couple of Everglades Society members get out of the bleachers and into the crowd pushing toward the door.

A moment later, all I could see of Socolow was the bald spot at the crown of his head. Then I felt a jab in my ribs and heard a weasel voice. "You and me, *muchacho*, we're going for a little walk."

Chapter 27

Shallow Waters

G<small>UILLERMO</small> D<small>IAZ</small> <small>HUSTLED ME OUT A SIDE DOOR.</small> H<small>E PUSHED ME</small> into the sunlight of the parking lot, the barrel of a .38 banging against my spine. We danced that way across the asphalt, Diaz steering me toward Nicky Florio's midnight-blue Bentley. People streamed by us, running. I tried to catch sight of Socolow but couldn't. Florio was already sitting behind the wheel by the time Diaz shoved me into the backseat, then climbed in after me. Florio started the engine, gunned it, and we fishtailed around a corner, burning rubber as we left the parking lot.

"You fucked me good, Jake." Florio looked straight ahead, an open palm pounding the top of the steering wheel. In the rearview mirror, I saw him glowering at me. "I gotta hand it to you, Jake. First you fucked my wife, and then you fucked me. I should have killed you along with Gondolier. You know how long I've been planning this? I started making nice with the Indians fifteen years ago. Fifteen years! It was my dream. I start by building stucco houses for them at cost, all the time planning for the future. It was all set up. First the bingo. We made money for them and for us, but that was chicken feed compared to what I had planned. A casino, and then the oil. Nobody could stop me."

We were doing seventy on a two-lane road. He shot a look toward the southeast and the Big Cypress Swamp. "Then you come along,

Jake. A half-assed ex-jock without a clue. Did you have a plan? Fuck no. All you cared about was screwing my wife and fucking me over. I cut you a break. I hired you on the Tupton case, you ungrateful piece of shit. Even after you screwed my wife, I let you live. But you gotta go fucking around with the Indians and the geologists. You stupid fuck, I would have dealt with you. You didn't have to go public."

"It was the only way to stop you," I said softly from the backseat.

"Once you knew about the oil, you could have come to me. I would have cut you in."

"I didn't want a piece of your action. I wanted you."

"Fine. You got me, pal. You got me good. Fifteen years of work down the drain. A lifetime of plans. Now what the fuck am I going to do with you?"

"Turn me over to Socolow," I said.

"Maybe I'll do that," he said. In the rearview mirror, I saw him smile, or at least bare his teeth. "In pieces."

"After what I've been through, you think you can scare me, Nicky?"

"Who gives a shit about scaring you when I can kill you?"

He swung the Bentley onto a gravel road. Diaz kept the gun leveled at me. The muddy bank of a canal rose above us on our left. Stalks of sugarcane towered over the car on our right. I had the claustrophobic sense of being in a tunnel. The sky was filled with black smoke, portions of the cane fields being scorched prior to harvesting. The fire burns off the undergrowth and much of the unwanted leaves, leaving the hard-husked cane intact. The air smelled sweet, like summer corn on the grill.

"Your face is going to be on the evening news," I said. I imitated his voice. " 'You sneaky bird-dogging son of a bitch, I'm gonna kill you.' How would it look if I turn up dead?"

"Maybe you won't turn up at all. Maybe you get buried under twenty tons of dirt." He looked toward the bank of the canal. "Hey, Guillermo, we got any shovels in the trunk?"

"No, boss, just a tire jack."

"Shit!"

Florio was quiet a moment as the car crunched along on the gravel road. He seemed to be thinking of what to do with me. Killing was easy. Disposing of the body was hard.

"We got a camera back there?" Florio asked.

"Don't think so, boss."

"Shit! Jake here likes to take pictures, don't you, lover boy? Wouldn't mind taking one home to Gina, maybe Jake's dick stuffed in his mouth like a cigar."

"Or a salami," I said.

"You think this is funny, asshole? I'm gonna watch you die."

"Nicky, think it over. It's too late. You can't kill me now. I was seen leaving the gym with your hired hand here. You just threatened me on videotape. Abe Socolow's figured out you're a scumbag and would love to bust you. Face it, Nicky. The game's over. Why make it tougher on yourself?"

"Because I owe you, big time, and because I can't have you testifying about Rick Gondolier. Face it, I can't afford to let you live, even if I wanted to, and guess what, pal, I don't want to. . . ."

I heard it then, the roar of the engine. At first, I thought it was a piece of equipment in the cane field, a harvester maybe.

". . . So what are your odds, Lassiter, six-to-five against?"

Then I saw it, above us, dipping down for a closer look. The helicopter with Hank Scourby at the controls. Florio saw it, too, and instinctively hit the brakes. "What the hell!"

"Even money," I said.

The copter hovered in front of us, dropping to just a few feet above our roof.

"This guy a friend of yours, Lassiter?" Florio yelled, jamming the accelerator to the floor. We bounced through puddles and potholes, my head hitting the ceiling. The copter hung there in front of us.

Over the noise of the copter and the racing car engine, I barely heard it. Not as much pop as a firecracker, the first gunshot missed. The second one pinged off the hood, and Florio nearly lost control, swerving toward the canal bank, then across the road toward the cane field, before straightening the wheel. I looked up, and there was Hank Scourby, door open, leaning out with his .44 Magnum, blasting away.

The next shot missed, then another ricocheted off the trunk. Finally, one squarely hit the front windshield, splintering it into a spider's web of fissures. Again, the Bentley swerved, but Florio kept driving, and the copter stayed with us.

Diaz lowered his window, stuck the .38 out, and fired two rounds toward the copter. He didn't appear to hit anything. He took a look at me, poked the gun out the window again, and I turned toward him. In a flash, the gun was in my face, the barrel pushing at my cheekbone.

"You want to try something, *abogado?*"

I shook my head, no.

Florio slowed down as the black smoke became thicker. The burning leaves now saturated the air, black papery cinders swirling in the breeze. Inside the car, the smell of the cordite combined with the sickly sweetness of the fire. Suddenly, Florio hit the brakes and slid to a stop. The copter wasn't visible. We were engulfed by clouds of smoke. Waves of heat from the blazing fields poured over us.

"If we can't see him, he can't see us," Florio said. "But we gotta get off this road."

We sat a minute, maybe more. Then I heard it again, growing louder. As it drew closer, the smoke was beaten away by the rotor. Suddenly, a clang from above. Scourby had set the copter down on top of the car. Now he was bashing our roof in.

Up, down, *bam*, *bang*. Twice more.

I slumped lower in the seat. Again, Florio hit the gas and took off, the copter in pursuit.

"There, boss." Diaz was pointing at what looked like a dirt path coming out of the cane field. It connected with the gravel road at a right angle.

Florio swung the wheel to the right and slid onto the path. It was narrower than the Bentley. We careened through the burning field, the car knocking down cane stalks with a *whackety-whack*, the wheels spinning in the soft earth. Singed leaves were plastered to our splintered windshield, smoke curling around us. The helicopter was nowhere to be seen, or heard.

Florio slowed as we entered a canebrake. In a moment, we were in an adjacent field. Here there was no fire, and the earth was soggy. Twice, our rear wheels spun helplessly, whining in the mud, but Florio kept the car moving, fishtailing his way onto firmer ground. Now, I saw them, a legion of cutters in tattered khaki work clothes and bandannas, wiry, dark-skinned men swinging machetes at the base of the stalks, cutting and gathering the cane. They wore shin protectors and thick Kevlar gloves like a platoon of hockey goalies. Hanging from their belts were flasks of energy-laced "petrol," a high-calorie brew of beer, sugar, and eggs. As we approached, they stopped and stared in wonder as our battered English sedan invaded their territory.

Again, we emerged into a clearing, and still we drove on. This time I saw the copter before I heard it.

Straight ahead.

Half a mile in front of us.

No more than ten feet off the ground, and aimed straight for us.

Hank Scourby was playing chicken with Nicky Florio. I didn't know who was crazier.

"Son of a bitch!" Florio cried out.

The copter dropped a couple of feet lower. On this path, its struts would come right through our windshield. Florio floored it, and we bounced through the mud on a collision course. At the last moment, with the roar of the car's engine lost in the drone of the copter, Florio swung it hard right, toward one of the burning cane fields, and we skidded and bounced over a muddy incline, the car flipping onto its side, tumbling me into Guillermo Diaz. The car continued its slide through the flaming brush, mowing down a row of cane, finally rolling onto its dented roof and slowing to a clunking, thudding halt.

I was upside down. My neck was twisted sideways, my head pressed against the ceiling, and my ears ringing. I hadn't felt like this since an offensive lineman grabbed my face mask and twisted my head around like Linda Blair in *The Exorcist*. Now my shoulder was squeezed against the door, and the backseat was a jumble of arms and legs: Diaz's and mine. I untangled my legs from his, and he screamed in pain. Then he moaned softly, *"Mis piernas tienen fracturas, mis piernas están rotas."* I groped for his gun, but I couldn't find it.

In the front seat, Florio was cursing. I heard glass tinkling. Florio was hanging on to the steering wheel but was upside down. He scrunched his neck and turned to face me. His face was studded with glass, rivulets of blood streaming into his eyes. He tried to reach into his coat pocket. "Where the fuck's my gun?"

Next to me, Diaz was still moaning. One of his legs was bent in a direction God never intended. I wrenched around, found the door handle, and yanked. It took two tries, then opened with a groan, and I climbed out and tumbled into the mud. One of the rear tires was still spinning. I lay there a moment, got my bearings, and scrambled on all fours, half crawling, half running away. Behind me there was a noise as Florio toppled out of the car. He was yelling at me, but I wasn't listening. I straightened up and did a poor imitation of a broken-field runner dodging stalks of sugarcane.

My black wing tips splashed through puddles of water. I kept running, keeping my body low, cutting back and forth from row to row. Flames rose from the undergrowth, and black smoke hung over the field, choking me. I tried taking shallow breaths, the heat crushing my chest. As I ran, I put my arms up to ward off the leaves, their jagged edges stinging the heels of my hands. I missed one, and it swatted me just under the eye, drawing blood. I pulled off my suit coat and wrapped it around my right arm, using it as a shield.

The first shot was a firecracker in the distance.

Unlike the movies, I didn't hear the bullet whistling by my ear, just a muffled *blam* from behind me. Second shot, same thing. I ducked out of one row and was suddenly left in an open field. I turned to go back into the forest of cane, but Florio was there, chugging after me.

Across the open field was a mud levee rising perhaps ten feet above the ground. The irrigation system. Everglades water would be running through the canal, draining the Big Cypress. I made a run for it.

The sound of the next shot didn't reach me until I spun and collapsed headfirst into the muck. It felt like someone had smacked me in the back. I rolled over and touched the front of my left shoulder. Wet with blood. A clean shot through the deltoid. What Charlie Riggs would call a through-and-through if he was examining a corpse in the red-brick building on Bob Hope Road.

My first reaction was surprise. What a lucky shot for a *pistolero* who probably never did anyone from more than three feet away, if he ever did anyone at all. Then anger. What an unlucky shot for me.

I was on my feet again, stumbling up the levee. Another gunshot plunked into the dirt near my feet. I instinctively ducked. I touched my shoulder. Very little blood flow, but it was beginning to hurt. Not a great, throbbing pain, not at all what I expected. More like a hot stinging, what I imagined it would feel like to get stabbed with an ice pick.

At the top of the levee, I slid down on my bottom. The water in the canal was maybe three feet deep. I waded across, climbed the levee on the other side, slid down again, and started running for the closest cane field. A mechanical harvester combine, a huge machine with tracks like an army tank, circled the rows. Like a giant snout, a green metal chute formed a V at the front of the machine, sucking the cane in, where rotating disks sliced close to the base of the stalks and sent the shards up a conveyor to a chopping drum.

I raced after the harvester, yelling at the driver, but he was sitting in a glass-enclosed compartment high above the machine, and he never heard me, never saw me behind him. I turned to see Florio sliding down the bank of the levee. He raised the gun, and I ducked and ran again, a zigzag route.

Another gunshot, but it was wild.

I headed into the rows of cane, trying to disappear. The air was heavy with soot, the cane thick and sturdy, twelve-feet high and ready for harvesting. With the irrigation gates opened and the field waterlogged, I wasn't running so much as slogging through the sludge. After a couple hundred yards, I became light-headed and wanted to sit down, but I didn't let myself. I felt the shoulder with my fingertips. The blood was still trickling out, and the pain had grown worse. My skin felt cold and clammy. I was short of breath, dizzy, and just wanted to sleep.

I stumbled a few steps and dropped to my knees. I crawled for a minute or two, then sprawled out, my head on my arms. I wasn't unconscious, but I wasn't conscious, either. My eyes were closed, and when I opened them, the world was gray. I closed them again. From somewhere far away, I heard a bird squawking, a moment later, the distant rumble of the harvester. Charred leaves fell from the sky, coating me with soot.

And then a splash. Soft enough to have been a frog in a puddle.

Another splash, then the unmistakable *splat-squish* of footsteps in the mud. I heard his breathing. Heavy, labored breaths. The rumble of the harvester grew louder.

I opened my eyes. Nicky Florio's Italian leather loafers, coated in mud up to his ankles, were six feet away. His back was to me. If I could get to my feet, I could blindside him, take him down into the muck. But there was no way to get up without rustling leaves and sucking up mud. By the time I was ready to pounce, he would have turned. He'd have a clear shot at me.

His shout startled me: "Where are you, asshole?"

I had to concentrate on not answering him. I pressed lower into the soggy earth. He turned slowly, looking left and right. One more quarter turn and he would see me. The noise of the harvester grew louder as it approached. When it came into view, Nicky spun that way, the sight distracting him, the sound muffling my movements.

As the rumble increased to a roar, I got to my knees. Then from a crouch, I stood up. I kept my eyes on Nicky, aware of the green steel monster chugging toward us, its tracks crunching fallen stalks and the burned debris on the soggy field.

I took one step, and Nicky whirled, either hearing me or sensing me there. His face was a mask of dried blood. A shaft of sunlight cut through the smoke and reflected a prism of colors from the shards of glass embedded in his forehead. His eyes were crazed with hate. The gun came up and pointed at my throat as I dived at him. Instinctively, I ducked my head to the left.

The gun was alongside my right ear when it discharged, breaking the eardrum. My good shoulder—the one without a hole in it— caught Florio in the chest and dropped him backward. The gun flew over his head and landed at the base of a cane stalk. I landed on top of Florio. I punched him with a right hand that had nothing behind it, and he gouged my right eye with his thumb, then clawed at my face. I grabbed him by the hair and bashed his head into the soggy ground. I wished we were on asphalt. He tried to knee me in the groin. I got two hands around his throat, but I had no strength, and he pried loose, then kicked at me, sliding out from underneath. I collapsed into the mud, my shoulder bleeding, my ears ringing, my eyes blinking.

Nicky got to his feet and came at me again. I was on my knees when he tried to kick me, but he slipped in the mud and fell on his ass. He got up again, and we came at each other, locking up like a couple of wrestlers. I pushed him back through the cane, the stalks bending and slapping at us. He tucked a leg behind mine and tried to trip me, but he didn't have the leverage, and I used my heft to drag him across my hip and put him on his back. He just missed being impaled on a sharp stalk sticking out of the ground.

I lunged at him and pinned him down by sitting on his chest. He yelled something at me, but I couldn't hear a thing. Again he growled, and this time I could read his lips.

"You son of a bitch, Lassiter. I always liked you, did you know that?"

I answered by smashing him in the mouth with a fist. "You're crazy, Nicky."

He said something else, and again, I couldn't hear a word. "What?"

"You stupid fuck!" he screamed, spitting blood onto my chest. "You always wanted to be like me, but you can't admit it."

That made me laugh. "You're out of your mind."

The harvester churned closer. "You admire me, because I do whatever's necessary to win," Nicky screamed. "I took Gina away from a spoiled rich kid, and you didn't. I work for myself and don't answer to anybody. What do you do, get pushed around by judges with their rule books? I take what I want, Jake, and you don't. I'm a winner. Can you fucking hear me, you punch-drunk second-string shyster?"

"You don't look like a winner," I said. "You look like a two-bit punk." This time, I gave him a short chop to the neck.

He gagged and forced a sick smile. Blood trickled from his forehead in a dozen meandering streams. "You stupid prick!" he yelled at me. "You still don't understand. It's not just that I was going to make you my partner 'cause you knew too much. I *wanted* you to be my partner. I *let* you fuck my wife. I knew all about it, even before I found the letter."

He twisted his head around, looking toward the approaching harvester as it bore down on us.

"I don't get it," I said.

"I remember you from when you played ball. I hung around training camp and knew half the guys on the team, but I've always been a loner, Jake. I was never on a team of any kind."

"Yeah, you were a jock sniffer. You were always one of the guys who wanted to belong, but you didn't, Nicky. You were a lowlife then, and you're a lowlife now."

His body shifted underneath me. "Yeah, but I got something you don't."

I looked him the question.

"The killer instinct," he said.

I drew my fist back to smack him again, but a pain stabbed me in the side. I looked down, my mouth hanging open in surprise. Nicky's hand was driving a sharp piece of cane into my flesh just below the bottom rib. He was twisting it, trying to dig deeper. It felt like a sword had gutted me. I reached down to wrest him away, and he used his free hand to yank me sideways. I toppled off him, the cane stalk still stuck in me.

He rolled over and got to his feet, his eyes searching for the gun. Behind Nicky, I saw the harvester approaching. The sight froze me. No more than thirty feet away, headed straight at us, stalks of cane disappearing into its mechanical maw.

Nicky saw it, too.

The gun was directly in the path between the machine and us. If we both dived for it, we'd be struggling there when the harvester chomped everything in its path. If one of us dived for the gun, he'd likely get it and roll out of the way.

One could live.

Or both could die.

I didn't like the odds. But then I wasn't a god.

I backed up, stumbling over severed stalks of cane. Nicky Florio dived into the row, sprawling headfirst in the mud. He speared the gun by the butt on the first try. He made his own rules and his own luck.

Ten feet away, the harvester boomed like pealing thunder, the tracks clinking, the blades *clop-clopping* through the woodlike stalks.

Florio had timed it just right, but with no room to spare. Gun in one hand, he braced himself with the other and tried to stand. His leather-soled loafers slipped in the mud, his legs churned, and his feet slid out from under him. He fell headfirst, both hands in front of him. He wriggled backward, his body moving, snakelike, getting his torso and head out of the path of the swinging steel blades.

Twisting like a corkscrew.

Backing out of harm's way.

Making it.

Everything but his hands.

Nicky Florio's hands were caught in the path of the V-shaped snout. He tried to pull back, but the steel held fast, yanking him higher toward the blades, dragging his body through the mud.

Clop-whomp-clop.

I never heard him scream.

On the conveyor belt, amid stalks and leaves, were two bloody hands, severed just above their knobby wrists. One hand still gripped a .38 revolver. The conveyor carried the hands higher, where they disappeared into the chopper drum. A whirring sound like wood through a sawmill; then, along with billets of sugarcane, bite-sized pieces of his fingers were ejected into the following trailer.

Nicky Florio lay facedown in the mud, his body twitching. He tucked both stumps under his armpits, trying futilely to stanch the blood flow.

He said something to me, but the words were drowned out in the noise of the harvester as it continued down the row. I leaned down next to him with the ear that could still hear. His face was in a puddle, his nose and mouth barely above the water.

"Tourniquet," he pleaded. His eyes were glazing over. "Bleeding to death."

I straightened and looked down at him on the soggy ground. "No, you're not. You're going to drown first, Nicky. The water level's been increasing ever since we got here. It's your water, Nicky. Enjoy it. Lick it up. Savor it as you would the finest French Bordeaux 1961."

"Stupid fuck," he said, his voice dying. "You could have been my partner. You could have been my friend."

He tried to stand, but he didn't have the strength. The effort sank him deeper into the puddle, and water began filling his nose. Blood pooled out from under him in the mud. He exhaled sharply, tried to hold his breath, then after a long moment, inhaled and choked, spitting out water colored with his own blood.

"Help me," he sputtered.

Again he swallowed water. The arms came out from underneath, the stumps spurting blood, and he struggled, trying vainly to flop onto his back. His face sank into water again, and his body went into convulsions.

I didn't help him.

I just watched him die.

I couldn't have saved him anyway. That's what I planned to tell myself later when I would ask the tough questions. Like what was I really feeling then? Joy? Relief? I would try to convince myself it didn't make me happy—it didn't make me anything—to see his blood stain the brown earth. But beneath the glib reply was something else, another question I couldn't answer. What was I really feeling then? Was it that I was safe from harm? Was it that Nicky Florio deserved to die? Or did it have something to do with Gina? Just what was it that made me want to see Nicky Florio die, and die hard?

Chapter 28

Playing with Pain

I LET CHARLIE RIGGS DO THE DRIVING. FOR THE PAST THREE weeks, I let him do everything. He had patched up my shoulder, front and rear, changed the dressings, shot me full of antibiotics, and slapped a patch on my ear. He had cleaned the wound in my gut and stitched it closed with needle and thread given to him by Betsy Ross. As far as I can tell, I'm his only patient who lived.

Charlie tossed some fishing gear into the back of his pickup, and we headed down Useless 1 to the Keys. First stop, Granny Lassiter's old house with faded yellow shutters and hard pine floors on the Gulf side of Islamorada. Granny crouched on the back porch hosing down a mess of grouper she'd caught just after sun-up. She wore khaki shorts with six pockets and a T-shirt emblazoned IF IT HAS TITS OR TIRES, YOU'RE GONNA HAVE TROUBLE WITH IT.

Granny was suntanned the color of mahogany bark. She hadn't worn makeup or a dress in thirty years. She smoked two packs of cigarettes a day and drank a fifth of her own moonshine a week. Without looking up from her filleting knife, she announced how damned fortunate that two strong men had arrived just when she needed some fresh coconut milk for a fish sauce. When neither Charlie nor I moved, Granny gestured at me with the head of a two-pound grouper. "Tree's right out yonder, Jake, in case you forgot where you once fell and broke your collarbone."

"I remember," I told her. "I was nine years old."

"Gave the boy a dose of my likker and set the bone myself," Granny said proudly, "and he don't seem no worse for wear."

For some reason, I wasn't in the mood to climb a tree. "I came here expecting tea and sympathy, and you want me to pick coconuts."

"Such a crybaby," she said, turning to Charlie. "I remember the first time he got his nose broke playing junior high football. Cater-wauled like a newborn can't find the teat."

"As I recall it, I stuffed cotton up my nose and played the second half. I always played with pain."

"That night," Granny said, staring off into space, "I had to give him a pint of the home brew to get him to sleep, he was whimpering so much."

"I said I always played with pain, not that I didn't complain about it."

Granny snorted her disapproval. "Jes' look at you now. Face scratched up like you spent a night with a she cat, arm in a sling, tummy bandaged, and here you come, lookin' for pity. What you need is some honest labor, 'stead of pushing paper and telling lies, which is what I figure lawyering's all about." She studied me a moment. "So climb that tree, boy, unless you're still afraid of heights."

Granny always taught me to confront my demons. "I've never been afraid of heights. It's falling that scares me."

Charlie harrumphed and told us to bicker all we wanted, he was going to sit in a rocker on the front porch and rest his bones. Granny went back to cleaning the fish, so I did what I was told. I wandered into her sandy front yard and took a look at the coconut palm, a healthy Jamaica Tall. The husks were tawny yellow, the nuts thirty feet off the ground.

I started shimmying up the coconut tree using one arm and both feet. Halfway there, I heard Granny yelling from the back porch. "Machete's in the toolshed, Jake. You remember how to use a machete, don't you?"

I remembered.

Charlie was snoring in the rocking chair when I set about making the coconut milk. I didn't use the watery liquid found inside the nut. That I just drank straight from the cracked shell. Then I dug out the white meat, poured hot water over it, and squashed the mixture into a thick cream. By this time, Granny was marinating the fish in a mixture of lime juice, pepper, chopped onion, and crushed garlic. When Granny was mixing the graham cracker crust for the Key lime pie, I made the fish sauce by heating the coconut milk with flour, butter, salt, and pepper. Then I sat down at the kitchen table with a coffee cup filled with Granny's white lightning. It singed the throat on the way down.

After she spooned the topping onto the Key lime filling, Granny sat down next to me. As she had done forever, she handed me the spatula and watched as I licked off the whipped cream.

"I was worried about you, son," Granny said. That was about as much of an endearment as you get from the old battle-ax.

"I love you, too, Granny."

She borrowed my cup for a sip, closed her eyes as it went down, and said, "C'mon, now. Wake up that old coot so we can eat. I'm not getting any younger."

After dinner, we sat on the porch, feeling the breeze, sipping whiskey, and talking. Charlie had heard it all, so he sat quietly while I told Granny everything, starting with Peter Tupton dead in a wine cellar and ending with Nicky Florio dead in a cane field. I told her how I dragged myself back up and down levees, through burning fields and into open spaces, before finding the overturned Bentley. Guillermo Diaz lay on the ground, moaning and praying in Spanish. Hank Scourby stood nearby, leaning on his helicopter, patiently waiting.

"I knew you'd be back," he said. "This one's got two broken legs, and he's none too happy about it."

I walked over to Diaz and leaned down next to him. "Nicky's dead. We're going to get you to a hospital, and after they glue you back together, I'm going to bring a court reporter into the room. You're going to go under oath and tell who killed Rick Gondolier and the circumstances of my killing Jim Tiger. Then when Abe Socolow comes to visit, you're going to do it all over again. Got it?"

His eyes were glazed over with pain. Spittle had dried in the corners of his mouth.

"Or," I continued, "we can toss you into an irrigation canal right now and leave you for gator bait."

"I'll talk," he said. "But you gotta do something for me."

"What's that?"

He winced with pain as he spoke. "They'll revoke my probation, won't they?"

"First thing, and if Abe Socolow's in the mood, you'll get charged with accessory to murder."

"That's why I need you."

"What for?"

"To be my lawyer, *naturalmente*."

We left early the next morning, again heading south on U.S. 1, the road that starts in Maine and ends in Key West, or is it the other way around? We stopped at a gas station in Marathon, where I bought some live grunt for bait and Chap Stick to lubricate the knots in the leader. I try not to be one of those guys who grumbles about the Keys being swallowed up by fast-food emporiums and hokey swim-with-the-porpoise shows, but there's no denying the truth. The drive numbs you with discount motels, T-shirt shops, and other touristy gewgaws and gimcracks lining each side of the highway.

Still, despite our best efforts to destroy the environment, Nature hangs tough. Bulldoze the trees, and the ospreys build their stick nests high atop our ugly telephone poles. Dredge ugly canals to cool nuclear power plants, and you've provided honeymoon suites for warm-blooded manatees. We think of man destroying Nature, and man does his level best to try. But Nature preceded us, withstands us, and probably will outlive us.

We rumbled over the seven-mile bridge. To the east, we call the water the Atlantic Ocean. To the west, it's the Gulf of Mexico. But under the bridge, it all looks the same.

We stopped at the Bahia Honda Bridge, unpacked our gear, and prepared to drop lines in the channel in pursuit of the great silvery tarpon.

"*Megalops atlantica*," Charlie said, wistfully. "What a fish. Hope you're prepared for a fight today. You going to use those grunts?"

"That's why I bought 'em."

"I'll stick with a four-inch George-R-Shad rubber fish."

Charlie hauled out a couple of six-foot bait-casting rigs with twelve-pound line. Standing on the catwalk, I tried a few practice casts with my good arm, dropping the bait near some pilings that looked like tarpon condos. If I got a bite, Charlie would have to help me with the reel. The wind was picking up, the clouds scudding across a gray-blue sky. A nasty gust nearly put my back cast into my ear. Behind us, cars were humming over the bride, headed for Key West.

We fooled around for an hour or so, doing no damage to the fish population. Even if we caught one, we'd cut it loose. Tarpon are too bony for eating, so the only use is to mount one and hang it in your den. I don't believe in killing animals for sport, and anyway, I keep my walls bare of diplomas, trophies, and plaques from the Kiwanis.

The sun had burned off the clouds by the time a school of the big ones came lazing into view, slicing through the pilings. They were rolling in the water, mouths open as if pleading to be fed. I dropped my grunt in the middle of the pack, and the strike came so suddenly I nearly lost the pole. When I got a grip, the pole was bowed toward the bottom of the channel, the tarpon diving, then running toward the open sea. The reel was whining, and I was giving line so fast, I imagined I had hooked an invisible speedboat. I dug my left arm out of the sling and held on with both hands. The pain was icy-hot, deep in the meat of my deltoid.

The tarpon jumped.

An impossibly high, wriggling jump, its blue-green stripe shining iridescent in the glare of the sun.

It smacked the water, swam and jumped, and swam some more. A five-footer, maybe eighty pounds.

I was soaked with sweat, my shoulder was throbbing, the stitches were tearing loose in my abdomen, and we'd only been at this a couple of minutes.

"You might want to start fighting him," Charlie said.

"What do you think I'm doing?"

We both saw it at once, a gray fin breaking the water, the smooth, swiveling motion of the fish powering its way toward its target.

"Oh shit," I said. "We've got competition."

"Quod avertat Deus!"

If there is any animal as ugly as the great hammerhead shark, I haven't seen it, With eyes at either end of a broad, flattened snout, the hammerhead looks like somebody rearranged its head with a shovel. This shark took the tarpon in one bite, snapped my line, turned, and was gone.

I wound in the lifeless line, dropped the rod, and leaned against the catwalk rail. "Just when you think you've landed one, you lose it."

"There are other fish in the sea."

"Damn sharks. Did you see the size of him, Charlie? Eighteen feet, I'll bet, fifteen hundred pounds at least, maybe a ton."

"No way."

"C'mon. That was the biggest shark I've ever seen."

"Non semper ea sunt quae videntur. Things are not always what they seem."

"I know, I know. You've taught me that before. But I *saw* it."

"You were excited. Your adrenaline was flowing. Your senses were distorted, much as a man hopelessly in love cannot accurately describe his lover. There is no objectivity in matters of passion."

"Charlie, this was a shark, not a woman."

"The distinction is, shall we say, *de minimis.*"

We would have argued it out a bit longer, but just then, a black limousine with dark, tinted windows squeaked to a halt on the roadway just above us. A uniformed driver came around to the back, opened the door, and a woman stepped out.

She wore a calf-length black suede dress with golden studs around the high neckline. It would have been a perfect dress for mourning, if you ignored the thigh-high slit up the side. I didn't ignore it. Her long butterscotched hair peeked out from beneath a broad-brimmed gray hat. Black sunglasses shielded her eyes. Her high heels clattered down the metal stairs to the catwalk, and the limo pulled to the end of the bridge.

Gina Florio lowered the sunglasses and looked at me with those dark blue eyes rimmed in black. "I waited for you to call me, Jake. I waited a week and then another week. And then I thought about it, and I knew you wouldn't. Whenever I'm available, you never call."

I didn't say a word.

Charlie Riggs cleared his throat. "I think I'll go clean some fish."

"We don't have any fish," I responded, as he walked away.

"Then I'll go to the market and get some," he called back.

"Anyway," Gina said, "I didn't hear from you, so I made other arrangements, but I wanted to see you before I left town."

That caught me by surprise. "I figured you'd be tied up with the lawyers for a while," I said. "The estate must be complicated."

Her smile was rueful. "Not really. When you have ten million in assets and twenty million in debts, it's really quite simple."

"I don't get it. I thought Nicky was loaded."

"Nicky was leveraged like you wouldn't believe. Everything he had, the bingo hall, the raw land, the apartment projects, even our house, was tied up as collateral for his loans. He'd lost a bundle in commercial real estate. Empty shopping centers were a huge cash drain, and he'd signed personally on every loan. The gambling and the oil were supposed to turn it around."

"There must have been life insurance."

"Pledged to the banks to secure the lines of credit. So were the cars, the boat, even my jewelry. Hey, I'm back where I started, Jake, except I'm older and wiser."

"I'm sorry. Not about Nicky. But I was hoping you'd be okay."

"I am okay. A girl uses her wits, or whatever her assets may be."

A charter fishing boat chugged under the bridge, three sunburned tourists saluting us with beer cans.

"So what now?" I asked.

"A long trip and short memories. I want to forget all about Nicky and his big plans."

The fishing boat picked up speed. For some reason, I wanted to be on it, headed for open seas.

"It'll take a while," I said.

She nodded. "You know what's funny? Nicky's plans would have worked. If it hadn't been for you, and of course, if Tupton hadn't . . ."

"Hadn't what?"

She shrugged. "Hadn't died."

"C'mon, Gina. I've known all along. Nicky killed him. You don't have to cover up for him anymore. Tupton found something in the den about the oil. Geologists' reports, maybe. Then he must have realized he was being bearded about the casino and the museum. Nicky wanted his blanket support, and if he got it, he would sneak the resolution through the Water Management Board that would let him drill for oil. Once Tupton learned the truth, Nicky couldn't let him live."

She was silent, and we both watched an osprey dive-bombing the water.

"You're half right," she said, which I figured was my usual batting average. "Tupton did find out about the oil, but there was something else, too."

"What?"

"It had to do with me."

"You? You killed Tupton?"

"No! Jake, I always told you the truth about Tupton. It was an accident. I just left something out."

"What?"

"Carlos de La Torre."

"What about him?"

"He was at the party. I'd been drinking a little too much, and Nicky was hobnobbing with all the politicos, and I was bored with the whole scene. Well, there's Carlos, oozing that Latin charm and flirting with me like he always did. First thing you know, he and I are in the guest bathroom downstairs. I thought I'd locked the door, but who barges in . . ."

"Peter Tupton."

"Right, three sheets to the wind and fading fast. He takes one look at us, goes, 'Naughty, naughty.' He says something about Nicky Florio screwing the Everglades and the sugar king screwing Nicky's wife. And he's laughing, a drunk's laugh. Maybe he wouldn't have said anything, but maybe he would have blurted everything out, thinking he was being hilarious, or maybe getting even with Nicky. Anyway, we couldn't risk it. Carlos zipped up, gives that big smile of his, and starts treating Tupton like a long-lost friend. 'Let's show Señor Tupton around.' So we do. We pick up two bottles of champagne and give him a tour of the house. He's weaving and staggering, but flattered by all the attention.

Finally, in one of the guest bedrooms, he just lies down and passes out."

"Then what? What did you and Carlos do?"

"We needed time to think, so we went back to the kitchen to talk. We figured when he woke up, maybe he wouldn't remember what he saw. Maybe he'd think it was a dream. I don't know. We were buying time. We just hoped for the best."

"So how did he get into the wine cellar?"

"It was late. All the guests had left. I'd looked in the guest bedroom, but Tupton wasn't there. I figured he'd gotten up and simply left. The caterers had cleaned up. I was downstairs and I hear this shout. Nicky found Tupton on the floor in the guest bathroom. He'd crawled in there, gotten sick, and curled up on the tile. Nicky's cussing up a storm about the fucking bird-watcher, just look at him now. Nicky said, 'Let's sober him up,' so he grabbed him by the wrists and slung him over his shoulder like a fireman."

"And took him down to the wine cellar."

"Right, but Nicky never thought Tupton would die. Just the opposite. He thought the cold would wake him up. It was an accident. Then Nicky figured you'd handle the trial for us, and in six months nobody would even remember Tupton's name." She sighed. "But things never work out the way you plan."

Just then, the limo reappeared on the bridge, this time pointed north. Its horn honked twice.

"Gotta go," Gina said. "Carlos is waiting."

"Here? He's in the car?"

"It's his, silly. And so am I. You haven't even congratulated me." She waved her left hand in front of my face.

"I'm surprised you can lift your arm," I said, examining a diamond that Liz Taylor would dismiss as too ostentatious.

"We're getting married in Mexico. Then a three-month honeymoon cruise around the world. Carlos says that when we get back, he'd like to hire you as a lawyer."

"Work for the sugar king? Forget it."

"C'mon, Jake. Your suspension will be over, and you'll need new clients."

"You don't have to do this for me," I said. "I'll be fine."

"It was Carlos's idea, Jake. He was impressed with you at the

Water Board hearing. So when I mentioned how you and I are old friends and how nice it would be if . . ."

The limo honked at us again. Gina slipped her sunglasses back on, gave me a peck on the cheek, and turned toward the metal stairs. "So long, Jake. Maybe I'll see you later, and maybe I won't."

"Oh, you will," I said. "You surely will."